I0718385

The Clio Project

A Military Time Travel Story

Mark S. Roberts

M&B Global Solutions, Inc.
Green Bay, Wisconsin (USA)

The Clio Project
A Military Time Travel Story

~ ii ~

Disclaimer
The Clio Project is a work of fiction that includes portrayals of the U.S. Air Force security police, bases, and their surrounding region. It is not intended to depict actual persons, organizations or places. The author took dramatic license with some descriptions of vehicle usage and associated weaponry to simplify the narrative. In the event you use any of the information in this book for yourself, which is your constitutional right, the author and the publisher assume no responsibility for your actions.

ISBN-13: 978-1-942731-34-4
ISBN-10: 1-942731-34-5

Published by M&B Global Solutions Inc.
Green Bay, Wisconsin (USA)

Dedication

To my wife, Lori, who supplied the encouragement I needed to finish a story that was more than thirty years in the making.

Also to all the men and women who have served in the U.S. Armed Forces, especially those with whom I had the privilege to serve.

Air Force Officers by Rank

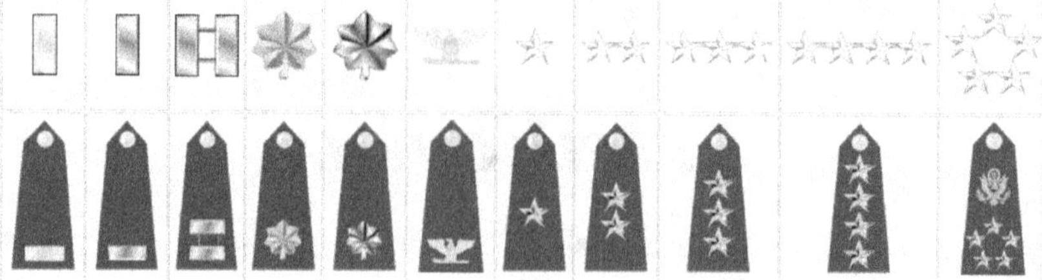

Insignia											
Air Force Service Dress Uniform Insignia											
Title	Second Lieutenant	First Lieutenant	Captain	Major	Lieutenant Colonel	Colonel	Brigadier General	Major General	Lieutenant General	General	General of the Air Force
Abbreviation	2d Lt	1st Lt	Capt.	Maj	Lt Col	Col	Brig Gen	Maj Gen	Lt Gen	Gen	GAF

Air Force Enlisted by Rank

Insignia	*No Insignia*										
Title	Airman Basic	Airman	Airman First Class	Senior Airman	Staff Sergeant	Technical Sergeant	Master Sergeant¹	Senior Master Sergeant¹	Chief Master Sergeant¹	Command Chief Master Sergeant	Chief Master Sergeant of the Air Force
Abbreviation	AB	Amn	A1C	SrA	SSgt	TSgt	MSgt	SMSgt	CMSgt	CCM	CMSAF

Contents

*"What then is time? If no one asks me, I know;
if I want to explain it to someone, I do not know."*

- St. Augustine

Chapter 1

"What's up, Nionee?" Technical Sergeant (TSgt.) Scott Rees asks as he walks toward Airman First Class (A1C) Raymond Nionee. The two U.S. Air Force Security Police (SPs for short) are watching the fire alarm flicker madly and the charging meter electricity level push itself to the maximum charge reading, but they hear no alarm.

"You ever see it do that before?" Nionee asks.

"Not that I recall," Rees answers.

Rees calls out to Staff Sergeant (SSgt.) Jack Bouvier while he quickly makes his way to the radio room.

"Sergeant Bouvier, check the meters. They're going crazy! I'm going to get Sergeant Shepard and have him check out the generator room."

Rees enters the radio room and presses the mic to talk.

"Security 15 to 15 Bravo!"

He releases the mic and waits for a response, but hears nothing except the hissing of radio waves. He presses the mic and calls the patrol again. This time he is rewarded with static and a faint voice.

"Security 15 this is 15 Bravo," comes the reply. "You're coming in broken, but go ahead."

"15 Bravo, I need you to proceed to the generator room and check it out," Rees says, this time with more volume. "The fire alarm and charging meter at Security 15 are showing a high power fluctuation. You copy?"

A couple of seconds tick by before Sgt. Thomas Shepard's voice comes back distorted and broken.

"Sec... A... Fif... co."

The signal is weak, but Rees knows Shepard has acknowledged and they are on their way. He glances up and sees Sgt. David Kriger, Airman Sean McGuire, and Airman Wally Harris standing in the controller area looking at the generator alarm with SSgt. Bouvier.

"You think it's on fire?" Kriger asks Bouvier.

"I don't believe so," Bouvier answers. "And the alarm didn't sound, only flashed."

"Could be a malfunction with the fire bells," adds McGuire.

Moving back into the room with the others, Rees tells Kriger to go outside and check out the radio in the Duck to see if he can contact the radio room. The Duck is the team's thirty-foot-long, amphibious armored vehicle.

"Give us a radio check," Rees says as Kriger walks down the hallway.

They listen to the Duck's heavy metal door squeak and hear Kriger clamber inside. A couple of seconds pass before there is static and Kriger's barely audible voice comes over the radio room speaker.

"Airman McAdams, call all the posts in the area and see if they can hear us or us them," Rees says. "Something is wrong, and it's not just the generator room. Something else is going on; I can feel it. There's a lot of static electricity in the air. I sensed it earlier, but didn't think anything of it."

After a few minutes of calls, McAdams reports that every radio check is the same: broken transmissions and static.

Bouvier turns with a furrowed forehead, wondering what in the world could be causing the interference.

"I felt it earlier and didn't think much of it, either," he says. "What about a downed power line near us?"

Before anyone can answer, an urgent yell from McAdams breaks their concentration.

"Sergeant Rees!" McAdams cries out. "The landlines are dead!"

"Did you try all of them?" Bouvier asks.

"Yes, sir," McAdams replies. "I tried calling everyone on the board. Lines are just dead. Even tried calling the outside lines. Nothing."

Rees looks perplexed and tells McAdams to check with Shepard to find out if they made it to the generator room. McAdams acknowledges the request and drops back down behind the wall where Rees can hear him talking on the radio.

Rees walks down the hallway through the Romeo team room and toward the back door. He wants to get an idea of what might be happening. Reaching for the doorknob, he receives a mild shock of electricity for the effort. He tries again and receives another shock, this time accompanied by an arc of electricity jumping from the knob to his hand. He holds onto the doorknob, absorbing the shock, and turns it to open the door so he can step outside.

Everything appears okay, except it's getting a little dark. Rees looks toward the generator building, for what reason he is not sure. It's too far away to see anything. He lifts his head toward the sky and turns in a circle to take it all in. The sky is a hazy, dark blue, not the normal blue of the sky, and he can't find the cause of the haze as it extends all around the area. It looks somewhat like a film, or giant plastic wrapping, or even a gigantic glass bowl has been placed over them.

Hairs on his arms are rising and he feels a tingling sensation throughout his body. The air is becoming hotter and a sudden vibration courses through his being. The electrical tingling becomes more noticeable. He looks at the tower and sees SSgt. Isaac Parks standing on the catwalk, looking toward the sky in confusion.

Parks looks at his hands and rubs them, and then looks up and spots Rees. He raises his hands in a "What the hell?" motion, and then places his hands over his ears. Rees is confused about what Parks is signaling and takes a step or two forward. He sees Parks then drop to his knees and open his mouth in what appears to be a scream. Rees is too far away to hear him, but Parks is obviously in pain and Rees begins an urgent trot toward the tower. However, his ears plug up after a couple of steps, somewhat like what happens in an airplane when the pressure changes with altitude.

Rees opens his mouth to release the pressure, but it isn't working. Taking a step back, he turns to make his way back into the building to tell Bouvier about Parks. He is thinking there should be safety inside the building, but safety from what he has no idea. He has that sensation you have as a child when you think a monster is emerging from the closet, but you will be safe if you can just pull the blankets over your head. This time it doesn't work.

As he turns, Rees glimpses Airman Harris, who has also made his way outside the building. Harris covers his ears and falls to his knees. As Rees moves toward him, the pressure becomes unbearable and he raises his hands to cusp his own ears. God, the pain. He tries to take another step and falls, unable to get up. He can sense the darkness envelope him. Ah, the sweet darkness that will take away the pain.

As Rees blacks out, he begins hallucinating and hears Bob Seger singing *Main Street* on an unseen radio. Suddenly, Seger's voice fades away and is replaced by that of a childhood friend who died long ago. He says, "Scott, we're here!"

In his mind, Rees asks his friend, "Yeah, so what?"

His friend keeps repeating, "Scott, there's nothing here, nothing here, nothing here, nothing here..."

Chapter 2

August is a hot and humid time of year in the Piedmont territory of North Carolina. Being outdoors can make a person miserable, tired, and just plain irritable. Serving in the United States Air Force frequently involves being out in the elements, although this is not a job one would consider hard, physical work. Well, sometimes, but that would depend on your Air Force Specialty Code (AFSC). Theirs is 81150, or Security Police Specialists, with their specialty being Security.

The career field splits into two categories, security and law enforcement. The latter features the ability to drive around in an air-conditioned vehicle, conduct traffic stops, and investigate crimes and such. The others get the "honor" of reporting to work at 0500 and sometimes sitting in a vehicle, whether it's a dark blue pickup truck, a Jeep, or armored vehicle, all without air conditioning, along with a partner with whom you ran out of things to talk about within the first hour of the shift. Though not demanding, it can become tedious and boring, along with being hot, but it is still work.

The day began as any other for Rees and his men, with no hint of the terrifying events to come. They were up before the sun peeked over the hills and stood guard mount with sixty-three other security policemen (SPs). Guard mount is the time when everyone shows for the day's duty and stands in rows to await the flight chief, a non-commissioned officer (NCO) who is in charge. It's basically roll call.

A flight is similar to an army platoon. A security flight provides security for aircraft, munitions, and the base perimeter. It provides mobile patrols and building security. Flights are broken into alphabetical order: Alpha, Bravo, Charlie, and Delta. Alpha is day shift, while the other three rotate between second and third shifts.

The guard mount area is located outside the rear of the security police station, or cop shop, with a corrugated roof as the only protection from the elements. Seeing "Ol' Sol" wasn't up yet, the real heat hadn't set in, but the humidity has no mercy on man or beast, no matter what time of day or night it is.

Two windows on the armory face the flight from the rear of the security police station. The armory secures the weapons, ammunition, radios, and other items until they are issued. It contains an assortment of death-delivering devices to include the armorer's bad breath, which always had the stench of Juicy Fruit chewing gum and the underlying reek of alcohol. It wouldn't be so bad if the guy didn't have such a loud voice and was always yapping, saying stupid stuff like, "Hey, ya want some ammo with that M-16? Gonna cost ya extra!"

Always a smart-ass comment, and he always leaned in close so the stench of his breath flowed over you like a whiff from a garbage bin containing empty beer cans. Everyone knew that he knew his breath stank.

Some guys are issued M-16 rifles with the M-203 grenade launcher attachment. The M-16 rifle is the standard issued weapon among all branches of the service. The M-203 is an updated grenade launcher that fires a 40-mm grenade. Other guys get the ground assault unit (GAU), which is an M-16 with a shortened barrel and collapsible stock.

Rees is from Yuma, Arizona. Yes, he's heard it before: nobody is from Yuma and everything in Yuma moves reeeeeally sloooowly. He is one of the few stationed here from a western state. Most of the flight personnel hail from the Eastern Seaboard. Rees stands six feet tall with a slim, all-around athletic build. He played basketball and baseball in high school. He has trouble keeping his dark hair and mustache within Air Force Regulation 35-10. AFR 35-10 covers the dress code as well as how you wear your hair, mustache, and grooming. Rees is the type of sergeant who likes his men and does what he can to take care of them. Most appreciate it. He tells them to always be honest with him. If they do something wrong and let him know, he will go to bat for them. But if he gets blindsided by his superiors about an airman or NCO screwing up, well, then they're on their own.

Facing the rear of the building and to the left are office windows for the assorted assholes the men fondly refer to as "back office personnel." They are the military equivalent of a civilian desk jockey or suit. Not really a bad lot, but you get a little envious when you're sweating your gonads off in the field and they're inside a cool, air-conditioned building. They get to come and go as they please, have lunch when they want, weekends and holidays off, make up rules for others to follow. Yep, come to think of it, they're assholes.

The flight chief, whose rank is master sergeant (MSgt.), is a big man standing six feet two inches and about 210 pounds, blond hair, with a great personality and professional attitude. He drives a newer Corvette and has a wife who is a real looker. The men in the flight have dubbed him "Captain America," a proper name they agreed. They don't call him Captain America to his face, even though they know he's aware of it.

Guard mount is where the security police flight personnel gather before going to their assigned posts. When the flight chief calls "fall in," they take their positions in line formation. He then has them stand at ease and conducts roll call, gives out posting assignments, briefings, and bulletin readings. Occasionally there will be an inspection, but normally the troops are forewarned so they can be their best. Everyone wears the new permanent press fatigue uniform with the updated subdued name tags and stripes (for those with stripes), having recently transitioned from the old cotton fatigues that featured blue and white name tags and stripes; highly polished black jump boots (bloused pants, of course), and a green web belt that contains handcuffs, flashlights, ammo pouches, and other items. To top it all off, they wear blue berets with the command crest attached in front. After guard mount, some switch out to the flight baseball cap or green fatigue cap.

Once in a great while, the flight is blessed with a visit from someone from the back office or even command to give someone an "attaboy," tell them about an upcoming base exercise (screwed again), or give an inspirational speech about how proud they are of them, often accompanied by some smartass in the rear row of formation softly humming the *Battle Hymn of the Republic* to snickers and snorts. This always gets a stern warning glare from Captain America. They even get an occasional visit from the orderly room personnel, explaining how they need to get the airman performance reports (APRs) in on time and travel vouchers done right, or other such mundane items. They listen like they care, because if the NCOs want their APRs going through, they must be nice to the orderlies.

On this day, they had none of that extracurricular activity, only the brief presence of a young lieutenant, who stops by to let them know he's alive. They don't pay him much attention because most of them have been security policemen longer than he has been a lieutenant, and he only visits when he feels they need to see him.

The flight goes to the armory prior to guard mount to gather their assigned weapons and equipment. They stand around and shoot the breeze until hearing the command to fall in. Rees walks to where Shepard is standing and stops next to him. Shepard is famed for his bullshit stories. Most are interesting, but the guys take them with a grain of salt. He is a big guy at six feet, one inch and 210 pounds, dark intense eyes, and at twenty years old he already has a receding hairline. Hailing from the mountainous area of the Carolinas, he is a true redneck reared in a backwoods cabin. He grew up hunting, fishing, knows how to dress his kills and clean the fish. He can cure and can goods. A true survivalist and self-contained person. Not having been around a lot of people growing up, he is considered a little uncouth at times, okay all the time. He also loves a good fight. He is a redneck, after all.

Next to him is Buck Sergeant (Sgt.) David Kriger, Airman First Class (A1C) Matthew Tosseti, and Sgt. Ben Montoya. Kriger is a good friend of Rees and hails from outside of Chicago. He's not very tall and has a great sense of humor. He has a ready smile and gets along with everyone. Brown hair and light blue eyes make him stand out in a crowd. He is one of the four medically trained personnel, or medics, in the flight who volunteered to take more medical training. There is no extra pay, but it looks good when promotion testing comes around.

Tosseti is the type of person who can find trouble wherever he is. He is a little rough around the edges and even has a mean streak in him, but he's one person you would want on your side in a fight. If he doesn't take a liking to you, it would be in your best interest to stay clear of him. On the other hand, if he does like you, he could be the best friend you ever had. Originally from Boston, Tosseti is an orphan and reared a street man, a fighter, and he won't take shit from anybody. He stands about five feet six inches, and his short-cropped, red hair fits the mold of an Italian-Irish brawler. Everyone says he looks like a miniature Incredible Hulk. He acts like the reference to the comic character insults him, but he actually likes it.

Montoya hails from Leesburg, Florida, a small town in the center of the state. He is a friendly guy, average build, sandy brown hair, brown eyes, and he always seems tanned. He has the faintest of a southern accent, even though he is of Cuban decent. Montoya smiles when required, but seems very serious most of the time and takes his job seriously.

They are listening to Shepard and shaking their heads, so Rees knows Shepard is captivating them with one of his tales. Sure enough, he hears Shepard spouting a tale about one of his escapades with a female. This is nothing unusual where Shepard is concerned and would be boring if told by anyone else. Without going into any of the sordid details, let's just say he has a way of making you cringe when talking about sex.

One thing about the military, the people are a close-knit group. It's a fraternity, a family of sorts. And like a family, not everyone gets along. Disagreements happen, but you're still a family. There's no way you will get sixty-three men together and expect them all to get along. Doesn't happen, but they are still a family.

Take, for instance, one night close to a year ago when half the flight was out at one of the local watering holes, a place called Bogart's Joint that since has burned down. Rees was sitting at a table with Montoya and his girl, Kriger with his girl, and Airman Nate Tucker. The others were scattered throughout the establishment, drinking their beers and talking. Suddenly, they heard a commotion at another table and saw three civilian gentlemen standing up and surrounding one of their guys. No one remembers the guy's name because he wasn't well-liked.

The guy was one of those who could get under your skin. You know he didn't mean to, but he couldn't help being an asshole. This was one of those times, and now he did it to some civilians. These guys weren't locals. The flight members knew most of the locals and they learned to leave the base personnel alone. These guys had been sitting with Airman What's-His-Name at a table in the center of the room. No one knows why nor did they care.

The civilians were so fixated on beating wants-his-name's ass that they didn't notice the others in the bar, one by one, were standing up and inching closer to them. Rees was transfixed on the scene and hadn't noticed Kriger leave the group. He heard glass breaking a minute later and thought nothing of it until Montoya slapped him on the arm to get his attention. Turning, he saw why.

Standing by a trash can near the jukebox was Kriger, who was breaking beer bottles. Grasping the neck of a bottle, he would break the base of it on the lip of the garbage can and hold the remnants up to inspect the jagged shards. He would then throw the broken bottle away, grab another, and do it again. This drew the attention of everyone in the bar, including the gentlemen who were about to whoop up on what's-his-name.

Kriger broke another bottle, examined the broken piece in his hand, and then looked at the three civilians who were holding what's-his-name. He looked from the bottle to the men, gazed around at everyone else, and smiled. He turned his head somewhat to take in all the flight personnel in attendance. Still smiling, he slowly returned his stare back at the three men and what's-his-name. The three civvies looked around and saw thirty men watching them, all slowly moving in their direction. This got their attention. They released what's-his-name, raised their hands in surrender, and backed off. They were told they were more than welcome to stay, but that what's-his-name's ass would not to be touched. They decided to leave. Good choice.

What's-his-name tried to thank everyone for helping him, but all he received was a "fuck off" and everyone went back to their tables. Ah family, gotta love 'em.

***

Captain America walked through the door into the guard mount area, and the flight members break up from their little cliques and stand in positions in squad order. They know the routine.

"Fall in!" he commands.

The men say their last few words and settle in to attention. As soon as everyone is in position, Captain America has them put at ease as he moves to the front position to address them.

"All right everyone, listen up for roll call and sound off when you hear your name."

He looks down at his clipboard containing the duty roster.

"Kriger!" he barks.

"Here, sir!"

"Romeo Three," Captain America replies, noting Kriger's posting assignment.

"Tosseti!" he barks again.

"Yo!" Tosseti comes back with his rough, thick Boston accent.

"Ten India!" the flight chief says, this time looking up from the roster to find Tosseti. "And Matt, please, let's not get into any mischief out there this time."

This elicits the usual snickers and laughs that come with having worked together for so long. Cops are mostly a tight-knit group of guys who can joke around and laugh at each other without someone getting their feelings hurt. This is one of those times.

"Fucks youse guys!" Tosseti rumbles. "Howz about I fuckin' bites youse fuckin' ears off, assholes. Just keep it up!"

His face becomes bright red as he speaks, making him look like a fireplug. It is all an act, but if you didn't know Tosseti, it could make you leery of him.

The flight chief breaks in on the oohs and ahhs.

"All right guys, settle down so we can get on with it."

They stop the laughing and settle into the routine of guard mount, listening solemnly as Captain America calls off names and assignments. After all the names are called and the last posts assigned, they have the privilege of listening to the weapon and vehicle safety briefing. This is always a little highlight in guard mount if any of the following apply: (a) the person giving it is an asshole; (b) he is terrified of public speaking, even in front of friends and co-workers; (c) he's a comedian, such as Kriger; (d) he stutters or stammers; or (e) everyone just plain likes the guy. It really doesn't matter. Someone always fits in one of the categories and catches hell from the rest of the flight.

Rees smiles, knowing he doesn't get the privilege of having to speak because of his rank. Been there, done that. RHIP (Rank Has Its Privileges.)

After accomplishing this task, the flight chief calls them to attention and asks, "Is anyone too sick, lame, or lazy to work?"

This always brings out the beast in the men, because they are all sick of the job and lame in the head, mostly due to alcohol consumption the night before. And of course, they're all too lazy to work.

No one would dare say this, but they do laugh and then shout out, "No, Master Sergeant!" at which time he commands them to "Post." This means the same as "Get your lazy asses outta here and get to work." The men disperse and collect their canvas equipment bags, which contain everything from helmets, flak vests, and gas masks to food, drinks and reading material.

For this shift, the majority of the flight is posted at the 7 and 15 areas. The 7 area is where the bombers are parked and the 15 area, which is where Rees and his team are unfortunate enough to be assigned, is where all the bombs are stored.

After everyone gathers their bags and equipment, they walk out of the guard mount area and head toward the road along the side of the station. The vehicles used to transport them to their destinations are parked there. Today, they have one bus and a flatbed truck. Being that there are fewer people going to the 15 area than the 7 area, Rees's group gets the truck. This isn't always so bad if you don't mind cramming thirteen bodies into the back of the truck. The driver and area supervisor ride in the front, of course. A breeze can help cool you off during the summer, but in the winter, man is that a bitch.

Rees climbs into the passenger side of the truck. Everyone else scrambles into the bed of the vehicle, helping each other up. When fully loaded, someone slaps the top of the truck and the driver pulls the vehicle out onto the road. They are on their way to the base's Munitions Storage Depot (MSD), or Mud Dump for short.

Rees closes his eyes and rests his head against the seat, listening to all the chatter and bullshit going on behind him. Shepard once again is going on about one of his sexcapades, while others talk about sports, the local bar they had been to, girls, and other trivial things guys talk about. Rees is minding his own business until he gets caught up in one of the conversations.

"Hey Ben!" he hears Tosseti yell over the wind.

"What, Matt?" Montoya asks back.

"I hear that queers wear cowboy boots!" Tosseti shouts for everyone to hear in his truly Tosseti voice.

All other conversations cease and everyone listens.

Montoya is silent for a minute and Rees thinks he is going to ignore Tosseti. Then Montoya speaks up.

"Matt, I don't know anything about that. You might want to ask Sergeant Rees."

"Sergeant Rees, hey chief!" Tosseti yells through the open rear window.

"What can I do for you, Airman Tosseti?" Rees asks with his eyes still closed.

"Sgt. Montoya says fer me to ask you if it's true that queers wear cowboy boots."

"Yes, Tosseti. It's quite true," Rees answers without moving a muscle.

This causes quite a stir and Tosseti loses it. Rees can hear the oohs and ahhs from the others, but Tosseti is getting animated. Rees opens his eyes and turns to see Tosseti holding onto the railing of the truck, shaking it back and forth, and making a sound that is in the proximity of a human laugh, or so Rees thinks.

Rees turns farther in his seat, looks through the open window and points at Montoya.

"Last time I conducted a dorm inspection, Sgt. Montoya had about a dozen pair in his closet," Rees says, perfectly happy to play along.

Tosseti completely loses it, shaking the railing so hard Rees thinks it might snap off like balsa.

"Ohhhh, he got you," Tosseti says to Montoya. "He got you good, slam!"

Montoya smirks, lifts his hand, gives the international one-fingered salute to everyone, and tells Tosseti he can go do something to himself that Rees doesn't think is humanly possible. Rees grins, snorts, and resumes his resting position to await their arrival at the Mud Dump.

Rees doesn't mind coming to work on a day like today. Sundays are quiet and no one is working except for them. Plus, they will be going on their three-day break after this shift. Rees is the area supervisor and stays in the building with the Reserve Force Team or Romeo Team, which is the mobile fire team. This is one of the easiest positions there is. It is comprised of a fire team leader, SSgt. Bouvier today, and three other team members whose job it is to back up any forces in need if attacked.

There are two Romeo teams, one in the Mud Dump and the other in the Aircraft Apron (AA), otherwise known as the Bird Cage. The Bird Cage is about a quarter of a mile from the Mud Dump and where the bombers are kept on standby. The Romeo Team drives an armored vehicle, official name "Cadillac Gage Commando," or M706 for the military, but unofficially it's called a Duck. It is an odd-shaped, amphibious armored vehicle that normally carries three people, but can carry up to nine. It has flat, sloping armor to help deflect bullets and heavier types of ordnance. The driver can look through a bullet-resistant portal in the front or open one of the front hatches and stick his head out. There are four large wheels and the vehicle can operate in water, thus the Duck nickname, though no one on the team has ever tried it, nor wants to.

The Duck has an M-60 machine gun in the turret. It is manned by Sgt. Kriger, who is also armed with a .38 revolver. Senior Airman Sean McGuire is armed with an M-16 and M-203 grenade launcher attachment. A1C Wallace Harris, likewise, is armed with an M-16 and serves as the driver and assistant gunner.

This is a plush assignment. Everyone sits around in the hardened bunker in a communal area and watches television, plays cards, eats, and does whatever they can to entertain themselves for eight hours. The only time they do anything constructive is when they have an exercise or go out to relieve another post for chow or a break.

The vehicle slows to a stop in front of the building and Alpha Flight members of the 13th Security Police Squadron have arrived at the Mud Dump for the day's duties at 0600 on August 9, 1980. They scramble off the back of the truck and go through checkpoints to enter the secure area and relieve the previous shift.

Rees exits from the front passenger seat and watches as the entry controller and alarm monitor walk into the building. The rest of the fifteen-man flight unloads their equipment and weapons, and then heads toward the entry control gate that leads into the depot and main building.

Bouvier asks Kriger to check out the M-60 machine gun mounted on the Duck as well as the Remington M-870 shotgun secured in a weapons rack inside. He turns to McGuire and asks him to check out the Duck itself; make sure it starts, lights are operational, etc., and for Harris to check the building for cleanliness. (Yeah, right). Tough jobs so far.

Rees goes into the Entry Control Point (ECP) room, or control room, to ensure everything there is operational and receive his debriefing from the off-going area supervisor. The Reserve Force stays in the Romeo room, which will be their tiny home for the next eight hours. It's about the size of a large living room, made of solid cinderblock and steel, and contains a table, chairs, couch, television, refrigerator, microwave, sink, and stove. Weapons ports, which are small openings that allow a person to fire a weapon out of if they are attacked, dot several places on the walls. The Duck is parked in the same room with them. It's just to the left as you enter the facility from the rear of the building. To the right is a hallway leading to the entry controller and alarm monitor area.

The alarm monitor, A1C Eric McAdams, keeps the aircraft posting board up to date, monitors the alarms to the bunkers and the radio, answers the phone, types the blotter (shift log), and is basically the lifeline to everyone in the area. The entry controller, A1C Raymond Nionee, monitors the entry and exit of personnel.

Nionee is from the Cherokee Nation and a great guy. He takes his job seriously and everyone likes him. Quiet most of the time, Nionee has a great sense of humor and throws a zinger at the others when the occasion arises. Rees never even knew Nionee was Cherokee until one day when Nionee called some guy a "usdi watali." When asked what the hell he had said, Nionee explained it meant "tiny dick" or "baby penis." Everyone got a kick out of that and began calling the guys on the other flights usdi watali whenever the chance arose. That really confused and pissed them off. Hell, it was more fun than calling them "bug fucker" or "mosquito dick."

The mobile posts outside are called 15 Delta and 15 Bravo, and each consists of a two-man unit operating M-151 Jeeps. They monitor inside the fence perimeter, responding to alarm calls and keeping checks on the static guards. The Jeeps are mounted with an M-60 machine gun, set up the way you see in the movies.

The static guard posts, which carry the official designation of Individual Visual Assessment (IVA), are stationed in the corners of the fence line obscured from the tower. They sit in a tiny gate shack containing a chair and a space heater for the winter.

It's early morning, but this time of year it becomes warm very quickly after sunrise. The area is quiet except for the constant sounds of insects. The river running just outside the base boundaries flows noisily and the sound echoes off the buildings and bunkers, making it quite soothing at times. It is usually like this on the weekends because no one is working in the area except for the security police (SPs). There are no trees, so no shade whatsoever. The area had been stripped of all trees and bushes to allow a clear line of sight for the guards and eliminate cover for anyone who might be in the area illegally. It makes complete sense, but when you're sweating your ass off during a hot August day like this, you just want some shade. Several roads crisscross the area to each weapons bunker, building, and fighting position.

This day isn't any different from any other day except something feels off. Rees can't put his finger on it, but something doesn't feel right. He shakes it off and goes about the day, settling in after conducting the checks and assuring all posts are manned. After sitting for a few minutes, he still feels like something is wrong. He walks outside and stands alone listening, to nothing. No insects making their insistent, nerve-wracking cries, no birds singing, nothing. Not until he thinks back on it does he realize there are no mosquitoes, no crickets, no gnats, no spiders, and no grasshoppers. Again, nothing. Even if someone had noticed and brought it to anyone's attention, he doubts they would have cared. He shakes off the feeling and returns to the control room, where Bouvier has just finished making out the chow relief roster for the day.

Bouvier glances down at McAdams, who is plotting the board, and asks him to call over to the Bird Cage and see if Security Alert Team 3 can handle taking a person with them. This two-man team roams the area of the base closest to the Mud Dump and the Bird Cage.

"Yeah, in a minute, I'm a little busy with the board right now," McAdams replies, not bothering to look in Bouvier's direction.

McAdams is one of the youngest among them, not just in the Mud Dump, but also the flight and probably the squadron. He joined the service at the age of seventeen and had to get his parents' permission to join, which from what everyone was told took some persuading as his parents are bona fide hippies. He stands about five feet nine, blond hair, 150 pounds give or take, and always has a lopsided smirk on his face. A smart mouth whenever he can, McAdams is on someone's bad side most of the time. It isn't always his fault. People tend to push him, including Bouvier. As a supervisor, he shouldn't, but they had their differences concerning a female some months back. They weren't the best of friends then and the young lady did nothing to help the relationship. McAdams is only an A1C and Bouvier is a staff sergeant, so he must check himself at times to keep from letting orders get personal. Rees gets along fine with McAdams as they, along with Nionee, date three women who are very close. In fact, two of them are sisters.

Rees hears Nionee utter a profanity. Turning around, he sees Nionee staring up at the generator room fire alarm and charging meter. It's impossible for them to know their lives are about to change forever.

Chapter 3

Rows of lights flash and flicker on consoles, illuminating the faces of people in the white control room. A quiet series of clicks and hums emitting from rows of large computer banks lining the walls permeates the room. Reel-to-reel tapes twirl and spin with their mass amounts of data. The barely audible sound of voices intermingles with the computer noise. Faces are still and serious as each technician stares at a green screen showing constantly updating data. Others read the printouts flowing from the machines.

Officers standing in the room stare alternately at the computer screens, then at the technicians, then up at a giant screen that almost fills one wall entirely. They wear worried expressions, expressions that come with responsibility. Things are not going as expected, with rank determining responsibility for specific assignments.

The huge screen is showing nothing of importance, but they can't keep their eyes off it. The snowy static and wavering lines are similar to television reception that isn't worth a shit. It might be nothing more than an annoyance for most people if this was a *Monday Night Football* game, but what they need to see now involves the lives of fifteen men.

Heads will roll, and roll hard and fast, if the Clio project is scratched due to technical difficulties or pure incompetence. These men of rank have a reason for their worried expressions.

Major General Richard Lucas watches through a window from a sound-proof office above that lets him see the goings on in the control room. He watches with a calmness that comes from years of dealing with heads of power and making decisions during conflicts and war. It is second nature to him. This is just another project. Granted, a project more interesting than any before, but still just a project.

Gen. Lucas turns his mahogany high-back chair from the scene below and pushes the off button on the speaker system that rests on the desk he has had since the Korean Conflict. The desk, given to him by an old colleague, goes with him wherever he is stationed. It is big, made of cherry wood with brass and silver fittings, and it feels a part of him. He is tired of listening to the confusion below. He is tired of things not going as planned. He is tired of being on the hot seat and the continuing harassment from government talking heads. He is tired of constant explanations of what was not going right, tired of the excuses. Lucas places his forearms on the desk and leans forward. He presses another button on a console.

"Shelly?" he says into the microphone as he turns to look back out the window.

"Yes, sir?" the voice of his secretary comes back.

"Please get in touch with the chief and tell him I wish to see him ASAP. Have him booked on the first flight out of Washington and report as soon as he arrives. You have that?"

"Yes, sir," she replies.

"Oh, and Shelly, will you bring me a cup of coffee?"

"Sure thing, General."

Lucas sits back in his chair and his thoughts turn to the chief – Chief Master Sergeant (CMSgt.) Joseph G. Black. "Chief" is the proper title of a chief master sergeant. The chief stands six feet four inches with 240 pounds of lean muscle. He holds a bachelor's degree in engineering and a master's degree in physics. He is also one of the youngest E-9s in the air force at thirty-two. The chief could have been an officer, but he preferred being enlisted. Started out enlisted and stayed enlisted. A chief master sergeant is considered upper management, and he has enough pull to keep himself in the field and not behind a desk.

Chief Black was assigned to an army unit in Vietnam when then-Major Richard Lucas made his acquaintance. The major was assigned to an intelligence squadron. Prior to that, he was assigned to the Air Force Office of Special Investigations (AFOSI or OSI for short). He met then-Staff Sergeant Black during briefings and was impressed with his quiet demeanor, watchful eyes, and a keen sense of intellect.

Black excelled in electronics, including the new computers. He took physics classes and admired Einstein. He wrote his thesis on the theory of time travel. The thought of sending a person through time appealed to his imagination.

Lucas heard an interesting story about Black that impressed him. The sergeant had ordered a handheld computer device from a Radio Shack retail store, which he tweaked to decrypt an enemy code. Black used it to feed the enemy false information, leading their patrols into ambushes. The result was the death and capture of numerous NVA (North Vietnamese Army) and the confiscation of maps, intelligence information, and equipment.

Lucas was amazed at how young Black was at the time and how huge he was. Black looked as though he belonged on a football field more than in a uniform. He knew Black played – he was given a full ride to the University of North Carolina – but he only played to keep his scholarship. His main drive was to get his degree.

Black was highly disciplined and carried himself confidently, but not cocky. Full military bearing, he was just as quick to smile, though it didn't always show through to the steel-blue eyes you could see a mile away.

The major kept tabs on SSgt. Black for a few years, and when Lucas was promoted to full colonel, he had the since-promoted MSgt. Black transferred to his squadron to become a member of his team. Col. Lucas took Black under his wing and the two became very close. Black became a personal advisor and a partner to his superior.

Black had always talked about time travel and Lucas became increasingly intrigued. He encouraged Black to keep at and even gave him access to working labs with a team of scientists. After a few years,

Black told the colonel he believed he had a working theory on how to make time travel a reality. Lucas was impressed when he read Black's proposal. He handed the report up the chain of command and a specialized group of scientists was assigned to his team. It took almost a year before the team informed Lucas it was ready to build a time machine.

The time machine was to be built at Area 51 in New Mexico, the classified base in the desert where top-secret projects are created, built, and tested. Within another year, a functioning small-scale time machine had been assembled. Col. Lucas told Black he wanted a demonstration so he could present it to those who held the purse strings. A bigger budget would make it possible to fabricate a larger machine. A date was set, and the wheels were put in motion.

Congressmen, senators, generals, and other VIPs were present on the day of the demonstration. Col. Lucas and MSgt. Black were on pins and needles. The model had not been tested because it could only work once before requiring a complete rebuild. The cost was enormous and the budget allowed for the production of just the one unit. Black was confident of success, but the slightest doubt is always present.

Lucas spoke to the group and explained what they were about to witness. The room filled with murmurs and whispers as disbelievers looked on in anticipation. The colonel introduced MSgt. Black, who approached the group.

"Gentlemen and sirs, what you are going to see is something which has never been tried before, so this will be new to us as much as it will be to you," Black said as he walked toward the covered time machine. "This is something that mankind has dreamed of for years."

He reached out and pulled the sheet off the machine. It was nothing impressive, just a large metal box that housed the actual working parts with a beam emitter attached to the top and a small control panel. It looked like something from a 1950s sci-fi show.

"I would like to introduce you to Clio," Black said. "Clio is the first machine capable of transporting objects, and perhaps people, through time."

The box itself housed the components, but the computers and main portions of the time machine itself were in a larger room, out of sight from the spectators. On the other side of the room was a small platform that held a small cage. The cage contained a guinea pig, banana, metal toy Jeep, folded shirt, a bullet, and a container of water.

"The objects you see are minerals and vegetable. A live subject in the guinea pig, and some materials someone may want to send to the future or the past," Black said as he walked to the control panel.

Flipping switches, he had everyone's attention as they strained to see what he was doing. Electricity permeated the room and the volume of murmuring increased. The beam emitter was aimed at the cage across the room.

"If I may have your attention please, we are about to begin. Everything is in order, so relax and enjoy the show," Black said with some showmanship.

With that, he pressed a final button and the cage began to shimmer. A haze thickened around the cage and a high-pitched sound grew to a painful level. Several guests placed their hands over their ears, others winced and squinted as they watched the cage shimmer even more. Then, it disappeared.

Every guest stood up with a look of astonishment on their faces. Some were intrigued, while others harrumphed and wore a look of skepticism.

"Where'd it go?" someone shouted.

"That's some smoke and mirrors," another yelled.

"Bullshit!" yet another exclaimed.

Col. Lucas came to the front with his hands raised, palms out, and asked everyone to calm down.

"Okay, what's the deal?" one congressman asked. "Is this a parlor trick?"

The colonel looked to MSgt. Black.

"No, sir," Black replied. "What you saw was what it is: time travel."

Black turned back to the console.

"Now, I'm bringing the cage back as we speak."

He adjusted a few dials and pressed a button. This time there was no static or haze, nothing. The cage just reappeared. The only thing different was the cage reappeared a couple of inches off the floor and four feet from where it had been moments earlier. The cage fell with a clatter and lay on its side, with the guinea pig appearing unharmed as it sniffed the air.

After a moment of shock, someone asked the obvious question of why the cage was not where it was when it had vanished. Black explained that the cage may have materialized on the side of a hill and rolled, or something may have kicked it. He could not be sure. As for it falling to the floor, he explained that the machine is programmed to materialize all objects a few inches off the ground so as to minimize the chances of them materializing inside the ground. He added that the same process occurred when the objects materialized in the past.

"Where did you send it? I mean, when did you send it? What time?" a congressman asked.

"Sir, the cage stayed where it was when transported," Black responded. "But for when, we sent it to the year 1776. A befitting time, we thought."

There were smiles from most, but the looks of doubt remained for others. Black patiently answered a rapid-fire barrage of questions while several people came forward to admire and examine the time machine.

Lucas and Black stood nearby and smiled with satisfaction. Clio had done its job and the two figured it wouldn't be long before funds rolled in and a larger version of Clio, called Clio II, could be in production. Once built, they would be ready for the next phase of the experiment: sending people back in time. They'd make history. The two men smiled at the thought.

Unknown to Lucas and Black, a lone senator stood unseen in the shadows, watching the two military men as they congratulated each other. Senator Herbert Minten wanted this machine and what it could do. He smiles and walks away, his mind already turning and thinking about leveraging the past to benefit his future.

***

The general was still smiling as he recalled the success of Clio's debut when Shelly walks into his office with a cup of steaming coffee.

"General Lucas?" she asks as she approaches his desk. "Sir?"

"Huh?" he says, looking up and breaking from his daydream. "Oh, yes, yes. Thank you, Shelly."

Shelly smiles and asks if there was anything else she can do for him. The general returns the smile, declines, and dismisses her. As she nears the door, he calls to her.

"Ah, Shelly?"

"Yes, sir?"

"Did you get in touch with the chief?"

"Yes, sir. I did. He said he should be here in about two hours."

"Good. Thanks again, Shelly. That will be all for now."

Lucas sits drinking his coffee and stares at his desk.

"What's going on out there?" he wonders. "God, I hope nothing serious has happened."

The lives of fifteen men are at stake. Even though they were deemed expendable, they are still men all the same. The general rises and walks to the window overlooking the control room. He stares at the giant screen still filled with static, white noise, flickering, filling the room with a reflective light much like a television left on after the broadcast has ended for the night. Coffee cup forgotten, he hopes everything has gone according to plan. He wonders what could be going through the minds of the men they had sent somewhere they were not meant to be.

***

Chief Black was reading in his favorite recliner when he heard the phone ring. He walks to the table and sees the flashing light on the black pushbutton phone indicating "Bank," the code name for the facility containing Clio II. Black switches on the crypto scrambler and picks up the phone, activating the automatic recorder.

"Chief Master Sergeant Joseph G. Black, go ahead Bank," he says into the receiver.

A hissing noise associated with a long-distance call fills the handset.

"Chief Master Sergeant Joseph G. Black, voice identification clear," a mechanical voice responds. "You may speak, Bank."

"Chief, Shelly here, the general wishes to see you. Priority item 2."

"Copy that, Shelly. I'll be there in approximately two hours," Black replies.

He quickly calls Andrews Air Force Base to make sure a jet will be waiting for him and heads out the door. Something must have gone wrong, he figures, otherwise Shelly wouldn't be calling. He knew something was bound to go wrong. Clio II was not ready to send people into the past. They needed to conduct more tests before embarking on such a high-risk action. They had all the time in the world to get this right, no pun intended, so why the hurry?

"Damn it," he thinks as he drives to the base. "No use speculating. I'll find out what the problem is in a few hours."

The chief parks his Porsche at Base Operations, exits and walks into the building. A C-20 Gulfstream is fueled, flight plans laid in, and the pilots on board and waiting for him on the tarmac. He walks straight through Base Ops and onto the waiting plane. Within a few minutes, the plane is taxing on the runway. Black sits back, looking out his window as they take off, concentrating on what may have gone wrong. He hopes it's not something that could be detrimental to the fifteen men used in the experiment. He kicks himself for acting childishly when the Bank Council told him it didn't matter if he was present or not for Clio II's activation. He knows he should have stayed to make sure everything went smoothly. The technicians running the program didn't fully understand Clio II and that the slightest variation could end in disaster.

"Fools," he thinks.

Black has nothing but contempt for the Bank Council except for his mentor, General Lucas, who has always stood by him. The council had pushed for an early test and politics won out. He knew this had put a strain on the general, put him between a rock and a hard place.

The flight was nearly over before the chief even realized it, being deep in thought as he was. The pilot's voice comes over the speaker announcing they are in final approach to Pope AFB. The jet rolls to a stop on the tarmac and Black walks down the steps onto the flight line, heading straight for Base Operations. He is greeted inside by some young-looking 2nd lieutenant, accompanied by a staff sergeant and two security policemen.

"Chief Black?" the lieutenant asks.

"Yes, sir," Black replies.

"I'm Lieutenant Harding from the Bank. We have a vehicle waiting outside for you. My orders are to see that you get to the Bank as soon as possible."

The chief nods his head, grunts something in acknowledgment, and follows the lieutenant out the front door. The staff sergeant and security policemen fall in behind the chief. The trip is uneventful, the lieutenant babbling on about how important it must be, what with the VIP treatment given to the chief.

Black feels stifled, not giving a damn about the lieutenant or the staff sergeant, but wonders again about why he is needed. All the while, he stares at the two SPs (security policemen). By the time they arrive at the Bank, the chief has it in his imagination to grab the lieutenant by the throat and crush it with his two fingers. Instead, he thanks the man for his help. He rolls his eyes at the two SPs as he exits the vehicle, and they grin and nod in understanding.

"These guys should be grateful they only had to ride with the lieutenant and escort me," he thinks of the SPs. "They could have been on the team that's God knows where and be dead by now."

He breaks from his musing and passes through the manned checkpoint, then on to the front doors of the Bank.

"Jesus," he thinks as he runs his identification card into a slot and types in a code. "Here I am making history and it feels no different than any other time."

The doors click open and he enters the building. Walking to a desk where another SP sergeant awaits, Black hands him his identification card. The sergeant checks his clipboard, hands the card back, and gives him an identification badge to wear. Black places the badge on his uniform shirt pocket and proceeds toward the elevators. He steps into the first one and says "Thirteen."

"Shift 13," a voice confirms over the speaker.

The doors close and the elevator begins its decent to the building's lower levels. The elevator stops at its destination and the chief emerges. Taking a right, he passes through another manned checkpoint and continues down the corridor to the general's office. He is greeted with a big smile from Shelly.

"How you are doing, Miss Moneypenny?" Black says in his best James Bond posh English accent.

Shelly smiles sheepishly and says without missing a step, "M is expecting you, James. Go right in."

Smiling, Black lays his cap on a table by the door and heads for the general's office. He takes note of the .45 caliber pistol Shelly keeps near her left knee behind the desk.

"Meant to ask, you any good with that thing?" he inquires.

She grins and replies, "Oh, you mean this little thing? Well, let's just say I will put down anything I want to very quickly."

"I feel sorry for anyone who attempts to try you, Shelly," the chief grins back.

He opens the door to the general's office, steps in, and closes it behind him. The earlier banter quickly forgotten, he is now all business.

"Hello, General," he says while closing the door.

Lucas looks up from his paperwork and a smile breaks across his face.

"Hello, Chief. Boy, am I glad to see you. Thanks for coming so fast. How was the flight? Not too dull I hope," the general says while indicating the chief should take a seat.

"Not too bad, sir. I was lost in thought for most of it, and as you know it's not a long trip," Black says as he walks toward the desk to salute.

The general leans back in his chair and returns the salute.

"How many times have I told you not to salute me when we're alone? No need for formalities."

"Sorry, sir. Don't want to get into a habit of not saluting a superior," Black says with a grin and takes a seat.

"Well, you don't know how relieved I am that you came," Lucas begins. "I know you're upset with the Bank Council and the way they handled this. And the way they handled you. Having said that, I've got a feeling something may have gone wrong."

Black leans forward, elbows on his knees, and clasps his hands. He looks at them a second and speaks.

"Sir, I didn't handle it well myself, but I'm here to do what I can to help. One thing I have to tell you, nothing better befall any of those airmen or there will be hell to pay."

Lucas stares at the chief for a few seconds, nods, and then rises. He walks from behind his desk and stands beside him.

"Let's take a walk down there and maybe you can let us know your thoughts."

The men take the short walk to the control room and Black stares at the giant screen for some time. He then makes his way over to one of the main consoles to review readouts, check displays, and observe the technicians. Walking over to a matrix printer, he scans several more pages of printouts showing operational readings on Clio. He collects the pages and asks a civilian technician to get him information on everything since the experiment started. The technician acknowledges the chief and scampers away as Black walks back to the general.

"Sir, is there a place for me to work?" he asks. "I'll need time to go over all the data and then maybe I can find out why we aren't getting any visual. It may be just a technical glitch or the shit may have hit the fan. Do we know if all the cameras made it to the timeline? Are they in place?"

Black turns and scans the pages as he heads toward the stairs. Lucas comes up beside him and keeps stride.

"As far as we know, the cameras were sent back without any problems," General Lucas replies. "We had a picture before the men were sent. The crew checked each camera and assured me they were all operational. Anyway, you can use my office, Joe."

"One thing for sure, this wasn't Clio's fault," the chief says. "I can already tell that human error was the cause."

"You can tell that by just scanning a few printouts?" Lucas asks.

"General, I designed most of that transporter. I built it. Hell, I watched it grow, you might say. I know that time machine more than anyone else around here, as you well know. I installed backup systems that no one is aware of. Not even you, sir."

The surprise on Lucas's face shows.

"What systems?" he asks.

Black chuckles and claps the general on the back as they reach the sliding glass doors.

"General Lucas, my friend, if Clio had any glitches during transportation, she is programmed to return whatever was being transported back to the original time and designation, then she is to shut herself down. She can't restart without my okay," Black explains.

"You're too much, Joe," Lucas says as he shakes his head. "But why didn't you tell me? Not that I'm upset, but I always thought we trusted each other better."

"Couldn't afford to, sir. You've been getting pressure from Washington, namely the Bank Council, about this project. What with them pushing up the timeline for the test and giving you hell about it, I didn't want something like this getting out. A guy has to have some secrets, you know. Besides, you know now and I'm trusting you will keep it between us."

General Lucas opens the door to his office and gestures for the chief to enter. It's not protocol, but no one saw except Shelly, and she knows their relationship is more than a supervisor and subordinate. Lucas walks to his desk and sits down, indicating that Black should have a seat.

"All right, let me get this straight," the general begins as he turns his chair around to look at the screen. "This means that if Clio didn't poop the chute, then someone on this crew did?"

"Yes, sir. That's about the size of it. Of course, I must go over all this data first," Black answers.

"Find it, Joe. We don't how much time we have, or rather how much time those men out there have. Hopefully they are all right, but we can't take too much time figuring this out. We need to know what's going on out there. Good God, man. They could still be traveling through time, not having reached their destination!"

"It doesn't really matter right now, sir," Black states. "Whatever has happened has happened. Not much we can do about it right now. If they're trapped in a time continuum, then they're stuck. If that's the case, we may still be able to save them. But if they're in a time warp, then they're gone. We won't be able to locate them. They could have even materialized inside a solid material."

Lucas snaps his head around toward the chief at that statement. Black raises his hand in a "hold on" gesture and continues.

"Not to say anything like that has happened and I hope it hasn't. I'll find out soon enough, sir. I'm hoping nothing detrimental has happened and we can get them back."

Chief Black rises and walks toward the general, placing the data and printouts on the desk.

"How long do you think it will take you, Joe?" Lucas asks.

"I don't know," the chief responds. "It could be a few minutes, a few hours, or worse-case scenario, a few days."

The general rises and walks to the door and asks Shelly to make a fresh pot of coffee. Black smiles and thinks about how coffee is a staple in the military, how it keeps things running and is an important morale booster. This is his last distracting thought as he blocks everything else out and immerses himself into the data spread out before him.

Two hours pass and the chief speaks only once during that time to say thanks as the general places another a cup of java in front of him. Suddenly, an exclamation breaks the silence.

"Damn!" Black says as he stares at the printouts.

General Lucas has not left the room the entire time and has been patiently waiting on a couch near the door. When the chief speaks, he stands and walks over to where Black is holding up a long page of a printout and staring at it.

"What have you found?" Lucas asks.

"Who's working the DSI? Sorry, the Degree Servo Instrumentation panel?" Black demands.

The general walks behind his desk and shuffles through papers.

"Well, there are three shifts ..." he begins before being interrupted by Black.

"No, no, I mean during initial sendoff?"

"That would have been Captain Henries. Why, does he have something to do with this?" Lucas inquires.

"Yes sir, and I need to see him right now!" Black exclaims. "Where in the hell did they get these people? Was anyone vetted, or did they grab the first sycophant in line for a job?"

Not bothering to answer the question, the general presses the intercom button on his desk.

"Shelly, get in contact with Captain Henries and have him report to me ASAP," he says.

In civilian terms, ASAP means As Soon As Possible. In military terms it means Right. Fucking. Now!

As soon as Shelly acknowledges the order, he turns to Chief Black and asks, "What did you find, Joe?"

Black tears off a section of the printout and discards the rest. Placing the printout on the desk, he turns it toward the general and points to a line of numbers.

"See these numbers here, sir?" he asks.

Leaning forward to get a better look, the general nods in acknowledgement.

"Well, these are parts of the numeric formula that adjust the elevation of materials and men sent though Clio," Black explains. "You remember the demonstration, when the items returned and materialized off the floor?"

The general again nods his head in affirmative and mutters, "Yes, yes."

"Well, look at those numbers here. There's a discrepancy between these numbers here and these over here," the chief says as he grabs another section of the printouts. "That means the elevation was off when the men got to their destination, which I believe they have reached, but they may have experienced trouble upon arrival. This also means Captain Henries was derelict in his duties. He was either unqualified to be at his station or asleep at the wheel. The amount of elevation the men and materials were to be upon arriving was off by, I don't know, several feet maybe. I'll have to take a deeper look into this, sir."

"So, the transported men and materials may have fallen several feet when they materialized?" the general asks with a perplexed look. "Okay, that could be a problem, but why isn't anything showing up on screen?"

Black drops the readouts onto the desk and looks at the general.

"Sir, the Degree Servo Instrumentation panel – the DSI – is not running in sequence, thus causing a simultaneity breakdown," he says.

The general looks perplexed and Black catches it.

"Sir, a simultaneity breakdown means events which are simultaneous as measured in one reference frame are not simultaneous as measured in another frame that moves relative to the first. It's like a phase shift. Okay, think of it this way: you're watching a football game on TV and listening to it on a radio. You hear the radio announcer call the play, and then a few seconds later the television shows it. There's a short delay between the two signals. That's what happened here. The DSI is not in sync with the monitors, so the delay is causing the monitors to show static. You won't see a thing until we adjust the DSI. It shouldn't take long once I get down there and have a chance to work on it."

The general nods in understanding, even though he doesn't. He just wants the damn thing corrected and doesn't want to get into a discussion about how to get it accomplished.

"The screen's not the priority right now," Black continues, again raising his hand before the general can break in, "getting the corrected elevation for the men we sent out is. I'll get that done and then work on getting you a picture."

The general watches Black for a few seconds and then thinks of something.

"What about Clio herself?" he offers. "Is she operational? I mean, once we get the picture back up?"

"Clio should be partially operational," Black answers. "I'll run some preliminary tests and a diagnostic check. She won't be able to transport the men back right now, but she could send or receive smaller objects, such as food, ammo, weapons, if need be.

"But humans?" he shakes his head. "She'll need a lot of fine tuning before that can happen."

"Just do what you can, Joe," Lucas says.

Black leans over the printout, grabs a pen, and begins making corrections. The general straightens himself up and tells Black to meet him in the control room when he's finished. As the general walks toward the door, Black leans on the desk and speaks without looking up.

"Richard," he says, causing the general to freeze with his hand on the doorknob.

Chief Master Sergeant Joseph Black has never called General Lucas by his first name. A small shiver runs down his spine as he releases the doorknob and turns to face the chief.

"Yes, Joe, what is it?" he asks.

Black scribbles on the printouts again, and in the same calm voice he always uses when upset or in deep thought replies, "Sir, we may have at least one man dead or injured. These numbers I was showing you are the degrees in elevation for the poor son of a bitch unlucky enough to have been assigned the tower detail. When he rematerialized, he didn't have the tower surrounding him. So I'd say since the elevation was off and he wasn't set to be near the ground, he fell about sixty feet. That makes him eligible for death or serious bodily injury, wouldn't you say, sir?"

Black continues to write on the printouts and never looks up. The general knows the chief is upset; not at him, but at the whole program being taken from him.

"Holy help Captain Henries," General Lucas thinks as he stands by the door watching the chief work. He doesn't know what to say. He has lost men before under his command, but that was war. This was different. This is peacetime. The general feels guilty because Black had warned the Bank Council that something like this could happen in their rush to proceed. After a few more seconds, he turns and exits the room.

The general walks through the lobby trying to reassure himself that military personnel die all the time during peacetime. Firemen, security policemen, both on duty. Test pilots, hell regular pilots give their lives when flying. This is the military, and this is a military experiment, and sometime sacrifices have to be made. Sometimes sacrifices come in the form of death.

General Lucas reaches the control room, and as he stands there watching the technicians and others go about their jobs, he thinks, "Who am I fooling?"

He is angry, too. If someone has died, then they died without knowing why and what was happening. This isn't about sending men on a patrol where individual tactics and training come into play. A man has a chance in the field.

These men didn't have a choice or a chance. They were snatched from their time on this earth and sent to a time when their great-great-great grandfathers had lived. They didn't have a chance to prepare before being whisked away to another time. Sure, their skills would come into play if they are still alive, as he hoped and prayed they are.

General Lucas scans the room once more and then turns his attention to the big screen. It shows constant static and snow, filling the room with a white noise. The screen is purported to be a window into history. The general watches, waits, and wonders where his men are. And more importantly, how they are.

Chapter 4

Rees awakes to open spaces surrounding him. His head aches and nausea churns in his gut like a bad hangover. Unable to move, he lay with his face on the ground. The smell of pine and the sting of needles pressing into his skin has the attention of his senses. He could swear he had been standing on concrete or asphalt moments earlier.

He notices the insects are back, as is the chirping of the birds. He can hear the wind rustling though the trees. He turns his head to look around and sees he is laying among spaced pine trees.

"How the hell did I get here?" he thinks.

Groaning and dizzy, he lifts himself into a pushup position, knees still on the ground. He lays back down and gathers enough energy to roll onto his back. The pain in his head quickly builds to a crescendo before settling into a dull throb. He opens one eye and sees the sky is clear, bright blue, and not a cloud in sight. It is boiling hot and he can feel sweat running down his face in droplets like tiny little warm springs. It's like one of those weekend mornings when you wake up but can't bring yourself to get out of bed. Just lay there and hit the snooze for another half hour. Maybe then he'd feel better.

Mercifully, he does just that because when he opens his eyes again, the nausea has passed and the pain in his head has receded enough to become tolerable. He sits up. Good, still no nausea.

He looks around and spots Airman Harris lying about fifteen feet away, also in a bed of pine needles. Rees stands, but too fast. He has to fight off another wave of nausea that thankfully dissipates quickly.

His web belt has twisted around, and as he straightens it, he sees his .38 and other items are still attached. Another good sign. Rees calls out to Harris, but no answer. He walks, more like stumbles, toward Harris's motionless form, still calling his name. Squatting beside him, he places a hand on Harris's back. Harris is breathing – a good sign – but Rees is not sure what to do next because his CPR and buddy care training didn't cover this. He's disoriented and confused.

"I need to get my shit together and figure this out," he thinks.

He hears a rustling noise and looks up to see Airman McAdams stumbling toward him. He looks like Rees feels: sick and with a look of confusion.

"You all right, McAdams?" Rees asks.

"Yeah, I-I guess so. Little dizzy. What's going on, Sarge? Where are we? One second I'm sitting at the desk, then I hear this noise, pain washes over me, and 'Bam!' I wake up to... this," McAdams says while indicating the area with his hand and noticing Harris on the ground. "Is he okay?"

Rees shrugs his shoulders and looks down at Harris's still form.

"Yeah, I think so. He's breathing," he answers. "I'm not sure what to do right this instant, but if we're all right, he probably is, too. We'll just have to wait and see."

McAdams points his thumb over his shoulder and says, "Airmen Nionee, McGuire and Sergeant Bouvier are over there."

Rees turns and sees the Duck. It's right where it should be if it was in the Romeo room. Kneeling beside it is Sgt. David Kriger, using the open hatch for support. Rees hurries to him and Kriger lifts his head in obvious pain, squinting with one eye closed and the other trying to focus. Rees knows how he feels and puts the breaks on Kriger's efforts as he tries to stand.

"Whoa, David. Not so fast. Take a few minutes to adjust," Rees says as he kneels beside him. "You'll get your feet back under you in a few."

Scanning the area, Rees can see boxes of grenades, rounds for the M-203 grenade launcher, two more M-16s, ammo, the M-60 machine gun, and an assortment of other items arranged the same as if they, too, were in the Romeo room. He informs McAdams that Kriger is okay and to bring the others back to the Duck if they have regained consciousness.

"What the fuck just happened?" Kriger asks. "My head feels like it's going to explode."

Rees gives Kriger a hand up. He wobbles, so Rees leans him against the Duck for support.

A few minutes later, McAdams returns with Nionee, McGuire, and Bouvier in tow. All are carrying their M-16s. McAdams says he came across his weapon where he awoke. Bouvier and Nionee have the same pained, confused looks as the rest of the group. Bouvier walks over to Rees and squats, looking weak and wearing a blank stare. He opens his mouth to speak, but Rees knows what he is going to ask and cuts him off before he can utter a word.

"Before you ask, I don't know," Rees says. "I've been awake for ten minutes and I don't know what, where, when, who, how or why."

Reaching inside the Duck, Rees retrieves his rifle, ensures a round is in the chamber and the gun set to safe, and then walks back to the group standing around Kriger. He sees that Bouvier has had Nionee set up the second M-60 facing outward.

"Good idea," Rees thinks. "Glad to see someone is relying on his training."

He has several thoughts racing through his head: Are they at war? He shakes the notion from his head. Time for that later. There are more immediate tasks to address. He instructs McAdams and Kriger to follow Nionee's example and set up a perimeter.

"Care to take a short stroll?" Bouvier asks Rees. "Maybe we can figure out where we are."

Rees agrees and they inform the others to keep an eye out. Before they have taken more than a few strides, the sound of a Jeep engine approaching catches the group's attention. Every man becomes alert and readies their weapons, each searching an area in front of them. Rees hears the bolt to the M-60 being racked. He looks over at Nionee, who gives him a thumb up. Rees signals him to wait until given the order before firing, and Nionee acknowledges.

The Jeep soon comes into view. It is being operated by Sgt. Shepard, with his partner, A1C Nate Tucker, in the passenger seat. Shepard looks dazed as he drives past their position. Rees stands and waves at him.

"Shepard! Sergeant Shepard! Over here!"

Rees doubts Shepard hears him, but the waving motion gets his attention. Shepard steers toward them, stops the Jeep, and jumps out.

"Gawd man. Gawd, what the fuck?" Shepard begins.

"Don't ask, because we don't know, either," Rees says. "We should get everyone together and try to figure this out."

Shepard looks over Rees's shoulder and sees Bouvier approaching.

"Hi ya, Jack!" Shepard says to Bouvier, then turns his attention back to Rees.

"There are more of us around," Shepard says.

"Yes, we know, Sergeant Shepard," Bouvier answers. "McGuire, Kriger, Harris, McAdams, and Nionee are over there setting up a perimeter."

As they speak, Airman Tucker exits the Jeep and approaches them.

"Hi," is all he says.

Tucker is one of two black airmen assigned to the MSD that day; Staff Sergeant Parks being the other. Tucker is one of the coolest guys you'd want to meet. He's from Martinsville, Virginia, and keeps a perpetual smile on his face. He's easygoing and a pleasant individual to hang out with. Tall and lean, he was a wide receiver for his high school football team, but he couldn't get a college scholarship. He decided to join the air force and try to get a degree while enlisted. He never has a bad thing to say about anyone and usually speaks only if he has something worthwhile to say.

The men begin talking at once about what is happening. Bouvier suggests they all move back inside the perimeter to continue the conversation. Shepard and Tucker relate their experiences first, stating they were in the generator room when they blacked out. When they awoke, they were in the same positions. The Jeep did not appear to have moved, but now the building was gone and they were in the woods.

"Sergeant Shepard," Rees says, "Sergeant Bouvier and I are going take a walk around. Try to figure out where are. Take the Jeep with Tucker and drive..."

"Yo, guys!" Nionee interrupts. "Listen! Something or someone is moving around out there."

The group grabs their weapons and again sets up a defensive position, scanning the surrounding area. Suddenly, they see Sgt. Ben Montoya and Airman Alex Steele moving toward them from around a pine tree. They are half carrying, half dragging Airman Steve Green, as well as trying to carry all their weapons. Rees points to McAdams and McGuire, and indicates for them to help. They jump up and run to assist. This is getting to be a reunion, but not the fun kind.

The new arrivals share basically the same story, one everyone now knows by heart. Rees finishes his version and tells Shepard and Tucker to go where Tosseti and Parks would have been, and see if they can retrieve them. This is the logical choice since everyone seems to have awakened in the same positions they were before. The Romeo team was in the same area they would have been if the building was still there when Rees ran outside; Shepard and Tucker came from where they would have been if they were in the generator room; and Montoya and his crew came from the area where one of the IVAs (static guard posts) should be, so it's a good bet they will find Parks and Tosseti at their posts as well.

The remaining men turn their attention to Montoya and Steele, who are holding onto a barely conscious Green as Kriger checks his vitals.

"What happened?" Kriger asks.

"He must have hit his head on the Jeep," Montoya explains. "Green was running toward the Jeep when the shit started to hit the fan. He was almost to it when he started stumbling. That's all I can remember before blacking out. When we woke up, he was like this."

Kriger scolds them for moving Green.

"Dumb asses," he chides. "He can have neck injuries, probably a concussion. One of you should have stayed behind with him and let the other find us."

"Where's the Jeep?" Bouvier asks.

"Can't get it started," Montoya answers. "Turns over, but it won't catch."

"Okay, we'll get to that later," Rees says.

The main topic of conversation among the group continues to be their situation. Where are they and what could have possibly happened to cause such confusion?

"What about a war?" Kriger suggests while working on Green.

As members of the military, this of course is the first idea on everyone's minds. But how would that have put them here? And where is here? Other ideas are proposed, but none hold water.

"Maybe a nuke went off somewhere," Montoya suggests.

Even if it did, where are the destroyed buildings? And how could the men be virtually unharmed, seemingly still in North Carolina? Rees walks over to the Duck and leans his back against it.

"If it was a high-yield burst on the ground, we would still see smoke, residue, something," he states. "If it was in the sky, we would have received an EMP burst that would have fried everything."

"What's an EMP?" Steele asks.

"Electro Magnetic Pulse," Rees explains. "It would have shorted out everything electrical. We currently have use of the vehicles and radios, so it's not that."

Montoya clears his throat and begins, "Hey you all, I saw a movie once," to the collective groans of the group.

"A movie, Sergeant?" someone asks, "Really?"

"No, listen," he continues. "What if this is a type of test? We are given some sleeping gas, then moved somewhere else and placed in the same positions. You know, just to see what we would do."

Now it's Rees's turn to contribute, being the science fiction guy that he is.

"What about time travel?" he adds.

This elicits a laugh from the group.

"You're kidding, right Rees?" Bouvier asks. "This is 1980, not the twenty-first century. We don't have the technology to build stuff like that or the knowledge. That's been a pipe dream for generations."

"Why not, sir?" Kriger says in Rees's defense. "That's no more a wild suggestion than Sergeant Montoya's test idea. Maybe this is a combination of both. We could be guinea pigs in a time travel test to see how we react."

Bouvier looks at Kriger, "You're not buying into this horseshit, are you?" he asks, pointing at Rees.

"Sergeant, we don't know anything, and guessing isn't going to help," Montoya says. "We need to move out of here, go see where we are, and find out what's going on."

"If we are part of an experiment, why us?" Steele asks.

The question creates immediate silence as the men look at each other. Finally, Rees has a thought.

"Guys, none of us is married, right?" he begins. "Some of you are orphaned, no families. I lost my folks a few years ago in an auto accident."

"I lost mine in a plane crash," Bouvier adds quietly.

"We all are orphaned, estranged from our relatives, or have lost our families one way or another," Rees adds. "There is no one to claim us missing. We are all perfect candidates for some type of mind game that if we didn't return from…"

"Then there would be no one to ask what happened to us. We're expendable," Bouvier says to complete the thought.

"What about our girlfriends?" Nionee asks.

The men turn and look at Nionee, who is leaning against a tree fiddling with a stick. He looks at each one and then rests his eyes on Rees.

Rees smiles and nods his head.

"I guess they either forgot about that or just dismissed the idea," Rees says. "Probably thought that with them being civilians, there wasn't much they could do. But that is a mistake on their part. You all know my girlfriend, Nora, and I can tell you she won't be sitting on her ass pining like a schoolgirl waiting for her boyfriend to call. She and her sister, Skylar, will be looking for answers. Their father is a retired lieutenant colonel and they know their way around the system. That, and the fact that McAdams's girlfriend, Ivy, has a lieutenant for a brother and he's stationed on the base. No, there will be questions asked and that should make whoever did this to us very nervous."

Silent nods of agreement, paired with dejected faces, slowly make their way around the group.

"Right now we need to get everyone together and scout out the area," Rees says, breaking the silence. "We'll split up into three teams. Sergeants Bouvier, Shepard, and Airman Tucker will be one team. They will take the Jeep to locate Tosseti. Sergeants Kriger, Montoya, and Airman McGuire and I will go on walking patrol to look for Staff Sergeant

Parks, who is – was – in the tower and shouldn't be too far away. I'm surprised he isn't here already. Airmen Nionee and McAdams, you stay behind to watch the camp and take care of Green. Airman Harris is still looking ill and will stay close to Green while the others secure the perimeter."

Rees looks up at the sky and checks his watch. Damn, still working. Not bad for seven dollars. It's 1832, or 6:32 pm civilian time. It will be dark in a couple of hours and the group will be spending the night in the woods. Rees is not too worried about finding Tosseti unless he has wandered off in a different direction. Each man grabs a radio and checks them to make sure they are working, which they are. Each team turns one on, leaving the others off to save the juice. The call signs are all 15. Sergeant Bouvier's team is 15 Bravo and the base camp is Security 15. These are the regular call signs, so they stay with what they know.

Rees orders the teams to return to camp in one hour no matter what, and with that they take off. Kriger gives last-second pointers to the men staying behind regarding Airman Green, and then joins his team.

McGuire takes point, followed by Rees and Kriger, carrying the M-60, and then Montoya with the M-203. They arrive near where they believe the tower should have been and fan out. It isn't long until they hear McGuire call out and hustle to where he is standing, looking down at Parks's broken body on the ground. They can tell he is dead by the angle of his neck and the grayish pallor his dark skin has turned.

Kriger sets down the M-60 and goes to check on Parks, shooing away the flies buzzing around. After a quick check, Kriger shakes his head.

"He's dead," Kriger confirms.

Rees stands there wondering where the tower is, or should be. They should be standing under it, by his estimation. His head is spinning. Lost in the woods, not knowing what is going on, this is surreal. The more he tries to figure out what is going on, the worse the situation appears. Rees sighs, removes his web gear and takes off his shirt.

"Give me your shirt, Montoya," Rees says. "McGuire, go get a couple of strong branches. We're going to make a litter."

"Sarge?" Kriger calls out to Rees, jutting out his chin toward McGuire, who is standing in frozen silence looking at Parks's body.

"Airman McGuire," Rees says quietly. Then a little louder, "Sean!"

"Huh?" McGuire reacts as he jerks his head up.

Rees walks over to him, placing his hand on the young airman's shoulder and gently pushing him away.

"Hey, go on now." Rees says. "Get the wood for the litter."

"Yeah... yeah, I'll go get the wood," McGuire says as he turns and walks away.

Kriger stands and moves over to Montoya and Rees.

"You know we can't afford for anyone to break down, right?" Kriger says. "It might seem cold-hearted, but we can't let Parks's death affect us right now."

"That's nothing we don't already know," Rees replies. "We'll keep an eye on him. This is scary for all of us. Some can handle stress better than others. We'll take Parks's body back to camp and figure out what to do with him there. We won't be able to keep him too long, though. Not with this heat."

Rees pulls out his radio, "Security 15, this is 15 Alpha."

A few seconds pass and then, "15 Alpha, this is Security 15, go ahead."

Rees hesitates and then puts the radio up to his mouth and keys the mic.

"Security 15, we've located Sergeant Parks. He's dead," Rees reports. "We're making a litter and bringing the body back."

Rees closes the mic and stands in silence. He is feeling a little disoriented. This is not supposed to be happening. He has seen the dead before, but not someone he knows personally. Certainly not in this manner.

The radio squawks. "15 Alpha, we did not copy, please say again."

Rees repeats his statement and then hears Nionee's voice.

"Roger, 15 Alpha, copy that. We'll await your return." Nionee then adds, "Also 15 Alpha, 15 Bravo has yet to find Tosseti. They believe he may have walked east and they want to follow."

Rees checks his watch. It's 1903, half an hour left until they need to return. He clicks the radio, "Do they know how much of a head start he has?"

"They know the direction, but they're not sure how long he has been gone," Nionee replies.

"It's your order to return within an hour," Montoya reminds Rees.

"Security 15, tell 15 Bravo they need to return at the agreed time, no matter if they find Tosseti or not," Rees says. "We can regroup and come up with another plan to find him if we need."

McGuire returns with two long poles and Kriger helps him make a litter using the shirts. Montoya and McGuire lift it up just as Nionee comes back on the radio.

"15 Alpha, this is Security 15," he says. "15 Bravo will look a little longer and be back on time."

Tosseti is a big boy and if anyone can survive on their own, it would be him. They begin their trek back to base camp and walk only a few feet when Kriger tells them to stop. They watch as Kriger walks a few feet to his right, bends down, and picks up something. Kriger snorts and walks back over to them, holding in his hand what looks like a cap.

"It's a kepi," he says.

"A what?" Montoya asks.

Kriger strides over and shows it to them.

"A kepi," he repeats. "It's a cap that soldiers wore in the Civil War. I bet some kids were playing around here and dropped it. That means we are near civilization, doesn't it? This is pretty authentic. Maybe it's one of those re-enactment caps. It's a rebel cap. Maybe Sergeant Shepard will want it since he's a backwoods country fuck. He'll hang it on his wall when we get home, remind him of his grand-pappy."

"Cut the crap and keep moving," Rees tells Kriger, thinking he knows what everyone is probably thinking: if they get home.

The group arrives back at camp and does their best to answer the flood of questions that come their way. Looking at his watch, Rees asks Nionee if he has heard from 15 Bravo. He has not, and there are only five minutes left.

"Security 15, this is 15 Bravo," Shepard's distinct southern drawl suddenly blares from the radio.

"15 Bravo, this is Security 15," Nionee replies. "Go ahead."

"We've found Tosseti and are en route back to camp," Shepard reports.

The group smiles at that bit of good news. Everyone is accounted for. Then they look at Parks's body and grow solemn again. A few minutes pass and the sound of the Jeep's engine approaches. The group already can hear Tosseti's loud Boston-accented voice.

"I'm fuck'n telling yas, this is some fucked up shit!" he says.

The Jeep stops and Tosseti is still talking.

"Some asshole has really done it this time. I'm gonna fuck up somebody's shit for putting me in this shit-hole situation. Motherfuckers!"

"Hey Tosseti, where the hell have you been?" McAdams calls out. "Lose your sense of direction, you Irish lug?"

Tosseti's face is red.

"I've been in the fucking woods, asshole, and I'm Irish-Italian, you thistle arse pipe blower!"

Tosseti turns toward Rees and demands, "What the hell is going on, Sarge, huh?"

"We don't know, Matt, not yet, but we're going to find out," Rees replies.

"This dumb fuck'n Yankee was wandering around lost," Shepard blurts out. "Would've died if we hadn't of found him."

"Fucks youse! Youse dim-witted, hillbilly redneck," Tosseti growls. "Why don't cha come on back to Boston with me? We'll see who's wandering around lost and who dies!"

Kriger walks toward Shepard and throws him the kepi.

"Here ya go you, hick, something for your trouble," Kriger says.

Shepard catches the cap and examines it.

"Where'd you get this?" he asks, turning it over to examine it more closely.

"Found it in the woods on our way back with..." Kriger's voice trails off as he looks at Parks's body.

The new arrivals look at the body and ask more of the same questions Rees and his team just finished answering. Rees looks at Harris, who is still looking under the weather, and excuses himself to check on him.

"How you holding up?" he asks.

Harris looks up with a weak look in his eyes. Whatever has happened to the group, it has obviously been harder on Harris. There is no doctor available, and Kriger is limited in his medical training.

"I'm feeling a little better, Sarge," Harris says quietly. "I'm still a little tired, but better than before."

Rees pats him on the shoulder and rises to meet Kriger, who is walking toward him after examining Green.

"How's Airman Green?" Rees asks.

"I believe he has a severe concussion," Kriger reports. "If we don't get him to a doctor soon, I'm afraid he could die."

"Really?" Rees asks. "Are you sure?"

"I'm not a doctor so, no, I'm not a hundred percent sure. But look at his skin tone. It has a bluish tint and his skull is slightly caved. I think he's in serious trouble."

Rees looks at the group of men gathered. He has one dead and two injured, including one critical and the other requiring observation. The rest are alive and apparently in good health. But God, where are they, and what is going on?

Doesn't matter. They are all together now and need to get down to brass tacks. They need to set a game plan and get moving. As darkness envelops them, they gather in closer to wait out the night and see what the next day has in store. There is strength in numbers, but they are obviously on their own.

Chapter 5

The sound of knocking on her bedroom door awakens Nora Miller from a deep sleep. Struggling to clear her head from a dream that seemed very real, she yawns and turns her head toward the door.

"Come in," she says with a groggy tone.

Her little sister, Skylar, opens the door and pokes her head inside.

"Good morning, sleepyhead. Time to rise and shine. Ivy's here waiting for you," Skylar says and leaves the door ajar.

Nora sits up, pulls back her long hair with both hands, and stretches. As she rolls out of bed, she tries to recall details of her dream that had something to do with her boyfriend and the military. The theme in itself is not surprising since her boyfriend, TSgt. Scott Rees, is a military man.

But this dream was different. More intense and just plain freaky.

Scott was in a war or some type of battle, but with whom it was not clear. He wasn't alone. There were others around him, and she feels good that there were. He was fighting in the woods and something was wrong with him. She remembers yelling for him, but no one could hear her. Concentrating hard as the dream wants to fade, she recalls something odd about his face and the way he was walking. The others in the dream began turning into skeletons, and then they fell apart. By the time she returned her gaze to Scott, he had aged noticeably in just a few seconds.

Nora shudders as she remembers becoming frightened and turning to flee through the woods. As she tried to make her way out, she saw several men on horseback galloping toward her. She couldn't make out their faces. They were blurry, moving. All of them were wearing vintage blue uniforms. One was carrying the Stars and Stripes, but it didn't have the right number of stars on it.

She heard a knocking and saw a cabin she hadn't seen before, as if it came out of nothingness. The knocking was coming from inside the cabin and she moved toward it. She vividly remembers her hand outstretched to grab the knob before being awakened by her sister's knocking. That's all she can remember and it gives her a strange, sad feeling.

Nora throws on her robe and leaves the bedroom, going into the living room to greet her friend, Ivy, who is sitting on the couch looking at a magazine. Ivy is an attractive blonde, about five-foot-four, with light blue eyes framed by crow's feet that are showing early for her age. They're not caused by age or worry, rather by the constant smile and laughter she displays.

Nora is physically the opposite, with dark hair, brown eyes, a couple of inches taller, and with a slightly bigger, curvier figure.

"Good morning, Nora," Ivy starts. "Damn, you look like shit. You out partying last night?"

Nora plops down in a chair and rubs her eyes.

"Yeah, I went to Bomber's Hole," she replies. "I didn't drink that much, though. Just didn't sleep very well last night. I had this weird dream about Scott."

Ivy shares that she also had a strange dream about her boyfriend, Eric McAdams. She explains how she saw him in the woods being pursued by men in gray and brown clothing.

"They looked like old-timey guys," Ivy says. "Eric was running, screaming that he was one of them, whatever that meant, but they still chased him, shooting. He kept running until he saw a cabin. He slammed open the front door and the room inside was full of computer banks. You know, the big cabinets with the reel-to-reel contraptions.

"Well, anyway, he ran behind one of those and pointed his rifle at the door. A young man entered the room and instantly aged into an old man. The further he walked into the room, the older he got. Then he turned to rot and dissolved into dust. It happened to everyone who came through the door. Then I woke up."

"Ivy, only you could top my wacky dream," Nora says with a wry smile.

Nora stands and goes into the kitchen, with Ivy right behind her. Nora pours herself a cup of coffee and lifts the pot toward Ivy with a questioning look.

"Yes, thank you," Ivy says. "Got anything to put in it, beside sugar?"

Nora grins and reaches for a bottle of liqueur in the cabinet. She turns and shows the bottle to Ivy, who smiles and nods her head in approval.

Ivy had met Airman First Class Eric McAdams when he was working the main gate as a member of the Elite Guard Section of the Security Police Squadron. She had entered the base to visit her brother, an officer assigned there. Ivy was instantly smitten with Eric's smile and the confidence with which he carried himself. She introduced herself and he invited her out on a date, which she readily accepted. They have been dating since, going on about six months now. A1C McAdams had since been rotated back to his security flight from the elite guard detail.

Blowing into her cup, Nora takes a sip and asks, "What are we going to do today?"

Ivy stirs her coffee with a thoughtful look on her face.

"Well, we could get the guys and maybe go to Raleigh," Ivy responds. "They are supposed to be on their three-day break starting today."

"That sounds fine to me," Nora replies as she gets up to grab the phone. "We haven't been there in a while and I'm sure the guys will go for it."

Nora dials the number to Rees's room and waits as it rings six times.

"That's funny," she says. "I was sure he'd be home. Come to think of it, he didn't call yesterday, either. He usually does after his shift."

Ivy mentions that she hasn't heard from Eric in a couple of days, either.

"Here, you give it a try," Nora says as she hands the phone to Ivy. "Maybe Eric knows where Scott is."

Nora lights a cigarette and walks into the living room while Ivy calls Eric's number and gets the same result.

"He doesn't answer, either," Ivy says as she hangs up the phone. "Maybe they're together or on their way here."

Nora returns to the kitchen as Skylar enters from the other side and grabs a cup for coffee.

"It's your turn," Ivy says in handing Skylar the phone.

"My turn for what?" Skyler asks.

"Give Ray a call and see if he knows where Eric and Scott are," she says, referring to Skyler's boyfriend, Airman First Class Ray Nionee. "Knowing those three, they're probably off gallivanting and didn't bother to ask us to go along."

Skylar dials Ray's number and listens to it ring for a minute before hanging up. She looks at the other two women, shrugs, and confirms that he didn't answer.

"Damn, those assholes," Ivy says as she sets down her coffee cup with a bit more force. "I bet they're out partying and didn't invite us. And they better not be meeting other chicks!"

Nora thinks for a minute and then announces, "We're going to the base and check things out. Maybe someone knows where they went. Scott wouldn't just up and leave without letting me know. At least I don't think he would. He's always been pretty straight with me."

"Ray is the same way," Skylar adds. "He generally lets me know what he's doing, as long as it's not classified.

"Not Eric," Ivy says with a laugh. "That wingnut will take off in a heartbeat and not say a word."

Fifteen minutes later, the trio are in Nora's car and on their way to the base. Ivy mentions she knows the guard as they approach the gate shack, so Nora rolls down the window for Ivy to lean over and talk.

"Hi, Jimmy," Ivy says to the guard with a touch of flirtation in her voice.

The guard leans down to the window and smiles as he recognizes Ivy.

"Hey, how ya doing, Ivy? Long time no see. Whatcha been up to?" he asks as he waves an authorized vehicle around them.

"Not too much. Have you seen Eric lately?" Ivy asks.

"Or Sergeant Rees?" Nora pipes in.

"No, can't say that I have," the guard replies. "But something screwy has been going on since yesterday. They had a recall and placed some of the B Flight security guys out in the MSD."

Ivy gives Nora a questioning look and returns her attention to Jimmy.

"So, you mean they're working?" she asks.

"No, that's just it," he says. "The crew out there yesterday didn't come in. The Bird Cage crew was at the barracks when I got there, but no one has seen anyone from the Mud Dump. Could be they were sent on some secret TDY or something. Who knows around here?"

The women look at each other with quizzical expressions. Ivy thanks the guard for his help and Nora drives onto the base, making a beeline straight toward the security police building. The trio exit the vehicle and walk into the station, where they are greeted at the window by the desk sergeant.

"Morning, what can I do for you?" he asks.

"We're trying to locate our boyfriends and have heard something about a recall," states Nora, who has no problem talking to military people because her and Skylar's father is a retired US Air Force lieutenant colonel.

The desk sergeant's smile falters as he tells them to wait a second. He picks up a phone, talks into it a few seconds, and then hangs up.

"Senior Master Sergeant Wright will be right up to assist you," he says with a smile.

It isn't long until SMSgt. Wright opens the door to the lobby and introduces himself. He explains that he oversees deployments for the squadron and will help them if he can. Inviting them into his office, he holds the door open as they file in. Nora begins the conversation as she takes a seat.

"Sergeant Wright, my name is Nora. This is my sister, Skylar, and our friend, Ivy. We heard there was a recall yesterday."

Wright smiles and nods. "That's correct," he says. "We initiated it yesterday morning."

Nora shifts in her seat.

"I know these are usually hush-hush, but we were wondering if we could find out if our boyfriends were involved," she says. "We haven't heard from them and it's not like them not to contact us."

Wright lights a cigarette and offers the pack to the women, who decline. He then reaches for a folder.

"Well, let's see," he says with a hint of hesitation. "What are their names?"

Nora gives him the men's names as Wright runs his finger down a page within the folder. He stops and smiles, looking at Nora.

"Ah, yes, here we are, Tech Sergeant Scott Rees. He is TDY," Wright stops and looks at the women. "That's short for temporary duty."

"We know what TDY means," Nora replies with an annoyed stare. "We are from military families."

Wright doesn't flinch at the rebuke, keeps his smile plastered across his face and continues.

"Yes, of course. Now, who are the others?"

"Eric McAdams," Ivy blurts.

He nods and again runs his finger along the paper until he finds the name.

"Yes, Airman First Class Eric McAdams is mobilized as well," he confirms. "And I'm sorry, what is Ray's last name again?"

"Nionee," Skylar replies, spelling the name.

"Yes, they have all been mobilized," he tells them.

"Well shit, that blows," Ivy responds.

Wright smirks at the salty language and asks if he can be of any more help. Nora asks if they can contact their boyfriends somehow and is told they cannot, classified operations and all.

"Can we at least know where they are, when they'll be back?" Nora asks.

The smiling Senior Master Sergeant again informs them, "No, classified."

Nora does not like the smiling sergeant one bit. She doesn't trust him and his fake smile at all. She is getting upset and the hangover isn't helping. She can't help blaming this man for Rees's absence, even though she knows the sergeant is just a cog in the military machine. Wright takes another drag off his cigarette, blows the smoke toward the ceiling, and crushes the butt in the ashtray.

"Sorry ladies, but the whole operation is classified, top secret," he says while getting out of his seat. "If I give any more information to you, it could be considered treasonous. Now if you will excuse me, I'll bet you all have lots to do, as I do. I'm sure you understand the need for secrecy."

Wright begins herding the women toward the door, but Nora isn't satisfied just yet.

"How can they go on a top-secret mission when they only have secret clearances?" she asks.

"They don't need top-secret clearances," Wright replies, the condescending smile firmly re-established on his face. "Granted, the deployment is top secret, but the men on the deployment don't need to know all the details. You see, this exercise is an exercise within an exercise. This is an experiment, something new. You could say a grand adventure for your men. Being new, it's something the air force is very excited about. I wouldn't worry ladies. When they return, they'll have quite the stories to tell you, I'm sure. All within reason, of course."

The smile does not reach his eyes and the women can sense it. Wright walks them to the door and into the hallway. They thank him for his help and exit the building.

The smile on Wright's face quickly fades and a serious expression replaces it. It is a look of concern that he is careful not to reveal until the women are out of sight. Returning to his office, he approaches his desk and opens a drawer to extract a strange-looking phone reserved for sending encrypted calls. He flips open a small box attached to the phone and dials a number. He hears clicks and bleeps, and then a voice comes over the receiver.

"Listen," Wright says into the phone as he swivels his chair to point away from the door. "We may have a slight problem we didn't foresee. There were some young women just here asking questions about their boyfriends. Guys who are on the assignment."

He listens briefly before continuing.

"No, no, of course I gave them the cover story, but at least one of them remained suspicious."

He listens again and stirs uncomfortably in his seat.

"Yes, I agree, but something has to be done about this. We will keep an eye on them and see what transpires. We will handle it if need be."

The sergeant ends the call and replaces the phone in the drawer. He takes a deep breath and exhales, a look of stress-induced fatigue evident on his face. Picking up the folder, he throws it onto the desk and turns back toward the window with his hands behind his head. A heavy sigh is all he can muster as he loses himself in thought.

Chapter 6

Senator Minten hates the United States Air Force. Well, not so much the military branch itself, just the people who make up that branch of service. He has a son in the army and a daughter in the navy. Both were groomed to serve him, if need be, in whatever capacity he can find for them in their branches of service. He figured any major projects awarded to the military would be given to the army or navy, not the damn air force. But it seems the air force gets all the good projects, all the time. Area 51 for one, Edwards Air Force Base for another, where all the cool gadgets are tested. He assumes the laws of probability would favor the other branches of service were due to receive their share of intriguing new projects.

Now the air force has been granted the Clio project. He can't really blame them, considering the man responsible for creating Clio is an air force enlisted man. A goddamn enlisted man, for all the nerve. Not even an officer. Why couldn't he have been army and an officer?

This means Minten now has to rely on his nephew to be the inside man. Captain Randall Henries is assigned to the Clio project, and Minten is hoping his nephew can provide some inside information he can use to take over the project. Henries has been lapse in reporting so far, and seldom does he have anything useful to contribute when he does report.

Minten is an ambitious, power-hungry man. Standing six feet five inches tall and muscular, he towers over most men and uses his physical presence as an intimidation factor. His dark, wavy hair and perfect white teeth disarm other politicians and causes their wives to swoon. He is the poster child for a perfect politician: handsome, conniving, and not averse to playing dirty. Most of his peers are afraid of him and he seems to always get his way, usually by bullying and making threats.

Minten became acquainted with the Clio project while serving on the House Committee on Armed Services. Since then, he has kept his ear to the ground, listening for any news about the project. He also made sure he became a member of the Bank Council, an unofficial group of powerful politicians for whom he feels nothing but contempt. These narrow-minded individuals don't know what they have in their control. The Clio project is the greatest achievement in human history and they have yet to understand its potential. They just want to play with a new toy and look back at history like a television program. Minten wants to use it to make history, reshape history, or even bend history to his will until he has the world in his grasp.

Taking control of the Clio project would almost guarantee Minten an enormous step toward the presidency. But why stop there? He figures that's peanuts compared to what he can do with that type of power. He could become king, no, emperor of the entire world. A god amongst men. He doesn't care who he must crush to get there and will go to any lengths to ensure his legacy. He has had his fingers in the Clio pie since witnessing the first demonstration, ensuring he was always in the loop. Now he wants the whole pie. Hell, he wants the recipe, bakers, and the entire kitchen.

One of the first steps Minten took as a congressman was creating the Military Intelligence Security Services, or M.I.S.S., under the guise of national security. This secret organization provides him with a vehicle he can use to throw the weight of his power around the military and gather information he can't get through regular channels. He also made sure the clandestine organization operates under black ops guidelines. It is known, but not known in political and military circles.

Minten placed John Clayborn in the role as M.I.S.S. director. Clayborn was a CIA agent in another life and has slowly worked his way up the food chain, but not as quickly as his colleagues. He didn't fit the profile the higher-ups thought a leader should look or act like. Minten found Clayborn to be somewhat desperate and easily manipulated. He had enough drive to succeed, but was expendable if necessary. If Minten needs to throw someone under the bus, Clayborn would be available to take the brunt of the punishment.

Clayborn has some good qualities in that he is moderately intelligent, knows how to take orders, and as loyal as a puppy dog. Clayborn reminds Minten of a pig rather than a dog. Short in stature, slightly overweight, with a receding hairline and pencil-thin mustache, he is known to tilt the bottle on more than one occasion. He is the perfect tool for Minten's selfish cause.

Minten is standing at his desk, staring at his wall of pictures, and thinking about his next move for Clio when his assistant informs him that Clayborn is in the outer office. He closes his eyes in exasperation, lets out a deep breath through his nose, and tells his secretary to send Clayborn in. Minten imagines Clayborn is about to grovel for something or bring bad news.

"To what do I owe the pleasure of your visit, Director Clayborn?" Minten asks in a sarcastic tone.

"Well, sir," Clayborn starts, stops, and then clears his throat, "Ah…"

Minten whirls around and glares at Clayborn.

"For god's sake, man. Grow a pair and spit it out!" he shouts menacingly.

"We received a call from the base," Clayborn quickly responds. "The sergeant in charge of the security police personnel called. It seems that some of the men sent on the classified mission have girlfriends who are asking about them."

Minten opens his eyes wider in mock shock.

"What, men with girlfriends? Oh my God. That's astonishing. Who would have ever thought men would have girlfriends. Stop the presses! Who fucking cares, Clayborn?"

Clayborn looks uneasy, just as Minten likes it.

"Sir, when the background checks were conducted on these men, they were picked because they had no ties with close family," Clayborn continues. "They didn't have girlfriends at the time. If you remember, you specified that if they disappeared, you wanted to make sure there would be no one to search for them. Well, since the project took longer to initiate than projected, the men had time to get acquainted with the women. Now that they are on assignment, the girlfriends are asking questions concerning their whereabouts."

Clayborn finishes and waits uneasily for an eruption.

Minten stares back for several minutes, not moving. Clayborn is getting worried when Minten suddenly blinks.

"Well, Clayborn, handle it. You can't expect me to do everything," he says. "I've more important things to do than solve your little problems. Good grief, man, it's girlfriends. Girls, not international terrorists. Handle. It. Clayborn."

Minten turns his back and Clayborn takes this as his cue to leave as quickly as he can.

"Oh, and Clayborn?"

"Yes, sir?"

"Don't ever interrupt me again with bullshit problems that you are supposed to take care of. Got it?"

"Yes, sir. Got it."

"And one more thing, John," Minten says as if the name leaves a nasty taste in his mouth. "Don't fuck this up."

Clayborn walks out of his boss's office, fuming at being treated like a dog. No matter, he has a job to do and leaves to seek out his problem solvers.

Chapter 7

It is dawn, around 0530, and the air is cooler. Everything is quiet except for the trees rustling in the slight breeze. Conspicuously absent is the usual faint sound of vehicle traffic coming from outside the base perimeter. But this isn't the base they know anymore.

Rees is making rounds, checking on each fighting position, when he hears what he believes is thunder. He looks up to see a few clouds, but not nearly enough for rain. He approaches Montoya and Nionee's position and squats beside them. They have dug a fighting position and are down inside.

"Do you hear that?" Nionee whispers to Rees.

"Yeah, I do. Sounds like thunder," Rees answers. "Not enough cloud cover, though."

Montoya, on the other side of Nionee, tilts his helmet back to expose his eyes.

"Sir," he says, "That's not thunder. Take a good look at the horizon."

Rees squints to see what Nionee is talking about. As his eyes adjust, he begins to make out flashes of light coming from the ground rather than the sky.

"Can it be ground lighting?" Rees asks, not wanting to believe the worst.

Nionee jerks his head up and snaps his fingers to indicate he has come up with an answer.

"We're at war," he says. "You know what that is? It's artillery."

"Could be, but we don't know enough yet," Rees says, keeping his eyes on the horizon. "Has anyone timed the sound interval?"

"I make it about four thousand meters," Montoya responds, noting the metric equivalent of two and a half miles.

Rees is growing more uncomfortable in the stifling heat and humidity by the second. Sweating like a witch on trial, he adjusts his flak jacket in an attempt to let in some air.

"I'm heading back to talk to Sergeant Bouvier," he states. "We need to figure out our next move."

Crouching low, Rees heads back to the Duck, where he finds Bouvier bedded down. Rees hates to wake him, but they need to get motivated. He kneels and shakes him lightly. It isn't much of a shake, but Bouvier bolts upright into a sitting position, and in his confusion grabs for his weapon.

"Whoa, buddy. Just me," Rees says, grabbing Bouvier's hand as it grasps the M-16.

Bouvier looks at Rees and snorts.

"Sorry, shit, didn't mean to do that," he says as he releases his grip on the weapon.

"Entirely okay, fully expected under the circumstances," Rees replies with a grin. "We are all on edge right now. Sorry to wake you, but we might have a slight problem."

Bouvier stretches and shakes his head.

"What's the problem, other than the obvious?"

"Not sure exactly, but I think there's a battle going on," Rees says as he glances over his shoulder.

The sounds he heard before have either stopped or are now out of range.

"We think there's a fight going on about two or three miles from here," Rees continues. "We could hear what we thought was thunder at first, but I think it might have been artillery fire. We could see flashes from the ground."

Bouvier stands, yawns, and rubs his eyes. He walks over to where there's coffee and pours himself a canteen cup full. Rees doesn't think Bouvier is ignoring him, but he's not speaking.

"Did you hear what I said?" Rees asks.

Bouvier takes a sip of coffee, winces from the heat, and blows into the cup.

"Yeah, I heard. Just thinking," he replies while holding out another cup for Rees.

"I'm at a loss right now. What the hell are we doing here?" Bouvier begins. "Are we at war? If we are, then this is a screwed-up way to start one. Any suggestions?"

"I think we should send out a team to reconnoiter the area where I saw the flashes," Rees suggests. "Send a second team out when the first returns and have them do a 360 sweep, maybe 400 meters out, and report back. Might give us a better idea of where we are."

"You're the boss," Bouvier says, taking another sip of coffee. "Want me to take the first team out?"

"No, thanks for volunteering, though," Rees replies. "I'll go and take both Jeeps and six guys."

"You sure about splitting us up?" Bouvier asks. "I know it's your call and I guess we need some answers. How long you think it will take?"

"Not sure. Don't want to be more than twelve hours," Rees says. "Radios won't work very far, so we will probably lose communications very quickly. We'll be on our own and so will you. We'll come straight back as soon as we find out anything. If something happens and you need to bug out, we'll need to set up a rendezvous point."

"Why not take the Duck?" Bouvier suggests. "More protection than a Jeep."

Rees shakes his head. "Too big and you can't see shit from it," he says. "I'd rather have speed and maneuverability."

Bouvier nods his understanding.

"I'll take Airmen Steele, Nionee, McAdams, and Tucker, and Sergeants Montoya and Shepard," Rees says. "Kriger needs to stay with you and take care of Green and Harris."

Rees leaves to round up the men and inform them of the plan.

"We're leaving by 0800, so grab something to eat," he tells them.

"Get C-rations and water for twelve hours, standard load out for your weapons. Steele and Nionee, you two are on the sixties. Everyone else, M-16s, and Shepard, grab one with a 203."

The men prepare their gear and by 0755 they're ready to go. Tucker gives them an azimuth reading, checks it on the map, and they head out. They drive straight toward where they saw the flashes of light earlier. Rees is in the lead vehicle with Shepard driving and Nionee and Tucker in the back. McAdams is at the wheel of the second Jeep, with Montoya in the front passenger seat and Steele manning the M-60. No one speaks, and Shepard has a strange look on his face.

"What's wrong?" Rees asks his driver.

Shepard looks at him and scrunches his face.

"This here is still North Carolina we're in. I mean, it looks like it, but it's just so different," he says. "The air smells funny and it looks like ain't no one been around here before. No trails, no trash, nothing."

Rees takes his meaning. The air does smell funny and he knows why. It's clean. There is no pollution, no engine exhaust, and no garbage.

"I know what you mean," Rees replies. "This does look like North Carolina, but are we still in the same area we were yesterday? I hear water running where the river should be, but that doesn't mean we are still in the same place."

Rees is still talking as they come upon a small hill and Shepard slows the Jeep to a crawl. Rees tells him to stop and radios the other team to stop behind them. He tells Shepard to proceed slowly and they crest the hill. Shepard stops the Jeep again and their jaws slack in shock. They stare in awe and horror at the scene revealed in front of them.

Bodies are strewn throughout the sparsely wooded area, some blown apart. Trees are blasted into splinters. This is a scene of slaughter, a scene of carnage. This was combat in its most brutal form. They have found the war zone they feared they were hearing.

Rees snaps out of his trance as the radio crackles to life.

"15 Charlie to 15 Bravo. 15 Charlie to 15 Bravo."

Rees keys the mic.

"Go ahead, 15 Charlie," he says weakly.

"What the hell's going on up there?" Montoya asks from the second Jeep.

"15 Charlie, come on up here," Rees replies.

A few seconds pass and the other team pulls up alongside. As soon as they do, the reactions begin.

"Oh fuck!"

"Sweet mother of God."

"Holy shit."

The reactions continue as someone begins puking.

Montoya crosses himself and mutters, "Por todo lo que es santo."

Rees orders the group to move out and they drive ahead to the battlefield below. He instructs the men to be vigilant as they come to a stop, telling Steele and Nionee to stay in the Jeeps to cover their 6 and 12. Rees orders Tucker and McAdams to set up on their flanks for protection. The M-60s are covering the front and rear.

They start walking among the dead and Montoya squats beside one of the bodies.

"What the hell is this shit?" Montoya says, not expecting an answer. "I mean, look at these clothes."

Rees does and sees the face of a very young man, in his teens he'd guess, wearing a blue wool uniform that looks to be that of a Union soldier during the Civil War.

"This is crazy," Rees thinks. "What in the gods is happening? This looks like something out of the history books."

All of the bodies are in some type of uniform, mostly dark blue, but there are some in gray and butternut-colored Confederate uniforms mixed among them. Montoya takes something off one of the bodies and walks toward Rees. He hands him a piece of paper, except it isn't just a piece of paper. It is money, old money with "Confederate States of America" printed on it.

Shepard searches another body and finds a wallet with the same type of currency. It also holds a black-and-white photograph of a young woman in a bonnet. It looks like an old picture Rees's grandmother has of her own grandparents hanging in her house.

One of the bodies dressed in blue has a different type of money on him.

"I think they called these greenbacks," Rees says. "Greenbacks were issued in the 1860s for currency instead of silver or gold."

Rees is getting a weird feeling. They have seen all they need to see.

It is time to get back and plan their next move. But before he can gather the men, there is a "boom" from what sounds like cannon fire in the distance. As the men turn in the direction of the sound, whistling sounds almost immediately fill the air, followed by huge explosions that throw them to the ground. They recover quickly and look around to see that one of the Jeeps is now a mangled heap. It is the Jeep that was being manned by Airman Alex Steele. Montoya and McAdams scramble toward what's left of the vehicle.

Steele is a bloody mess and there are no signs of movement as he lay several feet from the Jeep. Shepard and Rees scan for where the shots came from. Two more explosions heave the ground up to the left and right and McAdams begins screaming, writhing on the ground in pain. He grabs his leg around the thigh as blood seeps through his fingers.

"Shepard, Tucker, get fire in that direction!" Rees yells, pointing toward the spot where they can now see a cannon.

Nionee turns the M-60 toward the target and Rees hears its familiar "dat-dat-dat" sound. He watches Shepard drop to the ground and fire his weapon on full automatic.

"Sergeant Shepard! Stop firing!" Rees shouts. "They're too far away and you're wasting ammo shooting on full auto!"

Shepard rolls onto his side to stare at Rees and he sees a look of anger coming back at him. He stays that way for a few seconds before nodding his understanding.

The sound of pings and the slap of lead striking the wrecked Jeep catches Rees's attention. He gets to McAdams at the same time as Montoya. Tucker is there, too, and has the presence of mind to cover them. Rees and Montoya grab McAdams, who is still screaming, and drag him to the other Jeep. They lift him into it as Tucker gets behind the wheel. Montoya and Rees then run back to retrieve Steele's body and roughly toss him into the Jeep. Montoya jumps in as Rees clambers into the passenger seat.

"Shepard! Get in the fuckin' Jeep!" Rees screams.

Nionee is still throwing 7.62-mm rounds toward the area where they can see men behind the cannon. Shepard stands and fires a round from his grenade launcher and jumps in the Jeep. The round lands among some figures running toward them and explodes, knocking several to the ground. Rees returns fire and yells for Tucker to get them out of there, but there is no need as he is already turning the Jeep around.

Before they get moving, however, a howling noise behind them prompts Rees to look over his shoulder. He sees a platoon-sized group of men running down the slope toward them. More men are coming from the trees and a few stop to fire muskets at them.

"My God, muskets, really?" muses Rees.

Tucker hits the gas and drives back up the hill while the rest of the men stare at the sight behind them. Nionee opens up with the M-60 again and several of the charging soldiers fall with 7.62-mm rounds tearing into their bodies. Rees winches as he sees the head of one of the men explode in a red mist of blood. Shepard fires another 40-mm grenade from his launcher and it explodes amid the running soldiers. Hot shrapnel tears into a couple of them and they quickly fall. One man begins writhing on the ground in pain, clutching the area where a piece of shrapnel has struck him.

The attackers' ancient weapons are no match for the modern soldiers in the long run, but as Rees and his men have already witnessed, Civil War-era weaponry can still inflict damage and death. Steele is dead, McAdams is badly wounded, and they have just witnessed men who should be dead and buried for more than a hundred years chase them, shoot at them, kill them, and die by them.

The Jeep lurches and Rees nearly falls out before regaining his balance. They are driving north, or so he thinks. Doesn't matter. They'll get their bearings once they are clear of the madness that just unfolded. They drive a few miles to safety and stop. McAdams is swearing and in great pain.

"God dammit, I'm fucking hit!" he yells. "I'm gonna die. Fuck, fuck, fuck it hurts!"

Montoya hovers over him and Nionee jumps down to locate the first aid kit. He extracts a morphine syringe and hands it to Montoya, who injects it into McAdams's thigh. Within a couple of seconds, McAdams relaxes.

Tucker has his radio and is yelling into it, "Security 15, this is 15 Bravo!"

No answer.

"Security 15, this is 15 Bravo!"

Still no answer.

"God dammit, someone answer! Sergeant Bouvier, Kriger, anybody!" he yells some more. "We've been attacked, one KIA and one wounded. Please answer me!"

He turns and looks at the group with a panicked expression.

"We're too far out still!" he shouts.

Shepard stomps over to Tucker and snatches the radio out of his hand.

"Listen here, mother fuckers," he says into the mic with a low, menacing tone. "I know you can hear us, now answer the fuckin' radio, damn you!"

Rees grabs Shepard by the shoulder. He jerks away and glares at Rees.

"Don't fuckin' touch me, Sarge!" Shepard says through clenched teeth.

Rees raises his hands in surrender.

"We're too far away, Sergeant Shepard," Rees says in a calm tone. "Let's get our bearings and head back to camp."

"God dammit, Sarge. Alex is dead. What the fuck is going on here? Who are those guys? Rebels? Fuckin' rebels?!" Shepard asks as his voice escalates into a panic.

"I don't know what's going on any more than you do," Rees replies, "but we can't deny what we're seeing. We have to rely on our training and deal with this on our own for the time being."

Montoya looks up from tending to McAdams.

"Hey, Eric is out for now," he reports. "Maybe we should get going."

The group climbs back into the Jeep and drives about twenty minutes before Montoya tells them to stop.

"What's up, Sergeant?" Tucker asks.

Montoya looks at McAdams and turns his head toward the others.

"He's not going to make it, guys," he replies. "He lost a lot of blood. That round went clean through his leg and I think it nicked his femoral artery. We can't stop the bleeding."

The men watch as McAdams gradually drifts into death's arms. Airman First Class Eric McAdams dies at 1547. Now they are thirteen.

"We're going to have to bury them both," Rees says, referring to McAdams and Steele.

This causes an uproar from Shepard.

"Fuck that, Sarge. They come with us, damn you!" he exclaims as his face flashes red. "That's Alex and Eric you're talking about. We don't leave men behind!"

Rees spins and faces Shepard, getting in his face.

"You know what, Shepard, he was my friend, too," Rees seethes. "Don't forget, his girlfriend..."

Rees stops and thinks about that. Calming down, he continues.

"His girlfriend and my girlfriend, as well as Nionee's, are all friends. We all hang together, just like you and I have hung together. Just like all of us at one time or another have hung together. Remember that."

He turns away, trying to calm down. He knows a leader can't lose his composure in front of his men.

Tucker puts his hand on Shepard's shoulder.

"Sarge, calm down, we all know that. But Jesus, man, they're dead. We all know who they are, and Sergeant Rees didn't mean any disrespect," Tucker says. "We all feel like shit, but he's right. The Christian thing to do is bury them, and when the time is right we'll bring them home."

"God dammit... god dammit," Shepard sobs as he shakes his head. "I'm sorry, Sergeant."

"Forget it," Rees says. "We're all upset."

"Rees is right," Montoya states. "We can't drag them around with us in this heat. They'll be getting pretty ripe in a very short time. We've got to bury them."

"But we come back for them, right?" Shepard asks.

"Yes, of course," Rees says, not sure if he believes himself.

The group decides to drive a little further toward the river. The ground will be softer, and after they get a longitude and latitude reading, it will make the location easier to find when they return.

An area where the river has a large bend suits their purposes. They wrap both men in their ponchos and place the bodies into separate graves. They attach bayonets to the M-16s and stick them into the ground, placing their respective helmets on the butts of the rifles. Promising to return, each man says a few words and solemnly walks back to the Jeep.

Montoya is waiting there, eager to share a theory he has been developing.

"I think we're involved in some sort of government or military experiment," he says. "You know, like when they did those LSD experiments on troops and used them as guinea pigs during the atomic bomb tests. I think that's us. We're just guinea pigs in whatever this is. They're testing us under stress."

"But what about those other soldiers?" Nionee asks.

"So they knock us out, move us to an isolated location, dress a bunch of clowns in Civil War garb, and have them attack us?" Shepard asks.

Montoya rubs his stubble on his face.

"No, I believe Sergeant Rees might be right," he says. "I think we have been sent back in time."

The statement elicits the predictable "fuck that" reactions from the men.

"No, listen to what I'm saying," Montoya interjects. "Let's say the government does have a time machine. Just think of what that can mean. Say we are a fire team during the Vietnam War and the US is involved in a major campaign and loses a battle. Now, let's say our fire team, for some reason, is a contributing factor in that loss. We should have taken a different route to the conflict or set up at a different position that would have turned the tide to our side, whatever."

Rees begins to see where Montoya's line of reasoning is heading, and it appears Tucker and Nionee do, too, by the expressions on their faces. Shepard scoffs, but Montoya continues.

"Now, somehow we have survived this battle. The military brings us in, puts us in the time machine with specific orders to do something different that will change the outcome; somehow turn the tide of the battle to our favor."

Shepard slumps his weight backward against the Jeep, looks down, and shakes his head.

"Okay, Sergeant Montoya, that makes no sense, but it's better than anything else," he says. "So far."

"Makes sense to me," Tucker says with an affirmative nod.

"You think they know what's going on here?" Nionee asks.

Montoya lights a cigarette and hands one to Rees. He lights his and blows out a lungful of smoke, enjoying the relaxing effect.

"I'm betting they do, but I don't know how," Montoya replies.

Rees looks around at what is left of the team and can see the stress on their faces. They have all seen combat for the first time, and if their theory is correct, combat in a different era. He walks a few feet away and looks blankly into the woods, trying to clear his head.

"God, I wish I was home," he mutters to himself. "I don't need this shit."

He knows he signed up for duty and this could happen. Well, not this of course, but being placed in harm's way, sure. He never wanted to be in a war and always worried about the Cold War and possible nuclear war. But this is different. He hadn't prepared for this. How could he? Who would have ever thought the government was advanced enough that they could pull this off? A time machine, for Christ's sake! And worse than merely building one, having the audacity to send him and his comrades, his friends, to someplace in history so they can get their asses shot off? What the hell is that? And are they stuck here?

Too many questions and no answers. He takes the last drag from his cigarette, puts out the ember, and field-strips the butt. He looks at the almost-empty package he has in his pocket, realizing he's going to be hurting for a smoke soon when he runs out. Well, that's life; need to quit anyhow.

He walks back to the Jeep and sees Nionee now has a map on the ground with his compass out.

"I've got a good idea where we are, if this map is correct," Nionee begins. "I mean, if we are where we would be in our time… never mind. I've set our azimuth and have the grid coordinates for when we return for their bodies."

"What happens if we can't make it back?" Montoya asks as they get back into the Jeep. "I mean, what if we get yanked back to our time, or worse, we all die?"

"If we all die, then it doesn't matter," Nionee replies. "If we get back to our time, well, I guess we'll work it out."

Rees orders the group to move out and turns back forward in his seat. As they drive, his thoughts go to McAdams's girlfriend, Ivy. He wonders if she will ever know what happened to him. There is no chatter on the solemn drive back to the camp. It is the only place they can call home for now and the only place where friends wait for them.

***

It is 1319 and Ivy is sitting in Nora's house, drinking a Dr. Pepper and talking to Skylar, when she begins feeling ill. A migraine builds and by 1520 she has been sick twice. Nora and Skylar worry they may need to take her to the hospital. At 1547, the pain and nausea pass only to be replaced by feelings of emptiness and loneliness.

Ivy sits up on the couch and places her head in the palm of her hands, crying softly.

"What's wrong, girl," Nora asks.

Ivy sniffs and looks into her friend's eyes.

"Eric's dead."

Chapter 8

Rees and his men arrive at the base camp perimeter as the sun is setting. They radio ahead and Kriger informs them his team had to relocate the camp.

"When you get to the old camp, you'll understand," Kriger says. "Go on a compass reading of 76 degrees and travel about 1,250 meters to find the new base camp."

Rees's team proceeds as instructed and soon they understand why camp had to be moved. Stopping the Jeep at the old camp, they observe what is becoming too common of a sight: the bodies of young and old soldiers. They are also wearing the butternut and gray garb of Confederate soldiers, and their muskets, haversacks, bedrolls, and other items are strewn around the ground like the aftermath of a drunken slumber party.

Tucker and Shepard stare at a headless corpse with a large hole in its chest and one arm held on by a tendon. The coppery smell of blood mixes with feces to fill the air with stench, making it hard to breathe without triggering a gag reflex. The scene is fresh.

"Gawd, man, did our weapons do this?" Shepard gasps. "I had no idea."

"There's not much left of these guys to bury," Tucker says and walks away.

"We're not burying shit, guys," Rees says. "I'm sure someone will come along and take care of them."

Rees walks to where Nionee is squatting. He picks up a 7.62-mm shell casing and holds it up for him to see.

"One hell of a fire fight for sure. Would have hated to have been these guys," Rees says, waving the spent brass cartridge toward the bodies. "We got several hundred 7.62-mm casings here and there's a bunch of 5.56-mm casings around the perimeter. These guys must have wandered in and 'bam,' got an unfriendly welcome. We need to police the brass casings; don't want to leave them around."

"What about our guys?" Montoya asks. "I don't see any bodies here. They must be all right."

Shepard looks at Montoya.

"Well, no, Sergeant Montoya, you can't assume that, because we take our dead with us. Don't we, Sergeant Rees?" he asks sarcastically.

"That's enough of that Shepard," Montoya jumps in. "You know why we buried them. If there are other casualties, I'm sure they'll get buried where they are, too, so just stow it."

"Come on, y'all, let's get moving," Rees says, attempting to deflate the confrontation. "It's gonna be dark soon and I would rather get there with some light left. We don't want to be stumbling around in the darkness."

Nionee takes another reading and they head out. It takes time to find the new camp as the undergrowth grows thicker. The woods are pristine, untouched. Rees has never seen woods undisturbed by man. Even pictures of modern-day national parks can't help but show where man has disturbed the beauty.

They finally see the new camp set up on a small ridge, right below the crest. Rees can hear a river flowing somewhere nearby. Good, they will need the water. Bouvier and Kriger greet them as they exit the Jeep.

"Where's the other Jeep and the rest of your team?" Bouvier asks.

Rees shakes his head and takes a heavy sigh.

"We ran into some trouble," he says. "We came across a battlefield and were ambushed while checking it out.

"Ambushed? By who?" Bouvier presses.

"They looked like Confederate soldiers," Rees explains. "Airman Steele was manning the 60 when the Jeep took a direct hit from a shell or cannonball or whatever. He didn't make it. Airman McAdams took one in the leg and bled out on our way back. We buried them both. Here are their tags and the coordinates where they're buried."

Rees hands Bouvier the dog tags.

"Noticed you all had some trouble yourselves," Rees adds. "I'm assuming that's why you're here?"

Bouvier spits and shakes his head before speaking.

"Yeah, Tosseti heard a noise about an hour after you left. He alerted us and we stayed as quiet as we could, but a patrol walked into the perimeter. They spotted Tosseti, and that's when the shit hit the fan. It was a slaughter. Tosseti tried to get them to drop their weapons, but they took a shot at us so we opened up on them. We didn't mean to kill them all, but they wouldn't stop firing at us. It was over in less than a minute. Seemed like an hour."

"We didn't know who they were," Kriger adds as Bouvier takes a swig from his canteen. "Tosseti wanted them to stop, but it must have startled them. They fired those muskets. Muskets mind you. We didn't know who they were until it was all over. They dressed like Civil War soldiers. Gray uniforms, brass buttons, old money and pictures. What the hell?"

Montoya takes the rhetorical question as a queue to share his theory.

"Yeah, we found the same thing where we were," he says. "We have a theory that somehow the government has sent us back in time. For what screwed-up reason we don't know, much less how."

"Good God, Rees, you really think they have the technology to do something like that?" Bouvier asks.

Rees nods his head, "Yup, I do."

"Then why us?"

"Just think about it. We're all single, without families, no ties," Rees explains. "We've signed paperwork allowing them to abuse us anyway they see fit, all for the good of the country, national security, the American way, apple pie, et cetera, et cetera."

Montoya sits on the ground and lights a cigarette.

"That's all good and well, but we know people, people outside the base, girlfriends, acquaintances," he says. "Someone will notice we're not around."

"Sure, Ben, but the military can say we're off on a mission, TDY to another base, moved for some emergency," Rees explains. "They can keep us off the radar for a while. But I agree, eventually someone will look for us. In fact, I bet someone already is. It's just a matter of time before people realize we're missing."

Bouvier leans against a tree to take in the enormity of their situation.

"This is fucked up," he says. "Three dead, one seriously wounded, dying no less, unless we can get some medical attention for him. We don't need any more shit."

"I'm gonna check on the others," Rees says. "Make sure sentries are posted and trip flares are set up. Then I'm going to get a couple hours' shuteye."

After conducting his checks and assuring all is well, Rees finds a place near the Duck to relax. His mind wanders back to a few months ago, right after he met Nora at the All Ranks Club. He saw her across the room and introduced himself, asking her for a dance. She looked at him for a few seconds, smiled, and grabbed his hand, pulling him to the dance floor. They danced several songs, even the slow ones. Being this close to an attractive woman caused a heat to build in his loins. Nora noticed and made light of it, much to Rees's embarrassment.

They sat and talked until the club closed. He walked her back to her car and they made out for a few minutes, then made plans for a date. After their third date, Nora brought Rees to her home and introduced him to Skylar. He recognized her since she was dating Senior Airman Nionee.

Nora and Rees spent a lot of time together after that night and seemed a good fit. Their group soon included Ivy and her boyfriend, Eric McAdams, Skylar and Nionee, and Rees and Nora. They spent most of their days off doing things together; going to the lake, the mountains to visit Gatlinburg, and even a late-night trip to Myrtle Beach that featured Nora and Rees riding in the back of McAdams's truck.

Rees smiles as he remembers how he and Nora made love in a sleeping bag in the bed of the truck on the way down to Myrtle Beach. They thought they were being sneaky and no one would notice. That is until they arrived at their destination and McAdams complained that the shocks on his truck were probably worn out, the front end was out of alignment, and he had the hardest time keeping the vehicle on the road. Everyone got a laugh out of that.

He smiles at the memory, then realizes those good times are gone forever with McAdams's death.

Chapter 9

Captain Randall Henries arrives at the Bank and heads straight to General Lucas's office as ordered.

"What the hell do they want now?" he thinks while standing in the elevator.

Henries walks into the outer room and Shelly announces his arrival over the intercom.

"Have him come in," Lucas says.

Henries is already at the general's door before Shelly can say a word and she shakes her head in frustration. Henries strides straight to the general's desk and salutes, ignoring the third man in the room, Chief Joe Black.

Gen. Lucas looks up from behind his desk and stares at the captain for a second, then returns the salute.

"Captain Henries, please have a seat," the general says.

Henries takes a seat and immediately challenges his orders with a petulant tone.

"What's so important, sir, that I have to be called in?" Henries asks.

The general acts as if he didn't hear the slight and carries on.

"I'll tell you what's so damn important, Captain," he begins. "Your sloppiness and inattentiveness to detail on this project may have cost the lives of fifteen good men and damaged this program."

Henries leans back in his chair with a smirk, crosses his legs, and removes a non-existent piece of fuzz from his trousers. It is all the chief can take. He walks over to Henries, who acts as though it is the first time he is noticing someone else is in the room.

"Captain Henries, first off, you can remove that smirk from your face or I can remove it for you. Sir!" the chief growls. "And second, you had better hope to God those fifteen men are alive and well, or I'll personally see to it that you don't see daylight for the rest of your life, sir!"

Henries looks unfazed.

"Now listen here, Sergeant, and I use that word lightly. I don't like your tone," Henries says. "You can't talk that way to me. I'm an officer and I'll have your stripes. I don't know who you are and I don't care. I suggest you watch your step or I'll..."

That's all Henries can get out of his mouth before the chief backhands him hard enough to snap his head into the back of the chair, but easy enough not to remove his perfect teeth. Henries's hand goes to his mouth, and a look of pain and shock shows on his face. He looks at his hand, then at the chief, then at the general, and then back at the chief. Before he can say anything, the general orders the chief to stand down and points to a chair indicating for him to sit.

Henries jumps up and points his finger at Chief Black.

"You won't get away with that, striking an officer. I'll see to it you're busted down to Airman Basic and spend a little time in Leavenworth!" he shouts.

Black sits in his chair, his lips pursed in anger.

"You'll do no such thing, Captain Henries," General Lucas says sternly. "You're in no position to do anything. Now sit your ass down. I'll handle this little incident."

"Incident... Incident! You call this an incident?" Henries yells.

"Yes, Captain, it's an incident!" the general says in a louder voice. "You've got other things to worry about other than a rap in the mouth!"

The general walks closer to Henries and points an accusatory finger at him.

"You're here because of what you have done, or I should say did not do, while you were on duty during the departure of those men. You haven't met Chief Black before today, and we have reasons for that which you need not know. Chief Black is the architect behind Clio. We brought him back in to find out why we are having problems with the project and he found something."

Henries shoots the chief an angry look that at the same time is one of disbelief.

"He discovered that while you were monitoring the DSI panel, you missed something," General Lucas says. "That something may have had disastrous results. One or more of the men may have materialized several feet off the ground and fell the distance. I want to know what happened, Captain."

Henries looks nervous, yet defiant.

"I was monitoring my panel, nothing was wrong." he says. "I kept my eyes on the readouts the entire time. It must have been something else."

"Bullshit!" the chief spits.

"That'll be enough, Chief," Lucas says.

Turning his attention back to Henries, he continues.

"Captain Henries, this is a grave matter, and if you left your post or became distracted or anything you can think of that may have caused you to not monitor your station, we need to know. If you didn't, fine, but if you did, we need to know right now. It's a matter of life and death for these men."

Henries stands and becomes emotional, his face turning red with anger.

"Sir, I tell you I did nothing wrong, and I resent being treated this way and humiliated by this NCO."

"There will be a formal investigation into this matter," Lucas says. "For now, you are dismissed, but be where we can find you. Is this understood?"

"What about my duties, sir?" Henries asks.

"Pending the outcome of the investigation, you are relieved of your duties, Captain Henries," the general states. "Dismissed."

Henries protests, but General Lucas raises his hand to silence him.

"Captain Henries, you know the procedures as well as anyone and this has to happen. I shouldn't have to quote regulations to you."

With that, Henries stands to attention, salutes, does an about face, and walks to the door, giving Chief Black the evil eye before exiting.

The chief goes over to the general's desk.

"That went well," he says.

Lucas gives him a disapproving look and the chief raises his hands in surrender.

"General, I know that man is not telling us the truth," he says.

"You're probably right, Joe, but this will go under an investigation," Lucas replies. "We have notified the OSI as well as our own internal security, but for right now we need to get Clio up and running. We need to know what is happening to the men."

As if Clio has heard the general, the screen flickers and soon a picture appears. Chief Black's eyes widen and he speaks quietly.

"My God," he says.

The general turns to see what Black is looking at, slowly rising from his chair to give the screen his full attention. What he sees surprises him, but doesn't shock him.

***

The lieutenant has been working on the DSI panel for several hours. He is getting frustrated and beginning to think his efforts are for naught. Just as he is about to take a break, he stumbles upon the right adjustments and the screen comes to life. Momentary feelings of relief quickly turn to disgust as the screen flickers and shuts down again. He frantically makes more adjustments, and this time the screen stays on. However, his smile fades as the window into the past reveals a horrific sight. The other technicians in the room cheer and pat each other on the backs, but their smiles also fade as one by one they see the picture of death in front of them.

The screen shows an area filled with the mutilated bodies of men strewn about like so many discarded rag dolls. These are the bodies of soldiers who have encountered men from the future and the devastating weapons they brought with them.

The lieutenant breaks from his trance and pans the camera around for a better view. An incredible sum of death and destruction lay before them. Most of these technicians have never seen the aftermath of warfare. The camera shows a body with a missing head, and the lieutenant hears someone in the room retching. He counts thirty-one bodies, all in confederate gray. There are no security policemen to be seen. Hopefully that means there were no casualties.

The lieutenant looks up toward the general's office behind him.

"What's the old man want us to do now?" he thinks before returning his attention to the monitors.

***

General Lucas turns and faces the chief.

"What in the hell happened, Joe?" he asks.

Black stares at the screen, taking it all in. Despite being filled with anger, he also feels a small tinge of pride; anger because of the carnage he is seeing, and pride because his baby worked. They are witnessing the past. Clio II has done her job.

"Looks like our boys ran into a bit of trouble and we're seeing the results," Black responds.

Lucas stares at the screen in total amazement and then grabs his phone. An officer on the floor below picks up on the first ring.

"Yes, sir?"

"Major, where are our boys?" Lucas asks. "I don't see them."

"No... no sir, neither do we."

"Major, get to work finding those men!" Lucas yells. "Get the other cameras up and running and find them."

"Yes, sir. We're on it. I'll get back with you as soon as we have something, sir."

The general hangs up the phone and sits down. He can see Chief Black out of the corner of his eye as they watch the men working with urgency below them. Black leans on the window sill, transfixed by the activity. Even though the sight on the screen is terrible, he feels a tingle of excitement course though his body.

"We've done it, sir," he says. "We are looking at the past and we did that. This is one of the greatest accomplishments in history, right up there with the splitting of the atom and landing on the moon. Einstein came up the theory to split atoms and Oppenheimer made it work. Einstein came up with the theory of time travel and we made it work."

Black is excited and humbled by what he has done, but still says "we" as if the general has had a hand in creating it. Sure, he smoothed the way, but this has been the chief's baby all the way.

"Joe, it is you, my friend," Lucas says. "I can't take any credit for this. It is all you."

"If those men die out there, General," Black says forlornly, "believe me, I will take the credit."

***

Captain Henries arrives home and takes off his uniform jacket, throwing it across the room as he curses.

"God damn them!" he screams. "Who do they think they are? Rules, regulations, procedures. I did my fucking job. One tiny misstep and they act like the entire world's going to die. Fuck those cops. Never liked them anyhow. Fuck up my career will they?"

He walks over to the bar and pours himself a drink.

"Yeah that's right, something goes wrong, and they got to blame someone. Got to appease the bigshots and cover their asses," he continues ranting while taking a swig of bourbon. "Oh yeah, bigshot chief. Who the hell does he think he is, anyway? King Shit-heel, that's who!"

Henries pours another drink and lifts the glass to his mouth. The telephone on the countertop catches his eye and a smile breaks across his face. He picks up the Yellow Pages and thumbs through the book, the smile never leaving his face. He scans the pages and runs his finger down a column of names until he finds what he is looking for. Memorizing the number, he sets the book down, picks up the telephone receiver, and dials.

He places his glass on the open book and listens as the call connects. The heading on top of the page reads: "Television Stations."

Chapter *10*

Ivy feels much better the following day after a more restful night's sleep. She also looks to be her former self.

"That time of the month, girls," she says. "You know me, I can come up with some good ones and that was one of them."

Ivy, Nora, and Skylar drive to a local bar, still upset about not knowing what is happening to their boyfriends. They walk inside and look for a table as their eyes adjust to the darkness. Seeing an unoccupied table in the corner, they stride over and have a seat.

The bar is dimly lit and smells of beer and sawdust. General's Tap is a popular place on the weekends and periodically during the week, when "the Tap" runs contests and has drink specials. There aren't many patrons and the barkeep looks bored. A waitress comes over and Nora orders a Bloody Mary, Ivy a light beer, and Skylar a diet soda.

"I accept that the military does some unusual things, but something is going on here that just doesn't seem right," Nora says as she rubs her temples. "That sergeant is lying about something, I can tell. He is putting up the biggest front I've ever seen."

"Oh Nora, you're just being paranoid, that's all," Ivy says with what she hopes is a reassuring smile. "He said they were on a classified mission, exercise, whatever. I think it's neat, my Eric on some hush-hush mission. Kind of *Man from Uncle* shit."

Nora looks at Ivy and gives her a disbelieving stare.

"You are such a naïve optimist, Ivy," Nora says. "Besides, what about that little scene you pulled on us yesterday? That was pretty deep. And what about those dreams we all have been having? That's not a coincidence, is it?"

"I guess not," Ivy responds as she shrugs her shoulders, "but what does it mean?"

"I don't know," Nora replies. "Not yet anyway."

The waitress comes back to the table carrying their drinks and Nora's first sip brings on a coughing spasm.

"You okay there, sis?" Skylar asks as she reaches for her sister.

Nora lifts her head and pounds her chest twice with a closed fist.

"Yeah, yeah, I'm fine," she says in between coughs. "Went down the wrong pipe. God, I hate hangovers. Anyway, we've got to find out what is going on with our guys. It's great they may be on some top-secret bullshit mission, but I expect there's more to it than that."

Skylar takes a sip of her soda and sets down the glass, leaning on the table so she can speak in a hushed tone.

"Nora, what are you... I mean, what are we going to do against the whole United States Air Force? We've all seen the movies where the good guy tries to find out something about the government and then they disappear. I know that's far-fetched, but really, who do we turn to for help? If it's so secret, we aren't going to get too far. Even my guard friend, Jimmy, didn't know what was going on when we asked him."

Ivy finishes her beer and waves to the waitress to come over.

"Yu'uns want another round?" Ivy asks the girls.

"No, Ivy, and quit saying 'yu'uns.' Makes you sound like a hick," Nora scolds.

Ivy lifts her chin in an exaggerated look of dignity and searches for the waitress, who has not yet come to take their second order. Nora turns her attention back to her sister.

"Well, we can go to the local newspaper and see if they know anything," Nora says. "They get information most of us can't, and we can try the TV stations as well. It might not lead to anything, but it's a start."

"That might help," Skylar adds, "but what if they don't know anything or are unwilling to talk with us?"

"If that doesn't work, we go to the base," Nora states. "We ask around in the barracks. You know the guys, they will be more than willing to talk with us."

She smiles and pushes out her chest. Skylar moans, and Ivy looks down at herself.

"That's not fair and it's not funny," Ivy says.

Nora relaxes and takes on a serious tone again.

"Look, if that doesn't work, we'll figure something else out," she says.

The waitress finally arrives and Ivy looks at Nora, as if asking permission to get another beer. Nora gives her a scornful look and a dejected Ivy asks for the bill.

The girls leave the Tap and drive up Main Street, pulling into a parking slot in front of the *Daily Express News* building. They enter the reception area and ask the woman at the information desk if they can speak to a reporter about something concerning the base. The clerk tells them to go up to the third floor and ask for a Mr. Bill Rogers. They thank the clerk and head to the elevators.

"Hold on a second, girls," the clerk calls to them and holds up three identifications badges. "I'll need you to sign in and wear these."

The girls grab their respective badges and get into the elevator, where Ivy can't help but make fun of the reporter's name.

"You can call me Mister Bill, or you can call me Mister Rogers, or you can call me..." she says in a sing-song voice.

The elevator stops on the third floor and Nora shoves Ivy into the lobby, where she and Skylar follow.

"Very cute, Ivy," Nora says sternly, making it clear she is not amused.

The newsroom secretary gives them a friendly smile as they approach.

"Hi, can I help you?" she asks.

Nora takes the lead, as usual, and leans on the counter.

"Yes, you can. We'd like to see one of your reporters, a Mister Rogers," she replies, smiling back.

Ivy snickers and leans toward Skylar and whispers, "You can call me Mister Rogers, or you can..."

A sharp elbow to the arm from Skylar quickly quiets her. Ivy grabs at her arm and rubs it.

"Oww," she whimpers.

Nora shoots them an annoyed glance over her shoulder. Skylar looks somber and Ivy gives her an exaggerated sweet, innocent smile.

"Great," Nora thinks. "Here we are looking for information concerning the military and we look like the Three Stooges."

The receptionist points to a desk in the back right of the long newsroom and informs the trio that Bill is at his desk and they can go on in.

The girls walk through the sea of desks, most piled high with files and half-used notepads. They notice Bill's casual desk matches his appearance. He is in his mid-thirties with thick dark hair, dressed in faded blue jeans, a blue Izod pullover, and Adidas running shoes.

Nora stops in front of his desk.

"Mister Rogers?" she asks, with Ivy and Skylar standing behind her.

The reporter is looking for something in a file cabinet and turns toward the women. His smile seems authentic, not forced.

"Yes, that's me," he says. "Can I help you girls with something?"

"Yes, sir," Nora begins. "We'd like..."

Bill interrupts her by grabbing a piece of paper and exclaiming, "Ah, here's that sucker. Thought you'd escape from me, didn't you?"

He looks up at the three young women standing in front of him.

"Oh, shit, sorry," he says with an embarrassed grin.

He points to the chairs around the area and tells them to grab a seat.

"Please forgive me, deadline pressure. And, please, don't call me Mister Rogers. I'm Bill, Mister Rogers is..."

Nora smiles and finishes, "I know, your father."

Bill smiles back and shakes his head.

"Yes ma'am. I'm only thirty-three and I hate the Mister Rogers puns. Now, what is it I can help you with, now that I've found this elusive piece of paper?"

He grips his chair and takes a seat, leaning his elbows on the desk and looking at each of them. Nora likes this man, as does Skylar and Ivy. Of course Ivy likes him. Ivy likes everybody. It's a gift and a curse.

"My name is Nora Miller and this is my sister, Skylar," Nora says as she tilts her head in Skylar's direction. "And this is our friend, Ivy McKnight. We need some help, and this is the first place we thought of."

"Nice to meet you all," Bill says. "What is it you think I can help with?"

"Well, it's like this," Nora begins. "We understand you handle most of the stories from the base."

Nora waits for a reaction and Bill indicates with a nod that she should continue. She tells him what has transpired the last couple of days, even explaining to him about the dreams, Ivy's sickness and premonition, and everything up to them deciding to come to the newspaper.

Bill leans back in his chair, folds his hand across his stomach, and taps his thumbs together. He looks at them and smiles.

"Well ladies, that's some experience," he says. "Tell you what. I'm not sure what I can do, but I will investigate it."

He picks up a piece of paper and hands it to Nora.

"Funny, I just received this not two hours ago," Bill says as the girls all look at the paper. "It's an official press release from the base concerning a mobilization and some other basic PR crap. Not much. Just standard stuff we get all the time from them. But, there's one thing they haven't mentioned and I haven't gotten into yet, and that is the weather."

The girls look at each other with looks of confusion.

"What does the weather have to do with what is happening?" Nora asks.

Bill comes around to the front of the desk to sit on the edge.

"We received several calls from residents around the base telling us about a haze or fog or storm or something coming from a section of the base," he explains. "Not the whole base, just one area. Something is interfering with TVs, radios, and other electronic equipment, like being scrambled. Again, nothing big,"

Bill stops to pick up another piece of paper, this time handing it to Skylar.

"Then I get a call from a buddy of mine at one of the television stations and he tells me he received a call from a captain who claims to be part of a military project related to what is going on here and wants to meet," Bill continues. "My buddy isn't sure what to think, but he has an appointment to meet the captain and I'm tagging along. Now that I've heard your story, I'm definitely hooked. I might find something out that may help you, too."

"Is there anything we can do to help?" Nora asks.

"Nothing right now," Bill replies, "but give me your phone numbers so I can reach you. If I find anything useful or need some help or more information, I'll be in touch."

Bill stands and reaches out for handshakes all around.

"Thank you for the help. It was nice to meet you," Nora says as the girls stand up to depart.

Nora voices her eagerness to learn more during the elevator ride down.

"He's going to get somewhere with this, I just know it," she says.

When the door opens on the first floor, Ivy turns and walks backward to face the others.

"And he's kinda cute for an older guy," she says.

Skylar slaps at Ivy.

"Ivy, that's plain tacky. He's not old, he told you he is only thirty-three. Besides, he's probably married with three kids."

"Nope, no ring. I checked," Ivy says as she opens the car door.

Nora shakes her head and looks at Ivy in the rearview mirror, "Ivy, you're incorrigible."

"Doesn't matter, Eric's a lot cuter," Ivy responds.

Nora starts the car, backs out of the parking spot, and starts down Main Street. The discussion turns to the rest of the day's plans. Ivy suggests they go out on the town after getting something to eat.

"I don't think that's a good idea," Nora says.

"Why not?" Ivy wants to know.

"Look Ivy, you and Skylar can go out if you want, but Bill might need to get ahold of us for something. I just think it's a good idea if one of us is home if he calls."

Skylar and Ivy reluctantly agree, and they decide to grab some takeout on the way home.

***

After the girls leave the newsroom, Bill picks up his phone and calls the television station.

"Channel 11 News," a man's voice answers. "Can I help you?"

Bill switches the phone to his other hand and cradles it on his shoulder, using his head to secure it in place so he can write with the other.

"Yeah, hi, I'm Bill Rogers, *Daily Express News*, may I speak to Terry Jones, please?"

"Sure, wait a second. Yeah, he's here."

Bill can tell the man had placed his hand over the phone and can hear him call Terry's name.

"Hang on, he'll pick up," the man says, and Bill hears a click as another phone picks up.

"Terry Jones here."

"TJ, it's Bill."

"Hi Bill, what's up? You still on for the meeting?" Terry asks enthusiastically.

"Yeah, I'm still on. Listen TJ, I just had three girls come in with information that might tie in with what you're working on. They're worried about their boyfriends and how it's connected to the mobilization exercise. That and the whole fog and haze thing. And now you have contact with a guy who wants to talk. Too many coincidences, Terry."

Bill listens as his TV news friend tells him there were no flights off the base that day and the highway patrol did not get notification of any convoys leaving the base. It is a no-no not to inform local law enforcement when military vehicles will be traveling through towns and on the highways.

Bill leans back in his chair and rubs his forehead.

"Well, something is going on," he states. "I guess I'll see you later and maybe we can get something from this source of yours. I'll see you around six. Still at the Burger King, right?"

"That's right," Terry confirms. "See you then. I have a feeling this could be interesting."

Chapter 11

Captain Henries quietly eats his dinner as he works over details of the story he will tell the news media. He has already decided he cannot let them see his face and they will have to alter his voice if they want a taped interview. He can't afford to be caught; he is in enough of a mess as it is. After the interview, he will go back to command and grovel; make them believe he is sorry for his mistake, beg forgiveness, and ask for a chance at redemption.

"Those bastards are the ones who are going to be sorry, especially that fuckhead chief master sergeant," he says aloud to his empty kitchen.

Henries knows his career is finished, at least any hopes he had for advancement are gone. He will not get above the rank of captain because of what he considers one tiny mistake. He needs to strike first.

The bitter captain finishes his meal, showers, and dresses in civilian attire: jeans, tennis shoes, a chambray shirt, and jacket. He finishes with a baseball cap and glasses, and checks the time. It is 1613 hours (4:13 p.m.)

"I've got more than an hour to meet the TV guy and impress him with a true science fiction story," he tells himself. "He's going to shit!"

Henries grabs his car keys, checks his look in the mirror one last time, and walks out the door. He gets into his BMW and drives north toward the highway. Almost an hour later, he locates the warehouse and pulls around the backside to hide from view. He is early, which was his plan, to make sure the news crew is alone. At 1820 hours, he exits the car and enters the abandoned warehouse to wait. Things are going well so far.

***

Bill Rogers has gone home as well, picking up some fast food on the way and eating it on the drive.

"I've got to stop doing this," he thinks. "Going to get fat."

He lays out his change of clothes and goes to the couch. Pulling papers from his briefcase, he reads for about ten minutes before falling asleep. His catnap, however, turns into an unplanned hour-and-a-half slumber.

***

Terry Jones and his news crew arrive at the Burger King at 6:02 p.m. and wait for Bill. Terry is wearing his nice, on-camera clothes: a white button-down shirt, tie, and tan slacks. His dark blond hair just covers his ears with sideburns. He is well-liked by his peers and trusted at his job.

"If he doesn't show up within the next five minutes, we're going without him," Terry says to Doug Mead, his cameraman, and Mary-Beth Anderson, his sound engineer.

Doug takes a sip of his coffee and makes a disgusted look.

"When the hell did they make this crap, yesterday?" he moans.

Doug fits the stereotype of a cameraman with long, sandy hair, a receding hairline, and a thin beard. He is a good ol' boy from Tennessee who earned a scholarship to the University of Tennessee and took communication and film classes, which landed him a job with the TV station about five years ago. He has been with Terry the entire time. He has dreams of being a motion picture director one day and is using this job to build a collection of clips to get a foot in the door.

Mary-Beth stands about five feet five, and her short-cropped, brown hair makes her cute in a tomboyish way. She is ex-air force, having worked in communications. She did her four years and got out. She has worked with Terry about two years and enjoys her job. All three of them excel at what they do and have won many awards during their time together.

"Okay guys, time to get to work," Terry says as he stands to stretch and look around. "I thought Bill would have been here by now. He seemed pumped up for a story. Oh well, his loss. Let's move... don't want to miss out on a good story ourselves."

The team leaves the restaurant and climbs into the green and blue television news van. They arrive at the warehouse at 6:24 p.m. and park in front of the building.

"I don't see anyone," Doug says while unpacking his camera equipment.

Mary-Beth places her sound equipment on a cart and they proceed to the front door of the warehouse, unaware that Capt. Henries is watching them. Terry opens the door and sticks his head inside, blinking his eyes in an attempt to adjust to the low light.

"Hello?" Terry says tentatively as he enters the warehouse.

"Doug, let's have you set up the lights over there," he says. "It's cooler in here and we can't have the masses see him sweating."

Terry takes about four more steps when Henries calls out to him.

"Mr. Jones," Henries says.

Terry turns toward the direction of the voice.

"Is that you, Captain?" Terry asks, moving further into the warehouse.

"Yes, Mr. Jones, it is."

Terry moves to his right, trying to see around a stairwell so he can see the person speaking to him.

"That's quite far enough, Mr. Jones. I don't want you to see me," Henries says.

Terry stops and looks over his shoulder at his crew, who is standing just inside the doorway.

"Captain, I'm going to have my crew come in and set up, if that's all right with you," he says.

"All right, go ahead," Henries responds.

Terry waves his team toward a nearby area to set up.

"Is that him?" Doug whispers.

"Yeah, that's him. One paranoid sucker, too," Terry replies. "Doesn't want to be seen. I have a gut feeling this guy is a fruitcake."

"Camera won't be much use if we have no one to film," Doug leans in to say softly.

Terry looks around for an appropriate spot and sees what he is looking for. He turns back to his crew.

"I've got an idea," he says. "Move the equipment over there, where it's dark, in those shadows."

Terry points to an area barely visible in the darkness. They will be able to control the amount of light there better.

"We'll have him stand in the darkness so we can film him talking without showing his face," he says. "Just a silhouette of his body will be on camera."

The crew walks over to the spot and begins setting up. Doug takes light meter readings and Mary-Beth checks the background noise levels.

"You think he'll want his voice dubbed?" she asks.

"Oh, hell yes, don't all these whistle blowers?" Doug responds.

Terry walks closer to the captain's location so he can explain what they plan to do without raising his voice.

"Mr. Jones, please understand I do not want to have my face seen. I do not want my name used, and I want my voice changed so it's unrecognizable," Henries demands.

"We understand and we'll take care of that," Terry replies.

"Also, Mr. Jones, what I am about to do is very dangerous and can put you and your friends at risk," Henries adds.

"That's our job, Captain," Terry says. "Danger is sometimes a factor in getting an exceptional story."

Apparently reassured, Henries walks to the dark spot the crew has prepared for him and takes his position while Terry describes how the interview will transpire.

"First off, Captain, I will introduce you – not using your name or rank, of course – and tell our audience that we have a guest who works with a secret organization and has information he feels the public needs to know. I will introduce you and say, 'Sir, I understand you have come to us as a person working with the military and that you want us to know of a new project that will change the course of mankind. Will you please tell us your story?' Then I will turn it over to you. Is that okay with you?"

"That's fine," Henries says. "Just so nothing is said or shown that will lead anyone to me. Is that understood?"

"Understood. What do we call you? Mister X?"

"Do not insult me, Mr. Jones! I can always walk out of here and go to your competitors!"

"No, no, that isn't a putdown," Terry quickly responds. "I just think we might need a code name, you know, like Deep Throat was for the Watergate story. Tell you what, we won't use anything. We'll start the camera rolling and get this over with. Now, can you move a little more forward? We need to see your body in the light."

Terry signals for Doug to begin filming and Mary-Beth to record. Doug raises his hand in the air and counts off, closing a finger with each number.

"In five, four, three..." the last two numbers are silent, and he closes his finger down to zero, at which time Terry begins his introduction.

"This is Terry Jones with Channel 11 News, and I'm here in a secret location with a very important guest..."

The interview lasts about fifteen minutes, during which Henries details the military's time machine technology and the project taking place.

As the interview continues, a silver Ford sedan quietly pulls up next to the news van and four men in dark suits exit. The driver signals for two of the men to go around the back of the warehouse while he and the other man walk toward the front door. Moments later, a noise somewhere inside the warehouse catches Henries's attention and he becomes nervous.

"That's a pretty incredible tale, sir," Terry says. "I mean, time travel? Do you have any proof to back up your claim?"

"No, I don't have any proof with me," Henries responds, "but I can get you a picture of the time machine if needed."

Another noise in the otherwise-silent warehouse catches both men's attention.

Did you bring anyone else with you?" Henries asks. "I think someone else is here."

"Of course not," Terry replies. "You picked this location and it's been abandoned for years."

Suddenly, a single gunshot breaks the tense silence and a bullet strikes Henries low in the shoulder, causing him to spin around and fall as the bullet fragments inside him. Terry and his crew freeze momentarily, not comprehending what is happening. Blood quickly seeps through Henries's clothes where the bullet entered, and Terry takes a step toward the fallen officer.

A second shot rings out. This one hits Doug in the back of his head and exits below his right eye, taking part of his face with it. Mary-Beth screams as blood, bone fragments, and gore spray across her face. Her scream is cut short and turns into a yell of pain as a third round strikes her in the leg.

Terry stops in his tracks and looks as his friends fall to either side of him. He sees two men moving toward him, guns drawn, and takes a step to the right. His plant foot slips in Henries's blood and nearly causes him to fall. Catching his balance, he looks up only to come face to face with a man wearing mirrored sunglasses despite the low-light environment, grinning and pointing a pistol at his head. Terry tries to avoid the man's aim, but it's too late. The muzzle flash from the barrel of the gun is the last image he sees before he dies.

The man walks up and puts two more rounds into the reporter's body while one of his cohorts calmly walks up to Doug's already-lifeless body and fires two more rounds into him. A third man strolls up to Mary-Beth, who is writhing on the floor while holding her leg, and fires two more times. She stops moving.

All four men then walk toward Henries, who is curled up in pain from the gunshot wound to his torso. He gets up and tries to run away, leaving a trail of blood in his wake. The man with the sunglasses trips Henries and flips him onto his back, causing him to cry out in pain. The man smiles as places his foot on Henries's wound and presses down, causing Henries to scream in agony.

"Bad boy, Captain Henries, giving away secrets," the man says as he increases pressure on the wound.

"Tisk, tisk... sorry about the hole my man put in you. That must really hurt," he says, finally releasing the pressure so he can lean down.

Henries moans, trying to not pass out.

"What is that? I can't hear you," the man says sarcastically.

Straightening up again, he presses his foot on the wound, harder this time, as Henries screams louder.

"That's better. I would ask you what happened here, but I'm sure we'll find out when we review the tape. Well, it's been nice having this little chat with you. Sorry we had to meet under these circumstances."

He releases the pressure from Henries's shoulder, leaving the captain whimpering and rolling on the ground, gasping for air. As the man walks away, he nods to his associates to remove evidence of the interview from the news team's equipment. A final gunshot echoes through the cavernous warehouse as he exits the building.

Chapter 12

Bill Rogers wakes, yawns, stretches, and then bolts upright as he suddenly remembers his appointment with Terry Jones and his crew. He glances at the clock and throws his legs onto the floor, spilling the papers he was reading. He has only five minutes before the interview is scheduled to start.

"Damn it, Bill, you moron!" he curses himself. "Shit, shit, shit!"

The veteran newspaper reporter scrambles to retrieve his clothes and dress in record time. At least he placed his clothes out earlier. He gathers up the spilled papers and throws them into his briefcase, grabs for his keys, misses them, tries again. This time he gets them, but in his haste, drops them to the floor.

"Calm the hell down, Billy boy, you're not getting anywhere this way. No way you're getting to the meeting in time, no matter how much you hurry."

Bill takes a breath, picks up the keys, and leaves his apartment. It's not long before he forgets his own advice about calming down, spinning his wheels as he leaves the gravel parking lot. He realizes as he turns onto the freeway that he is lucky Terry gave him the warehouse location for the interview, otherwise he might miss the whole thing.

Bill accelerates to 75 miles per hour in the 55 zone and hasn't even gone a mile when he hears a siren and notices blue lights in his rearview mirror.

"God dammit, I don't have time for this shit!" he says between clenched teeth as he pulls over to the shoulder of the road.

The officer sits in his squad for a couple of minutes as Bill impatiently drums his fingers on the dash.

"Must be running the plates," he guesses.

Finally, the patrolman exits the squad and approaches.

"You in some kind of hurry there, sir?" the officer asks. "Clocked you at 78."

Bill smiles and tries playing the politeness card.

"Yes, sir, I am. I'm with the press and I'm late for an interview on the other side of town. Twenty minutes late."

The officer pulls out his ticket book and begins writing.

"So, you're a reporter, are you?" he asks.

"Yes, with the *Daily Express News*," Bill replies with the fake smile still plastered to his face.

"I'll need to see your license, registration, and press credentials, too," the officer says.

Bill fishes in his glove compartment for the requested items and hands them over.

"I'm sorry, officer. I know I was speeding. It's just that this is a very important interview. I'll slow it down. I'm not going to make it on time anyhow. I might be able to catch the television crew I'm supposed to meet before they wrap it up and get something from them."

The officer stops writing and looks at Bill.

"Tell you what I'll do for ya, Mister… Rogers," the officer says as he scans Bill's press credentials for his name. "You boys at the press have been decent to us lately, so I'm going to cut you a sprout. Slow it the heck down and try to get there in one piece. Ain't nothing worth getting yourself or someone else killed over."

He hands the paperwork back to Bill and says, "You have a good night now, ya hear?"

"Thank you, officer," Bill says with a legitimately grateful smile.

Bill checks the time. It is 6:41 p.m. He pulls back onto the highway and keeps to only slightly over the speed limit the rest of the way. Ten minutes later, he sees the warehouse district to the left and exits the highway. He turns onto the service road and glimpses the green and blue Channel 11 News van parked in front of a warehouse. He glances at the van and sees no one inside.

"Good, that must mean they're still doing the interview," he thinks.

Bill parks behind the van and gets out of his car. Noticing the van's sliding door is ajar, he opens it and peers inside. No one is there, so he closes the door and walks toward the open front door of the warehouse. Listening briefly, he's not able to hear the sounds of any talking.

"Terry? You here?" Bill calls out as he pokes his head inside.

There is no answer. Cautiously, he enters the dark warehouse and struggles to see anything in the dim light. He calls out for his friend again. Still nothing. As his eyes adjust, he is able to make out some shapes in a far corner.

As he moves closer, his jaw drops at the sight of four bodies strewn across the concrete floor amongst broken camera and recording equipment. He sees Terry lying in a pool of blood, or at least it looks like Terry. It's the right hair color, but the back of his head is missing.

Bill's heart rate begins to race in near panic as he quickly takes in the entire scene. Suddenly, a hand grabs his pants leg and he lets out a small yelp, nearly causing him to jump out of his skin. He looks down and sees a woman reaching for him. She is covered in blood.

"Help me," she moans in a weak voice.

Bill gathers his senses and squats next to her.

"Oh, God… Mary-Beth!" he says, finally recognizing her through all the blood. He grabs her hand, not knowing what else to do. "What happened? Who did this to you?"

"Men… with guns… suits," she says, gasping for air.

Bill leans in closer and she clasps his arm, pulling him to her.

"Time machine… he says… time machine… the base," she says in a voice now no louder than a whisper.

Not sure what she is talking about, Bill gently pats her hand.

"I'll go get help, be right back," he says, not knowing if she could hear him or not. "Everything will be fine. I'll be back."

Bill runs outside and heads for the TV van, figuring it would have a two-way radio connection with the studio. He quickly locates the radio and sees a small sign stating the van's engine needs to be running. Cursing, he turns and runs back into the warehouse, knowing he is wasting valuable time. He goes to Terry's body and feels for the van keys in his dead friend's pockets, almost retching in the process. Finally discovering the keys, he runs back to the van, nearly slipping in the blood on the way out.

"So much blood," he thinks.

Bill starts the engine and grabs the mic.

"Hello, hello, anyone!" he shouts. "Hello, I need help, please answer!"

Releasing the button, he listens to the static. A few seconds pass and then a voice comes over the radio.

"This is Channel 11 control. Who is this?"

"This is Bill Rogers from the *Daily Express News*. I'm at an abandoned warehouse just off the freeway and there has been a shooting involving your people. Get the police and ambulance here, now! Three people are dead and one is badly wounded."

"Give me your exact location," the studio attendant replies. "I'm getting the police on the other line."

Bill complies and then explains he was there to meet Terry Jones and his crew for an interview, but was late arriving. A shiver runs down his spine as he realizes if he had been there on time, he likely would be laying there with them.

The radio crackles and the voice comes back on. "Stay there. Help is on the way."

Bill acknowledges, throws the mic on the front seat, and runs back into the warehouse. He goes straight to Mary-Beth. By this time, however, she is dead.

Very quickly, the scene is swarming with state troopers, county sheriff's deputies, EMTs, and other news agencies who were monitoring radio scanners. Bill talks with a detective, who is taking notes.

"Mr. Rogers, just what was this interview about?" the detective asks.

"It had to do with the base," Bill responds, still in shock. "Mary-Beth Anderson said something about a time machine and spooks. That's all she said before..."

The detective looks up from writing and stares at Bill.

"A time machine and spooks, huh? Sounds like she might have been delirious from blood loss, in shock."

Bill nods his head.

"I don't know anything about that," he says. "I do know something is going on and I'm going to find out what it is. I just lost a good friend in there and I need to know why."

The detective asks a few more questions before telling Bill he is free to go, but to stay available in case they need him for further questioning. Bill walks away and gets into his car. He sees his camera on the passenger seat and gives it a reassuring pat.

Chapter 13

Rees is sound asleep, dreaming of the men he killed in the field the previous day. The other members of his unit are dead in the dream, and he is running from a massive, unending horde of dead Civil War soldiers. They are right behind him and he is too afraid to turn and look; terrified that if he does, one of those zombie-like soldiers will be staring him right in the face.

They are yelling at him in a weird chorus, a chant, "Go back... Go back..." over and over, then it changes to, "You don't belong here... You don't belong here!"

Rees can hear a set of footsteps gaining on him and then feels a boney hand grab at his shoulder. He wants to scream, but as is the case in most dreams, he can't. The creature's face is so close that Rees can smell its putrid breath.

"Sergeant Rees," it whispers, "you need to leave."

Rees opens his eyes with a start and sees that Sgt. Kriger is shaking him by the shoulder, saying his name in an attempt to wake him. For a few seconds, Rees thinks Kriger is the corpse from his dream, still holding onto him. Then he realizes where he is.

"Shit, sorry," Rees says as he struggles to sit upright. "What is it?"

Kriger grins, "Having one hell of a dream there, huh Sarge?"

"Yeah, I was at that," Rees replies while blinking away the sleep and forcing a smile. "What time is it anyway?"

"Well, considering where we are, that term doesn't really apply now does it?" Kriger responds before adding that it is almost 0700.

Rees grabs his gear and walks over to a clearing, staring at the sun beginning to show in the east. Kriger stands beside him.

"Not something you'd see in the twentieth century. Clear skies like this," Kriger comments. "No planes from the base or traffic noise, no pollution, still pure. No modern civilization around to fuck it up. Oh well, soon enough. Anyway, we're about to go on another patrol."

"On whose orders?" Rees demands.

Kriger shrugs and opens a can of C-rations, then offers some to Rees.

"On whose orders?" Rees asks again.

"We were talking about it a little while ago that if we are still in the same geographic spot we were when we left the Mud Dump, we figure the town of Hendricks Hill is not too far in that direction," Kriger says, pointing with the can in his hand. "Figure we'll take a patrol and check it out."

"Oh, so you guys are running the show now, without consulting me?" challenges Rees.

"You were out of it and Bouvier didn't want to bother you. He figured you'd be okay with it anyhow, seeing we need some answers."

Kriger takes another bite of his C-rations, looks at it disappointingly, and throws it down. Rees stares at the discarded can and lets out a bemused snort.

"What's so funny?" Kriger asks.

"Modern man has struck before his time," Rees says, nodding toward the metal can on the ground. "Never mind. What were you saying about Hendricks Hill?"

"If we find it, it probably means you're right with your time travel theory," Kriger responds as they walk toward the Duck. "Also, we might find out something useful, like exactly what year we're in and where we are."

The pair walks up to Bouvier, who is talking with Tucker, Tosseti, and Montoya.

"How's Airman Harris?" Rees asks the trio.

"He won't last too much longer unless we can get him medical treatment that we can't provide," Bouvier says, looking despondent.

Bouvier updates Rees on their discussion regarding a potential patrol, and Rees reluctantly agrees with him.

"I'll lead the patrol and take the Duck," Rees says. "We'll see if we can locate Hendricks Hill. The Jeep doesn't provide enough protection in case of another attack. The other guys might still be alive if they had been in the Duck instead of that Jeep. I should have listened to you, Jack."

Shepard climbs into the driver's seat and starts the engine, and Bouvier stands by the open hatch as they settle in.

"You know you're going to give me a complex taking all the patrols yourself," Bouvier says.

"As Captain Kirk would probably say, 'Captain's prerogative,' " Rees says with a smile.

"Just be careful," Bouvier replies. "Don't get caught, or worse, get killed. Just find out what you can and get the hell back here. We'll stay in radio contact with you as long as we can, then you're on your own. Good luck."

Bouvier closes the hatch and the patrol drives off.

Shepard drives close to where they started and pulls to a stop. Tucker and Tosseti exit the Duck and go on foot ahead to look around. They return about fifteen minutes later and Tosseti is smiling gleefully.

"Geez, I didn't get a look at this mess we made," he says. "We really fucked 'em up, didn't we?"

"Yeah, we did. What's so great about that, Tosseti?" Kriger demands. "Killing people we don't know and having them kill us. Yeah, fuck'n great!"

Rees quickly changes the subject.

"What's it look like? Are we clear to move on through?"

"No, there are soldiers there, searching the bodies," Tucker replies.

Tosseti, still grinning, informs the group that the soldiers ahead are all in blue.

"You know what that means don't you?" he asks.

"Yeah, fuck'n Yankees, that's what!" Shepard answers. "Let's go in there and kill 'em all, fuck'n blue bellies! We killed some Rebs, now let's kill some Yanks, even it up!"

Tosseti turns on him.

"Fucks youse, man. Goddamn Rebels couldn't do shit during the war and can't do shit now," he says in anger.

Shepard lunges for Tosseti and lands a blow to Tosseti's face before anyone can react, driving the smaller man backward. Tosseti recovers and returns a punch to Shepard's midsection. The other men finally react and get them apart, but it isn't easy considering their size and frame of mind. Rees has no patience for this type of in-fighting.

"That's enough of that shit from you two," he says, getting in both of their faces. "We ain't killing anyone if we can help it. You all get that? This ain't no picnic and we don't have time to be going at each other. We are going into town to find some answers, not go on a killing spree. I just want to get in, then get out, hopefully with some information that will be useful. How about you get your shit together and start acting like professionals?"

Shepard and Tosseti nod their heads in agreement and the others release them.

"Now get in the Duck and let's get going," Rees concludes.

Nionee is understandably nervous as the only Native American soldier in the squad. Still, he can't help but smile at Shepard and Tosseti.

"You know I always get a thrill out of watching a couple of white guys try to kill each other, especially over a bunch of white guys fighting a war trying to kill each other. Only time in history you all weren't trying to kill my people," he says.

Tucker snorts at that comment and gives Nionee a high five.

Tosseti and Shepard look at each other and then Tucker, then back at Nionee, simultaneously giving him their middle finger.

"Fuck you," they say in unison.

Nionee flips them off as he starts the engine.

"No, fuck *you*," he says as he places the big vehicle into gear.

"All right guys, knock it off," Rees orders after watching the spat play out. "We have a job to do so quit the grab-assing and stay alert."

He turns back in his seat and faces forward, smiling to himself that airmen can be at each other's throats one minute and then joking and smiling the next.

"Yup, just like family," he muses.

The group works their way toward town by giving the boys in blue a wide berth so they can make it past without incident. They come upon a farm about twenty minutes later, but decide not to stop. At 1024 hours, they see Hendricks Hill ahead and find a place to park out of sight. Tucker, Tosseti, and Nionee stay behind to watch the Duck and cover the backs of Rees and the rest as they walk to town.

"This should be interesting," Rees says. "It's going to be hard enough explaining who we are, much less explaining how come we have a black guy and an Indian with us, so you two and Tosseti need to stay here."

As Rees and his team quietly approach the town, they can see people dressed in period-appropriate farmer attire, barefoot kids running around the yards, people in horse-drawn buggies, and men on horseback. The airmen look at each other and Rees has to smile. What a sight they are seeing. It's like looking at old photographs come to life. People are going about their business in the 1860s. This is incredible.

The team moves stealthily along the back of a building, looking for a way inside. Not finding a back door, they take a chance by going around to the front. Rees peers around a corner and sees a man and a woman in the street, but too far away for them to spot the team. Rees removes his cap and motions for the others to do the same. They stand out enough as it is. He signals for Kriger and Shepard to follow him as he scrambles up on the front porch to peek into the window.

He sees a man behind the counter in what looks to be a hardware store, looking at something in his hands and talking to another man. Rees opens the door and all three enter the store. The man behind the counter looks in their direction and begins to speak, but stops. His eyes widen as he takes in the sight of the three airmen, and the other man turns and has the same expression. The storekeeper drops the object he has been holding and it explodes on the wooden floor. Whatever it was must have been made of glass.

"Sweet Lord and Jesus!" he exclaims and then stammers, "What do you want? Who are you? You Yankees? What kind of uniforms are those?"

Kriger and Rees move further in while Shepard turns to the door and keeps watch. Rees walks up to the counter to engage the store owner.

"Sir, we are not Union nor Confederate, we're..."

Rees hadn't thought this through. How much will he tell people they come across? He looks to Kriger for support, but gets a lopsided grin for his effort.

"Your call," Kriger says.

Rees looks back at the man and says, "We are an independent faction of the military, neither North nor South."

"Y'all gots to be spies or sump'n. How come you got no accent? And that fella there," he says while pointing at Kriger, "he sounds like a Yankee."

Rees smiles at that.

"Yes sir, he is, and I'm from the Arizona Territories, Yuma actually," Rees says, trying to use a nonthreatening tone. "Sergeant Shepard over there by the door is from the North Carolina mountains, outside of Asheville."

Shepard turns from his post near the door and waves. The two men exchange looks and the storeowner continues.

"Some secret stuff our boys been working on, fancy army duds and such?"

Rees looks down at his uniform then at Kriger, who shrugs.

"Well, sir, you can believe what you want," Rees replies.

Suddenly, there is a noise from the back of the store and Kriger rushes into the back room to see what is going on. He comes back a minute later with a young woman in her early twenties with long, blonde hair.

"I found her under a table. Must have hid when she saw us," Kriger explains.

The storeowner takes a step and Rees puts his hand up to stop him. He looks at Rees, then at the young woman.

"You just let her be, you hear me?" the man says. "She ain't caused no trouble."

"Calm down, sir," Rees says. "We aren't here to hurt anyone."

He nods for Kriger to let the young woman go and she runs straight into the storeowner's arms.

"Pa, who are these men?" she asks, still trembling.

"Just some fellas passing through," he tells her and looks at Rees, who nods his head in the affirmative.

"That is correct, just passing through," Rees responds. "May we ask your names, please?"

"My name is David Olsen, and this is my store. This is my daughter, Sarah, and that there is Mr. James, one of my best customers."

Rees snaps a look at Kriger, who returns the wide-eyed glance.

"You hear that? David Olsen," Rees says. "You think this David Olsen might one day have a descendent named David Olsen III who becomes a prominent judge in this area?"

"Could be," Kriger replies.

"What are you boys talking about?" Olsen demands.

Rees quickly changes the subject.

"Sir, we're only here for some information. We kind of got lost, but figure we are in North Carolina and this is Hendricks Hill, correct?"

"Yes."

"Okay, and can you tell us what year it is?" Rees asks, hoping the question doesn't raise a red flag.

Mr. Olsen looks perplexed and pauses before answering.

"It is 1862," he says with a quizzical look.

"August?"

"Yes... even if y'all are lost, how can you not know what month and year it is?"

Rees was not shocked by Olsen's answers, and from the look on Kriger's face, neither was he. The information merely confirmed what they already suspected.

"Hey, there's a guy with a badge and a gun coming this way," Shepard calls out from the front of the store.

Rees runs to the front and looks out the window.

"Shit, we don't need this," he says under his breath and returns to the counter.

"Mr. Olsen, there's a sheriff or deputy coming this way. We do not need him to find us and start asking a bunch of questions or trying to arrest us. He will lose and we are on an important mission for both governments, I can't explain anymore. Is there a back way out of here?"

Olsen points to the room where Kriger found Sarah.

"There's a window in there," he says. "It opens up to the alley."

The men start for the room when Kriger yells, "Watch out!"

Rees sees Kriger draw his .38 and fire a round, at the same time he hears the sound of another pistol shot as the store customer yells, "Damn Yankee spies!"

The wood by the door frame splinters next to Rees's head, wood fragments peppering his face. Turning and reaching for his pistol, Rees catches a glimpse of Mr. James holding a pistol in his hand before a shotgun blast from Shepard lifts the customer off the floor. The force of buckshot striking his chest flings James across the room and into the glass window, the shards causing further damage to his already-dead body.

Mr. Olsen looks at James's body with his mouth open and Sarah clasps her hands over her mouth in terror. There is yelling in the streets and people are running toward the store.

"Kriger, let's go now!" Rees says with force as he grabs Kriger's arm.

Shepard is already running for the back room and is out the window in a flash. Rees pulls on Kriger again until he snaps out of his shock and follows Rees into the back room. Kriger clambers out the window first, hitting the ground running. Rees can hear people shouting and turns to Mr. Olsen, who has followed them into the room.

"I'm sorry, Mr. Olsen," Rees says. "We weren't here to cause trouble, just needed information. I hope you can forgive us."

He doesn't wait for a reaction and scrambles through the window.

As Rees runs to catch up with Kriger and Shepard, he looks over his shoulder to see someone stick their head out of the window. The person yells and indicates to others that the men are heading toward the woods. This causes the airmen to double-time their speed.

They slow after a few hundred meters and Shepard lets out a whoop as they crest a small hill. They go on for about another hundred meters before stopping to catch their breath. They can hear the townspeople in the distance looking for them. They start off again and soon make it back to the Duck, where Tucker, Tosseti, and Nionee are waiting for them.

"Gawd man, you should have seen it!" Shepard says with an adrenalin-fueled laugh. "We were running to beat the gun. Those poor suckers didn't know what to think. They thought we were Yankees, you believe that? Damn Yankees! They freaked, really totally freaked. It was great, man. I just blew the shit out of this dirt fucker who tried to shoot Sergeant Rees in the back."

Rees walks up to him with a hostile look.

"Sergeant, that is enough! This isn't a game and there's nothing funny about killing a man, or almost getting killed ourselves. What is wrong with you?"

Shepard takes a step back and looks aghast at Rees's reaction.

"Shit, sorry. Didn't mean noth'n by it."

Rees turns away in disgust and heads toward the Duck.

"Sorry sir," Tucker interrupts, "but we have a little situation here, too."

"A little situation?" Rees asks. "What kind of situation?"

Tucker tilts his head toward the door of the armored vehicle and walks toward it. The others follow. They get to the right-side door and look inside to see a scrawny boy of about fourteen or fifteen, wearing a tattered shirt, bib overalls, a pair of worn leather shoes, and an old felt hat. He barely notices the men staring at him as he looks through a *Playboy* magazine with a strange look on his face.

"Who in the hell is this?" Rees asks Tucker.

"This here is Billy Olsen," Tucker replies. "He says his father owns the hardware store in town. Tosseti thought it would be a good idea to give him some reading material. Kept him from asking too many questions."

"Unbelievable," Rees grumbles, shaking his head.

Kriger walks over and grabs the magazine from the boy, waving for him to get out of the vehicle.

"Hi Billy, I'm David," Kriger says. "I'll hold onto this, sorry."

"That there picture book is great!" Billy says. "Ain't never seen no color pictures, and ain't never seen no necked woman before! Can I keep it?"

"Probably not," Kriger answers. "It wouldn't be a good thing if other people saw this."

"Suppose you're right. Y'all from the future, huh?" Billy asks in wonder. "Don't care for that noise box you got, though. That's not any music I know, just noise."

Tosseti takes that as his cue to go inside the Duck and turn on the cassette deck. It blasts out a Van Halen song, making the boy contort his face in discomfort. Tosseti switches it off after a few seconds. Rees snatches the magazine out of Kriger's hand and holds it up for Tucker, Tosseti, and Nionee to see.

"Really?" he asks, not expecting a response.

Tosseti shrugs, Tucker looks sheepish, and Nionee raises his hands in surrender from the driver's seat of the Duck.

"Don't look at me, Sarge," Nionee says. "These two yahoos did this on their own."

"Sergeant Kriger is right, Billy," Rees tells the boy. "We can't have you running around with this in your possession."

"Aw, shucks, mister," Billy says, looking downtrodden. Then just as quickly, he lightens up. "Y'all sure are dressed funny, and this here thing is funny-looking, too. Tucker says it's like a wagon, but without horses."

"That's right, Billy," Rees replies. "Like a wagon without horses."

Rees glances at his watch and his men take the hint they need to move on. Tucker rests his hands on Billy's shoulders.

"Hey buddy, we got to go, but it was sure nice meeting you," Tucker says, trying to sound upbeat.

Billy smiles and Kriger walks over to him.

"Listen Billy, we met your father and sister," he begins, and Billy's smile falters a little. "They are all right, but a man tried to shoot us and we had to shoot back, and we think he's probably dead."

Billy's face turns serious and Kriger looks to Rees for support.

"Billy, please don't tell anyone you saw us or where we are," Rees says. "We are lost and trying to get home. We're not trying to cause any trouble. Do you understand?"

"Yes, sir. I won't," Billy replies.

With that, the youngster scampers off and the men climb into the Duck. Shepard starts the engine and they head north.

"Ah shit," Tucker says after a few minutes, holding his beret and looking around on the floor for something. "Lost my crest."

"It probably fell off when you were helping make a juvenile delinquent out of Billy," Kriger suggests, getting a laugh from the rest.

"Don't sweat it," Rees tells Tucker. "It'll show up."

After taking a looping route around town, the men arrive at camp and relate their experience in town with the rest of the unit.

"Oh great," Bouvier groans. "That's all we need is to be the subject of a search party. Word spreads fast in these parts, you know."

"I'm not happy about it either, but what's done is done," Rees responds. "For now, let's just stay put and see what happens."

The twelve men, including two injured, are lost in another time and have no idea what is in store for them. Some of them slump in depression, resigned to a bleak outlook, while others believe their prayers will be answered.

Chapter 14

Shelly hands Chief Black another cup of coffee and leaves the office. He takes a sip and looks in the direction of General Lucas, who is leaning on his desk and deep in thought.

"Don't fret it too much, sir," Black says. "You'll give yourself an ulcer."

The general gives a short chuckle and starts to say something when the phone rings.

"Yes, what do you have?" he asks, and after a short pause, "What do you mean you have *some* of them?"

Lucas looks up at the screen and Chief Black goes to the window to look for himself. The camera shows five of the security policemen and a boy in his mid-teens. The men are standing in a semicircle around the boy, who is sitting inside the side door of the Duck. Lucas reaches down and turns up the audio feed from the camera, but receives only white noise for his efforts.

"Major Hess, where in the hell is my audio?" Lucas demands. "All

I'm getting is static!"

"Sorry, sir, the picture finally came back on, but we still don't have sound," the major responds. "We are working on it and hope to have something for you shortly."

Lucas turns back toward the window and looks at the screen, willing it to give him sound.

"Major, do what you can, but I want some audio and I want it ASAP, you got that?"

"Yes, sir."

Almost as though the screen can hear the general's threatening tone, the audio crackles to life. Lucas looks at the chief with a boyish grin on his face. Standing a little taller, Lucas adjusts his uniform.

"What did you expect?" he says. "I didn't get this far in the service by not having people obey me?"

They turn their attention back to the screen in time to see the boy scurry off into the woods. The audio begins to clear up as the technician adjusts wavelengths, just in time to hear one of the sergeants tell the others that they need to leave. The men then get into the Duck and drive away. The next words Lucas and Black hear send chills down their spines.

"What the hell are we going to do now?" another of the sergeants asks. "We shot a man in Hendricks Hill!"

Chief Black looks at the general and the general at him. Both look disbelievingly at the screen with what they heard, but they know it must be true. They knew something like this could happen.

The security policemen inside the Duck look worn and tired. General Lucas asks Black to get him the intelligence on all of the men on the mission. The chief goes to his briefcase and extracts several files that contain information on each man, including their photographs.

"General, I have the information right here," he says. "They are good men and I can tell you a lot about each of them."

Black lays the files on the general's desk and Lucas half turns to pick one up.

"Who are the sergeants in charge?" he asks.

"Sir, that would be Tech Sergeant Scott Rees and Staff Sergeant Jack Bouvier," Black answers.

"That must be Rees with them now," the general notes.

"Yes, sir, that's correct."

The general thumbs through some of the folders, pausing now and then to read.

"I can tell you who the rest of the men are," Black says. "The Buck Sergeant is David Kriger and the stocky, red-headed man is Airman First Class Matthew Tosseti."

As the camera pans, the chief identifies the driver as Senior Airman Ray Nionee, the tall black man as Airman First Class Nathaniel "Nate" Tucker, and the larger man as Buck Sergeant Thomas J. "TJ" Shepard. The general compliments Chief Black on his recall.

They turn their attention back to the screen and listen to the conversation. Rees is telling his men that there is nothing they could have done to avoid the shooting. It was self-defense. The other big sergeant, the one with the heavy southern drawl, keeps saying, "Fuck it. It didn't mean a thang." He seems like a mouthy person in the general's mind.

Lucas hopes the incident actually was self-defense, because he doesn't want to think the men on this mission would murder people. People can do strange things under pressure. The mission was designed to see what they would do under pressure, and this is an early wake-up call. Now that they have visual and audio, the general will see it first-hand.

Gen. Lucas and Chief Black continue to listen as the SPs discuss their situation. One of the men seems to find it amusing while the smaller NCO – Black says Kriger is his name – tells the man to shut up. The airmen then sit silently, staring at nothing. The general and the chief have seen those looks before from others who have been in the shit.

"Those men have killed for the first time, Joe," Lucas whispers. "I sent men back into a time and a war they have only learned about in school. It's a shame that even though we are making history, we have sent men to their deaths to achieve it."

The general feels ill in realizing the looks on the men's faces likely means they have witnessed the deaths of friends and comrades. Chief Black also knows that look and joins the general in despair.

The in-vehicle camera shows the men pile out of the Duck upon reaching their destination. The screen view changes to outside the vehicle and the camera pans the area, revealing a makeshift camp. Chief Black takes it all in, his photographic memory recording everything he sees. He counts each man as they come into view and places them with the file he has on each. He applauds the security procedures he sees in place: good fields of fire; 360-degree coverage; they probably have an LP-OP (Listening Post, Observation Post) out, too. He doesn't like the number of men he counted, though. He can only see ten. He asks the general permission to use the phone to the control room.

"Major Hess, please have the camera move over to the Jeep," Black says.

As the camera moves over to the Jeep, he sees what looks to be two men sleeping. The camera zooms closer and he sees the men are injured. That brings the total count twelve. The general knows what Black is thinking.

"Joe, if you notice, there's one Jeep missing. I bet there's a patrol out, that's why three men are missing."

The chief grunts in acknowledgement. He had been focused on the count and hadn't noticed the missing Jeep. The general also notices the two men on the ground. Rees and Bouvier go to the Duck and sit down, themselves watching as Kriger goes to the two injured men. Rees leans his head back against the vehicle and closes his eyes.

"How are Harris and Green doing, Sergeant Bouvier?" he asks.

"Not too well, Sarge," Bouvier replies.

Bouvier draws up his knees and crosses his arms over them to rest his head.

"We're tired, Scott, and sick of this shit," Bouvier says. "I want to know why the hell we are here. Who did this, and for what purpose? We all do our jobs, go to work when needed. When did we get asked if we wanted to come here? We aren't prepared for this. What did we do to deserve this? It might have been different if we have been prepared. We might not have lost Parks, Steele, or McAdams. And now we've got two injured men lying over there and they need medical attention now. Kriger's not qualified to do more than he is, poor bastard. Fuck, this sucks!"

"Jack, man, don't let it get to you," Rees says. "We need you here with us."

Bouvier lifts his head and looks at Rees.

"Look, Jack," Rees continues, "we've made mistakes. What did you expect? This is new to all of us. We've never been in a situation like this.

Hell, I bet no one has. We have been trained, but have never been in combat until now. And we didn't train for what has been thrown at us. We've got to hold on and hope we get back to where we belong, as I'm sure we will. I don't see the powers that be just leaving us here. I'm sick of it, too. We've already lost three good men, friends, but don't forget we have those guys out there to care for. They're counting on us for leadership. So do not fold up on me, my friend, okay?"

Bouvier sits up straight and arches his back.

"I hear you. Points taken," he responds, seeming to have shaken off his gloom. "Okay, what do you have for me?"

Their conversation answers several questions that the general and chief had. They continue listening without even blinking, afraid even that little motion will deprive them of seeing or hearing one word. Both have the same reaction as they take in the fate of the three missing men, whom they now understand are dead.

Gen. Lucas picks up the phone and tells the major to continue monitoring the situation and let him know of any developments. The general turns and lowers the blinds to the picture window and turns off the audio. The chief moves to the chair across from the general's desk and sits down wearily. Both men remain silent for a brief period, each with his own thoughts. Finally, General Lucas speaks.

"Three good men dead, two others injured. God dammit, it's my fault. I should have been better prepared for this. If I would have just fought a little harder with the Bank Council, put my foot down, they would all still be alive!"

"Sir, that's bullshit and you know it," Black responds. "The Bank Council would have done it with or without your approval, and you and I both know that. Besides, I'm the one responsible. It's my project."

The general gives the chief a hard stare.

"I don't want to hear that talk from you," he says. "You were the only one fighting tooth and nail to delay the project, demanding more tests. You made more noise about this than anyone else. Hell, you even quit at one point."

"Yes, sir, that's true. But I could have thrown a monkey wrench into the works, withheld vital operational information from key players, anything to keep Clio from initiating a start-up sequence. If I had known I would be responsible for the deaths of men, murder even, I would never have made her. I should have gone in there and smashed the whole thing to smithereens!"

This irritates the general. He's not upset with Chief Black, his friend, but at the Bank Council for putting them in this predicament. He sits up higher in his chair, his back straight as a general should be seen, not slouching over his desk. He speaks firmly, but softly.

"I'm giving you an order right now, Chief Master Sergeant Black."

The chief's eyes widen. "An order?" he thinks.

"I don't want you talking like that ever again. You do not get to blame yourself. You don't get to bear all of this on your shoulders alone. Now get over this self-pity and back on track. Do you understand me?"

"Yes, sir, loud and clear!" Black replies, looking directly into the general's eyes.

"Good, now we've already placed these men in harm's way and I'm sure they're scared, angry, confused, and in a position none of us like," General Lucas says. "The way I see it, the Bank Council wanted to see how the men would react when placed in a situation like this. I'm not sure why they chose not to prep the team, but that's a moot point now. Anyway, I think they have been through enough and we should have enough substantial information. The Bank Council will not agree, I'm sure, but that's too bad. There will be time for future experiments, and right now we know that Clio works. It will need fine tuning, but that's for another day. Right now, we need to get those boys home."

"I agree whole heartily," the chief says with a smile.

The two begin going over the next phase of the plan when the telephone rings from the floor.

"Yes?" the general asks.

"Sir, I thought you would want to know how the men died," Major Hess replies.

The general glances at the chief.

"Yes, Major, we would. Hold on, I'm putting you on speaker so the chief can listen in. Okay, go ahead, Major."

"Yes sir. Well, it seems a patrol was ambushed and two of the men were killed. Airman Alex Steele was manning the M-60 in a Jeep when it was struck by cannon fire. A firefight ensued, and Airman Eric McAdams was shot in the leg and bled out on the way back to the staging area. The third person was Staff Sergeant Isaac Parks. He was manning the control tower when they transported. They discovered his body and it's assumed he died from a fall."

"Major, was he in the location he would have been if the tower was still there?" Lucas asks.

"Yes, sir. It seems when he transported, he was not lowered to ground level," the major answers. "When he materialized, he likely fell to his death."

Black's face becomes a mask of red with the anger engulfing him. The general is feeling at least as angry, if not more so.

"Thank you for the update, Major. Find out what you can about the injured men, too."

The general disconnects the call and immediately presses the intercom button for Shelly.

"Shelly, get me that sorry excuse for a captain in here right now," he says. "Tell Captain Henries that doesn't mean ASAP, but right the hell now."

Shelly acknowledges and the general turns his attention to Chief Black.

"That sonofabitch is out of here!" General Lucas fumes. "I can't believe the Bank Council picked an idiot like him to work on a project as complex and important as Clio. Goddamn Bank Council and their political appointments. Just because your uncle's a senator doesn't mean you should be placed in a sensitive position. That waste of an officer cost the life of a good NCO."

"Yes, sir," the chief stares blankly, "but it would not have happened if..."

The general points his finger at Black.

"Chief, I already gave you an order about blaming yourself," he says.

Black nods his head in agreement and continues, "Sir, what I was going to say is those pinheads on the Bank Council are the ones responsible for this incident. They put the man in a position he should not have held. They placed people in positions I would not have allowed. Not only did they not listen to you or me about further testing, they bloody put politics in front of safety."

The intercom buzzes and the general pushes the talk button.

"Did you get in touch with him, Shelly?" he asks.

"Sorry, no, sir. I tried his home, no answer. Then I called places he's known to frequent and no one has seen him. I'll keep trying, sir."

The general thanks her and sits back in his chair, resting his elbows on the arms and placing his fingers into a steeple, tapping his index fingers together. Black watches him, but doesn't say a word.

"Joe, I know the captain was upset when he departed and his attitude is something less than to be desired," the general begins. "Do you think he is capable of doing something stupid? I mean, doing something that can jeopardize this project? I know he is an officer, but he is an ambitious one who was politically appointed to this position. Then we berate him, hell, literally threaten him."

"Sir, I don't know the man, but I do know his type," Black answers. "If he thought going behind our backs and working the system would hurt us and benefit him in any way, then my answer is yes."

Before they can continue, Shelly knocks on the door and enters quickly.

"Sorry, sir, but you'll want to see this," Shelly says as she hurries over to the television.

She switches it on and in a few seconds the screen comes to life. It shows some young women in bathing suits doing exercises. Shelly rolls her eyes as the general and chief stand there wondering what she is doing.

"Sorry, general. That's HBO," she says, quickly changing the channel. "It's one of the channels that came with the new cable system. One of the installation crew must have had it on."

She finally locates the channel she is looking for and the screen shows a local reporter standing in front of a warehouse cordoned off with yellow police tape. In the background are police squad cars, fire department vehicles, and ambulances with their blue and red lights flashing in the darkness. Policemen and other emergency personnel are milling around as the reporter speaks into his microphone.

"Officials have not given us much more information concerning the horrific scene behind me, which was discovered earlier this evening by a local newspaper reporter. All we know is several bodies were found in the warehouse, apparently killed by gunfire. It's still not known why this happened or who the victims are, and we are told there are no leads at this point. This is Frank Gray, reporting live for Channel 11 News."

Shelly turns down the volume and looks to the general.

"Thought you might find that interesting, sir," she says and turns to leave.

"Shelly?" the general calls to her.

"Yes, sir?"

"Have you had any contact with the captain yet?"

"No, sir. I've tried everyone I know, and I have asked everyone to keep an eye out for him and inform us ASAP if they see or hear from him."

"Thank you, Shelly. That will be all for now."

Shelly leaves and shuts the door behind her as General Lucas turns toward Chief Black.

"I've got a bad feeling about this, Joe," he says. "A really bad feeling."

Chapter 15

Bill Rogers drives straight to the newspaper office as fast as he can, this time being careful not to get pulled over. He parks in his designated slot, exits the vehicle, and scurries into the building. A security guard who has replaced the information clerk this time of night nods at the reporter.

"Evening, Bill. Working overtime?" he asks in humor.

"Yep, gotta get a new pair of shoes," Bill replies as he signs in and hurriedly heads toward the elevator.

The doors open on the third floor and he walks into the near-empty newsroom. Heading straight for his desk, he sets down his camera and plops into his chair, weary from the night's events.

"What the hell have I just seen?" he thinks to himself. "What is going on?"

Leaning back in his chair, he rubs his eyes and face, takes a cleansing breath, blinks, and looks at the phone. He picks up the receiver and dials the number Nora Miller gave him. She picks up on the second ring.

"Hi, Nora, it's Bill from the newspaper. Do you think we could meet? I might have something for you and your friends, but would rather not talk on the phone."

"Sure, Bill. Sounds intriguing," Nora replies. "We'll meet you at the Copper Nickel in about an hour."

Bill pushes the disconnect button on the phone, releases it, and immediately dials the number for his editor, Mike Thornton. He quickly gives his boss a *Reader's Digest* version of what has happened.

"Jesus Christ, Bill. You okay?" Thornton asks. "What the hell have you stumbled onto?"

"I'm not sure; it happened too fast," Bill replies. "I'm going to meet with some people who might help me out on this. They have ties with some guys on the base and it might be related."

"Keep me posted," Thornton orders, "and let me know if there is anything I can do to help."

"Just be ready to clear me for things if needed," Bill answers. "I'm not sure how far I can get on the base, but I might need a bit of your pull."

Bill grabs his camera and heads downstairs to the photo lab. He will barely have enough time to develop his film before meeting Nora and the girls.

***

Inside of a van parked outside, a Military Intelligence Security Service (M.I.S.S.) technician removes his headset and looks over his shoulder at another man standing behind him. The van is adorned with the logo of a national delivery service, but that is the only thing "normal" about this vehicle. Inside are advanced electronics, surveillance and communications monitoring equipment, and night vision cameras. You name it, they have it.

"What do you want us to do?" the technician asks.

The other man takes a cloth from his pocket and cleans his mirrored sunglasses.

"We'll keep an eye on him and whoever it is he's supposed to meet," the man says. "Let's just see where this takes us."

The technician nods and replaces his headset. Switching frequencies, he contacts other members of the M.I.S.S. and advises them to maintain surveillance. They are to have no contact with the subjects.

"All units acknowledge and are awaiting further orders," he reports. The man places the sunglasses back on his face and smiles.

"Good, very good," he says.

***

Bill goes into the darkroom and begins preparation to turn his 35 mm film into photographs from the warehouse. After nearly an hour of work, he has all the pictures hanging on a wire to dry. He looks at each of them and puts his fist to his mouth and bites it.

"Good God, what have they done to my colleagues, my friends?" he thinks to himself. "Oh Terry, what did you get yourself into? Jeez, what have I gotten *myself* into?"

"What is going on?" he says aloud. "I've got to make sure this doesn't end here. I'm going to find who did this to you, Terry, I swear."

He gathers the pictures and takes them back to his desk, placing them in his briefcase. Closing it, he looks at his watch and realizes he needs to head out to his appointment with Nora and the girls.

***

After Nora finished talking with Bill on the phone, she hung up and noticed Ivy and Skylar watching her.

"Well?" Ivy asks, "What's going on?"

"Bill Rogers wants to meet with us at the bar," Nora replies. "He says he has something to tell us, but wants to do it in person."

The local television news is playing in the background and the sound is low. Skylar looks at the screen and a curious look crosses her face. She walks over to the set and turns up the volume as the anchorman is recapping the evening's big story. Four bodies have been found shot in an abandoned warehouse in the industrial district.

"Hey, girls, come look at this," Skylar says.

"Channel 11 News has learned that three of the victims of this horrific act are members of our news team," the newscaster says with difficulty.

Taking a deep breath, he continues.

"Our own Terry Jones, Mary-Beth Anderson, and Doug Meade have been identified as three of the four victims. The fourth victim's name is being withheld for what we are being told are national security concerns. All we can tell you at this point is our crew was on assignment to meet with an unnamed source. Terry had told our assignment editor that he was working on what could be a major story."

The anchor concludes by informing the audience that the station will continue monitoring events as they unfold.

Skylar reaches out to turn the volume back down.

"Shit!" Nora exclaims. "Are those the people Bill was supposed to meet with?"

Skylar looks stricken.

"What if it is? Do you think he's involved?" she asks.

Nora gives her a scornful look.

"Come on, Skylar. You saw the man. Does he look like a killer to you?"

"No, not really, but we don't know him," Skylar responds with panic in her voice. "Hell, we just met him and only talked for a few minutes!"

"Skylar, he's a newsman, not a killer," Ivy pipes in. "Besides, he's cute."

"Cut it out," Nora scolds. "Listen, we're going to meet him in an hour. I say we get there early and watch for him. See if he's alone. Just a precaution. I don't think we'll need it, but better safe than sorry, right?"

***

Bill drives his car into the bar's parking lot and finds an open spot. He gets out and walks toward the main entrance, paying little attention to the delivery van parked on the far side of the lot. The three women watch from their car as he goes inside.

"I think it's going to be all right," Nora says. "Let's go."

Bill enters the bar and opens his eyes wider to adjust to the low light. Scanning the room, he notes that it's fairly busy for a weeknight and begins looking around for the girls. He has no luck at first glance, so he heads to the bar and orders a drink while continuing to check out each patron and keeping an eye on the door. A few seconds later, the three young women walk in and he gestures them toward a nearby empty table.

"What the hell is going on, Bill?" Nora demands.

Bill is taken aback and stares at her, then looks at Skylar and Ivy.

"What do you mean?" he asks.

Nora leans closer.

"Were you involved in what happened at the warehouse tonight?" she asks, her face searching his.

Bill shakes his head.

"Hell no. Well, not in the manner I think you're asking," he replies. "Yes, I was there, but after the fact. How do you know about the warehouse?"

"We just saw it on the news," Skylar interjects.

"I see. Well, do you remember when I told you I was supposed to meet with a buddy of mine? That is Terry… was Terry," he corrects himself. "We've known each other for years and occasionally we throw each other a bone. I was supposed to meet him and his crew at a restaurant and then go with them to interview this mystery man who claimed to have information about something going on at the base. Anyway, I fell asleep on the couch and overslept. By the time I got there, everyone was dead."

He shutters at the memory and then continues, keeping his voice barely audible over the jukebox.

"I arrived at the warehouse, went inside, and found four people shot. Three of them were my friends. Mary-Beth was barely alive said something to me. She was dying, and what she said didn't make much sense. I think what she was trying to say was that men in suits shot them. She also said the man they were interviewing – and I'm guessing here – told them something about a time machine on the base."

Bill finishes his story and then watches for a reaction from the three women sitting across from him. Before anyone can say anything, the tension breaks as a waitress stops at the table to take their drink orders.

After the waitress leaves, Nora sits back and looks at Bill.

"A time machine, Bill? Really?" she asks incredulously.

Placing a hand on the table, Rogers leans in and quickly looks around as though making sure no one can hear him outside of the three girls.

"Hey, I'm just telling you what she said," he says with conviction. "And what's so crazy about that story? Why would men in suits – what, CIA, NSA, Secret Service, OSI, I don't know – come in and kill them? What if what the mystery man told them is true? You think the government would want something like that getting out? What if other world powers found out about it? Hell, what if the public found out about it? There would probably be a panic!

"Think about it. What if you could go back in time? What if you could change the course of history, like stopping Lincoln's assassination, or killing Hitler before his rise to power, manipulating the stock market... hell, anything would be possible. I'd say that would be worth keeping as a national secret, wouldn't you?"

"Yu'uns can't be serious," Ivy says with a skeptical smile. "So, you think my Eric and the others are on some time trip thingy? Please. I know I'm gullible, but again, please."

Nora gives Ivy a look that says she's thinking about the story for a moment, and then jumps in.

"All right, let's say the mystery man said something about a time machine," she begins. "Who is he and how can we prove it?"

"Hold on a minute," Bill says. "I have something in my car I want you to see."

He gets up and moves toward the exit, passing the waitress with the drinks on her way to the table. He fails to notice two men at a nearby table who are acting like they're watching the dancers on the floor, but actually they're observing Rogers and the three women in conversation.

Bill retrieves his briefcase and returns to the table. He opens it and takes out a folder containing his photographs. Placing his hand on the folder, he tells the women what they are about to see.

"I took these at the warehouse tonight before the police arrived, because I knew they would usher me out right away," he says. "What I found were two dead men in Terry and Doug, Mary-Beth, who was dying, and the dead mystery man. I have to warn you, these are graphic."

He opens the folder and shuffles through until he finds the picture he is looking for. It shows a man lying on his back with a gunshot to his forehead. He looks to be military, right down to his haircut.

"Oh my God," the girls gasp virtually in unison.

"This is the mystery man," Bill explains. "We need to find out who he is and what he was trying to tell Terry and his crew before they were all killed."

Ivy is shaken, but clears her throat as she stares at the picture.

"I might be able to help there," she says with a wan smile.

"How?" Skylar asks as all eyes turn to Ivy.

"My brother, silly. Remember, he's a lieutenant in the base personnel office."

"Oh shit, Ivy, I completely forgot." Nora says, perking up. "Do you think he will help us?"

"Of course he will. I'm his little sister," Ivy replies. "He can't say no to me."

"Are you sure?" Bill presses. "I mean, there might be some sensitive stuff here, classified. This could get dangerous."

"Oh, I'm sure," she says.

Bill returns the pictures to the folder and places it back into his briefcase.

"I'll get you a copy of this picture yet tonight," he says. "First, I'll doctor it up so there's no evidence of a gunshot wound. See what you can find out about this man and that will be our first good lead."

As the group walks toward the exit, one of the men at the nearby table says something into a hidden microphone. Bill and the women go to their separate vehicles and drive out of the parking lot, all heading to the newspaper building. A few seconds later, the lights of the delivery van turn on.

After the short drive, Bill leads the group into the building and they register with the night guard. They take the elevator to the editorial department and the women wait for Bill at his desk as he works on the photograph in the lab. It takes time, but the veteran newsman is as good in the darkroom as he is with journalism. Finally, he returns with the doctored photo.

"Wow, you made him look like he's sleeping," Ivy says.

"Sleep of the dead," Skylar deadpans.

"Well, anyway, here you go," Bill says as he slips the photo into a large envelope. "Good luck, and please let me know as soon as you find out anything."

"We'll go to the base first thing in the morning and pay a visit to Lt. McKnight," Nora states.

With that, Bill walks the women back downstairs and to their car. They bid him goodnight, unaware they are being watched.

Chapter 16

"Oh, hell no!" First Lieutenant Vincent (Vince) McKnight exclaims in an angry voice.

"Aw... come on, big brother. This is important," Ivy begs him.

As soon as he hears his sister's request regarding the photo she holds of a dead man, Vince throws his hands in the air and walks away.

"Please? Pretty please?" Ivy persists as she scampers after him.

Vince is the officer in charge (OIC) of his section of the Civilian Base Personnel Office (CBPO), and he has no need to have his sister demand such as request. He storms into his office and turns toward his baby sister. She stops short and stands just outside the open door with a pleading, forlorn look on her face. He points at her with a dour expression and then at the floor of his office, indicating she should come in and stand where he's pointing. She grins and scampers inside.

"Shut the door behind you," he tells her unceremoniously.

She happily complies.

"Do you know what you're asking of me?" he demands. "This can get me an Article 15, or worse, a damn court martial! I can't go snooping around personnel files and pulling out information. I can't do it for me; think what will happen if I get caught doing it for a damn civilian. I can't believe you!"

"Nora will give you a blowjob," Ivy says with a mischievous grin.

Vince jerks his head in her direction.

"What!? No! What's wrong with you? I'm going to talk to Mom about where you came from, 'cause you ain't no kin of mine. And I don't want a... no, I want nothing from Nora. Shit, Ivy!"

"I'm kidding," Ivy laughs. "Anyway, Nora would kill me if she knew I told you that."

"Not funny, Ivy. Not funny at all. This is serious, and I won't do it."

Ivy gets a serious look on her face and this worries Vince. She has always been the most carefree person he knows, and she seldom becomes serious.

"Look, Vinny, this is crucial and it may be dangerous," Ivy says, "but I – no, we – need to know."

"You're just playing Nancy Drew with the Hardy Girls and some newspaper man," Vince says. "This can land us all in jail!"

Ivy draws in a breath and lets it out, and then holds up the picture again.

"This man tried to talk with a television news crew," she explains. "Now he, along with the entire news crew, are dead. Eric, David, Ray, and a bunch of others are missing. This man knew something, and I want to know what that was. You've got to help us. You can do it without anyone becoming suspicious, c'mon."

"No, if he is military and dead, they'll be closely looking at his profile," Vince responds. "Too dangerous, no."

"God dammit, Vince, grow a pair of balls for once!" Ivy replies, trying to keep the volume of her voice under control. "This is just like you, scared of your own shadow. You aren't going to make anything of yourself if you don't take a chance once in a while. I love you, one way or the other, but you are, by God, gonna get me this info, you got that?"

Softening her tone, she continues, "Don't go through computer channels. That would raise suspicion. Look it up the old-fashioned way, by hand. Not everything is on the computer anyway."

Vince walks behind his desk and sits down dejectedly. Placing his elbows on the desk, he cups his hands and uses his thumbs to support his chin as he ponders his little sister's suggestion.

"All right, I'll look into it," he says with an exasperated exhale.

Ivy starts to get giddy, but Vince holds out his hand for her to calm down before she gets started.

"You'll owe me big time for this, and you'd better hope to God I don't get caught," Vince says, pointing an accusatory finger at Ivy. "I'm not promising you anything here. I'll see what's on file and get what I can, but don't get your hopes up. If the OSI has the files already, I won't be able to find anything."

Ivy jumps up and runs to her brother to give him a kiss, but he stops her.

"No, no, not here," he says. "You know better."

She stops short and draws herself up into attention and gives a half-ass salute.

"Yes, sir, lieutenant big shot, sir, thank you, sir," Ivy says in her most manly voice, and then drops the salute. "No, truly Vince, thanks. And yes, I'll owe one. Maybe Nora will give you a BJ after all."

"Get the hell out of my office," Vince says sternly, flapping his hand in a go-away motion. "I'll be in touch if I find anything. Again *if* I find anything. Now shoo, little girl."

Ivy leaves her brother's office and walks out of the building to find Nora and Skylar standing by the car. Nora is leaning on it, having a smoke, and talking with Skylar. Skylar juts her chin toward Ivy, indicating to Nora that Ivy is coming up behind her.

"Get anything out of big brother?" Nora asks as Ivy approaches.

"Yup, took some doing, and you'll have to give him a hummer for the info," Ivy says with a smile, winking at Skylar.

Skylar grins, but Nora looks annoyed before giving a lopsided smirk.

"Huh? Right," Nora replies.

"I did tell him you would, but he turned it down," Ivy says with a laugh.

Now it is Nora's turn to look surprised.

"What do you mean he turned it down? What man in his right mind will turn down a blowjob?" she asks with a chagrined look. "What's the matter, is he queer or something?"

"Guess you're not his type," Ivy shrugs.

"Look at me, I'm every man's type," Nora gloats as she put her hands on her hips. "Just kidding, I know your brother and he knows you, bitch. Now, what did he say?"

"He said he'd see what he can do, but didn't promise anything," Ivy says. "That's all we can hope for at this point. And I did really tell him you'd give him a BJ, Nora. Now let's get out of here."

The girls pile into the car and head toward the gate. Looking in the rear-view mirror from the front seat, Nora repeats, "And I am every man's type!"

***

Lt. McKnight sits behind his desk, wondering what to do next. He has heard the news report of the deaths at the warehouse, but can't believe his little sister and her friends might be involved in something so serious.

He remembers there were several files on security policemen pulled recently, and that arouses his curiosity. Nothing unusual about that. Happens all the time when base personnel are sought for special duty assignments, going on temporary duty (TDY) assignment, or even a promotion. There are dozens of reasons why personnel files might get pulled. But from what Ivy tells him, this might mean something more in this case.

"Or," he thinks. "It can be nothing and it gets me in hot water."

Finally, he makes up his mind, gets up from his chair, and walks out of the office.

"Airman Garcia," he calls out to the A1C sitting at her desk.

"Sir?" she replies.

"I'm going to the main building if anyone needs me."

"Yes, sir. If anyone asks, can I tell them when you'll be back?"

"Maybe half an hour," he says, glancing at his watch.

"Yes, sir."

Vince walks through the lobby and exits the building. He briefly considers taking his car the short distance to the main CBPO building before deciding to walk. It's too nice of a day to be in the car, he thinks.

Fifteen minutes later, a plain-looking government vehicle pulls into a parking slot. Two men in suits exit the vehicle and enter the CBPO office. They approach the senior airman at the main desk and ask to speak with Lt. McKnight. The airman asks if he can say who is looking for him and the men pull out their M.I.S.S. badges and identification cards. The airman looks at the badges and his eyes widen.

"Thank you, I'll check," he tells them and picks up a phone to contact Airman Garcia.

The airman learns McKnight has left the building and passes on the information to the M.I.S.S. agents.

"I'm sorry, sir," he says to the man closest to the desk. "I'm afraid you missed him. Lt. McKnight's assistant says he left about fifteen minutes ago, but that he should be back shortly. If you care to wait…"

"Where'd he go?" the second agent interrupts.

"I don't know, sir. He left and told his assistant he'd be back in about half an hour."

The agents turn and leave without saying another word.

"Assholes," the airman thinks to himself.

***

Vince looks over the shoulder of a sergeant working a computer inside the main CBPO building. The sergeant is searching information on personnel working special assignments.

"Sir, this will go quicker if you can give me a little more to go on," the sergeant says. "There are a bunch of special duty assignments listed in here."

"Anything that involves a special duty at Pope within the last month or two," Vince replies, referring to the big North Carolina air force base.

The NCO sighs and types again. The screen runs for a few seconds and then shows a list of base personnel TDY to Pope.

"This is all we have, sir. Only three personnel assigned from here."

"Print that for me, will you?" Vince requests.

The NCO complies and Vince goes to the dot matrix printer, tearing off the printout with the names. He thanks the sergeant and heads toward the file room. He opens the file drawers and starts with the first name on the list, Second Lieutenant James Emerson. He locates the file and opens it to compare Emerson's official photo with the one he has of the dead man. Nope, not him. Next.

Opening another file drawer, he pulls the file for Captain Randall Henries. He opens the file and stops. Vince doesn't need to look again at the picture he brought with him. This is the man. Closing the file, he shuts the drawer and places Henries's file inside the one he brought with him. He leaves the room and quickly walks through the main lobby.

"Sir," the NCO calls out.

Vince freezes. He knows he is to sign out any files and none are to leave the facility. He turns to the NCO.

"Sorry, sir," the NCO says, "but I'll need you to sign the log saying we used the computer."

"Shit," Vince thinks as he cringes inside. "Now there will be a paper trail of me being here. Nothing I can do about that now."

He smiles at the NCO.

"Of course, Sergeant," he says and walks over to him.

Vince takes the offered pen and scribbles an illegible name on the form, thanks the NCO again, and leaves the building as fast as he can without bolting. Instead of going back to his office, he heads for the Jet Hawks recreational center, where he can grab a bite to eat and read the file without drawing any attention.

He gets his food and finds an empty table a comfortable distance away from others. Looking around to make sure no one is watching, Vince takes a bite of his sandwich and begins reading about Captain Henries. Time passes quickly as he reviews the file and eats his lunch.

"Shit," Vince thinks, looking at his watch and noticing almost an hour has passed.

He closes the folder, places it back into his briefcase, and walks to the main desk staffed by a female A1C.

"Airman, can I use the base phone please?" he asks.

She lifts the phone onto the counter and walks away to give him privacy. Vince calls his office to check in with Airman Garcia.

"Personnel office, Airman Garcia, may I help you?"

"Airman Garcia, it's Lieutenant McKnight," he says, looking around to make sure no one is eavesdropping. "I took longer than expected with what I am doing. Anything going on?"

"No, sir, nothing earth-shattering," she replies. "There were a couple of men here to see you not long after you left, though."

"Do you know who they were, what they wanted?" he asks.

"Senior Airman Pickett talked with them, not me," she replies. "All he said was that they claimed to be from an organization called M.I.S.S. When he told them you were out, they left and did not leave a message."

Vince straightens up and this time looks around more intently.

"M.I.S.S?" he thinks. "Oh shit."

He returns his attention to Airman Garcia.

"I'm going to be a little longer. I don't know when I'll be back," he says and quickly hangs up.

Thinking for a minute, Vince realizes he has all he needs on Captain Henries for Ivy and decides to return the file. But first he needs to let Ivy know about the captain.

Vince thanks the airman behind the counter and hurries out of the building. He walks to a payphone along the side of the parking lot and dials Ivy's home number. When she doesn't answer, he calls Nora's house and Skylar answers the phone.

"Is Ivy there? This is Vince," he says with a sense of urgency.

"Hi, Vinny," Skylar says. "Yeah, she's here. I'll get her."

Vince hears Skylar call for Ivy, and a couple seconds later she picks up.

"Hi Vinny," she answers. "What's up?"

"Listen, Ivy," Vince says as he looks around nervously. "This guy's name is Captain Randall Henries. He's assigned to an EMS squadron, but doesn't work there. Captain Henries is TDY to a top-secret project at Pope Air Force Base. He has a degree in electronics from MIT and his uncle is a senator from Massachusetts. He's well-connected, and from what I've read on him, a bit of a screw-up. He used his political connections to get into the air force and land choice assignments. Doesn't get real complimentary reviews. Usually does just enough to get by and looks to climb the ladder the old-fashioned way, sucking up and pulling his family into it to get what he wants.

"I don't know what he's doing at Pope, but it must be something big. I have no idea why he would be talking to the press, because that's career suicide as well as getting a possible court martial. And one more thing, Military Intelligence & Security Service agents came by the office looking for me. They go by M.I.S.S."

"Who?" Ivy asks. "Why?"

"They're a secret organization within the military that few people even know exists," Vince explains. "I can't be sure, but it's probably got something to do with you being involved in this and then coming to my office. Now I have this dead man's file on me and it can't be a coincidence. Listen, I know you won't, but try for once and stop right now with your junior varsity detective work. Stop it right now, and let the police and air force handle this. You can't afford to have M.I.S.S. on your ass and neither can I. If this is something that causes them to take notice, we can get in a shitload of trouble."

Ivy sighs into the phone.

"Thanks for getting the information," she says. "And you're right, I won't listen. We need to know where our men are, and with what you've given me and with the help of our reporter contact, we may be able to get some answers. I'm not worried about the M.I.S.S. We're civilians, so they can't touch us. Thanks again, big brother."

With that, Ivy hangs up before Vince has a chance to protest. Looking around quickly, he grabs his briefcase and heads back to the main CBPO building. He waves to the NCO who helped him earlier and the NCO gives him a quizzical look.

"I left something in the back room," Vince says, trying to sound matter-of-fact.

The NCO nods and returns to his work. Vince hurriedly walks back to the file room and returns the Henries file to its place in the cabinet. When he returns to the lobby area, he sees two men in suits waiting.

"Lieutenant McKnight," one of the men says.

His tone is that of a statement rather than a question. He speaks as though he already knows Vince.

"Huh, yeah, I'm Lieutenant McKnight," Vince says.

Both men hold out M.I.S.S. badges and identify themselves.

"Lieutenant McKnight, you must come with us, sir," the man orders.

Vince looks at one of the M.I.S.S. agents and then the other. Then he looks over their shoulders to where he can see the NCO and others watching. One of the agents turns to see what Vince is looking at, and then leans in to whisper in his partner's ear.

"What's this about?" Vince asks.

"Sir, you need to come with us," the man says sternly. "Now."

Not wanting to make a scene, Vince walks out the front door with the agents and into a waiting unmarked government vehicle.

Chapter 17

General Lucas switches his office TV to a different channel in an effort to find more on the warehouse district story. Not finding anything, he turns to Shelly.

"Get in touch with the OSI commander and have him call me immediately," he says, referring to the Office of Special Investigations.

Shelly acknowledges his order and leaves the room. The general turns down the TV volume, but leaves the screen on. He sits impatiently at his desk as Shelly's voice comes over the intercom.

"Colonel Grayson is on line one, sir," she says.

Lucas thanks her and picks up the phone.

"Colonel Grayson, thanks for calling so quickly," Lucas says.

"No problem, sir," Grayson replies. "What can I do for you?"

"There's been an incident at an abandoned warehouse just off the highway. Are you familiar with the area?"

"I can do one better than that, sir," Grayson says. "My people are already on it."

"Why am I not surprised?" Lucas says. "I had a feeling you were going to tell me that. You have a reputation for always being on top of everything."

"I have a preliminary SITREP for you," Grayson adds, using military shorthand for a situation report.

Lucas raises his eyebrows and looks at the chief while putting the call on speaker.

"Go ahead, Colonel."

"As I'm sure you already know, three of the four victims are from a local TV station. The fourth victim is one of ours, a Captain Randall Henries out of..."

"God dammit!" Gen. Lucas swears as he slams his hand on the table. "I'm sorry, Colonel. Continue."

"Yes, sir. It looks like the captain was there for an interview and all four were shot. From what it looks like to our team, he was shot in the shoulder, then tortured, and then shot in the head execution-style. The others look to have taken rounds from a distance and then also shot execution-style. The video and audio recordings are missing. We don't believe this was something that just went wrong. This was planned."

"Colonel, Chief Joe Black here. Were there any witnesses or evidence left behind?"

"Chief, there are no witnesses we can locate, but there is another reporter who arrived on scene after the fact," Grayson replies. "He's a local newspaper man who apparently was supposed to be there for the interview. He was late arriving, lucky for him. Anyway, he called it in and the police already questioned and released him by the time our people arrived.

"As far as evidence goes, there are bloody footprints and one shell casing. We pulled national security needs over the local and state police, and took control of the evidence. It's being looked at as we speak. We don't know how many shooters were involved. We won't know any more on that until we have autopsy reports and take a more thorough look at the crime scene. We are guessing that most of the shots are from .45 caliber pistols, just from looking at the wounds. We should have more information shortly, ballistics report within an hour."

"Thank you, sir," the chief says, indicating to Gen. Lucas he is finished with his questions.

"Colonel Grayson, do you have the name of this reporter, and if so can we get in touch with him?" Lucas asks.

"Yes, sir. His name is Bill Rogers, *Daily Express News*. My people have been to his office and his home, but no contact yet. They will stay on both scenes and wait for him."

Gen. Lucas thinks for a second before responding.

"Colonel, once you find him, please transport him to the Bank and do not question him."

"Yes, sir, understood. I'll notify you once he is en route."

"Thank you, Colonel," the general concludes. "That will be all for now."

Gen. Lucas leans on his desk with both hands, then sighs as he pushes off and stands up straight.

"What the hell was Captain Henries doing there?" he asks the chief rhetorically. "What was he thinking he was going to accomplish? Getting back at us? All he would have done was get himself arrested and a court martial. Damn fool."

Chief Black walks around the room shaking his head.

"I don't know, sir, but this isn't good. Thank goodness OSI arrived and took over the scene or this could be worse than it is."

"Quite right, Chief," the general says with a nod. "Could be worse. Now we have to get in touch with this reporter fella and see what he can tell us."

***

Ivy hangs up the phone after talking with her brother and immediately informs Nora and Skylar what Vince said about Captain Henries.

"We've got to get in touch with Bill," Nora says, reaching for the phone.

Skylar places her hand on top of Nora's to stop her. Nora looks at her sister questioningly.

"What's the matter?" Nora asks.

"I'm not liking this," Skylar says, shaking her head. "I might be getting paranoid, but what if we're being bugged? I've had this feeling we're being watched. I know it's probably my imagination running loose, but I can't help it. We've been asking questions and getting the runaround. We may have stirred up a hornet's nest with the military."

Ivy gives Nora a sideways glance.

"Skylar might be right," Ivy says. "I've had that feeling, too. Can't put my finger on it, but something is not right."

"Okay, what do you want to do, little sister?" Nora asks.

"Well, for starters, we're not using the phone," Skylar replies, throwing up her hands as though the phone is too hot to touch. "I think we should drive to the newspaper and try to find Bill there. If not, we'll try his home. This way we can keep an eye out for anything suspicious."

***

Bill stayed in the newsroom after the girls departed with the doctored photograph. He is full of nervous energy, something every good journalist has when chasing a big story. He starts working on an article, trying to get a feel for what he wants to tell his readers without sounding crazy, but finds that challenge easier said than done. It's two in the morning and he is crashing despite the earlier adrenalin rush. He decides to get some sleep in the back room of the editorial department rather than going home.

The newspaper has a room set aside for reporters to use when they need to get a few winks before getting back to work. The room contains a cot, table, chest of drawers containing blankets and pillow covers, and even a separate bathroom with an assortment of personal hygiene items.

Bill grabs a fresh pillow case and a blanket, takes off his shoes, and lays down on his back, staring at the ceiling. He stays that way for a few minutes before drifting off to sleep.

Downstairs, two OSI agents enter the security guard's after-hours area.

"Good evening," the lead agent says. "I'm Agent Von and this is Agent Beltranee with the Air Force Office of Special Investigations. "Can you tell us if Bill Rogers has come into the building tonight?"

"Yes, he has," the guard answers. "Mr. Rogers came in with three women, but the women left a while ago. I assume Bill is still here, since he has not signed out."

"Mind if we go upstairs to see if we can find him?" Agent Von asks.

"Be my guest," the guard replies. "I'll need you to sign in first and wear these visitor's badges."

The guard has the agents sign in and directs them upstairs to the newsroom. They check the area near Bill's desk, the men's restroom, the lunchroom, and the darkroom, but their subject is nowhere to be found. The entrance to the back room where Bill is sleeping is not obvious. It is in the archives area and appears to be a closet.

After taking another unsuccessful look around, the agents decide to leave the building and give the guard their cards on their way out.

"Have Mr. Rogers contact us if you see him," Agent Von says. "He's not in any trouble, but this is of great importance. We are investigating a shooting and need his assistance."

The guard nods and the agents depart, turning their attention next to Bill's residence.

Nora, Skylar, and Ivy arrive at the newspaper building at eight o'clock sharp and go to the front receptionist desk. The night guard has departed with the start of the new business day, and the receptionist smiles as she recognizes the three women.

"Good morning, ladies. How can I help you today?"

"We're here to see Bill Rogers again," Nora replies. "He should be expecting us."

"You know, I just got here and haven't seen Bill yet. Hold on a sec and let me check."

The receptionist picks up the phone and calls up to the newsroom, speaking briefly to someone before hanging up.

"That was the editor," she says. "He said Bill is indisposed for a little while, but for you ladies to go on up and wait for him at his desk. Remember, you'll need to wear these visitor badges."

The three women thank the clerk and stride to the elevator for the ride to the third floor. The newsroom receptionist greets them at the door and tells them to go on in and wait by Bill's desk. About fifteen minutes later, Bill comes around the corner and smiles when he sees them. They giggle at his rumbled appearance.

"Sorry ladies. I fell asleep in the back and haven't had time to change," he tells them while running a hand through his hair.

"Ivy's brother got us some information on this dead guy," Nora says, laying the picture on Bill's desk. "His name is Captain Randall Henries. He is assigned to an electronics squadron, but apparently is doing something for a top-secret project at Pope Air Force Base. He seems to be the nephew of a senator, and was assigned to this project because of that. Ivy's brother says the guy doesn't have that great of a track record, so that's the only reason he can think of to explain why Henries was sent there. What the project is, he didn't know."

Bill sits back and thinks for a second.

"You know, a few years back there was talk of an experiment of some importance being conducted for a group of senators, congressmen, and top brass at Pope," he says. "The media wasn't invited, but it leaked out anyway. The news agencies went bonkers and threatened the air force and the government with lawsuits, but of course they denied everything. Then they used the old 'national security is in play' argument and that we had no business knowing what they were doing."

Bill goes to a nearby file cabinet and begins rummaging through it.

"Now, we didn't think much about it at the time," he continues. "The military has always been secretive with everything they do, so we just chalked it up to it being their typical secret squirrel shit. Ah, here we go."

Bill pulls out a folder and comes back to the desk while flipping through some pages.

"Seems that the experiment involved some type of matter transference machine. You know, *Star Trek* 'beam me up' stuff."

Grinning, he notices the blank looks on the girls' faces.

"You know, a matter transporter?"

Again, they look back at him without a clue what he is talking about.

"Okay, they were working on a device that can break down all the molecules in an object or even a human body into atoms," he explains. "Then they send those atoms through a beam, kind of like a radio or television signal, to another device somewhere else. From one side of the world to somewhere else in the world. When your atomized molecules reach the other device, you are re-integrated and voila! You're somewhere else in the blink of an eye."

"Bullshit," Nora says in disbelief.

"Hey, I said that's what people thought was going on, but no one ever found out anything more about the project. We were shut out and told to stand down. Now, there are a few journalists who don't like being told no, so they snooped a little more. They didn't find out much, but the rumor is that it wasn't a matter transporter the military was working on after all. It actually was a time machine."

Nora rolls her eyes back, Skylar slowly shakes her head, and Ivy giggles.

"What the hell, Bill?" Nora groans. "Really, that same time machine nonsense you mentioned Mary-Beth mumbled something about just before she died?"

Bill holds up his hand.

"Hey, now hold on a minute and let me finish. It gets better," he continues. "The two reporters who were working this story died. They were from separate news agencies. The story goes that one reporter went on vacation and was lost in a boating accident in Bermuda or Jamaica or someplace down there. They never found his body. The other crashed his car on I-95. Funny thing is he was heading north and he didn't live in the area where he is killed. He wasn't on assignment and nobody knows why he was in that area when the accident happened. No witnesses, nothing. They say he was drunk, but he wasn't a drinker. This can't be a coincidence. Something happened to them, and I bet the government is involved. They got too close to the truth and I bet they were both killed for it."

"Look, Bill," Nora says as she looks him square in the eyes. "I'm sorry, but I just can't buy into this science fiction crap."

"All right, don't buy into it, but just go with me for right now," Bill replies. "Listen, I know it might be farfetched, but I want to pursue this. Something happened out there and you know it, otherwise you wouldn't have found me. This is what I do. I take stuff that seems trivial and dig deeper."

"Nora, what about the feeling we're being watched?" Skylar interjects.

"What, who's watching you?" Bill asks sharply.

"We all have had this feeling we are being followed or watched since we started this little investigation," Skylar responds.

Bill thinks back to the bar and the two men at the table who didn't seem to fit the mannerisms of the other patrons. Then he thinks about the delivery van he has seen at all times of day. He has seen it more often than usual.

"You know, now that you mention it, I think we are being watched," he says. "Nothing I can confirm, but, yeah, I got that feeling, too. Have you noticed a delivery van hovering around you?"

The women look at each other and shake their heads no.

"Do you think my brother will be all right?" Ivy asks quietly. "I mean, Vinny took a chance getting that information for us. What if he was seen?"

Skylar places a hand on her shoulder.

"I'm sure he's fine," she says. "Why don't you call him? I bet he's back to being the same old boring officer we know and love."

Bill points to the phone on his desk.

"You can use mine, or if you want some privacy, go over to Tom's desk. He's out this week."

Ivy looks at the other desk and walks over to it. She picks up the phone and dials, turning slightly away to shield her voice. Everyone watches as she talks out of earshot from the group. A few minutes later, she hangs up and returns to the group.

"I spoke to Airman Garcia, Vinny's assistant," Ivy reports. "She says that Vinny left right after I did. He told her he would be gone about an hour, but that was yesterday and he hasn't returned. I don't like this."

"Ivy, if you want, you can take my car and go to the base and wait for him, or even look for him," Nora offers.

"I'll go with you," Skylar adds.

"Yeah, okay," Ivy smiles wanly. "He's probably goofing off some-where. Sure, let's do that."

Nora gives Skylar the car keys with instructions to call as soon as they find out anything.

"What are you and Bill going to do in the meantime?" Ivy asks.

"I'm going to look more into this time machine theory and see what information I can get," Bill says. "Nora, you're more than welcome to join me."

"I'm up for that," Nora says enthusiastically. "I like mysteries."

Ivy and Skylar take the elevator downstairs and immediately spot a delivery van parked down the street.

"You think that's what Bill is talking about?" Skylar asks, subtly nodding in the direction of the van.

"Could be, but they deliver packages all over town," Ivy counters. "I can't see it being the boogeyman."

Passing the van as they drive away, Ivy and Skylar turn to look at the driver, who smiles and waves.

"I've got a feeling they're on to us," Skylar states.

***

OSI agents Von and Beltranee arrive back at the *Daily Express News* building shortly after 9:00. The receptionist sends them up to the editorial floor, where they find Bill and Nora at his desk. They approach and show their identification.

"Sir, I'm Agent Von and this is Agent Beltranee with the Air Force Office of Special Investigations. We are investigating the attack at the warehouse and understand you are a witness to the incident."

"I was there after the fact, not during the shooting," Bill clarifies. "I didn't see it happen."

Agent Beltranee looks at Bill's desk and notices the photo of Captain Henries.

"Where did you get this?" he asks.

"Well, I, I, err," Bill stammers. "Okay, I took some pictures before the police arrived. It's my job."

Agent Von grabs the picture from his partner and takes on a stern expression.

"Mr. Rogers, we'll need you to come with us," he orders. "You're not necessarily in trouble, but we do need to speak with you."

"I'm not going anywhere with you," Bill says defiantly.

"Mr. Rogers, this is a federal investigation involving the death of a member of the United States Air Force who was involved in a highly classified project," Agent Von says. "We can detain you or you can come voluntarily."

"Then she comes with me," Bill says, pointing his thumb at a surprised Nora. "She is part of the investigation I'm conducting and knows as much as I do. If that's all right with you, Nora?"

"Sure, you bet," Nora replies.

The agents stare at Bill and tell him to wait a minute. Agent Von walks away and pulls out his radio. He talks into it briefly and returns to inform them that Nora can join them.

"Please grab anything useful and come with us," the agent says.

Before the foursome can leave the newsroom, Bill's editor, Mike

Thornton, storms out of his office like a mad bull and stomps over to the OSI agents.

"Just what the hell do you think you're doing?" he demands. "This is a goddamn newspaper, and we have First Amendment protections. Why are you harassing my reporter?"

"Sir..." Agent Von starts.

"Don't fucking 'sir' me, you little twerp," Thornton yells. "This man isn't going anywhere."

"Sir, please. He's not under arrest, but this is a matter of national security..."

Thornton interrupts again.

"National security, schmurity!" he belts.

Nora looks to Bill and mouths the words, "Security, schmurity?"

Bill shakes his head, waves his hand dismissively, and mouths back, "He's on a roll."

"I'm calling our attorney and he'll get to the bottom of this bullshit!" Thornton says and turns to leave.

Agent Von becomes very serious, and in a loud, stern voice says, "You need to stop right there or it's going to get ugly."

The editor stops and turns, glaring at the OSI agent.

"As I was saying, sir, this is a case of national security," Agent Von continues in a slightly calmer voice. "This man is coming with us voluntarily or I can bring the might of the US Attorney General's office as well as our Staff Judge Advocates Office to serve you with warrants, injunctions, and whatever else we need to make your life miserable. Or you can cooperate, and Mr. Rogers and Miss..."

Von looks at Nora, who stares for a few seconds.

"Oh, Miller, Nora Miller, Nora," she blurts out.

Agent Von turns back to the editor.

"Miss Miller can come with us for questioning as well. They are not suspects, but witnesses, and we will return them unharmed and well-taken care of. Mr. Rogers may even be able to write an interesting article, and I say 'may.' Now, do you want to sound off some more and be all blusterous or can we do this in a civil manner?"

The red-faced editor stands flabbergasted, his mouth opening and closing like a largemouth bass.

Bill breaks the tension.

"Boss, let it go, I don't mind. And as he says, this might be interesting."

"Okay, go ahead, but you," Thornton growls, pointing his finger first at Agent Von and then Agent Beltrane, "you better be sure he returns unharmed. Oh, and that goes for the young lady, too. Got it?"

"We got it, and thank you," Agent Von replies with a thin smile. "You've made a good decision."

"Don't fucking tell me I made a good anything," Thornton roars, not wanting to back down in front of a newsroom full of reporters. "Now take my reporter and get the hell out of my building."

The agents look at Bill and Nora.

"Are you ready?" Agent Von asks.

Bill nods and grabs his things, putting them in his briefcase.

"Don't worry about my editor," he says. "Sometimes he thinks he's Perry White."

Agent Beltrane pushes the button to the elevator and glances at Bill.

"So, I guess that makes you Clark Kent and this is Lois Lane?" he says, playing off the *Superman* reference. "Don't worry. As I said, I think you will find this to be quite interesting."

Chapter 18

"Crap, just what we need," Rees mutters as a light rain begins making faint splattering sounds on his helmet.

He pulls a poncho over his head and wanders over to where a few of the guys are relaxing, enjoying chow, and drinking coffee. Kriger hands him a cup of coffee as Nionee, Shepard, McGuire, and Tucker eat their C-rations nearby.

"Hey guys, did I ever tell you about the first time I met Sean?" Rees asks.

McGuire looks at Rees and shakes his head.

"Ain't no call for that, Sergeant Rees," he says, slightly annoyed.

Rees grins and proceeds with his story.

"Anyway, McGuire comes to the flight and I go to greet him. I introduce myself and he tells me his name is Sean McGuire. 'Well damn, that's a good old Irish name you have there,' I tell him. McGuire stares at me with his forehead furrowed and says, 'It's not, I'm from Tennessee.'"

Rees takes a sip of coffee as the guys snicker at McGuire's expense. It's good to see them in a better frame of mind.

"Damn, I sure could get good and drunk right now," Shepard says.

"Yeah, a drink sounds good right about now," Tucker agrees.

"Is that always your answer to everything? Alcohol?" McGuire asks, shaking his head. "That's not the solution to our problems."

"Oh, this coming from a Tennessee boy?" Shepard retorts. "Weren't you born with a bourbon bottle in your hand?"

"Well, McGuire, actually alcohol is a solution," Tucker says matter-of-factly, generating laughs from the guys.

"What?" asks a bewildered McGuire.

"If you look at it scientifically," Tucker says with a smile, "alcohol is a solution."

This gets empty C-ration cans thrown at him and a frustrated Mc-Guire looks dumbfounded.

"Shut the hell up, whatta you know?" he says.

Rees asks Kriger to join him in checking on Green and Harris, while Nionee says to no one in particular that he needs to see a man about a horse and walks a suitable distance away to relieve himself.

As Nionee unzips his pants, he hears a peculiar "whirring" noise. He strains to listen. There it is again. He realizes it's coming from close to the ground, about fifteen feet away. He steps over to a tree and crouches. Leaning in closer, he sees what appears to be a tiny camera. He takes an angled flashlight off his belt, ensures the red lens is in, and turns on the light.

"Holy shit," he whispers to himself before standing up and hurrying back to the group.

"Hey guys, you've got to come see this!" Nionee announces.

"What is it?" Shepard asks.

"I think it's a frigging camera," Nionee answers excitedly.

"A camera? Out here?" Tucker says as the group quickly gets up to follow Nionee back toward the woods.

When they arrive at the spot, Nionee turns on the flashlight.

"See?" he says.

"Sure as shit, it's a camera all right," Shepard confirms. "McGuire, run back and get Sergeant Rees. Tucker, go relieve Sergeant Bouvier and have him come see this, too. Now go!"

Rees is standing with Kriger by the Duck as they make a cover out of ponchos to keep Green and Harris dry. They hear someone running toward them and look up to see McGuire in full stride.

"Sergeant Rees!" a wide-eyed McGuire says as he tries to catch his breath. "You gotta come see this. Nionee found a camera in the woods!"

"A camera? Is it one from the Mud Dump that transported with us?" Rees asks.

"Don't know, Sarge," McGuire says with a shrug. "I was told to come get you."

Rees grabs his rifle and follows McGuire back to where the others are standing, arriving at the same time as Bouvier.

"What's going on, Sergeant Shepard?" Bouvier asks.

"Nionee found a camera," Shepard responds, pointing toward the edge of the trees.

Rees walks to where Nionee is pointing his flashlight and squats down to look. He reaches down and picks up a small, black camera that is unlike any he's seen before. It is on a little stand and has a small motor that allows it to turn, tilt, and pan.

"This didn't come with us from the Mud Dump. Someone put this here to keep an eye on us," Rees observes, handing the device to Bouvier.

"Huh. We'll just take this little thing with us," Bouvier says. "Maybe we can get some answers about why we're here."

"McGuire, go relieve Sergeant Montoya and have him meet us at the Duck," Rees says.

"What do you want Montoya for?" Bouvier asks.

"Ben's a camera bug," Rees explains. "I thought we could let him take a look at this thing and see if he knows anything about it."

McGuire heads off to retrieve Montoya, and when he returns, Bouvier hands him the camera. Montoya's eyes nearly pop out of his head.

"Jesus, where'd you get this?" he asks.

"Nionee found it at the edge of the woods over there," Rees explains.

"I need to look at this a little closer," Montoya says, peering intently at the device. "Let me take this into the Duck so I can have more light."

He opens the hatch and climbs inside the vehicle while the others wait impatiently outside.

"Well, what do you think?" Rees yells in. "Ever seen anything like that before?"

"I'm not sure, but I think it's a Vidicon camera," Montoya answers. "This is some state-of-the-art shit here. It's almost indestructible, waterproof, shock resident. And the size of it... jeez. I don't know, I've never seen technology like this. See this area on the front with tiny groves? This is a microphone. Whoever placed this here is listening to us, too."

Bouvier takes the camera from Montoya and sets it under the poncho canopy for a better look.

"Rees, what do you think?" he asks.

"I think whoever sent us here is watching and listening," Rees replies, stating the obvious.

"Agreed," Bouvier nods. "They've probably placed them all over the place to keep tabs on us. We're like little rats in a maze, and they want to see how we react in this environment."

"Another thing y'all," Montoya interrupts. "This thing is powered by a small battery pack, but it doesn't have enough juice to transmit very far. There's got to be a major source of power elsewhere to send the signals. This is a technology I've never seen before; I mean, futuristic, science fiction stuff."

"Where would this source be?" Rees asks.

"Could be anywhere," Montoya replies. "It might even be underground. I don't know. Like I said, this is stuff I've never seen before."

"Is this thing on?" Bouvier asks while looking into the camera.

"Oh yeah," Montoya nods. "It's working."

"So they're watching us, listening to us right now?" Bouvier says. "They know everything we're doing and going to do? So now they know we're going to look for more cameras at daybreak."

"Couldn't they just take the cameras away?" Montoya asks. "I mean, using the same technology they used to send them, and us, here in the first place?"

"I don't think they will," Rees answers. "That would leave them blind. Remember they want to watch us, so I'm sure they have more of them around here."

"Good point," Bouvier says as he places the camera under the poncho. "What say we have a one-sided chat with our friends from, God knows where... Air Force, Pentagon, NSA, CIA?"

The group watches as Montoya adjusts the camera so it's facing the

Duck and tilted upward, making it possible for whoever is watching to see their faces. He gestures to Rees that the stage is his.

"I am Tech Sergeant Scott Rees with Staff Sergeant Jack Bouvier of the Security Police. We don't know who you are or what you hope to accomplish, but we have two injured men here who need immediate medical attention. They could die without it, and this is in addition to the three others who have died since being here. At least one of those deaths, I feel confident in saying, is on you.

"Apparently you are watching us and trying to see how we will act under pressure. We don't know how or why, but it seems you have somehow sent us back in time to a period that was a sad chapter in our nation's history. We have already taken some lives as well as lost some of our own. For now, we are going to stay put and not give you another show. You can return us to where we belong, if that's possible, or just leave us here.

"I don't know what will happen to the...," Rees pauses to come up with the correct term. "Time lines. I know about the butterfly effect theory, and if it's true, we may have messed up a bunch of butterflies. You might know, but I'm not counting on it. I hope you got what you want and are planning on bringing us back, because we've had enough of this shit. Now get us the fuck outta here and get these men some help."

Rees steps back and Bouvier steps forward.

"Now, unless you have a way to contact us, we're through for now," he says before turning off the camera.

The rain is beginning to let up and the group can see purple on the horizon.

"The sun will be up shortly. You think there's more of those things around?" Bouvier asks, pointing to the camera.

"Yeah, I do," Rees replies.

"Think we should look for them or just leave them be?"

Rees glances at the woods as he thinks for a second.

"Naw, just leave them," he says. "We don't need to be traipsing around the woods looking for the little buggers. We probably wouldn't find them all and I assume they could just send more anyway."

"Yeah, you're probably right," Bouvier nods.

Rees walks over to the Duck and calls for Montoya to join him there.

"Get some help and inspect this vehicle inside and out for cameras,"

Rees orders. "It makes sense they would have at least one in there to follow our every move. I'll grab some of the guys to help me look over the Jeep, too."

Half an hour later, the teams have found a total of ten tiny cameras, four in the Jeep and six in the Duck.

"Damn," Bouvier says, "That's a lot of cameras. Well, at least we know they're keeping tabs on us."

"What should we do with them?" Shepard asks.

"Nothing," Bouvier answers. "There are probably so many other cameras in the area that we'd never find them all. It would be a waste of time. Plus, who's to say we won't need them to get us out of here?"

"Good point," Shepard acknowledges. "In the meantime, we need to take care of ourselves right here and now. We need guys back on perimeter security and a team to head down to the river for water."

"We have two water bladders in the Duck," Bouvier says. "Shepard and Tucker, grab them and whatever canteens we have and take the Jeep to the river. You should be able to get a couple of days' worth of water. Just one of you collect water, the other keeps security. You see anybody, stop and retreat here. We're trying to stay out of sight until we can get out of here."

Chapter 19

General Lucas and Chief Black are staring at the two NCOs' faces that are filling the screen in the control room, shaking their heads in disbelief.

"What a goddamn clusterfuck," Lucas says.

Chief Black asks a technician to replay the video for them. The fact the men have found at least one of the cameras and have a good idea what is happening to them has dealt a severe blow to the Clio project.

"What now, sir?" Black asks. "We can't bring them back just yet. Not until we recalibrate Clio, check the displacement fields, and ensure all capacitors are aligned. We have a ton of work to do to make sure we don't make any more mistakes."

"Do what you have to do to make sure Clio is in complete working order," Gen. Lucas replies. "All we can do for now is wait until you give the go-ahead and hope nothing else happens to those men."

The general looks tired as he moves behind his desk. No sooner has he sat down than Shelly's voice comes over the intercom.

"General Lucas?"

"Yes Shelly, what is it?" he responds in a voice that hints at exhaustion.

"There are two OSI agents here with a couple of guests," Shelly answers.

"Send them in," the general says, suddenly energized.

Shelly opens the door and the two OSI agents enter, followed by Bill and Nora.

"Sir, I'm Special Agent Von and this is Agent Beltrane. With us are Bill Rogers of the *Daily Express News* and Nora Miller his, uh, his companion."

Bill and Nora were still getting their bearings after the helicopter flight that brought them to Pope Air Force Base. Upon landing they were blindfolded and transported to the Bank, where they were searched, scanned, given a disclosure form to sign, and warned of prison or worse consequences if they said a word about this to anyone. They were handed badges and then escorted to the general's office, wherever that is.

The general comes out from behind his desk and approaches Bill and Nora.

"I'm General Lucas," he says, shaking both of their hands, "and this brute is Chief Master Sergeant Black."

The chief shakes their hands, surprised at the strong grip from both civilians.

"Glad to meet you both," he says.

"Please, be seated," the general says, extending an open hand toward the chairs near his desk. "Can I get you anything? Coffee, water, soda? Are you hungry? I can have the cafeteria make you something if you like."

"I could use a cup of coffee, black," Bill says.

"Just a Diet Coke for me," Nora adds.

"Shelly, please get drinks for our guests," the general says before looking at the two OSI agents. "Gentlemen, thank you for being so prompt and getting our guests here so quickly. I'll inform your commander you will be returning soon. Dismissed."

Agent Von thanks the general, nods to the chief, and returns the small wave that Nora gives them. The agents move aside on their way out to let Shelly pass with the coffee and soda. Chief Black takes a chair by the wall in front, and the general half-sits on the front of his desk to address Bill and Nora.

"Bill Rogers," the general begins, looking at a printout of Bill's background. "Thirty-three years old, graduated journalism school at the University of Tennessee, 3.5 GPA, worked at local newsrooms in Tennessee, Kentucky, and then offered a job at the *Daily Express News*. Been there what, four years now?"

"Actually, it's been five years now," Bill corrects him.

"Five, well okay," the general says, raising his eyebrows.

He then turns his attention to Nora.

"Nora Miller, I will be discreet about your age, born at Chennault Air Force Base. Father is a retired lieutenant colonel. You have a big brother in the navy and you live with your younger sister, Skylar."

He looks at Nora, who sits silently, and then at Bill.

"I have files on both of you since we found out you were coming. I also have a file on your sister," he nods to Nora, "and your friend, Ivy."

Nora is taken aback, but maintains her poise.

"The reason we asked you here..." the general begins to explain.

"You mean forced us here, don't you General?" Bill interrupts.

The general turns and smiles wryly.

"Yes, I guess we did. Really didn't have a choice. You stumbled onto something that isn't known to anyone outside this building and a few politicians. You have signed the disclosure form and we will hold you to it. After I explain what is going on to you, we will also have Skylar and Ivy sign as well."

"Where are they?" Nora asks, now shifting nervously in her seat. "Did you bring them here, too?"

"No, oh no, they're fine," Gen. Lucas says with a reassuring smile. "They're still back where you last saw them. We'll get in contact later. We're just curious as to why you and the other two ladies are asking about men who you were told are off on assignment?"

Nora stares at the general and comes to the edge of her seat.

"Well, General, I've been around the military my entire life and I know bullshit when I hear it," she says without trying to hide her anger. "Those guys aren't TDY. It doesn't happen that fast. There's no war, no conflict, unless you're keeping something from the citizens of the United States. There's nothing happening that would have them deploy that fast. The guys didn't have time to notify family, friends, get personal things done, like powers of attorneys, wills, payment plans for their homes, apartments, cars. No, General, this is something else."

Gen. Lucas looks over to see Chief Black chuckling, and he can't help himself from smiling as well. Nora looks at Bill, then the general and the chief.

"What's so goddam funny?" she demands.

"Smart lady we have here, General, sir," the chief says, walking behind Bill and Nora toward what they see as a shaded window.

Chief Black raises an eyebrow in Lucas's direction and the general nods in affirmation before continuing.

"As I said, what I'm about to show you is highly classified and you're the only civilians to be let in on this. What you see may seem like science fiction, but it's not it's..."

"Time travel," Bill interjects, eliciting a shocked response from both military men.

"Why yes, Mister Rogers, it is time travel," Gen. Lucas responds. "May I ask how you came to that conclusion?"

"Let's just say there have been other reporters looking into rumors of this type of activity going on around other military bases. I had a feeling it was something like this," Bill says, turning to Nora with a wink. "Told ya."

Gen. Lucas presses a button on his desk that makes the wall and blinds separate, bringing the control room into view. Bill and Nora can only see the top portion of the large screen from where they are sitting, so the general motions for them to come forward to the window. Exchanging glances, they both stand and approach, taking in the view of the busy control room below and then the activity on the screen.

Nora places a hand over her mouth.

"Oh my God. That's Scott, my boyfriend!" she exclaims. "Where the hell is he? What's he doing, and who is that on the ground? Oh shit, that's Steve Green and... and is that Wally Harris? Oh hell, it is. What's going on? What's wrong with them? Where are they?"

The general and chief remain silent as Nora stares at the screen. She finally turns to look at them.

"What's going on, General? And no bullshit about time travel. Where is my boyfriend, and Skylar's and Ivy's boyfriends?"

"You said you were going to explain this to us, General," Bill adds.

"Okay, please calm down," Gen. Lucas says. "Please have a seat and we'll explain everything to you."

Nora crosses her arms in a stubborn pose and Bill places a hand on her shoulder, giving her a gentle nudge toward a chair. She relaxes a bit and sits down.

"Chief Black, fill them in on what we know so far and answer any questions," the general says.

The chief stands in front of Bill and Nora, takes a deep breath, and rubs his hands together as he organizes his thoughts.

"You see, I discovered a way to displace time several years ago," he begins. "I have always had an interest in time travel, so I studied and worked, and finally came up with a working model of a time machine. After a demo to the military brass and politicians, I got the okay to proceed and make a full-scale time machine. I finished it with the help of many others a couple of years ago. Before I could fine-tune it, so to speak, the powers that be – we call them the Bank Council – decided they wanted a full-scale test using people. I was against this because I wanted to run more tests, a lot more tests, before trying it with humans. We had conducted tests with objects and animals, and most were successful."

Bill quickly raises his hand.

"What do you mean most?" he asks.

"Well, that's why I wanted to run more tests, so we could get it right every time," the chief replies. "We had a few mistakes with the elevation actuator and worse, having things materialize inside solid objects. We, I, can't let that happen to people, so I put up a fight to stop a full human trial. My pleas fell on deaf ears, however, and I was ordered to get the machine up and running. I couldn't do that in good conscience, so I quit. I was afraid this might happen, but I let my anger get the best of me and like a petulant child, I took my marbles and went home."

The chief leans back on the general's desk and sighs.

"That was a mistake, and one I'm sorry for," he continues. "The Bank Council went ahead with the experiment without me a few days ago, and security policemen assigned to a weapons storage area were the guinea pigs."

"Why those men?" Nora asks, her voice rising in anger. "What made you decide to turn our boyfriends and the rest of their flight into guinea pigs?"

"They picked men who had no families, none close anyway," the chief answers. "These men were selected over time and brought here from different bases. They were then assigned to one squadron and one flight. None have living parents, wives, or children. One thing we didn't take into consideration was girlfriends. This obviously was a major oversight that has come back to bite us. The project was given the green light and Clio – our name for the time machine – was activated, sending the men on a journey."

"A journey where?" Bill asks.

"They were sent to the year 1862, during the height of the Civil War," Gen. Lucas answers.

"Why then?" Bill asks.

"The politicians, scientists, and military brass wanted to see how they would react in a time of war, in a different era," Chief Black explains. "They wanted to see how they would cope with the stress of being displaced in time as well as possibly seeing combat."

Bill starts to ask another question, but the chief holds up his hand to stop him.

"I know, why then, and why not World War II or World War I or even Korea? I can't say," the chief admits. "Someone liked the Civil War period is all we can guess. What we actually wanted to do was send them back to a time where they wouldn't have to interact with anyone, for the first test trial anyway. I wanted to inform them first and ask for volunteers. The Bank Council overrode everything I asked for. But none of this matters now. It's done, and I should have been here and maybe the problems that arose... well, maybe I could have prevented them."

"What problems?" Nora asks, growing more perturbed by the second.

"Joe, remember what I said about that," Gen. Lucas tells the chief.

Chief Black nods and looks at Bill and Nora.

"What problems?" Nora repeats, this time with more force.

The chief shakes his head and takes an anguished breath.

"We had an officer here who was working one of the panels that controls the elevation of arrival for the men," he says, averting his glance away from Nora and Bill. "When one of them materialized in the past, he was about fifty feet off the ground and fell to his death."

Bill's jaw drops and Nora gasps.

"Who was it? Tell me!" she cries.

"A sergeant by the name of Parks," the general answers.

"Isaac? Isaac Parks?" Nora demands.

Nodding, the general answers, "Yes, I take it you knew him?"

"Of course I knew him," Nora says incredulously. "I know everyone on the flight!"

"Yes, I suppose you would," the general says sadly, turning toward the window. "There's more. Besides the two men you saw who were injured, there have been two additional deaths."

He turns back and looks at Bill and Nora. Nora is pale and has grabbed the arms of the chair in anxious anticipation.

"Airman Eric McAdams and…"

Nora's mouth drops open, "No, no fucking way!"

"And Airman Alex Steele."

Nora shakes her head, rising to her feet in a rage.

"You fucking bastards! What have you done?" she yells. "You sick, twisted bastards!"

Nora takes a step forward and Bill grabs her arm to prevent her from attacking the general.

"Let fucking go of me!" she shouts, and jerks out of his grasp.

She strides toward the general, who stands fast. The chief watches nervously, ready to react if needed as Nora gets in the general's face.

"You arrogant assholes, playing God," she says, her voice building to a crescendo as she unintentionally spits a little on the general's uniform. "What gives you the right to play with men's lives, huh? What right? And you, Chief, why in God's name would you build such a thing and then allow it to be used against your good sense? Now I've got to tell my best friend that her boyfriend is dead; dead because you two thought it would be fun to experiment with others' lives. Why the hell didn't you use it on those politicians? Or better yet, yourselves?"

Shelly opens the door with her weapon at her side. The general sees her and shakes his head, and Shelly backs out the door. The general returns his attention to Nora.

"I'm sorry, Miss Miller, I truly am. I'm as sick as you are about this. Hell, we both are. That's why Chief Black is here. Believe me, we're doing everything we can to bring those men back. We want you to know what has happened and we're hoping that no one else gets hurt before we can get them home."

Nora glares at the general and Bill places his hand on her arm.

"Nora, calm down," he says softly. "Let's have a seat."

Nora yanks her arm away and storms back to her chair, still glaring and clenching her teeth. She crosses her arms and turns her head away from the men as a tear forms in her eye and runs down her cheek.

"Who is the officer who caused the problem?" Bill asks. "I assume he's been relieved of his job?"

"The officer was Captain Henries," the chief begins. "I say 'was' because he is the man you saw at the warehouse. We came down hard on him and he apparently took it very personally, deciding he was going to get back at us by conducting an interview with your cohorts. And you. You were very lucky you were late in arriving."

Bill shutters at the thought.

"So, what now?" he asks.

"Now we fix the problem and bring those men home," Gen. Lucas answers in a firm tone. "Then I will work on getting a congressional hearing convened to look into the Bank Council and those responsible for pushing for this project to happen before it was ready. When that happens, Mister Rogers, the cat will be out of the bag and I believe you will have an exclusive."

Bill nods almost imperceptibly while Nora closes her eyes.

Chapter 20

Skylar and Ivy drive back out to the base to look for Vince, and after being waved though the gate, head straight for his office building. Ivy points to Vince's car in the lot as they pull in next to it.

"He must have come back after all," Ivy says.

The senior airman behind the counter knows Ivy, but he has not seen Skylar before. Straightening up, he gives Skylar a once over, which she notices and mentally rolls her eyes.

"Airmen, what a bunch of horn dogs. Why do they have to be so obvious?" she thinks, forcing a smile as they approach. "Honey and vinegar, honey and vinegar."

"Hey there," Ivy says, leaning on his desk.

"Hello," the airman replies.

"My brother in his office?"

"I don't think so. Haven't seen him, but he may have come in while I was on break," he replies as he picks up the phone. "Let me check."

Ivy turns around and leans back on the counter, using her elbows as support. She lifts one foot and twirls it in circles in an attempt to appear nonchalant.

"Sorry, Ivy, he hasn't come back," the airman reports.

"But his car is in the parking lot," Ivy protests, sounding alarmed.

"I don't know what to tell you," he says with a shrug. "Airman Garcia says he hasn't been back and she hasn't heard from him."

"Can we talk with Airman Garcia?" Skylar asks.

"Yeah, I guess. I'll call her back."

"Never mind, we'll just go back there," Ivy calls over her shoulder, as she's already through the partition and on her way toward Vince's area.

Airman Garcia looks up as they walk toward her desk.

"Hi, Ivy. Sorry, but I don't know where your brother is," she explains before Ivy can say a word.

"Did he say where he was going?" Ivy asks.

"No. He said he was going out and would be gone about half an hour," Garcia replies. "He called, though, to say he'd be a little longer. Sounded like he was in a rec center from the background noise I heard."

"When did he leave?"

"It wasn't too long after you were here."

Ivy and Skylar thank Airman Garcia and leave the building, waving to the senior airman up front as they head out the door.

"Where to next?" Skylar asks Ivy.

"Let's try the rec center," Ivy replies. "Maybe someone there will remember seeing him."

The rec center is only a couple of blocks away, and the absence of traffic makes it obvious that the unmarked car behind them appears to be following them. The vehicle looks to be government, but it carries standard North Carolina plates. Still, with the black wall tires and two obvious-looking G-men inside wearing those signature sunglasses and suits, Skylar knows the car is government.

"Now what do we have here?" Skylar says.

"What?" Ivy asks from the passenger seat.

Noticing Skylar looking in the rearview mirror, Ivy turns in her seat and looks out the back window.

"What is it? What are you looking at?"

"That green car back there," Skylar replies. "See it, with the two typical government-looking agents in it?”

“Yeah, I do,” Ivy responds. “I’ve been seeing more of them around the last couple of days, now that I think about it. Probably something to do with all the base activity.”

“Could be, but they’re always where we are,” Skylar notes, “even when we’re in town. I’ve got a feeling they’re watching us. And what about those delivery vans we keep seeing? I don’t like it.”

“Hey, don’t sweat it,” Ivy tells her friend while trying to sound calm. “We’ve done nothing wrong.”

“Oh, and having your brother sneak a look at a personnel file is doing nothing wrong?”

“What, oh that, come on, that’s nothing.”

“If you say so, but unless we find Vince, I’m going to stay paranoid,” Skyler admits. “If that’s okay with you?”

Only a handful of patrons are inside the rec center when the women arrive. A couple of sergeants are playing pool and a few airmen are drinking beer and watching television.

“Wow, this is a real happening place,” Skylar observes.

Vince is nowhere to be seen, so the women go to the counter and ask the airman on duty if she has seen a first lieutenant recently.

“Oh, yeah, there was a lieutenant here earlier,” she says. “He was sporting a personnel function badge and asked to use the phone.”

“Why would you notice that?” Skylar asks.

“Oh, kind of a hobby,” the airman replies proudly. “I like to keep track of the different squadron personnel who come in here. I keep a little journal with who comes in, and it helps me to recognize different function badges. My supervisor likes it. He says it shows initiative.”

“Did you see where he went when he left?” Ivy asks.

“Matter of fact, I did. He was cute, so I watched him as he walked out,” she says. “The funny thing is he goes to a payphone, talks a few minutes, and then leaves. I don’t know where he went after that. I got busy.”

The women thank the airman and walk toward the exit.

“That must have been when he called us,” Ivy says quietly to an agreeing nod from Skyler.

On their walk back to the car, they notice the same unmarked car parked a short distance away. The window reflection prevents them from seeing inside, but they assume the two suits are on duty.

"I've had enough of this horseshit!" Skylar says. "Those assholes. I'm tired of them following us."

"Come on, you can't be sure they're following us," Ivy responds. "It could be just a coincidence."

"Nope, they're following us, I'm sure," Skylar says, and heads back toward the rec center.

"Hey, where you are going?" Ivy asks, hustling to catch up.

Skylar practically stomps to the counter and asks the airman if she can use the phone.

"Who are you calling?" Ivy demands.

Skylar puts the phone to her ear, dials a number, and smiles as she sees Ivy's expression change when she realizes who she is talking to.

"You're crazy, girl," Ivy says. "I hope you don't get someone in trouble. Like us."

Skylar hangs up and again they exit the building.

"Let's see how they like these apples," she remarks as they get back into the car.

Skylar backs out of the stall and drives onto the main street that leads off the base. She watches her rearview and sees the unmarked vehicle pull out after them.

"Yup, they're following us," she tells Ivy.

Ivy turns and looks.

"I'll be damned, you may be right," she says.

Skylar is doing the speed limit and the unmarked vehicle speeds up a little to stay close. The next thing Skylar sees is a set of blue lights atop a security police squad car that has pulled up behind the unmarked car. She hears the siren's "whoop" for a second, and watches as the unmarked vehicle pulls to the side of the road.

Skylar smiles and Ivy opens her mouth to say something, then closes it. The women drive off the base engaged in laughter.

∗∗∗

SSgt. Jensen and Sgt. Allen sit briefly in their squad car as Jensen runs the unmarked vehicle's plates. They come back as "Not on File," with a contact number to call if there is anything that arises relating to the vehicle. Jensen doesn't like that, and the two officers approach the unmarked car.

"What the hell do you think you're doing, Sergeant?" the car's driver demands in an unfriendly tone.

"License, registration, and proof of insurance, please," Jensen says politely, but sternly. "Sir, do you know how fast you were going?"

"This is bullshit," the driver says as he pulls out his wallet and displays his M.I.S.S. badge.

"I asked to see your license, registration, and proof of insurance, not your badge," an unimpressed Jensen says.

"You are making a big mistake, Sergeant," the driver threatens. "Do you know who we work for?"

"No, I don't, and what's more, I'm not interested in who you work for," Jensen retorts. "What I am concerned about is if you have a driver's license."

A second squad car pulls up behind the first and two more security police join the stop. The M.I.S.S. driver tries to open his door, but Jensen puts his hand on it to keep it closed while moving his other hand to the butt of his revolver.

"Sir, I didn't ask you to get out of the vehicle, I asked to see your license and registration," Jensen orders, this time with more force.

The driver points to the glovebox and tells his passenger to open it. As he does so, the passenger's jacket opens to reveal a shoulder holster containing a .45 automatic pistol.

"Gun!" Allen yells as he draws his service revolver and points it at the passenger, while Jensen points his at the driver.

"Hands up! Touch the roof!" Jensen shouts.

The driver, looking like he could spit nails, slowly raises his hands.

"Now, with your left hand, reach out and open the car door from the outside, then slowly exit the vehicle," Jensen orders.

The driver does as he is told. Allen watches the passenger as Jensen and one of the other patrolmen secure and search the driver, taking his weapon. Once he is secured, they do the same with the passenger.

"Your ass is grass, Sergeant. You hear me?" the driver fumes. "I'll fucking have your ass, your stripes!"

Jensen has the driver by the arms and leads him to his patrol car.

"Gentlemen, you are being detained for possession of a firearm on a federal base," Jensen states.

"Screw you," the passenger pipes in. "We are government officials.

You, you're nothing but Keystone Cops."

Jensen looks at the driver's badge and identification listing him as a member of the Military Intelligence Security Service.

"Please, you expect me to believe these are real? M.I.S.S.? Really? You couldn't come up with something cooler than that?" Jensen says mockingly. "What's the matter, someone else take all the good acronyms?"

The others laugh as they place the two agents in separate squad cars for the ride back to the station house.

***

Skylar and Ivy continue their drive home, chuckling at the scene that was beginning to unfold in their rearview mirror. Skylar can't wait to call the "cop shop" as soon as they step into the house. She dials the number and asks to speak with Sgt. Jensen.

"Chucky!" Skylar says. "Thank you so much."

"Hey, my pleasure. These two guys are a couple of jerks," he says. "I have no idea what M.I.S.S. is, but I've got a feeling they are for real. Who they work for is anybody's guess."

"What are you talking about?" Skylar asks, wrinkling her forehead.

"Yeah, it was on their card," Jensen replies. "It stands for Military Intelligence Security Service, whatever that is. They're not air force and no one here knows anything about them. Any idea why they were following you?"

Skylar explains what they are trying to do without getting into too much detail.

"Oh shit, Skylar. What's going on out here is hush-hush. We're not even supposed to talk about it. You two should stay clear of this and let the military do its job," he warns. "You wouldn't want to get in trouble now, would you? Hang on a second."

Jensen places his hand over the receiver and talks to someone else. He comes back on after a few seconds.

"Listen, the boss is piping hot that we brought these two in," he says. "I've got a feeling they might just be who they say they are. Keep your heads down and back off anything that has to do with what's going on out here. This is some top-secret shit we aren't even supposed to be privy to, much less ask questions about. I don't know what's going on and everyone's uptight, but we have been assured everything is fine.

Your boyfriend and the others will be back soon, some sort of top-secret mission, okay? Hey, I gotta go, time for an ass-chewing. Seriously, stay away. If these guys are spooks, they will have the full weight of the government behind them. They can be dangerous."

Skylar thanks him again for helping out and hangs up the phone.

"Well?" Ivy asks.

"He said they claim to be government agents from something called the Military Intelligence Security Service, or M.I.S.S."

Ivy gives Skyler a funny look.

"Yeah, I know. Who? Chuck didn't know either. He'd never heard of them," Skyler continues. "He said we should back off. I think we should just stay here for now and wait to hear from Bill and Nora."

Chapter 21

Sgt. Shepard and Airman Tucker drive the Jeep about a mile from the camp before finding the river. They park in foliage down an embankment and walk the forty meters to the river's edge, Shepard carrying the bladders and Tucker the canteens.

"You take watch and I'll fill the containers," Shepard says quietly.

Tucker walks off a few meters and squats, keeping an eye out for anything unusual, while Shepard heads to the edge of the river and gets to work filling the first bladder. After filling both bladders, he motions for Tucker to help carry them back to the Jeep.

"Shit, these are heavy fuckers," Shepard swears under his breath as sweat pours down his face.

After placing the bladders in the Jeep, Tucker again takes up a security position while Shepard heads to the river to fill the canteens. Halfway through filling the first one, Shepard hears a noise and freezes. Straining to listen, he realizes the sounds are approaching voices and horses.

"Shit, just what we need," he thinks, quickly capping the canteen and scrambling up the embankment to Tucker's position in the bushes.

"We might have company," Tucker whispers, raising his M-16.

The sound of horses approaching grows louder, and Tucker and Shepard see six Union soldiers on horseback heading their way. The two shrink lower into the overgrowth in the hope that the passing cavalry patrol will fail to notice them and the Jeep parked below the embankment.

Shepard looks past the bushes and catches sight of the second canteen lying on the ground, near where the patrol is heading.

"Dammit," he curses himself. "Must've dropped a canteen."

The Union soldiers are talking to each other when the lead man raises his gloved hand for the others to stop. He is looking straight at the canteen and climbs off his horse. Shepard and Tucker hold their breath and pray he will just grab it and go. There's not a thing they can do about it at this point.

"It's only a canteen," Shepard thinks. "Probably not like any canteen they've seen, but hopefully they'll just assume a soldier dropped it."

The Union sergeant, from the look of his stripes, picks up the canteen by its olive drab holder and displays it for the others to see.

"What is it?" one of the men asks.

"I'm not sure," the sergeant replies as he grasps the cap and turns it. The cap falls off and dangles by the chain attachment.

"What the...?" the sergeant comments.

He turns the canteen upside down and a small amount of water pours out.

"Oh, it's a canteen," he says.

"Looks kinda like a bullseye canteen, doesn't it, sir?" one soldier says.

"Don't guess so. Never seen one like this. Has this cap thing that turns, not a stopper, and I don't know what this is," the sergeant says, displaying the hard-plastic cap dangling from the metal chain.

He pops the snaps that hold the canteen and removes the shiny metal container. He looks inside and sees the cup, pulling it out.

"Well I'll be dammed!" he says, looking at the cup and placing it on the bottom of the canteen. "This ain't one of ours, that's for sure."

"It sure can't be the Rebels' either. They ain't got the brains to come up with something that fancy," another adds to the laughs for the group.

"Well, I reckon I got me a fancy canteen here then," the sergeant announces, putting it in his travel bag. "You know, I think we should scout around this area and see if we can find anything else interesting."

Shepard grits his teeth and makes a face as the soldiers dismount and walk in their direction.

"God dammit," he mouths through clenched teeth as Tucker looks at him with a worried expression.

Shepard shakes his head, resigned to the fact they will have to take action. He flicks his selector to semi-auto, shows Tucker what he has done, and Tucker follows suit. The Union soldiers are within a few meters of their position as Shepard slowly rises and points his rifle. Tucker hesitates for a few seconds, then stands and raises his rifle to waist level and also aims at the soldiers.

"That's far enough, blue bellies," Shepard says, realizing he has always wanted to use that phrase.

The soldiers halt and look at the two strangely dressed men pointing what looks to be weapons at them.

"Put your hands in the air," Shepard orders.

The men stare, but don't move.

"I said put your hands in the air. Now!" Shepard yells. "Tucker, go get their guns."

"What are we going to do with them?" Tucker asks.

"Right now, I don't care," Shepard replies, "but I want these men unarmed."

The Union soldiers are not big, the tallest is maybe five feet, eight inches.

"Miniature soldiers," Shepard thinks as he suppresses a snicker.

Before Tucker can move, one of the soldiers opens the flap for his pistol, and that's all it takes for the shit to hit the fan. Shepard shoots the man square in the chest, driving him back into his horse. The horse jerks from the impact and bolts.

The Union sergeant fires a round from his pistol that just misses Shepard, so close that he can feel the breeze of the ball as it flies past his head. Tucker drops to the ground, takes aim at the sergeant's head, and fires and a 5.56-mm round that finds its mark.

Shepard ducks as more rounds speed past him, quickly ducking for cover behind a tree. He shoots twice at a soldier reaching for his pistol, and the man is dead before he hits the ground. One of the rounds strikes a horse, who rears and takes off running, trailing blood from its wound.

Two of the soldiers ride away on their horses while the last soldier on the ground takes off running. Tucker takes aim and shoots him in the back, dropping him on the spot.

Shepard steps out from behind the tree and takes aim at the two men riding off. He fires right when the trailing rider turns the horse around, and the bullet strikes the horse's head. The horse dies instantly and traps his rider under its weight. The other soldier rides off in a gallop and is obscured by trees before Tucker or Shepard can get off a shot.

"God dammit!" Shepard swears as the horseman fades from view.

Shepard and Tucker run to where the fallen soldier lays under his dead horse. The man raises his hands in surrender.

"Please don't kill me, please!" he cries out with an Irish accent, wincing in pain from the weight of the horse. "Please, God, get this here horse off of me."

Tucker points his rifle at the stricken soldier and the man's eyes grow wide.

"Oh God, please, I'm a beggin' ya. Don't shoot," he repeats, this time in a softer tone.

Shepard places his hand on Tucker's rifle and has him lower it.

"He's not going anywhere," Shepard says as he kneels beside the man. "What's your name?"

"Andy, Corporal Andy O'Toole, 3rd Regiment Maryland Volunteer Cavalry, 1st Brigade."

"Where's the rest of your unit?" Shepard asks.

"Our diggings are close to two miles back that way," O'Toole replies, jerking his head in the direction of the escaped rider.

"This isn't good," Shepard tells Tucker. "When his companion gets back to the unit, they'll probably send out a larger search party to try and find us."

"What about him?" Tucker asks, nodding toward the stricken cavalryman, still pinned by his dead horse. "Should we shoot him, leave him, or what?"

"No, we take him with us," Shepard answers. "He might be able to give us more information. He is a soldier, and though the Geneva Convention wasn't around then – or now, or whatever – we still need to abide by it. He's a POW. Get his weapons, and I'll get the Jeep so we can move this animal."

Shepard turns toward the soldier and decides to share some information in a display of good faith.

"My name is Sergeant Shepard," he says, "and this is Airman Tucker."

The soldier stares in disbelief.

"What? I ain't ne'r seen uniforms like that," he says. "You some new type of greyback? What's an airman, and what are you doing with a darkie?"

Tucker looks at the soldier and smiles.

"Darkie, huh? That's a new one," Tucker says. "I've been called a lot of things, but never that. I say we just shoot him, Sergeant Shepard."

Shepard grins, knowing Tucker is joking.

"Naw, that would be a waste of a bullet," he says. "We could hang him, though."

The soldier looks terrified as Tucker and Shepard laugh.

"Don't worry," Shepard tells the man with a reassuring smile. "We're going to get this here horse off you, at which time you will be our prisoner. We won't hurt you, but if you try to run, attack us, or do anything I don't like, I will kill you. And don't call Airman Tucker a darkie or anything else other than 'sir.' You got that?"

O'Toole nods his head fervently.

"Yes, yes, sir. Just please get this critter off me."

Tucker searches the soldier and takes everything off him that could be used as a weapon, while Shepard jogs off to retrieve the Jeep. He starts the engine and O'Toole's eyes grow wide as the Jeep crests the hill.

"Jesus, Mary, and Joseph!" he exclaims. "Who are you? Where did you get that thing?"

Shepard climbs out of the Jeep and grabs a few feet of nylon cord.

"Don't worry about anything you see and quit asking questions," he says. "Now, I'm going to tie this rope around the horse and pull him off you."

Tucker gets a large branch to use as a lever to lift the horse enough so O'Toole can slide out.

"Keep an eye on him in case he tries something funny," Shepard warns.

Tucker nods his understanding and locates a good-size branch not far away. He slides it under the horse near O'Toole and poises himself to lift. Shepard ties the rope around the horse and then to the Jeep. He climbs back behind the wheel, starts the engine, and drives slowly until the rope becomes taut.

"Go!" he shouts to Tucker.

The horse slides off O'Toole easily as the soldier yelps in pain. Shepard stops the Jeep and comes back to see how O'Toole is doing.

"Let me see," Shepard says, kneeling down so he can feel along O'Toole's leg. "It's not broken, so you're lucky there. See if you can stand."

O'Toole rises slowly, favoring his left leg.

"I hate to do this, but we're going to have to secure you," Shepard says, producing a pair of handcuffs and leading his prisoner over to the back seat of Jeep.

O'Toole stares in awe at the vehicle, then at the mounted M-60 machine gun.

"What the...?" he asks, then remembering what Shepard told him, he closes his mouth.

Tucker jumps into the Jeep and trains his rifle on O'Toole as Shepard starts the engine and speeds back to camp.

***

"Jeep coming in!" Airman McGuire shouts from his fighting position.

Rees and Bouvier walk to where they can pick up the rumble of the engine, and within a few seconds they see the Jeep carrying three passengers. The two men exchange glances as Rees raises an eyebrow. Shepard drives the Jeep into the encampment, turns off the engine, and leans on the steering wheel as the men look incredulously at a grinning Tucker and the Union soldier in the backseat.

"What the hell?" Rees asks, walking toward the Jeep.

"Sorry, y'all. Couldn't be helped," Shepard tells the group. "Damn Yankee cavalry patrol snuck up on us. We had to fight our way outta there. Killed four men in the process."

"And a horse," Tucker adds.

"Yeah, and a horse," Shepard continues. "One soldier got away and we captured Corporal O'Toole here. We shot this guy's horse. Lucky for him, because I was aiming for his chest. Anyhow, the horse fell and trapped him, injuring his leg. I didn't want to shoot him in cold blood, so we made him a prisoner and a present to you," he finishes with a grin.

"What the hell?" Rees says again. "Airman Tucker, get him outta there and bring him to the Duck."

Tucker helps O'Toole out of the Jeep and holds his arm as he leads him to the Duck.

"Sergeant Kriger!" Rees calls out as they approach the Duck.

Kriger looks up from where he is examining Airman Green.

"Oh my, what do we have here?" Kriger asks.

"Check out this prisoner's leg," Rees requests.

O'Toole stares wide-eyed at the Duck as Kriger examines his leg. Kriger reports the prisoner has suffered only a bad bruise, possibly a sprained knee as well, but nothing serious as far as he can tell.

"Corporal O'Toole, is it?" Bouvier asks the young man.

"Yes, sir. Corporal Andy O'Toole," he replies.

"He's with some Maryland cavalry unit," Shepard interjects. "They have their camp a few miles northeast of us. Also, one of the group escaped and probably skedaddled back to tell them what happened. All he really will be able to report is that they got ambushed. I don't believe he had much time to get a real good look at us, but I could be wrong. Bet they'll send a search party out, though."

"That right, Corporal?" Rees asks. "Will they send out a patrol?"

"Might'n," O'Toole nods. "We're a scoutin' party, checking the area ahead. We're part of a small battalion shy of where you jumped us. There's a brigade about sixty miles further north heading this way."

Looking around at the men and equipment, he adds, "I'll say one thing, you lads sure ain't no Little Coots. None like I've ever seen anyway."

Rees and his men have no idea what O'Toole is talking about.

"Jesus Christ!" Bouvier exclaims. "A damn brigade, and it's headed this way? We've got to get out of here. We do not want to tangle with them, no matter how modernized we are."

"I agree," Rees adds. "I hope the bastards who have sent us here are working on getting us back."

Rees moves to the camera on the side of the Duck.

"Hey, you, assholes observing us," he says into the camera. "Now we're fucking up your timeline by killing more soldiers, and look here, we've got us a real live prisoner. Listen up, fuckwads, I assume you've been listening and realize we can't fight off a brigade of soldiers. So get your shit together and get us the hell home! Got it? Good!"

Rees finishes by giving the camera a middle finger salute, then turns around to address Bouvier.

"We need to break camp and find a spot deeper into the woods where no one can find us," he says. "We'll either be safe until the powers that be can find us a way home, or we'll have to wait out the war and assimilate into society and live out our lives here."

"I hope you're joking, Rees," Bouvier replies. "Let's keep our hopes up and pray they'll get us out of here before too long. I don't expect I can live here."

Bouvier walks away and Rees calls out to him.

"Oh, Jack? By the way..."

"Yeah, what is it?" Bouvier says as he pauses.

"You know what they say about assuming, don't you?" Rees asks.

"What's that?

"If you assume something," Rees says, "you're making an 'ass' out of 'u' and 'me.' "

Bouvier glares at Rees to let him know he is the ass.

Chapter 22

General Lucas is staring out the window at the control room screen, watching and listening to Rees rant at them through the camera. The general wishes they could get things moving faster. They need to get those men back.

"Joe, do we have access to those experimental cameras?" Gen. Lucas asks Chief Black. "You know, the flying ones. What do you call them?"

"Helicameras, sir, or helicams for short," Black replies. "They seem to work fine; we just haven't put them in the field for real. I think I can get my hands on four or five of them. What are you considering, sir?"

"I would like to send them there," Lucas replies, pointing at the screen. "I would like to deploy one above our boys, one over the town, and another in the area that soldier told them about. We need to locate that brigade, see what they're up to, which direction they're marching, and maybe help our boys avoid contact. Has there been any progress with Clio that we can use her to transport those helicams?"

"Yes, sir," Black answers enthusiastically as he walks toward the door. "She is capable of handling that. I'll see to it that the helicams are delivered ASAP."

"Thank you," Lucas says before turning to his guests. "Now, Mr. Rogers, Miss Miller, we're going to work on getting the men back. As you heard, we can deliver more cameras and hopefully that will assist the men in averting any more danger. There is no guarantee, but it might help."

Nora has settled down some, but is still angry.

"Not a guarantee, well ain't that par for the course with y'all," she says. "Why don't you just bring them back, get to work on that solution, huh, General?"

"Miss Miller...," the general smiles.

"And quit calling me Miss Miller," Nora snaps. "That makes it sound like I'm an old spinster teacher or something. Call me Nora."

"Okay, Nora," Lucas acknowledges with a nod. "That's exactly what we're doing as we speak. Chief Black has the team working around the clock to get Clio working perfectly so we can return them home. The Bank Council has been advised of this and we're not waiting to hear from them. Once the chief gives us the green light, we will bring everyone home."

"And how long will that take?" Nora demands.

"I'm hoping it's not too long," Lucas answers. "We have identified the problem, now it's just a matter of getting everything aligned and in perfect condition first. I'm no scientist, but the chief is. He will get the settings corrected and Clio functioning properly. He wishes those men were back more than anyone, but we also can't risk transporting them until we're sure Clio is working safely."

Nora looks at Bill and starts to ask him a question when Chief Black returns to the office.

"The cameras will be here within twenty minutes, General," Black says. "I'm going downstairs to arrange everything for their departure."

"Chief?" Bill interrupts before Black can leave. "Can you tell us how this time travel works?"

"Mr. Rogers, are you familiar with quantum mechanics or space time with curved timeline speculation?" the chief asks impatiently. "How about multi-dimensional probability distribution?"

"Ah, no, none of it."

"How about a black hole?"

"Yes, that I am aware of," Bill replies, pointing a finger at the chief.

"Well good, but that has nothing to do with time travel," the chief says, shooting down Bill's enthusiasm. "Look, Mr. Rogers, this is a complex machine. Unless you have any sort of scientific background, you're not going to understand anything. Don't try. Just report what we let you report and you'll get a great story for later."

The chief looks at Bill like he is a child who needs to understand that crossing the street without looking both ways is bad. Bill nods his head in resignation. The chief smirks as he nods to the smiling general before walking out.

"Well, that was embarrassing," Bill thinks.

"Well, that was embarrassing," Nora tells Bill with a grin.

***

Chief Black goes to the control room to update the personnel on the plan for the helicams. Fifteen minutes later, the helicams arrive and the chief rechecks Clio's settings to confirm the machine's readiness before going back upstairs.

"Ready to go, sir," he tells the general upon entering the office.

"Good, good. Now there's one more thing I want to do before we ship them off," the general says.

Walking over to his desk, he pulls out a cassette tape recorder and rummages through a drawer to find a blank tape. He attaches a microphone, sets it on the table, and looks up as Chief Black, Bill, and Nora watch with curiosity.

"I thought we might want to send a message to our boys," the general explains. "I see they have a... what do you call those big cassette players they use for music?"

"A boombox," Nora answers.

"Right, a boombox. Well, I see they have one and it gave me an idea," the general continues. "Since we are sending the cameras, maybe we can also send a little encouragement. We can inform them of our progress in getting them home. The hell with the Bank Council, these men deserve to know what's happening to them. They need to know they are not forgotten or alone. Nora, I'd like you to record a message as well. I believe it will be a morale booster for your boyfriend as well as the other men. A voice from home. Would you like to record something?"

"You bet your ass I would," Nora says, standing up to walk toward the table.

"Great, but I'll start," the general says. "First, I'll explain the situation and then I'll turn it over to you. Please be as brief as you can; we don't have much time until launch."

Gen. Lucas and Nora record their messages in one take, and the general pops out the tape to hand to the chief.

"Chief, I assume you can rig something so a helicam can drop this off?" he asks.

"Yes, sir," Black replies. "Not a problem."

"Will it take long?" Lucas presses.

"No, sir, I already know what to do. I'll get it set up in no time. Everything else is a go. Once I get the rig set up and you have the tape ready, we'll launch them."

"Great, thank you, Chief."

Chief Black strides from the office and heads back toward the control room. He stops by Shelly's desk on the way through, and an item on her desk catches his eye.

"Shelly, you mind?" he asks with a nod toward the item.

"Of course not, take what you need," Shelly says with a curious smile.

The chief grabs what he needs and proceeds to the control room. He has a simple mechanism in his mind's eye for releasing the cassette tape. Grinning to himself, he walks into the launch area and picks up one of the helicams. A lieutenant walks up beside him and watches closer, smiling as he sees what Black is doing.

The chief finishes his task and looks around for a small object to use as a test. He attaches it to the helicam, grabs a controller, and directs the helicam to fly a few feet off the ground. He triggers his drop mechanism and smiles at the success.

"That didn't take long and it didn't cost the taxpayers a dime," he tells the assembled personnel. "Okay, we're a go. Prepare for activation on the general's orders."

The chief returns to Gen. Lucas's office and informs him that everything is ready to go. The general picks up the phone and tells the control room's officer in charge to proceed. Bill, Nora, and the chief join the general at the observation window.

"What happens now?" Nora asks.

"We'll start up the sequence program and initiate Clio's drive system," the chief explains. "Once she's warmed up, we'll deliver those cameras back to 1862. We will send the cameras to different areas so they can give us a birds-eye view of what's going on. Of course, we'll also drop off the cassette tape for the men to listen to."

The control room is full of activity as Gen. Lucas gives the order to begin. Nora and Bill watch in amazement as the area around the helicams shimmers and becomes hazy, fading in and out of focus. Suddenly a small flash occurs and the cameras disappear. Nora and Bill look at each other, eyes wide.

"Now that's some magic trick," Bill says.

"That's no trick, Mr. Rogers," the general replies. "That's science; a science made possible by the chief here. Now, keep an eye on the screen. We should be getting video from 1862 any moment now."

Everyone turns their attention to the control room screen, and within a few seconds a picture begins to come into focus. The control room technicians adjust their dials and finally a clear, aerial shot of some woods comes into view.

"Which camera is that?" the general asks.

"That's camera one," the chief answers. That's the one that will follow the SPs and carries the cassette."

The group watches in fascination as the helicam flies high above the trees. It begins to descend once the technician operating the device sees the encampment on the ground. The camera zooms in on the activity below, revealing the faces of the men as they look up into the lens.

"They probably hear the helicam motor," Chief Black explains.

The helicam moves closer to the SPs, drops suddenly, and then pulls back up almost as quickly.

"What happened there?" Nora asks.

"Nothing to worry about," the chief replies. "Everything is fine. That was just a maneuver the helicam had to make to deliver the cassette."

The chief had attached a paperclip to the bottom of the helicam, bending one end so it could hold the cassette though one of the tape's reel holes. The helicam tilted forward slightly, dropped, and then halted, causing the cassette to slide off the paper clip.

They watch as one of the men picks up the cassette and hands it to Rees. Nora gasps at the sight of her boyfriend, putting her hands over her open mouth. The helicam rises a few feet and remains steady, showing Rees as he walks back to the Duck.

***

Airman McGuire is the first to hear the whirring of the helicam, telling the others to hush and listen.

"What are we listening for?" Tucker asks, not yet hearing what McGuire does.

"I hear something now, too," Nionee says.

The men look skyward, trying to find the source of the noise.

"I see something!" McGuire shouts. "It's a small helicopter, one of those toy ones, except this one is square."

"Watch out!" Shepard yells as the helicam descends suddenly and releases an object.

The object hits the ground and bounces on the thick layer of pine needles. By now, the rest of the team has walked over to check out the cassette tape and watch the helicam. Tucker picks up the tape and hands it to Rees, who has also joined the group after hearing the commotion.

"That little helicopter dropped this," Tucker explains.

"Someone obviously wants us to listen to it," Rees says. "Let's pop it in the boombox and see what's on it."

The group walks to the side of the Duck, where Rees takes out the boombox and places it on the hood of the Jeep. He inserts the tape, and presses play, stepping back so the others can gather around. A baritone voice immediately fills the speakers.

"Gentlemen, my name is Major General Richard Lucas, commanding officer of a branch of the air force not listed as any squadron. We are a section that consists of scientists, physicists, engineers, and others assigned the task of developing new and innovative technology. You no doubt have seen a few of our inventions, including the small cameras and the helicam that is currently flying above you and delivered this cassette tape. I am here with Chief Master Sergeant Joseph Black, who I will tell you more about later.

"First, I want to personally apologize for the position you are in. I'm sure you all have a hundred questions, but unfortunately I can't answer them right now. I want to assure you we are doing everything we can to bring you home as quickly and as safely as possible. I wish we could have a two-way conversation, but for reasons unbeknownst to us, we can only receive communications from you and not transmit; thus, the necessity for the tape you are listening to.

"As to when you are, if you haven't figured it out already, you are in the year 1862, during the Civil War. You are exactly where you were geographically when you arrived at the Mud Dump, only now you are in the same place about 120 years in the past. Let me explain how that happened. Some time ago, Chief Black discovered a way to traverse the laws of time, and after years of research, he finally produced a working time machine. An early version was used for a demonstration to military brass and politicians, who then gave the green light for a larger machine.

"Problems arose when the politicians decided we needed an oversight committee and one was thrust upon us. We call it the Bank Council. The council pushed hard to have a human test conducted much sooner than we would have liked. The chief fought hard for more time to conduct much-needed tests. He wanted to ensure that it would be safe before sending men through. I fought for this as well, but in the end, we were overruled and a human test was ordered. The council chose each of you to be subjects in this project because you do not have any immediate family, as well as for your job training and psychological makeup.

"I know you are angry, especially concerning the loss of some of your comrades. I am deeply sorry and angry as well, as is Chief Black. There have been some complications, some of which you are aware of. That's why we've sent in the helicams to help, including the one that delivered this cassette. We will keep one over your camp, one over the town nearby, and the other we will be sending northeast to keep an eye on the Union troops that we understand are coming your way.

"We can't talk with you, but we can hear you through the cameras. If you see the helicam move, that is our signal for you to follow. If the Union forces move toward your position, we will have the helicam lead you in the opposite direction. Our team is here twenty-four hours a day and will be here until your safe return. If you need to speak to us, go ahead, we'll hear you. Again, please be assured we are doing everything in our power to get you back safely and quickly.

"Now, gentlemen, we have someone here that you all know, one of you more than the others."

The men exchange glances as the sound of movement and people talking in the background comes through the speakers. The microphone makes a noise like it is being adjusted, followed by the sound of a familiar, feminine voice, and she clears her throat.

"Hello, y'all, this is Nora Miller."

The men immediately look at Rees, who pushes in closer to the boombox as the guys move out of his way.

"Hello, Scott," Nora continues. "I hope you are okay, and I want you to know I love you and I'm going crazy. I don't know where to start."

The general's voice briefly becomes audible before the tape goes silent.

"What happened? What's going on?" Rees demands.

As suddenly as the mic had shut off, it comes back on and Nora continues.

"Sorry about that. The general just wanted to make sure I don't say anything classified, like I know anything classified and you don't have the right to know anything classified," Nora says, accentuating 'classified' like it is a dirty word.

"I'm here because Skylar, Ivy, and I got wind of something going on at the base. We did some digging, and it brought attention upon us and a newspaper reporter, Bill Rogers, who is also here. Bill was helping us find out what happened to you boys. Well, now we know. Skylar and Ivy are all right, but they don't know we're here – yet. I've been told by the general and the chief that they are working as fast as they can to get you home. I didn't believe them at first, but after being here and watching what everyone is doing, I do now. They are trying and are upset about what has happened.

"Guys, I'm sorry about Isaac, Alex, Wally, Steve, and Eric. Ivy doesn't know about Eric. Well, she doesn't really know, although she had a premonition the other day that he had died. Damn, that girl is strange. That's why we love her. Okay, they want me to wrap this up. Scott, you keep your head down, don't be a hero, and don't die. You do, and I'll kill you."

The men all smile and look at Rees, who chuckles softly.

"I love you," Nora concludes. "Hell, I love all of you and want you all home so we can have a big ol' party. Okay, I gotta go. You all remember, we're watching, so don't be jerking off or running around naked or stuff. Except Scott, of course. I'll see you boys when you get home, which I know will be soon. Take care and be safe."

Rees can hear Nora sniffle as she backs away from the mic, and then the general's voice comes back on.

"Okay, men. Stay alert, stay safe, remember your training, and we will see you soon, very soon. We can't send anything else to you as this puts a strain on Clio, that's our time machine's name. Too many uses and it will delay our efforts to get you home. It shouldn't be too much longer. We will be able to fill you in on everything when you return. Good luck and Godspeed.

"Oh, and Sergeant Rees, we know you're upset, but please don't give a major general the middle finger. Very disrespectful. Again, stay safe."

With that, the recording stops and Rees turns off the boombox. He puts the cassette into his fatigue pocket and catches Bouvier's glance. He also can't help but notice grins on the faces of the rest of the men generated by the general's last comment.

"Well?" Rees asks.

"Sounds like they're trying," Bouvier replies, shrugging his shoulders. "Or so the general would have us believe. I guess we'll see. It was a nice touch having Nora on there. Made it more personal and gave it a little more credence."

"That's true," Rees nods. "So, I guess we stay here and keep watch over the little whirly bird there. What did he call it?"

"A helicam. What a name," Bouvier says. "I thought those scientist types had more imagination than that. Still, that's some cool technology. Wouldn't mind having one to fly around myself. You know, check out the neighborhood pools."

Bouvier looks at Rees with a wicked grin and winks.

"Pervert," Rees coughs.

"Nearly all men can stand adversity,
but if you want to test a man's character, give him power."

- Abraham Lincoln

Chapter 23

Senator Herbert Minten studies the report delivered by M.I.S.S. director John Clayborn. The report outlines every action that has taken place pertaining to the Clio Project, including what is happening at the Bank and the base. It also reveals what has transpired with his nephew, Captain Henries.

"That fucking idiot!" Minten thinks as he re-reads the description of his nephew's attempt at betrayal and subsequent killing. "If only he had called me instead of trying to take things into his own hands. That moron could have ruined everything. He could never see the big picture. Always wanting it now. Couldn't wait, had to have it now. That's what happens when your mommy and daddy give you everything."

It never occurs to the senator that he also gave in to his brother-in-law's pleas to secure an important job for his son. Minten wanted a mole on the inside of the Clio project, but would have preferred almost anyone else. He never thought of his nephew as a self-centered megalomaniac, at least not to the degree that would lead to his demise. It also never occurred to him that his nephew would betray him.

Shaking off these thoughts, he continues to read the report and focuses in on the three women and the reporter. They are pursuing information related to the men being used in the experiment and could be a problem. Minten reads the last part again and looks up into the despondent face of Director Clayborn.

"And what exactly do you mean by 'the reporter and Nora Miller are at the Bank?' " Minten asks. "And what is that about your men being arrested?"

"Actually, sir, they aren't under arrest," Clayborn replies. "They are just being detained."

Minten looks up at the director and examines him like a scientist observes an insect. Clayborn's facial features are strained, and a nervous tic starts on one side of his cheek.

"Is that your attempt at humor, Clayborn?" Minten snarls. "Because if it is, I'm not finding anything funny in this report. Detained, arrested, incarcerated, I don't give a damn. You are supposed to have the best men on this and here they are in the custody of the military police?"

Clayborn is too intimidated to correct his boss about the air force having security police, not military police.

"Well, sir, they weren't expecting any flak from the base personnel," Clayborn stutters. "Most people just look at the badge, see they look like government agents, and take it at face value. M.I.S.S. is not well-recognized, and clearly the SPs weren't impressed with the badges. But, the agents are in the process of being freed as we speak. We reached out to our man on the inside and he's dealing with it."

Clayborn watches Minten's face and waits for another tirade. It doesn't come.

"All right, John. What about the other two women?" Minten continues. "The ones who got away from your men? Where are they?"

"We assume they went home. As far as we know, they are not aware that the reporter and Miss Miller are at the Bank. The other team is moving to their home and should be there soon, if they're not there already. They will fill me in as soon as they learn more."

Minten drops the report on his oversized mahogany desk. Pressing his knuckles on the surface for support, he leans toward the director.

"I'm tired of this bullshit," he says after an uncomfortable pause. "This has been a disaster since the beginning. That asshole chief thinks Clio belongs to him when we are the ones who paid for it. Then pulling that crap about wanting to do more testing and more delays, and quitting after being informed there would be no more tests, no more delays. Damn, I hate the military! I should have had more inside people. This should have been run by my people, by me, not some crackpot Bank Council who prefers the military manage it."

Minten stands and turns around, looking at the wall of photographs behind him. Most feature himself with various government leaders. Some are from various branches of the U.S. Government, some from other countries, and one is with the president. There are also a few photographs with actresses and actors taken during photo ops in his attempts to appeal to the voters.

"Tell you what, John," Minten says, still admiring his wall. "How about we take control of this situation. Here's what I want you to do..."

***

General Lucas smiles at Nora and tells her she did an excellent job on her recorded message. He could tell by the men's reactions that it had given them a morale boost.

"Thank you, General," Nora smiles back. "That puts me more at ease, and I accept that you are trying to get them back. I'm still mad that they were sent there in the first place, but realizing you're working on the problem helps."

The general nods his appreciation and is about to describe the next steps when his intercom buzzes.

"Yes, Shelly?"

"Sir, Colonel Grayson is here to see you."

General Lucas glances at the chief with a confused look as to why the OSI commander would be there.

"Yes, Shelly, show him in," Lucas says and glances toward the door.

The door opens a few seconds later and Colonel Grayson strides in. Ignoring the two civilians in the room, he stops in front of the general and salutes.

"Well, this is unexpected, Colonel Grayson," Gen. Lucas remarks, returning the salute.

"Yes, sir. I know, but I wish to talk to you in person about what we uncovered," Grayson says in a very serious tone. "It concerns the request you made earlier."

Grayson then glances questioningly at the two civilians in the room. The general notices the look.

"Colonel Grayson, let me introduce my guests," Lucas says. "This is Bill Rogers of the *Express Daily News*, and this is Miss Nora Miller. Her boyfriend is one of the men on assignment with us."

Nora looks at the general, puzzled, and shakes the colonel's hand.

"Please call me Nora," she says, releasing his grip.

"Colonel, these are the two people I had your agents bring in earlier," Gen. Lucas explains.

Grayson nods his understanding.

"And I believe you have already met Chief Black," Lucas continues.

"Yes, Chief Black and I go way back," Grayson says as he shakes the chief's hand. "How are you doing, Joe? It's been awhile."

"I'm fine, sir. Thanks for asking," the chief replies. "And yes, it's been some time since we last spoke."

After the formalities are concluded, General Lucas indicates for Grayson to take a seat while he moves behind his desk.

"Before we get started, Colonel, you should know that Mr. Rogers and Miss – I'm sorry, Bill and Nora – are cleared to hear anything in this room," the general states. "So please speak freely with what you have to tell me."

The colonel sits straight in his chair facing the general.

"Yes, sir," Grayson says, taking a deep breath. "Well, you asked me to check into M.I.S.S."

"Yes, I did," the general acknowledges, then turns to address Bill and Nora. "M.I.S.S. is the acronym for Military Intelligence Security Services. They are a secret government agency that showed up out of nowhere. Some of their agents have been sticking their noses into the Clio project. I have asked Colonel Grayson to see what he could find out about them. Go ahead, Colonel."

Nora and Bill look at each other, both thinking the same thing about the acronym.

"Quite right, sir," Grayson continues. "They did just come out of nowhere. As far as we can tell, they are a covert group recently introduced.

We did a little digging and found they are working for Senator Minten. They were formed by the Bank Council, but it seems they report to a director named John Clayborn. Director Clayborn is...."

"I'm quite familiar with Mr. Clayborn," the general says, holding up his hand. "Go on with the rest."

"Yes, sir. Well, it seems the agency was organized about the same time as your section was introduced. We don't know how many agents they have or where they are based. If they report to Minten, then it's reasonably safe to assume they are out of Langley or close to it. We're still looking into that."

"What have they been up to lately?" the general asks.

"We found out they have been very busy running around town and on the base," Grayson replies. "In fact, two of them are currently detained. They were stopped by a base patrol for following a couple of civilians. Apparently, the civilians noticed they were being followed and called the Law Enforcement desk. A patrol was dispatched to the area and pulled over an unmarked government vehicle. The two individuals identified themselves as M.I.S.S. agents. The SPs had not heard of them, so they detained them and took them to the police station. As far as I know, they are still there. There have also been complaints about delivery vans parking on the streets. We believe some them are M.I.S.S. surveillance vehicles."

Nora perks up when she hears about the two civilians and raises her hand.

"Yes, Nora," the general smiles. "What is it?"

"Colonel, these two civilians, do you know who they are?"

"No, ma'am," Grayson answers. "All I know is it was two females and they called the LE desk to inform them about a suspicious vehicle."

"Is that important?" the general asks.

"I think that might have been my sister, Skylar, and our friend, Ivy," Nora says proudly. "It sounds like something Skylar would do. As I told you earlier, we had a feeling we were being tailed. Sorry, didn't mean to interrupt."

"Quite all right," the general says. "Anything else, Colonel Grayson?"

"No, sir. Do you want us to do anything with the two detained agents or follow up on these complaints concerning the delivery vans?"

"No, Colonel. Just have your agents keep an eye on them when and if they are released. Same goes for the vans, just monitor them. No action needed at this time. Senator Minten is an ambitious bastard who would love nothing more than to take complete control of the Clio project. It doesn't surprise me one bit that he has his own government police force. Don't interfere with them unless they break the law. And please keep me posted on any developments."

"Yes, sir."

The colonel stands, salutes, and leaves the office as General Lucas walks over to Nora.

"Nora, I would like you to get in touch with your sister and Ivy," he says. "Let them know you and Bill are safe. I'm sure they're worried. However, please don't tell them anything about this."

Nora starts to protest, but the general raises his hand to stop her.

"Please let me finish," he continues. "Tell them you were following a lead that took you out of town, but you are with Bill and are all right. Explain to them they can expect a visit from our OSI agents and to do as they ask."

"What are you going to do with them?" she asks.

"We will have them escorted here, just like the two of you," the general explains. "They will go through the same process as you. Once that is completed, you may fill them in on what is transpiring here. Is that understood?"

"Yes, General. It is," Nora beams. "Thank you."

***

Skylar and Ivy are still having a chuckle over the predicament they left the two men in who had been following them. Skylar is concerned by what SSgt. Jensen told her about the two men, though. If they are part of some government agency branch, she and Ivy might have bitten off more than they can chew. Jensen hadn't even heard of them. Meanwhile, Ivy was thinking about Vince and what a predicament she may have gotten her brother into.

The phone rings and Skylar notices she has been holding a beer for some time, but has yet to take a drink. She sets down the bottle and goes to answer the phone.

"Hello?" she asks tentatively.

"Hi, little sister. How's everything?" Nora says jovially.

"Holy shit, Nora. Where the hell have you been?" Skylar gushes.

"You won't believe what's been going on around here."

She excitedly begins to explain what has happened when Nora cuts her off.

"Skylar, Skylar! Listen up," Nora shouts. "I know all about your ordeal. I'll explain how later, but for right now, listen to what I'm telling you, okay?"

Skylar is taken aback by Nora's statement and Ivy notices her surprise.

"Is that Nora?" Ivy asks. "Is she all right?"

Skylar nods in the affirmative and puts her finger to her lips.

"Nora, say that again, Ivy interrupted me," Skylar says, generating a middle finger salute from Ivy.

"I said I'm with Bill," Nora says. "We are following a lead and it paid off. I can't tell you anything right now, but soon. Just keep an eye out and expect a visit from some OSI agents. They are going to stop by and pick you up. They will bring you to my location, and then I'll be able to explain everything. It will all be cleared up when you arrive. Can you do that?"

"Yes, but what's going on, Nora? Now you have me worried," Skylar replies with anxious confusion.

"Your questions will have to wait," Nora says. "Don't worry and just trust me on this. I've got to go, but I'll see you soon."

Skylar hangs up and turns to Ivy, who has a quizzical look on her face.

"Well, was that Nora?" Ivy asks. "Where is she? Is she with Bill? What did she say? Is she all right? Is she coming back soon?"

"Yes, yes, Ivy, that was Nora. Jeez, chill, will ya?" Skylar replies, slightly irritated. "She said she has a lead. Well, she and Bill have a lead, and she said they found out something."

"What is it?"

"She wouldn't say. All she said is that we are to wait here for some OSI agents to arrive. She said they will pick us up and take us to where she and Bill are, then she will tell us what's happening."

"That's it?" Ivy asks incredulously. "Not where she is? Nothing about what's happening now?"

"Look, Ivy, that's all she said," responds an exasperated Skylar. "She says we are to wait for the agents and go with them."

"What if she was under duress or whatever you call it?" Ivy asks suspiciously. "Maybe she had a gun to her head or something."

"No, she actually sounded good," Skylar explains. "Really, like she is excited and wanted to tell me more, but couldn't. I trust her on this. We'll just have to do as she asks and wait. We don't really have a choice."

Chapter 24

A delivery van parks down the street and out of sight from Ivy and Skylar's location. A technician inside the van pulls back one of the headphones from his ear and turns to look at the man wearing sunglasses.

"We are going to lose them if they get picked up by OSI," the technician warns.

"Don't be an idiot," comes the stern reply from the man in the sunglasses.

The technician takes the rebuke in stride.

"We have our orders," adds the man in the sunglasses." We'll just have to get to them first. How soon until our agents are released from custody?"

The technician looks at a computer and scrolls through a couple of screens.

"They're being released right now," he reports. "They should be contacting us soon."

The man in the sunglasses nods and sits back in his chair to wait.

***

"Just who in the hell do you think you are? Who told you to detain two government agents, huh?" SMSgt. Wright loudly demands of SSgt. Jensen.

Jensen stands at attention, seemingly unfazed by the berating he is receiving.

"Sir, they were acting suspicious," Jensen explains. "After we stopped them for speeding, they brandished a weapon. There was enough probable cause to detain."

"What the fuck did you just say to me? You telling me the law? Why you little piss-ant!" Wright yells, punctuating his reply with a small spit on the 'p' sound. "Don't you dare try to tell me what probable cause is."

"No, sir, I wouldn't dream of it, Sergeant," Jensen answers as he holds his composure.

"Don't get fucking smart-mouth with me, you little cocksucker," Wright continues, getting right up into Jensen's face. "I ought to have you written up and make you a Tread. See how you like guarding aircraft instead of law enforcement duties. How'd you like that, asshole?"

"I wouldn't really like that, Sergeant."

"Shut the fuck up. That was rhetorical. Goddamn smart-ass kids nowadays," Wright snarls. "Did the man not show you his government badge?"

"Sergeant, I have no idea what he showed me," Jensen says, holding a snicker. "It was a badge, but really, M.I.S.S. as the acronym? I thought he was some nutcase playing cop or something. I haven't heard of them. Hell, no one here has."

"That's not your fucking call to make, you jackass!" Wright bellows. "Next time you feel like playing Adam-12 out there, stop and think before you pull some boneheaded, asinine bullshit like today. I do not – repeat, do NOT – like getting a call from the commander, who does not like getting a call from Washington, D.C."

Jensen jerks his head slightly to look at Wright in surprise at that statement.

"That's right," Wright continues. "The commander got a call from Washington, D.C., concerned about two of his fine agents being treated like common criminals on our base. Now, get the fuck out of my office."

Jensen does an about-face and leaves the office. Shutting the door behind him, he sees Sgt. Allen and some of the others from his flight standing in the hallway waiting for him.

"I take it that went well?" Allen asks with a smirk.

"Oh yeah, you should try it sometime," Jensen responds. "Builds character."

The men walk through the hallway and are in the process of leaving the building when they see the two M.I.S.S. agents retrieving their belongings from the front desk. Both groups glare at each another, with the agents displaying a look of pure contempt. They start to walk past the security policemen and the lead agent stops to stare at Jensen.

"You better watch your back, grunt," the agent growls. "You just fucked with the wrong organization."

"Zoomie," Allen says.

The agent turns towards him with a scowl. "What?"

"We're called Zoomies, or Flyboys, or Zipper-heads," Allen tells the agent. "Grunts are army."

The rest of the SPs snicker at the scene.

"And we only allow other branches of the armed forces to call us that, is that understood agents…?" Jensen adds, fishing for their names. He could look at the report, but this is more fun.

The agents' faces go red as they storm out of the building. The lead agent points his finger like a gun at the SPs before the door shuts behind them.

***

The M.I.S.S. agents get into their vehicle and radio the command van, which instructs them to meet at its location down the road from the Miller house, where Skylar and Ivy are waiting.

The SPs walk out of the building and watch as the agents depart.

"Okay, we'll just call them Agent West and Agent Gordon," Jensen says, referring to the two main characters from the popular 1960s television show, *The Wild Wild West*.

"I think they look more like the team from *Lancelot Link*," Allen quips, referring to the children's show that featured a cast of chimpanzees. "Either way, I don't trust those assholes."

"Me, neither," Jensen adds. "And I've got a feeling they aren't finished bothering the girls. You guys up for a little unpaid overtime?"

"Count me in," Allen says as the rest of the SPs enthusiastically agree. "We need to be ready to help the ladies out if it comes down to it. Our missing brothers will expect it from us."

"All right then, let's see what these boys are up to," Jensen says. "You know it won't be long before they show up at the girls' place. Everyone change out of uniform and meet at the main gate in ten."

The SPs disperse and reconvene a few minutes later as planned. Jensen and Allen take Jensen's car and lead the way on the short drive to the house. Jensen stops his vehicle a block from the dwelling and the others park behind him, exiting their cars to gather around him.

"Okay, this is just a recon mission," Jensen tells the group. "Keep your eyes peeled for any shenanigans from our boys from M.I.S.S. Spellman, you and Morgan go around the back. Sanchez, you take Hernandez and cover the west side. Nicholson, you take Burns and Meyer and cover the east side. Sgt. Allen, Kowalski, and I will remain here. If you see anything suspicious, don't act, just send a runner back to me. All right, let's go."

As the men break for their positions, Jensen calls out softly to them, "Remember, take no action, not unless your life or the girls' lives are in danger."

Jensen looks toward the house and can faintly make out the front porch from his position. He scans the street and decides they are in a good spot. Scrunching down in the seat, he makes himself a low profile while keeping an eye on the house.

"This could take a while," he tells Allen and Kowalski.

But he is wrong.

***

Skylar and Ivy have freshened up and are a little anxious about what is going on. They both trust Nora and know she wouldn't put them in harm's way, but they also realize they have stumbled onto something that is generating more attention than they would like.

"I don't know what to think about Nora," Skylar says. "She has been very cryptic, but I sensed excitement in her voice. She said she is with Bill, and he seems a capable person, so we will have to take a chance on them knowing what they're doing."

"I don't like waiting around," Ivy responds as she paces around the living room.

"Go make us a drink," Skylar smiles, trying to put her friend at ease.

"That'll give you something to do."

Ivy stares briefly at Skylar in contemplation before turning to walk into the kitchen. Skylar can hear her opening the cabinets and the clink of glasses, followed by the refrigerator opening and the rustling sound of the ice container being removed. A sound outside catches her attention. Perhaps it's the OSI agents Nora mentioned would be coming. She heads to the window and looks outside, but there is nothing there. She shrugs and walks into the kitchen to see if Ivy needs help with the drinks.

***

Two plain-looking government vehicles pull up and park in the street, two houses down from the Miller house. Four men exit and gather to talk. After conferring with each other, two of them get back into a vehicle and move forward to park in front of the house. The other two men walk through a neighbor's yard and head for the back of the home.

***

Jensen sits up when he sees the two vehicles pull up. He slaps Allen's arm, which catches Kowalski's attention as he leans forward, resting his hands on the back of their seats.

"What's going on?" Kowalski asks.

"Two cars just stopped and those guys got out," Allen explains, pointing to where the men are standing.

"Well, I'll be damned," Jensen says. "It's our two best friends, West and Gordon. And hey, they brought more friends."

"What do we do?" Kowalski asks the sergeants.

"We wait and watch," Jensen says. "Be ready for anything."

Sanchez and Hernandez are out of sight on the west side of the house, using bushes to obscure them. Hernandez takes hold of Sanchez's arm when he hears someone moving close by. Hernandez squats and places a finger to his lips, pulling Sanchez down with him. He points at his own ear and then in the direction of the noise. Sanchez nods his understanding when he hears the noise, too. They watch as two M.I.S.S. agents carefully make their way through the neighbor's backyard and proceed toward the Miller house.

Spellman and Morgan, watching from the rear of the home, see the same two men emerge from the bushes at the edge of the neighbor's yard. Spellman gives a jerk of his head toward the street, indicating

Morgan should go tell Jensen what's happening. Morgan silently backs away and makes his way around the house to where Nicholson, Burns, and Meyer are concealed. He stops long enough to hand signal what he sees and continues on toward the vehicles. Stopping along the line of trees next to the road, Morgan leans imperceptibly around a tree. He can see agents West and Gordon sitting in a car in front of the house. That means he won't be able to get to Jensen's vehicle without being seen, so he moves back a little into the trees and waves his hands, hoping to get Jensen's attention.

In the car, Jensen, Allen, and Kowalski are busy watching West and Gordon. As Kowalski leans back to rest his shoulders, he glimpses movement to his left. Sitting forward again, he looks out the side window and catches a glimpse of someone waving their arms.

"Hey guys," he whispers, "look over there to your left. At the woods."

Both men in the front seat turn and see what Kowalski describes. Jensen rolls down his window and Morgan moves out enough so he can be seen by the SPs in the car, but not the M.I.S.S. agents. Using hand signals, he tells them about the two others in back. Jensen gives him a thumbs up as West and Gordon exit their vehicle and proceed to the front door of the house.

"Here we go," Jensen says, nodding toward the agents.

***

The two M.I.S.S. agents go to the front door and knock. After a few seconds, Skylar answers.

"Can I help you?" she asks.

"Yes, ma'am. I'm Agent Von and this is Agent Beltrane. We're with the OSI and I believe you are expecting us," West says with a smile.

The M.I.S.S. brass has checked on local OSI agents and discovered that Von and Beltrane are the two agents who escorted Bill and Nora to the bank.

"Oh, right, come on in," Skylar tells them.

The fake OSI agent smiles, thanks Skylar, and both men enter the home.

***

Jensen waits until both men enter the home before having all three SPs exit his vehicle. Looking around to ensure no one else is watching, they get on the sidewalk and casually walk up to the front of the home and wait outside the house.

Morgan is making his way back to Spellman's position and is almost there when he trips over a root and stumbles. He catches himself before he falls, but he has made too much noise. Both of the M.I.S.S. agents in the backyard look toward the woods and begin walking toward Spellman and Morgan's position.

"Ah shit," Spellman says to himself, realizing he must make a quick decision.

Without further thought, he stands and walks into the backyard to face the agents. When he is clear of the woods and in plain sight, he stops and acts surprised to see them. The agents reach for their weapons, placing their hands on the butts of their guns. Spellman reaches behind him and places his hand on the butt of his own gun.

"Whoa there, fellas," Spellman says, cocking his head and using what he hopes is a slurry-sounding voice. "Don't get antsy now. We don't want to do anything stupid now, do we?"

"Just who the hell are you and what are you doing here?" one agent demands.

"Hey, I'm just a horny guy looking to get some action from the girls inside," Spellman says. "Who the hell are you guys?"

"We're federal agents on assignment. I'll need to see your hands. Now!" the second agent orders as he starts to pull out his Smith & Wesson M-13 revolver.

"I don't think that's going to happen there, mister federal agent. And I wouldn't draw that gun out any further if'n I was you," Spellman says, jutting out his chin to indicate the agents should look behind them.

The second agent does and sees Sanchez and Hernandez pointing their weapons at them. Before the agent can say anything, Morgan comes out from the woods with his weapon drawn as well. Nicholson, Burns, and Meyer walk into the clearing at that moment, each of them also brandishing weapons. The M.I.S.S. agents keep their hands on their weapons, but don't finish drawing.

"Now listen here, boys. We're federal agents and we're here because of a threat to national security," the first agent announces. "The women in this house are under suspicion for treason and you're interfering. If you don't want to find yourselves in federal prison for aiding and abetting, as well as interfering with a federal investigation, I suggest you put down those guns and move along."

Spellman looks at Nicholson and chides the agents, "What do you think there, Sergeant? Think we should drop our guns and skedaddle?"

"Well, let's see," Nicholson says to the agents. "We are security policemen, which makes us federal as well. So, naw, we ain't leaving. In fact, we want you to take out *your* guns and place them on the ground."

The first agent shakes his head.

"Military Police don't…"

"Security Police," Nicholson corrects, but the agent ignores him.

"Military Police don't have jurisdiction off base. Posse comitatus."

"Yes, you're right," Spellman says, "but we can exercise our rights and duties as citizens to make a citizen's arrest. Plus, Airman Hernandez, Staff Sergeant Jensen, and I are reserve deputies for the county. Furthermore, you're on private property, which makes you trespassers, and we know the owners. They won't approve of you walking around their backyard brandishing guns."

"We're federal agents."

"So you've said," Spellman replies. "But I've seen nothing to prove you are. You could just be a couple of perverts stalking young women alone in the house. How do we know?"

The confrontation suddenly stops as a ruckus coming from the front of the house distracts the group.

***

West and Gordon are eager to get going and want the girls to leave with them.

"Skylar and Ivy, right? If you're both ready, we should leave. We need to get you to your destination," West urges, opening the front door and indicating the women should walk out.

Skylar and Ivy grab their personnel belongings and walk out onto the front porch.

"And just where is it we are going?" Skyler asks as they walk down the steps.

Jensen can hear the conversation from his position and is wondering the same thing.

"Yes, 'Agent West,' just where are you and 'Agent Gordon' taking them?" Jensen asks the agents, who are surprised by the presence of the three SPs on the sidewalk.

The names West and Gordon confuse the faux agents, and Skylar and Ivy look just as surprised. It takes only a second for Skylar to recover.

"Sergeant Jensen, what are you all doing here?" Skylar asks. "And who are West and Gordon? These are OSI agents, Von and Beltrane. Aren't they?"

"Von and Beltrane?" Jensen snorts. "Sorry, Skylar. I know Von and Beltrane, and these two are not them. These guys actually claim to be agents with M.I.S.S., the agency I told you about earlier. In fact, these are the two goons who were following you earlier today."

"Oh, it's real now, you interfering little piss-ant," an angry West snarls. "You're about to find out just how real when we slap cuffs on all of you, throw you in a deep hole, and lose the key. You are so fucked."

Ivy moves away from Gordon, who makes a grab for her. Ivy squeals and slaps him in the face, giving her enough time to get away before he lunges for her. Simultaneously, West grabs Skylar by the arm. Skylar stomps hard on his foot, causing him to release his grip and curse in pain as Skylar runs toward the security policemen.

"You fucking bitch!" West yells as he pulls his service revolver. "All of you are under arrest!"

Jensen already has his pistol out and levels it at West.

"Drop it!" Jensen orders.

West turns his gun toward Jensen, and with a scowl on his face raises it to fire. Jensen doesn't wait, pulling the trigger three times. The first two rounds hit West in the chest. One round drives straight through his heart, stopping it instantly, and the second round to the left side of West's chest damages his lung. The third shot strikes him in the forehead, causing his head to snap back. It is a classic demonstration of the Mozambique Drill for which Jensen is trained to perform as a Tactical Neutralization Team (TNT) member. Two to the chest, one to the head. West is dead before he hits the ground.

Gordon reaches for his weapon, but hesitates when he hears the shots. He turns to watch as his partner falls, and Allen and Kowalski use the opening to tackle him. They take his weapon, pin his arms behind his back, and get him handcuffed. Gordon swears and threatens them the entire time.

Ivy walks up to Gordon as the SPs subdue him.

"See what happens when you fuck with us, dickhead?" she yells while bending over Gordon.

Ivy prepares to kick him in an uncontrollable rage, but Kowalski stops her. He holds onto her as she yells and thrashes about, trying to get to the restrained agent.

Jensen stands frozen. He has shot another human being. He is on the TNT and has known this could happen, but this isn't what he expected. It's different now that it has happened for real. He breaks from his reverie and walks to where West is laying, checking the body for any signs of life. Finding none, he shakes his head and stands.

Skylar walks over to Ivy and takes her from Kowalski, hugging her and telling her everything will be okay. Ivy calms down and cries into her friend's shoulder. Skylar looks at Jensen and mouths the words, "Thank you."

Jensen smiles sadly and nods. Then he remembers that Morgan signaled there are more agents in the backyard. He turns and is about to say something to Allen and Kowalski when gunfire rings out from the rear of the house.

***

Spellman is still in conversation with the two M.I.S.S. agents in back when he hears shouting and gunfire coming from the front of the house. A couple of the SPs take their eyes off the agents, who think this is a good time to finish drawing their weapons. It isn't.

Hernandez and Spellman see what's happening and yell for them not to draw, but it's too late. Both agents have their weapons drawn and pointed at one security policeman, then the other, turning from one man to next.

"Okay, this is how it's going to be," the first agent commands. "I'm going to radio this in and we're leaving. More of our agents will be en route and you guys can leave or wait around; it's up to you. Hang around and you're going to be arrested. Oh hell, doesn't matter, leave and we'll still be on your asses."

"No, that's not going to happen," Spellman replies. "You're going to disarm and we're taking you into custody. Now drop the guns."

"Fuck this, we don't have time for this shit," the first agent says as he fires, striking Spellman in the chest and sending him to the ground.

The second agent takes aim at Sanchez and Hernandez, but his indecisiveness costs him. His shot goes wild, missing both. Sanchez and Hernandez return fire and their shots hit the agent, who makes a guttural sound as he falls backward into his partner. The collision causes the first agent to fire slightly off-target at Morgan, but the bullet still hits him in the upper left shoulder. Morgan yelps in pain, drops his gun, and reaches for his shoulder as he falls back into the woods.

Three of the SPs charge the first agent and knock him to the ground before he can recover and take another shot. Meyer wrestles the gun away, breaking the agent's wrist and a finger in the process. The pain makes the agent scream. He fights to get them off, but to no avail. There are too many SPs on him, and the agent finally surrenders. The SPs roll the agent onto his stomach and handcuff him, and he yells in pain as the cuffs bite into his broken wrist.

By this time, Jensen has run around the corner of the house and sees the security policemen on top of the agent. He takes in the scene quickly before noticing Sanchez and Hernandez running toward the woods and Morgan writhing on the ground in pain.

"Oh shit, Morgan! What happened?" Jensen asks no one in particular.

Hernandez points at the dead agent nearby.

"That puta madre shot them," Hernandez says with anger in his voice and emotional pain evident on his face.

"Them?" Jensen thinks, trying to absorb the gravity of the situation.

Then he sees Spellman's body laying prone on his back, a dark pool of blood forming around him. Meyer is kneeling beside him, frantically checking for vitals that are quickly disappearing.

"Oh my God, no!" Jensen yells as he raises his hand to his mouth, then rubs his face with both hands. "God dammit. This isn't supposed to happen. Mother fuckers. They're going to pay for this!"

With sirens now approaching, Jensen quickly composes himself and orders the security policemen to safe and secure their weapons.

"Stay where you are and don't move or touch anything. You all know the drill," he says. "The police will want our weapons for ballistics. Cooperate with law enforcement as well as OSI. I suspect they will be here soon, too."

Jensen takes one last look around the backyard, and one longer look at Spellman's body, before walking back to the front of the house and waiting for the local authorities to arrive. He sees Kowalski leading Ivy and Skylar back into the house. That's a good idea, he thinks, getting them someplace familiar and away from this scene. It's going to be a long night. SMSgt. Wright will be thrilled to hear this news.

Unnoticed amid the chaos, the delivery van parked up the street slowly drives away.

Chapter 25

"God dammit, Clayborn! I can't believe the incompetency of your organization! Why in the hell did I entrust you with being the director of M.I.S.S.?"

Senator Minten stands behind his desk staring daggers at Director Clayborn, who is frozen in place like a frightened child. Clayborn opens his mouth to speak, but stops as Minten raises a finger in warning.

"Don't you dare answer that question. It was rhetorical!" Minten snarls, raising his hands in front of his face and gritting his teeth in frustration. "Ughhh!"

Minten takes a deep breath and appears to calm somewhat as he leans on his desk in resignation. Clayborn takes this pause as an opportunity to explain what happened at the house.

"Sir," is all he gets out before the senator jerks up his head, looking at him with disdain. Clayborn knows he must tread lightly.

"Sir, the teams weren't expecting base personnel to be at the house," he explains. "Well, certainly not armed base personnel. The women could have had a few friends there and that would have been fine. The agents could have handled them, told them that…"

Minten has had enough.

"Shut the hell up, you incompetent boob. I don't want to hear what your asinine teams could or could not have done. I only wanted to hear they detained the women and put them in the hole with everyone else. That's all. Is that too much to ask from your 'elite' agency?"

"Sir, even if we had taken the women, we couldn't have held them for long," Clayborn replies, shuffling nervously in front of the senator's desk. "We can't go around taking citizens and base personnel from their homes and places of work without drawing suspicion. Someone will eventually come looking for them. That's actually what started this mess."

"Again, I ask, is this too much for you and your so-called super agents to handle? Picking up a couple of girls?" Minten declares, not wanting to hear any more of Clayborn's excuses.

"No, sir. We can move forward on this," Clayborn answers. "We can finish the task, I assure you."

"Your assurances just inspire me with confidence," Minten replies, his words dripping with sarcasm. "It hasn't happened so far. You now have two dead agents, one in the custody of local authorities, and another under guard at the hospital. Oh yes, that really fills me with confidence."

Minten turns and looks at his wall of fame and thinks quietly for a few seconds. Clayborn is about to ask for permission to leave when the senator suddenly turns around and faces him. Clayborn shudders at the evil expression Minten has on his face and dreads what he is about to hear next.

"I've had it with incompetency," Minten states. "I'm taking control of this situation right now. In fact, I am taking control of everything. The Bank Council, the asshole general, the chief master sergeant who thinks his shit doesn't stink, all of the personnel involved, everything. We're going to take control, even if we must use force to take it. We. Will. Take It. This will be my legacy. Clayborn, we are taking over the Clio project!"

Yep, Clayborn did not want to hear that.

***

Von and Beltrane, the real OSI agents, arrive at the scene of the shootings in what should be a quiet, residential neighborhood. There is activity everywhere with police, paramedics, detectives, security police, and news crews milling about. Blue and red lights flash from several emergency vehicles, giving the area a surreal look in the gloom of dusk, like a mad hatter's carnival ride.

"Staff Sergeant Jensen?" Agent Von says as he approaches the sergeant, who is leaning against a police vehicle watching the commotion.

"Huh? Oh, hey guys," Jensen replies in a weary tone. "I thought some of you would show up. Coincidence it being you two."

"Why is that?" Von asks.

"Ah, you haven't been brought up to speed yet. Well, you see that corpse lying in the front yard?" Jensen explains, pointing at West's body. "Well, supposedly that's you, Agent Von. And a guy claiming to be Agent Beltrane is in jail for now."

Jensen smirks at the two confused agents and lights a cigarette. He inhales and blows out a lungful of smoke, still watching the two men grapple with the situation.

"Somehow they got your names and were posing as you both," Jensen continues. "They were here to collect Skylar and Ivy, and take them God knows where."

"Who the hell are these guys?" Von says, shaking his head. "Nobody had heard of M.I.S.S. until recently. They must have a lot of pull to discover what we are up to. Which brings us to why we're here. We didn't come because of what happened. We were coming here to collect the two women and take them to meet their sister and her reporter friend."

Jensen takes another drag off his cigarette and looks at the glowing ember. He slowly exhales the smoke and looks at the two agents.

"Where you taking them? Or am I not supposed to ask?" he says finally.

"We're not supposed to tell you, but they will be in safe hands, I assure you," Von replies. "There is a bigger picture here you have not been made aware of. It has something to do with the missing SPs from the Security 15 area. This mess here is part of it, too. We know why they were interested in Miss Miller and Miss McKnight; what we don't know is what they wanted them for. I'm sorry you got involved."

"I'm actually not sorry," a somber Jensen says. "We stopped something from happening that more than likely would not have ended well for those two women. I'm just sorry I lost a man in the process and have another one seriously injured. I'm sorry these assholes wouldn't listen to us. I'm sorry they tried to kill us. But I am not sorry for being involved. This is my job, same as it is yours."

Jensen finishes his cigarette and field strips it as Von looks on.

"For what it's worth, you and your guys did a hell of a job here," Von says with conviction. "You can be proud of yourselves."

Von pushes himself away from the vehicle he is leaning against, takes a deep breath, and prepares to carry on.

"I've got to gather the young women and escort them to the next location," Von says. "You gonna be all right?"

"Yeah, I'll be fine, thanks," Jensen replies as a faint, melancholy smile shows on his face. "You be careful yourself and keep them safe."

"We will," Von says reassuringly. "We are on alert now that these guys have shown us their true colors."

Von walks away a few feet, stops, and turns back toward Jensen.

"Oh, by the way, you don't have to worry about Senior Master Sergeant Wright anymore."

"Why do you say that?" Jensen inquires, cocking his head in surprise.

"He's been under surveillance for a while now. Apparently there were multiple calls made from his office to D.C., so we asked ourselves why an enlisted man needs to make so many calls to D.C., as well as receive them. It seems he has been talking to a Director Clayborn, a lot."

Jensen raises his eyebrows and waits for Von to finish.

"Clayborn is the director of M.I.S.S." Von adds.

"What are you saying? That Wright is working for M.I.S.S?"

"It sure looks like he is," Von continues. "We're not sure, but after what's been happening around here, we found it prudent to relieve him of his position, at least until we find out why he's in contact with M.I.S.S. so much. Hey, it could be nothing, but you know us, everyone's a suspect. Besides, no one knows anything about this M.I.S.S. agency. Do they even have federal jurisdiction? We plan to find out. I'm just telling you about this because of the encounter you had earlier with him."

Jensen displays a look of surprise as Von raises his hands in a surrender gesture.

"Hey, we are the OSI, we know everything," he says. "Anyway, he won't be bothering you about today's incident. Go home, have a drink, relax. I know it will be hard. Taking a life is not what we want to do, but it's what we're trained for. You did your duty. You and your men did their duty. You protected the people you're supposed to protect. I'm sorry I can't tell you more of what's happening, but trust me, it will all work out."

Agent Von walks no more than ten feet away when he sees another unmarked government vehicle approach. He watches as two men exit. They're not FBI, not detectives, and certainly not OSI. They could only be M.I.S.S.

"Was wondering when they would show up," Von mumbles to himself.

Von looks beyond the vehicle and sees two more government vehicles pull up. One he doesn't recognize, the other he does. It belongs to his commander, Colonel Grayson. Both vehicles stop, and the commander and another OSI agent get out of the first car to meet with three men who exit the second car. They confer for a few seconds and then walk toward the crime scene. Von watches as an M.I.S.S. agent wearing sunglasses approaches him.

"Who's in charge here?" the M.I.S.S. agent demands.

"Sunglasses? Really, at night?" Von asks aloud.

The agent ignores the remark. Von points to the OSI commander and the group of men with him.

"Well, now that they're here, I would say it's them," Von says.

The M.I.S.S. agents turn to see who Von is pointing at. They stand still as the commander and OSI Agent Stanton come toward them. Following the commander are three other men, all wearing suits, whom they assume to be FBI. The group walks right past the M.I.S.S. agents and straight to Agent Von.

"Agent Von, SITREP," the commander orders.

"Sir, I just arrived myself and have only talked to Staff Sergeant Jensen, one of the SPs, and…"

"Excuse me!" the M.I.S.S. agent with sunglasses breaks in, storming up to the group. "I asked, who is in charge here?"

Colonel Grayson forces a good-natured smile and turns to face the man.

"Well, technically there are a few of us in charge, multi-jurisdictional you see," Grayson says calmly. "The sheriff over there, along with his detectives, are processing most of the crime scene since it involved civilians and it's his county. I oversee the military portion of the investigation because air force members were involved.

"These fine men here," Grayson gestures to the three men in suits, "are with the FBI, so they're in charge of the entire scene because the air force is a branch of the federal government and two of the deceased are quasi-federal agents. That answer your question?"

The man with the sunglasses stands as tall as he can in an attempt to display dominance.

"Well, I am Special Agent in charge of M.I.S.S." he says. "As of right now, I'm taking control of this investigation. What I need from you and your men is to gather the two female witnesses and all the personnel involved in the shooting, especially those who are responsible for the deaths of our two agents. After that, I want them handed over to me for transport to our location for in-depth interviews..."

Colonel Grayson moves quickly into the M.I.S.S. agent's personal space and hovers over him. The agent stops talking and stands with his mouth open, not finishing his sentence.

"Oh, I'm sorry, were you trying to order me, the sheriff's department, and the FBI around?" Grayson asks, not expecting an answer.

The M.I.S.S. agent's face becomes red with anger.

"Listen here, whoever you are. This is an M.I.S.S. investigation," the agent claims. "Those were my men who were investigating a possible treasonous act by the two women in question."

Col. Grayson catches a glimpse of the three smirking FBI agents.

"Nobody here recognizes your authority," Grayson begins. "We don't even know what M.I.S.S. is. I know you report to a Director Clayborn, who reports directly to Senator Minten. But that's all we know, which means you don't even get to play in this sandbox. In fact, I think we need to detain you for interference of this investigation, as well as unauthorized surveillance, trespassing, firearm violations, attempted kidnapping, sedition, and whatever else we can find on you. Let's let everyone get in on the fun. Agent Von, why don't you have that security police staff sergeant, what's his name?"

"Staff Sergeant Jensen, sir."

"Yes, Staff Sergeant Jensen," Grayson continues. "Have him, along with yourself and a sheriff's deputy handcuff this man and his partner, and take them to the base for safekeeping."

"Be glad to, sir," Von smiles. "What about the previous assignment concerning the two women?"

"Thank you, almost forgot," Grayson says. "Yes, after you get the men together to take these um, persons in, go ahead and finish that assignment. I'll let the sheriff know we're taking the young ladies with us. Thanks for reminding me."

The M.I.S.S. agent with the sunglasses reaches inside his coat, but that's as far as he gets before two of the FBI agents quickly grab and disarmed him.

"Now son, that was a stupid thing to do," Grayson says. "Now I have to add attempted murder to your list of stupidity."

Chapter 26

Chief Black has been showing Bill and Nora around the Bank offices and answering questions as best he can. The three walk into General Lucas's office in time to see him place his phone back in the cradle. The general looks up at them with a grave expression.

"What is it, sir?" the chief asks.

"That was Colonel Grayson, the OSI commander," Gen. Lucas replies. "There's been an incident at Nora's home."

Nora's eyes grow wide and concern comes over her face.

"Are Skylar and Ivy okay? What happened? Tell me!"

"I'm sorry, I should have worded that better. Yes, yes, they are safe," the general answers. "In fact, they're on their way here now. Agents Von and Beltrane are escorting them, so you know they're in good hands."

"Christ almighty, this just keeps getting better and better," Nora says, breathing an exasperated sigh of relief and plopping into a chair.

Bill sits next to her and places a hand on her shoulder for reassurance, while the chief takes the chair in front of the general's desk to await details of what happened.

"The two M.I.S.S. agents who were following Skylar and Ivy were released from custody, but the apprehending NCO was wary of them," Gen. Lucas explains. "So he, along with a few of his fellow SPs, decided to watch your home. Turns out the NCO has good instincts. Von and Beltrane were on their way to pick up Skylar and Ivy and bring them here. However, the two M.I.S.S. agents got there first, posed as Von and Beltrane, and tried to get Skylar and Ivy to go with them. The sergeant and others from his team confronted them and additional M.I.S.S. agents outside the house, and shots were fired."

Bill perks up at that statement and Nora utters a small gasp.

"Did anyone get hurt, General?" she asks. "Who is the NCO, and the others?"

"Yes, a few people were hurt, but not your sister or Ivy," the general responds. "They are fine and on their way here. Two M.I.S.S. agents were killed, another injured, and one more arrested. Unfortunately, one SP was killed and another is in the hospital with a serious gunshot wound. The NCO is Staff Sergeant Charles Jensen, and he is okay. Why, do you know him?"

"Yes, we do," Nora replies. "What about the other SPs?"

"Sergeant Jack Spellman was shot and killed," the general answers, checking his notes. "Airman First Class Billy Morgan was shot in the shoulder and is in serious, but not life-threatening condition. When it was over and the local and base authorities had arrived, two M.I.S.S. agents attempted to take control of the scene and get their hands on Skylar and Ivy."

"What happened then?" Bill interjects.

"Colonel Grayson had them apprehended," the general answers with a smile. "They are now guests of the security police hospitality house."

"Are Skylar and Ivy really okay?" Nora asks. "How long until they get here?"

"I'm sure they're shaken up a bit, but they really are okay," the general replies. "They should be here in less than an hour. Don't worry, you can meet them when they arrive and help as they go through processing."

"Thank you, General." Nora replies, genuinely pleased.

"General, Chief, when do you think Clio will be ready to bring those men back?" Bill asks, changing the subject.

The general looks to the chief, gesturing that he should answer.

"I'm not positive, but it shouldn't be too much longer," the chief replies. "Sometime tomorrow, mid-morning maybe."

"We might as well go down to the chow hall and get something to eat while we wait for Skylar and Ivy to arrive," the general says. "It's on me."

***

An announcement comes over the PA system that Skylar and Ivy have arrived. The general waves an SP over to their table in the chow hall and instructs him to escort Nora to meet her friends and help with entry processing.

"Um, sir?" the chief says. "It might go smoother if I go with her."

"You're probably right," agrees Gen. Lucas as he motions for the chief and Nora to follow the SP out of the chow hall.

Bill stirs the remaining food around on his plate, catching the attention of the general.

"Food not to your liking, Bill?" the general asks.

"No, no. It's not bad," Bill smiles. "I thought it would be horrible, but it isn't."

"That's because we are the Bank," Gen. Lucas says proudly. "We only get the best services personnel in the air force, next to Air Force One. You're just lucky the army isn't running this project, or worse yet, the marines."

Both men chuckle at the general's obvious bias.

"What now, General?" Bill asks. "I mean, what happens when you bring those men back? They can't go back to normal duties, can they? There's got to be some psychological damage, as well as physical injuries to some of them. You're not going to make them disappear, are you?"

Bill's reporter brain has kicked in. He can't help it. He's trained to see a boogeyman behind every tree; big brother lurking around every corner; corporate greed playing a role in important decisions. His skeptical mind begins to see a conspiracy forming.

"Bill, Bill," the general says.

"Sorry, General, my training gets the best of me sometimes."

"Well, we need people like you asking questions. I don't always agree with the press, but you are a necessary evil," the general says with a sly grin.

"Okay, you got me," Bill replies. "But, seriously, what is going to happen to them?"

The general takes a sip of coffee and sits back, eyeing the reporter and contemplating the appropriate response.

"Bill, I need you to trust me on this," he says after a brief pause. "Nothing unwarranted is going to happen to those men when they return. They are pioneers and heroes. I will do everything in my power to ensure they are taken care of. They will be allowed to return to active duty. Not immediately, mind you, but sometime in the future if they so wish. They'll be compensated for their sacrifices. As we told you, we did not want to do it this way, so I have a moral obligation to look out for them when they return. I can't tell you what we will do to help return them to the real world.

"You have been given a free pass on things that no other reporter will ever be allowed to see. Having said that, I cannot tell you everything. Some parts are highly classified."

"Fair enough, General," Bill responds. "I do thank you for the opportunity you have given me."

The two men finish their coffee and head back to the general's office to await Skylar and Ivy's arrival. General Lucas knows he will have to break the bad news to the reporter concerning his article. There is no way the world can know of the Clio project. Not now, at least. That much is certain.

***

Skylar and Ivy are awestruck and still excited about their helicopter ride to the base as they enter the Bank complex. Nora sees the expression on the girls' faces and remembers the feeling. Skylar breaks into a wide smile when she sees Nora standing near the first checkpoint.

"Nora!" Ivy squeals, breaking into a run with Skylar in tow.

The three exchange enthusiastic hugs, but Skylar and Ivy notice Nora's solemn demeanor.

"What is it, Nora?" a worried Skylar asks.

"I'll tell you both in a little while," Nora answers. "They need to get you processed and inside before we talk. I'm sorry, but we must do this first."

Skylar and Ivy don't press the issue, although they obviously want to know more. Chief Black listens to their conversation from a few steps away and takes Nora's comment about going through processing as his cue to join them.

"Skylar, Ivy, meet Chief Master Sergeant Joe Black," Nora says. "He is a vital part of this operation and has been treating Bill and me very well. Once you're cleared, we'll explain everything we can."

"Nice to meet you, ladies," the chief says, shaking their hands. "Nora has talked a lot about both of you."

"All good, I hope," Ivy replies with one of her patented smiles.

"All good," the chief confirms with a reassuring smile of his own before motioning for a guard to take the women to the processing area.

"Ladies, please follow this SP and he will escort you through processing," he says. "Nora can go with you."

The chief instructs the SP to ensure the women are processed expediently.

"If any questions arise or anyone tries to delay things, they will need to talk to the general," he tells the SP. "And they do not want to talk to the general, if you catch my drift."

"Yes, sir. Understood," the SP replies.

The women complete processing in about thirty minutes and the SP escorts them to Shelly's desk outside the general's office. They are eager to rejoin Nora and find out what was weighing so heavily on her mind.

"Hello, ladies. My name is Shelly and I am General Lucas's assistant," Shelly says. "Can I get you something to eat or drink?"

"No, we just want to find out what's going on," Ivy says.

"Let me see if I can bring you inside," Shelly replies.

Shelly buzzes the general to let him know the women have arrived.

"That's great, Shelly," General Lucas says. "Show them right in."

Shelly opens the door to the interior office and the women see the chief and Bill standing alongside General Lucas. Chief Black makes the introductions.

"Skylar, Ivy, this is Major General Lucas, commander of this operation," the chief announces.

"I'm so glad to meet you," the general says, walking around his desk to shake hands with the new arrivals. "I'm also glad that both of you are safe. My apologies for the situation you were placed in, and I want you to know we are looking into it. There will be hell to pay."

Nora clears her throat to attract the attention of everyone in the room.

"General, you won't mind if I use your office to speak with my sister and Ivy alone, would you?" she asks.

It takes the general a second to realize why Nora is making this request.

"No, no. Of course not," he replies. "Bill and Chief Black, please come with me and we'll get some coffee. When you're finished, tell Shelly and she will let us know."

Chief Black holds the door open for the general and Bill. He follows behind while giving Nora a cheerless smile and closing the door behind him.

Nora pulls up a chair and sits down, motioning for an apprehensive Skylar and Ivy to do the same. Nora studies her hands, trying to figure out the best way to tell them about Eric and the others. She takes a deep breath, releases it, and looks them both in the eyes.

"Ivy, Skylar, I am so sorry," Nora begins. "Before I explain what has happened, I have bad news."

Nora looks at Ivy and reaches for her hands. Ivy pulls back, scared.

"It's Eric, isn't it? He's dead," she says, emotion already overcoming her before she hears the answer.

"I'm so sorry, Ivy," Nora says. "God, I am so sorry."

"I knew it. I told you he was dead. God dammit, I told you. That night I had the premonition. God dammit!" Ivy says, breaking into tears.

Skylar and Nora go to Ivy as she sobs uncontrollably, her tears dampening their clothes as they fall from her checks to their shoulders. The three stay that way for several minutes, shaking with emotion until Ivy makes a last sniffing sound and sits up straight. Nora grabs some tissues off the general's desk and gives them to her.

"Who else?" Skylar asks, looking sorrowfully at Nora. "Who else is gone?"

Nora grabs her sister's hands and takes another deep breath before answering.

"Ray and Scott are all right, for now. Ricky and Alex are gone. Wally and Steve are hurt. The rest are okay," she says.

It takes a few minutes for Ivy and Skylar to gain their composure. Finally, Nora stands up as a signal that the time has come to reunite with General Lucas, Chief Black, and Bill.

"Ivy, are you going to be okay?" she asks.

Ivy looks wrung out and despondent, but she is able to muster a small nod.

"Okay, I'll have Shelly get the guys back in here," Nora says.

The three men come back into the room a few minutes later, each casting a wary glance at Ivy as they enter.

"Miss McKnight, I want you to know how sorry we are for your loss," General Lucas begins. "I know that doesn't mean much coming from us, but please believe me when I say we are angry about this, too. I know I'm not as upset as you must be, but we do feel the loss. I don't know how much Nora has told you."

"Nothing yet, General," Skylar speaks up angrily, "other than you got some of our friends killed."

"Skylar!" Nora exclaims. "The general didn't get them killed. Let us explain. Believe me, I was spitting nails when I first arrived and wanted nothing more than to strangle both these men. But after being here for a while and seeing what they're trying to do, working to get the men back and understanding what happened in the first place, I've decided they are earnest in what they are telling me. Please, give them a chance to explain."

Skylar trusts her older sister and nods in acceptance. Ivy is silent, hanging her head and dabbing her tears with a tissue.

"Nora, you can explain what is going on if you'd like," the general says in what he hopes is a comforting tone.

"Girls, come here," Nora says, walking to the window that overlooks the control room.

Skylar stands and joins her at the window, but Ivy stays seated.

"Come on Ivy," Skylar says softly, bending down to place a hand on her friend's slumped shoulders. "You need to know. Come on."

Skylar helps Ivy stand and they walk the short distance to where Nora is waiting. They can immediately see the giant screen, and as they move closer, the commotion going on in the control room below comes into view. It is an awesome sight, shocking in its complexity and impressive in its scope.

Nora fills them in about the time machine and Chief Black's role in its development. Skylar and Ivy are at the same time astonished and unbelieving.

"Keep your eyes on the screen," Nora says, directing their gaze to the far wall. "What we're seeing is a video image being sent by a small, remote-controlled helicopter hovering over the area where our guys are."

The general calls the control room and instructs Major Hess to switch the view. A few seconds later, the screen shows a small group of security policemen milling around a Duck. Skylar looks at Nora, then everyone else in the room.

"So, you're telling me we are looking at them in the year 1862? Bullshit," Skylar says, shaking her head and pursing her lips. "It's a trick, Nora. Come on, right?"

"No, it's really happening," Nora responds. "I even recorded a message to them on a cassette tape that they sent to the guys. I watched the tape vanish and then show up where they are. I even watched as they listened to it."

"If that's true, then I want to speak with Ray," Skylar demands.

"I'm sorry, Miss Miller," General Lucas explains, "but we can only receive audio from the men at this point, not transmit to them. That's why we had to use the cassette tape."

"Why not?" she challenges.

"We have no idea," the chief interjects. "It's something we have to work on, but for right now that's all we have."

"So, what happens next?" Skylar inquires.

"They are working on the time machine right now," Nora replies. "It has a few problems they are fixing. Chief Black says it will be ready, what, mid-morning today maybe?"

"Yes, sometime later this morning," the chief confirms.

After a few more questions, the general suggests passing the time by getting something to eat and drink in the chow hall. It will be several hours before Clio is ready, and some rest will do them good.

Ivy, especially, needs to shut down for few hours. She picks at her food and says little as Nora, Skylar, and Bill discuss the incredible situation in which they find themselves.

Once they are finished, an SP escorts them to living quarters where they can rest and freshen up for what promises to be another high-stress day. The morning will arrive soon enough, and everyone wants to be ready for whatever fate awaits them and the men.

Chapter 27

Senator Minten sits in his limousine, car-phone to his ear as he talks with M.I.S.S. Director Clayborn.

"Do you have everyone we need?" Minten asks, closing his eyes as he listens to Clayborn's response. "I don't care what it takes. Just get the men ready, equipped, and on the plane."

Clayborn's answer obviously does not sit well with the senator as he suddenly leans forward in anger.

"No, I don't want you talking to the base commander, you idiot!" Minten says, his voice rising in volume. "He would inform General Lucas of our arrival and that's not what I want. We are going to go in as if it's a surprise inspection from me and move in on the Bank. I want this to go like clockwork. Like *The Taking of Pelham One Two Three*."

Minten pulls the phone from his ear and looks at it with disgust before ripping into Clayborn again.

"*The Taking of Pelham...* It's a movie! Never mind, you fool."

Minten takes a deep breath and continues.

"We go in with smiles and pleasantries, all friendly and cordial. Then once inside the Bank, Wham! We take over. I can't wait to see the look on Lucas's face when I go strolling into his office, informing him I am relieving him of his post. He'll shit! I can't wait."

Minten listens to Clayborn briefly before cutting him off.

"I don't care what you fucking think, you imbecile. Do what you're told. When I arrive at Andrews, you had better have the plane loaded and everyone ready. No excuses or your ass is grass. Do you understand me? Now quit wasting my time and get to work."

Minten hangs up the phone and complains aloud, "Good grief, where do I find such incompetency?"

"Did you ask me something, sir?" the driver asks, looking in the rearview mirror.

"Oh, you think I was asking you for an opinion? Well, I wasn't," Minten sneers. "Now shut your pie hole, pay attention to the road, and get me to the fucking base. Jeez, again incompetency."

Minten pushes the button to close the tinted glass partition that separates him from the driver.

The car arrives at the airfield after sunrise and a master sergeant from base operations opens Minten's door. The senator exits and does not acknowledge the sergeant's presence. The sergeant shuts the door and hurries ahead to open the door to the base operations building. Minten hurries through the terminal and opens the door leading to the tarmac, not waiting for the NCO to do it for him.

"Incompetent boobs," Minten mumbles as he storms across the tarmac to the waiting aircraft and Director Clayborn.

"Everything ready?" Minten asks.

"Yes, sir," Clayborn replies. "We should have ample men to get the operation underway."

"Don't be so dramatic, Clayborn. Operation underway. Just say you have sufficient men to get the job done. And you had better, or you will hate to see me again."

"Uh, sir... Am I not going with you?" Clayborn asks.

Minten stops at the bottom of the passenger stairway and looks at Clayborn like he is an insect.

"You're kidding right? You've got to be kidding. I want men there to run this operation. Real men. Now go back to your office and play director and direct something. Hell, go back to your office and play with yourself for all I care. This had better go well or...”

He concludes by sliding his finger across his throat in a slicing movement.

Clayborn stares at the senator as he walks up the stairs and disappears into the jet.

“We’ll see about that, you piece of shit,” Clayborn says under his breath as he throws a halfhearted salute toward the aircraft. “Yeah, we’ll see all right. Fuck you!”

Clayborn turns and storms back toward base operations as an idea begins forming in his head.

***

Senator Minten’s aircraft arrives fifty minutes later at Pope AFB, North Carolina. It taxis and comes to a halt in front of base operations. Maintenance crews rush out to secure the aircraft, placing chocks on the tires and immediately beginning the refuel. Security police move into position around the aircraft. General Beck, the base commander, and other personnel are at the bottom of the stairway waiting for the doors to open.

Beck is somewhat concerned about this unscheduled visit. He doesn’t like it when politicians show up unannounced. It means they are up to something designed to make themselves look good and can only make him, his personnel, and the base look bad.

“This is some bad juju,” Beck thinks.

The aircraft door opens and Minten steps out, all smiles as he sees the entourage waiting for him at the bottom of the stairway. The general smiles back and both men read each other perfectly. These are the smiles of professional politicians, getting ready to see whose is bigger. But first they must put on the show for the minions. The senator walks down the stairs with his hand extended.

“General Beck, great to see you,” Minten says in an overly friendly tone. “Sorry for the unannounced arrival, but something important arose. Time sensitive, you might say. We didn’t have the opportunity to inform you we would be here until airborne. Again, my deepest apologies.”

“Not a problem, Senator Minten. Always glad to have our civilian leadership stop by. Keeps us on our toes. We are here at your pleasure, sir. Now if you'll come with me?"

The general releases Minten's hand and gestures for the senator to take the lead as they walk toward the base operations building.

"General Beck, can we speak privately for a minute?" Minten says out of the corner of his mouth.

The general's smile never wavers.

"Of course, sir. Why don't we step into base ops and find a room. Quieter there, away from the flight line noise and prying ears."

"That's fine, General," Minten replies. "Please lead the way."

Beck does as he is instructed and walks into base operations. The personnel inside stand to attention until the general waves them off. He points to a door leading to a small conference room, telling his escort to wait until he returns as he and Minten step inside.

Minten walks to the far side of the conference room and gazes out the window. Clasping his hands behind his back, he studies the aircraft that just delivered him to the base and watches his M.I.S.S. agents unloading equipment and gear.

"General Beck, again I'm sorry for the intrusion," Minten begins. "Don't worry, I'm not here to conduct any inspection or look at your soldiers. No tour, no escorts needed. In fact, I only need one thing from you."

Beck winces internally at Minten's reference to the base personnel as soldiers rather than the airmen he knows them to be, but he will not give this power-hungry mongrel the satisfaction of a reaction. Minten turns to eye the general, who is patiently waiting for this blowhard politician to get to the point, and purses his lips in disappointment when he does not receive the reaction he was hoping for.

"As I said, sir, we're here at your pleasure," Beck replies, in complete control of his emotions. "What can I do for you?"

"That's the attitude I like, General. I guess that's why you are a general. You know where your bread is buttered," Minten says as he struts across the room, purposefully not paying attention to the general.

The senator believes it's best to use confident body language to let others know he's in charge. Let the general know he's the person who needs to jump when you say so. Make him wonder what you're after.

"I assume you are aware of the Bank," Minten states, finally facing General Beck.

"Yes, sir, along with the deputy base commander, OSI commander, chief of security police, and of course those assigned to the facility. No one else is privy to what is out there."

"Good, good," Minten nods. "It's always a pleasure to know that security is a priority with you and your people. You are also aware that I am essentially in charge of this program? It's my baby, so to speak."

Minten smiles at his own quip and the general returns the smile, as required.

"I know that you have some influence over the program, but I did not know you are in charge," Beck says. "I was under the impression General Lucas is in charge, with a civilian committee oversight."

Minten's face changes from a smiling politician to the devil incarnate, if only for a split second. The general is taken aback, thinking he must have misread the senator. When he looks again, Minten's friendly, though forced smile has returned.

"No, General Beck. I am in charge. That's why I'm here. This is not a surprise inspection on you. It's a surprise inspection on the Bank."

Beck is confused. Why would there be an inspection on a top-secret facility from a senator? This is not right. But then, there are things he is not made aware of and details for which he does not have clearance. He knows about the secret facility on the base, but he doesn't know what goes on in there. He's heard stories of an offshoot of Area 51, Roswell, and other rumors. This is expected when anything secret is involved. Military personnel gossip and speculate on everything they are not privy to. The senator must be in charge, Beck reasons. Why else would he be here?

Minten clears his throat, interrupting the general's thoughts.

"Are you listening, General?"

"Yes, sir. Yes I am."

"I will need your security police tactical team," Minten demands. "What do you call them?"

"That would be the TNT," Beck replies, concerned about where the conversation is headed. "Stands for Tactical Neutralization Team."

"Yes, fine, I will need them. They will report to the leader of the M.I.S.S. team. They are unloading their equipment now. My men, along with your TNT guys, will assist on the inspection."

"Senator Minten," Beck interrupts. "The TNT is used for emergencies. They are trained for hostage situations, barricaded suspects. They are the equivalent of the civilian SWAT. They aren't trained to conduct inspections."

"They are trained to protect people, are they not? Well, that's why I want them. I need them to cover my guys while here. This will give them some on-the-job training. Please don't worry, General. It will be fine and I'm sure they will enjoy it."

"Yes, sir. Whatever you want."

"Yes, General, that's what I want," Minten says with a cocky smirk. "Also, my guys will need a place to set up, a base of operations you might say. Do you have anything available?"

"I'm sure I can find something for you," Beck responds. "Now, if that's all, I will get your team together and direct them to the location."

"Yes, General Beck. I am through. But I need you available in case I require something else."

"Yes, sir," Beck replies as he turns to leave the room.

The general walks toward the ops desk to use the phone. The bad feelings that cropped up during his conversation with the senator have not gone away. They have only intensified. There is something fishy happening here, and he doesn't like it.

"Cry 'Havoc!', and let slip the dogs of war."

- Mark Antony in William Shakespeare's *Julius Caesar*

Chapter 28

"I am happy to confirm that Clio is up and running!"

The control room erupts in cheers at Chief Black's announcement. The tension among the Clio project's technicians was palpable as the chief personally conducted a quality control inspection of the entire system. Now Clio is ready to bring the men home.

"That's great news, Chief. When do we start?" General Lucas asks from the phone in his office. His words are punctuated with a level of joy normally reserved for great victories.

"Once the power cells are fully charged, we'll be ready," Chief Black replies. "We should be able to start within two hours. My best guess would be around 0945."

"I'll inform our guests. They should be up by now and ready to come back in here," the general says. "I must notify the Bank Council, too. You know, I'm surprised they haven't been in here making our lives miserable. Well, we shouldn't look a gift horse in the mouth, I guess."

"Yes, sir," the chief agrees. "I'll stay here and monitor everything myself this time. I'm not leaving anything to chance, especially after what happened last time."

General Lucas looks at the chief, who is standing below him in the control room. He nods and both men hang up their phones. Shelly is delighted at the news as well and asks the general if he would like her to contact the guests.

"Always one step ahead of me, aren't you?" he smiles.

"That's why you pay me the big bucks," Shelly replies with mischief in her voice.

"After you inform our guests, please contact the Bank," the general continues. "Let me know when you have them on the line. I want to tell them about this myself."

***

Nora, Skylar, Ivy, and Bill are in the chow hall, quietly having breakfast and drinking coffee.

"You think we should go back up to the office now?" Skylar asks. "We should hear something soon."

"We can't just go marching up there," Nora scolds. "The general said he'd let us know when they're ready for us."

No sooner had she spoken than a runner came in and informed their security police escort to bring the guests to the general's office.

"Psychic now, are we Skylar?" Ivy asks.

Ivy seems much better this morning. A few hours' sleep did her good. She is still grieving over Eric, but knows she has to carry on for the others. She will deal with the pain later once the men are home.

The SP escorts the group to Shelly's office, and once inside the general's office they can see something is happening. The general is smiling and the control room is busier than it was the night before.

"Tell me Clio is ready to go," Nora says, eyeing General Lucas.

"She's ready to go," the general replies to a joyous response from his guests.

"When do we start?" Skylar asks after the group calms down.

"We still have a few things to do," the general replies, checking the clock on the wall. "We should be able to start the process around 0945. The chief is charging the power cells and running final checks. He wants everything perfect this time."

The group moves over to the window to watch the activity below, the three women holding hands.

***

"Major Hess?" the technician operating the helicam calls out.

"What is it, Lieutenant Reynolds?" Hess responds, leaning over the technician's shoulder to look at his monitor.

"Sir, we may have a situation here. I've picked up something and you should see it," Reynolds states. "I was monitoring Hendricks Hill and saw a large force of Confederate troops massing west of the town. They aren't moving; looks like they're going to bivouac for now. They're probably there to secure the area around the town."

The major looks on quizzically.

"But that's not what concerns me," Reynolds continues. "I flew a little higher and spotted smoke southwest of the town. I flew even higher and toward the smoke. It's coming from numerous campfires being extinguished. Sir, it's a whole battalion of Confederate soldiers."

"Put it on screen," Major Hess says with alarm.

The screen switches from an overview of the SPs to a view showing hundreds of Confederate soldiers. They are breaking camp and most of them are already in columns, ready to march.

"Where the hell did they come from?" Hess demands. "Never mind, where are they going?"

"They will run right into the SP encampment if they march the direction they are facing, sir," answers the lieutenant.

"Dammit!" Hess mumbles as he picks up the phone to the general's office.

General Lucas and everyone in his office can see what is on the screen. The general is about to call Major Hess when his phone buzzes. He snatches up the handset.

"What are we seeing, Major?"

The general's face remains neutral as he listens to Hess explain what is happening.

"All right, Major. Get the chief up here right away," Lucas orders. "Don't let him stonewall you. Tell him what's happening and that I need him here, now."

"Yes, sir."

The general hangs up the phone and is engrossed in thought when he notices the others staring at him. He has forgotten they are even in the room.

"Oh, I apologize," he says. "What you are seeing is a battalion-sized Confederate force breaking camp. They are starting their march, and as our luck would have it, they are heading straight for our boys."

Everyone begins asking questions at once and the general raises his hands to silence them.

"Before you get worked up, remember we told the guys to follow the helicam if it starts to move away," he reminds them. "We will do just that and lead them in the other direction. No problem."

"Are you sure they're headed for our guys, General?" Nora asks.

"Not positive, but I'd rather the men move away just in case. Better safe than sorry, right?"

***

Senator Minten is in the large conference room with his M.I.S.S. team, which is geared up and ready to move out. The air force TNT men also are there, but confused as to their assignment. The lieutenant in charge of the TNT team is not certain he and his men should be here. This isn't what they are trained for, but orders are orders. The senator sees his concerned look and goes over to him, putting on his best fake smile.

"Lieutenant, I'm glad you and your team could join us," Minten says. "I'm sure you are wondering why we asked for you. Well, this is going to be a very special inspection of the Bank facility."

The TNT lieutenant gives him a puzzled look. He has never heard of the Bank. The senator recognizes this and realizes he has to change his tactics.

"I'm sorry, that's what we call the facility we are going to inspect. It's a classified area," Minten says with a dismissive wave of his hand. "You don't need the details, as I'm sure you and your team aren't cleared anyway. Your team is to remain outside the facility and secure it after I go inside to inspect. You will keep anyone from coming in after us, no matter who or what. Is that understood?"

The lieutenant looks at Minten and wants to ask questions, but he thinks better of it. If he had more time in service, more experience, he would feel more freedom to ask. But as a 2nd lieutenant, he does not, so he keeps his mouth shut.

The senator takes the lieutenant's silence as confirmation that he understands the senator's order.

"Good, now let's get moving," Minten says to the M.I.S.S. team as he walks out the door.

The group climbs into several vehicles for the short drive to the Bank. They pull up to the gate manned by two SPs, upon which the senator exits his vehicle and approaches, all smiles.

"Good morning, gentlemen. I'm Senator Herbert Minten. I'm in charge of this facility and we are here on a surprise inspection."

The two SPs look at each other and the senior airman speaks up: "Sir, we know who you are, but we have no word on an inspection."

"Well, of course not. It's a surprise inspection," Minten replies with a wide smile. "Now, if you check my credentials, you will see I have the authority to enter this facility."

The SPs check the senator's credential and hand it back to him.

"Sir, you are cleared to enter, but your team does not have authorization," the airman states.

"They have authorization on my say-so," Minten retorts, clearly losing patience. "They are my inspection team and they will be coming inside with me. Do you understand?"

"Sir, I'll have to get clearance for this," the airman replies as he starts toward the phone.

"Stop right there, son," Minten commands.

The senator's condescending attitude rubs the SP the wrong way. Clenching his teeth, the SP turns around and walks back toward his demanding visitor.

"Senator Minten, I happily refer to you by your title as you expect. I have a title as well. I am a senior airman, so please refer to me by my rank or designation of airman. Not 'son.' Now I need to get clearance before you or your team are allowed entry."

With that, he turns back around and heads toward the gate shack.

Minten nearly blows a gasket. Who does this child think he is? He is about to launch into a tirade when the 2nd lieutenant steps up to intervene.

"If I may, sir?" he asks the stunned senator.

"Uh, why yes, be my guest." Minten stammers.

"Airman?"

The senior airman stops and turns to see who has addressed him.

"Yes, sir?" he responds with a salute.

"Listen, this was cleared by the base commander. Here's the authorization," the lieutenant explains, reaching into his vest pocket and pulling out a sheet of paper. "If you call this extension, it will connect you to the general's office. He will tell you to let us in. This is a surprise inspection after all."

The senior airman studies the form and goes into the gate shack to call the number. After a brief conversation, he hangs up the phone and instructs the other SP to open the gate for the senator's group. The base commander's office has approved their entry, and the senior airman is in the clear. He has done his job.

The turn of events stuns the senator. How in the hell does this squeaky-clean 2nd lieutenant have an authorization form for them to enter?

"Oh well," he thinks. "Doesn't matter. We're on our way in now. Lucas, your ass is mine."

He almost giggles, but catches himself.

***

After seeing the senator off, M.I.S.S. Director Clayborn goes back to his office and considers what he should do next. Fighting with his conscience, he finally makes a decision. He makes several calls to members of the Bank Council and then one more to General Beck, the base commander.

The general is not shocked by what Clayborn tells him, but he is concerned he might not have time to do anything about it. He already cleared Minten and his team for entry into the Bank some time ago.

Beck does leave instructions with the TNT leader to keep him informed of any deviation of an inspection from the senator and his M.I.S.S. team. Now he can only wait and hope he won't hear from him.

Chapter 29

Kriger is giving Rees an update on Green's concussion symptoms and a still-woozy Harris as they stand near the Duck. Harris has woken up and is improving, but still is not feeling 100 percent. Kriger has higher hopes for him now that he has gotten some fluids down as well as part of a candy bar.

Rees runs his hands over his face and feels his days-old stubble as he half-heartedly listens to Kriger's report. He looks at the others and sees that everyone is getting a little ratty as well, not to mention being out of their salty, sweat-laden regulations. He smiles at that and thinks, "Fuck 'em."

"What?" Kriger asks.

Rees realizes he must have said that out loud.

"Uh, nothing," he replies. "How's our Union boy doing?"

"He's not a problem. Just sits there quietly and eats," Kriger says. "He told us he hasn't had this much food since leaving home, and certainly not this type. The boy likes the C-rations, especially the fruit."

"Just make sure he doesn't eat all the apricots," Rees smiles and points at himself. "Mine, my friend. All mine."

Kriger chuckles, but before he can say anything else they are interrupted by Shepard, who is yelling and pointing to the sky.

"Hey, y'all, look at that!" Shepard says. "The little helicopter is going ape-shit."

The men look to where Shepard is pointing and see the helicam is bobbing up and down, back and forth, and spinning.

"I guess they want our attention," Bouvier observes.

The helicam flies away, almost out of sight, and then returns.

"Oh shit," Rees says and looks at Bouvier, who also understands.

"Oh shit is right," Bouvier replies and then raises his voice for the group to hear. "Everybody! Grab your things and let's get moving. Remember what the general said. If there is trouble heading our way, the copter will lead us away from it. Now get moving!"

"What about Green and Harris?" Kriger asks.

"I'm good to go, Sarge," Harris says with the most energy he has displayed since his injury.

He quickly sits up, but still looks a little out of it.

"I feel a lot better and I don't want to be a burden," he adds.

"If that's true, then I want you to watch over Green," Rees says. "We'll put him in the Duck and secure him the best we can. It might get bumpy, but we have no choice."

Harris agrees to the assignment and Kriger helps him to his feet. Tucker and Nionee get Green into the Duck, and Kriger helps Harris inside. Kriger follows and begins arranging a few sleeping bags on the floor, one on top of the other. He uses a rope to secure Green inside his sleeping bag, and then cuts a blanket into a makeshift neck support for Green's head.

"Not sure if this will work, but at least it should keep his head from jostling around," Kriger explains.

"What about Corporal O'Toole, the Union soldier?" Bouvier asks as he walks over to Rees. "You think we should let him go?"

"I don't know," Rees responds, quickly running through possible scenarios in his head. "He might be useful if we come across more of his buddies. We might need him as a bargaining chip."

O'Toole anxiously listens to Rees and Bouvier, looking from one to the other.

"If you let me go, I won't say anything about where you are. Honest," he says.

"Sorry, son. You're coming with us," Rees replies. "We won't hurt you, but you might be needed. C'mon, let's get you in the Duck. Don't do anything dumb and we'll see about letting you go later."

O'Toole is disappointed, but nods his understanding and they help him into the Duck.

The rest of the men are busy grabbing and stowing equipment, making sure nothing is left behind for the Civil War troops to find. After all the equipment is secured, they congregate next to the Duck.

"I'll take the Jeep with Shepard, Tosseti, and Tucker," Rees says. "The rest of you in the Duck. McGuire, you drive, and Montoya, you get on the sixty. Kriger and Nionee, you keep a watch out the rear."

The men acknowledge their assignments and gather their gear. Rees places his pot helmet back on his head and shrugs into the heavy, olive drab flak jacket. The jacket isn't worth a hill of beans in stopping much more than a slow-moving piece of shrapnel. Stopping a bullet is out of the question and wearing it in this heat it is oppressive. He often wonders why they haven't developed something that will be more effective in protecting them. Guess it's cheaper to have them die.

"I reckon I'll man the sixty in the Jeep," Shepard says.

"Fuck youse. I got it," Tosseti counters.

"You two shut up. I'm tired of you bickering," Rees commands. "Tucker's got the sixty. Shepard, you're up front with me. You've got the 203. Tosseti, in back, cover our six. Now get in."

The three climb in and Rees starts the Jeep. Looking over his shoulder, he sees that McGuire is already driving the Duck toward them. Rees scans the sky to locate the helicam and signals its operator to lead the way. It begins to fly away and the small convoy quickly follows.

There is no way for the group to know what the helicam is leading them away from or where they are headed, but they're about to find out.

***

Chief Black is watching the scene unfold on the screen and is amazed by what it shows.

"My God," he says, eyes wide with wonder. "You see old pictures of them, but watching an actual battalion-sized army of Confederates is incredible. But that's not why you asked me here, is it, General Lucas?"

The general understands the feelings the chief is having. He feels the same way. Watching history unfold in front of you is not something you experience every day. He can't imagine having to lead that many men without the modern equipment and communications the military possesses today. Vehicles, automatic weapons, radios – Civil War soldiers had none of them. Radios are the number one item, since communication is key to winning any battle. How the hell did they get orders to each other back then? He breaks from his musing and turns to the chief.

"I asked you here because the men are all right for now, but we need Clio to get them out of there immediately," the general says.

"Not too much longer, General," the chief responds. "I've finished all my checks, now we're just waiting on the power cells to charge."

As they talk, the screen changes again. Bill is the first to notice.

"Hey, now what are we looking at?" he asks.

Everyone in the room turns toward the screen, which now shows a different aerial view of a different army.

***

Major Hess is at another station, looking over the shoulder of Lt. Gordon, another technician who is operating a second helicam.

"Okay lieutenant, what have you got?" asks an exasperated Hess.

"Sir, after hearing what Lt. Reynolds did, I decided to do the same thing, kind of," Gordon replies. "I've got what looks to be a battalion of Union troops, sir."

Hess looks closer and can see a column of men in blue marching along a dirt road. They are being led by men on horseback. He figures they must be dismounted cavalry, followed by regulars, and then the cannon.

"Where did they come from?" Hess demands. "I thought you were monitoring the regiments further north."

"I was, sir. Like I said, after what Lt. Reynolds did, I wanted to look around, too. This battalion must have broken off, crossed the river somewhere, and are heading southwest. They are heading straight for the Confederate Army."

"And our guys are damn smack in between them. Shit!" Hess yells.

Hess looks up at the window and sees everyone in the general's office either looking at him or the screen. He snatches the phone at the same time as General Lucas.

"Now what, Major?" Lucas asks tersely.

"Sir, it's the Union Army. A battalion-size force, with dismounted cavalry and cannon. They are marching toward the Confederate Army and our men are in between them."

"Well, Major, have your helicam operator that's leading the SPs get them out of there."

"Sir, if they head west, they will run into the mass of troops outside the town," Hess explains. "On the east, they face the river. The Duck might get across, but the Jeep can't and they can't swim it."

"Well that's just dandy, Major," the general snaps, then closes his eyes and takes a breath. "I apologize, Major Hess, it's not your fault."

"No need, sir. I quite understand. What do you want us to do?"

Chief Black walks up to the general and asks to be put on speaker phone.

"Major Hess?" the chief begins.

"Yes, Chief?"

"Can you have your helicam fly along the river? There must be a bridge somewhere near there, otherwise the town can't conduct trade."

"Good idea, Chief," Hess replies. "We'll do that."

Hess hangs up and passes on the suggestion to Lt. Gordon.

"General if we can find a bridge, we may be able to get them across it and out of danger," the chief tells General Lucas. "Clio should be ready to transport them by then."

"Let's hope the helicam can spot that bridge and fast," the general says.

About ten minutes lapse with no report from the floor, and the general is growing impatient. He is just about to call Hess when the major buzzes in.

"Sir, we found something," Hess reports in a tone that carries more concern than General Lucas was expecting. "There is a train bridge close to a mile from where our guys are. The problem is the Union Army is closer to it then we are. It's our opinion they are going for the bridge with the goal of capturing it. We believe the Confederates are marching to the bridge as well, to secure it. It's going to be a race. Our guys might not make it before the Union troops arrive. We really don't have a choice, though. At least until we activate Clio."

"Thank you, Major," the general replies. "I'll get back with you."

Lucas replaces the handset and looks at the people in the room with a sigh.

"Seems we can't catch a break," he says, and goes on to explain the situation. "We have no way to inform the men and we can't have them stop or the Confederates will catch up to them. If we try to get them to the bridge, they will more than likely run into the Union army. Either way, they are going to have a fight on their hands."

"General?" Nora asks, drawing his attention. "I'm no military person, but it seems to me they need to try for the bridge. Maybe if the helicam moves faster, they will get the hint that they need to speed things up. I think they will have a better chance crossing the bridge than staying put. Just my two cents' worth."

The chief smiles and nods at the general. The general thinks for a second and picks up the phone.

"Major, our best option is the bridge," he tells Hess. "Have the helicam speed up and hopefully the men will try to keep up. We believe this gives them the best chance."

Unknown to the general, Senator Minten is heading for the Bank facility at this moment, supported by M.I.S.S. teams carrying semi-automatic rifles and pistols. They are going in as an assault team, not an inspection team. As they pass through the gate, the TNT team 2nd lieutenant walks into the gate shack and dials the base commander's number. He is clearly disturbed by the sight of civilians carrying weapons into a top-secret facility.

***

Rees is driving at a steady speed, keeping up with the helicam ahead and making sure the Duck maintains pace behind him. They are heading north, so he assumes there is some type of danger coming their way from the south. Rebel troops maybe? His mind is wandering when Shepard slaps him on the arm.

"Sarge, that helicopter is speeding up," Shepard says with alarm. "What the heck?"

"Damn, you're right," Rees mutters. "We'd better step on it or we'll lose it. Must be something urgent going on."

Rees presses on the gas pedal and accelerates to keep up with the helicam, dodging trees and trying to keep the little machine in sight. Shepard turns to check the Duck and sees Bouvier raise his hand in a "What the...?" gesture, and then grab the dash to hold on for dear life.

Shepard gives him a shrug indicating he doesn't know. They drive for almost a mile and then clear the trees. Rees drives outside the tree line for a short distance and then slams on the brakes. Shepard places his hands on the dash to keep from striking his head or being ejected. Tosseti isn't so lucky, losing his balance and falling onto the floorboard. He expels a few choice words at his misfortune.

Tucker was already holding onto the sixty, trying not to fall out of the Jeep as they careened through the woods. He recovers first and sees why Rees hit brakes. He pulls the charging handle on the sixty to make it ready.

As the others recover, they see it, too. Union cavalry, ground troops, and artillery are massed in front of them. There are hundreds of regulars, all in lines, marching their way with the cavalry to the left. Looking further behind, they can see rows of cannon situated on a rise.

"Look over there to the right," Rees says. "The helicopter was leading us toward those train tracks and a bridge, but we're too late."

McGuire parks the Duck next to them and Bouvier gets out to talk with Rees.

"This doesn't look good," Bouvier says in stating the obvious.

"No, it doesn't," Rees agrees. "I assume we were going for the bridge. I don't know why they would lead us straight into the Union Army, though, unless they were hoping we could get here before them."

Bouvier looks around and quickly surveys their options.

"I say we go west or turn around and go back," he says.

"They must have had a reason for us to go this way," Shepard interjects. "Reckon there's worse trouble to the west and behind us?"

"Well, we can't go through them," Rees states.

"Hey guys," Montoya says. "You might want to see this."

Rees gets out of the Jeep and looks at where Montoya is indicating from the turret. He can see movement in the woods. It's more soldiers, and they're heading toward them. And this time they are wearing the gray uniforms of the Confederate army.

***

Chief Black returns to the general's office to give his boss the update he's been waiting for.

"It's almost time now, General," he reports. "We can start up Clio in a few minutes. Once she's online, it's just a matter of throwing a few switches and we should be able to get our guys back."

"Sounds good, Chief," General Lucas responds. "Make it happen as quickly as possible."

The chief acknowledges and turns to head back down to the control room. As he leaves, he glances at the women and Bill.

"Tell you what," he tells them. "Why don't you four come with me? You might find this interesting and can get a better view of what is happening. If that's all right with you, General?"

"That's fine with me," Lucas says as his guests jump out of their seats. "Give me a wave when you're ready to activate Clio the second she is ready."

***

Senator Minten and his team of M.I.S.S. agents enter the facility and approach the first security checkpoint. Minten turns to his team leader and puts his plan into action.

"Agent Sterling, have one of your men relieve this fine gentleman of his post," Minten says.

"Yes, sir," the agent replies, signaling for two of his men to replace the guard.

The SP doesn't understand what is happening, and when he stands, the M.I.S.S. agents raise their weapons in his direction.

"Hey, what's... whoa there," is all he can say before the agents disarmed and handcuff him.

"Good work, men," Minten says in a cocky tone. "Now shall we move this along? As we proceed, please relieve any of these cops of their weapons and duties. I want to lock this place down as quickly as possible, and that includes shutting down any outside communications."

Minten strolls through the hallway toward the next checkpoint.

***

Chief Black enters the control room with Bill, Nora, Skylar, and Ivy right on his heels. The guests are trying to watch everything at once and Bill is frantically scribbling notes. The chief talks with Major Hess, who assures him everything is a go.

The chief picks up the critical Inabular device and places it into a slot on Clio's frame. He issues final instructions to everyone in the room.

"Where will you send them, Chief?" Nora asks. "I mean, they aren't where they were when you transported them the first time."

"We'll bring them here, on this base," he assures her. "There's plenty of open area and we already have a place picked out. You'll see them on the screen when they arrive. Just a few more minutes and they'll be back."

The chief looks up toward General Lucas and gives him a thumb up. The general returns the gesture and the chief issues the ignition order for Clio start-up. A hum fills the control room as technicians flip switches and adjust dials. Clio is alive.

General Lucas looks at the screen and his face changes as he sees what is happening. He reaches for the phone and rings Major Hess.

"Major, get me four screen shots of what's happening with our boys," he says in near panic. "I want this covered from all angles."

Hess, as well as everyone else in the control room, was busy getting Clio started and had not been paying attention to the screen.

"Oh my God!" Hess exclaims.

He quickly orders a technician to get camera angles from the helicams, the Jeep, and the Duck. The technician obeys and the screen shifts until there are four camera angles displaying each viewpoint.

***

Rees and his men are staring at the predicament in front of them, first at the Confederate soldiers and then at the Union troops. Montoya keeps his sixty pointed at the Confederate soldiers in the trees.

"What do we do now?" Montoya asks no one in particular.

We need to get out of here, that's for sure," Shepard says.

Rees agrees and points to an opening on the left. The opposing armies are about a mile from each other, but they are closing in and the security policemen are stuck in the middle. Rees climbs back into the Jeep as Bouvier runs back to the Duck. They put their respective vehicles into gear and speed off toward the crest of the hill, straight toward the Union lines and away from the Confederate troops. Rees wants to get as far away from both as he can, then make a dash for the opening on the left and hope to outrun both armies.

As Rees begins the turn to the left, he realizes the Union cavalry has spotted them and is moving into a position to block their escape. He doesn't know what the Union soldiers think they're doing, but of course they have no idea who the security policemen are or what devastation they are capable of inflicting upon them.

When Rees sees what is happening, he slows the Jeep to a stop and the Duck pulls alongside. Bouvier gets out and again comes over to discuss the situation.

"Okay, this is a crock," Bouvier says. "Sergeant Rees, we've got to go through them."

Looking behind them at the Confederates emerging from the woods and then at the line of Union soldiers and cannon, Rees agrees they seem to have no choice. The rebels are lining themselves up for battle against the Union troops, who are still marching toward the SPs. Bouvier grabs his binoculars and looks at the artillery.

"They're loaded and ready to fire," he reports.

Rees looks at the Confederates and sees they appear to be aiming their muskets at them, but likely are aiming at the Union troops. Or so he hopes.

Before they can do anything, a volley of cannon fire erupts from the Union army. The SPs jerk their heads toward the sound and can hear the whistling of the cannon balls as they fly over their heads. To Rees's amazement, he can actually see the black balls as they soar over them as if in slow motion. The SPs stand there dumbfounded and awed by the sight. That is until the balls explode within the ranks of the rebels, then the scene turns to horror. Steel fragments fly in different directions. Several pieces decimate rows of men, cutting them down and sending bodies flying, some exploding in sprays of red mist.

The Union artillery fires a second volley, and this time one of the cannon balls strikes the Duck with a resounding "clang." The ball hits the slope of the upper part of the vehicle and nearly takes off Montoya's head, flying up and away from them with a whistling sound. The men drop to the ground, except for Airman Tucker.

"Fuck this shit!" Tucker yells as his M-60 begins chattering.

Rees looks toward where Tucker is aiming and watches as several Union soldiers in the front rows start falling. The sixty is cutting them down way before they can even get in a range of the security policemen.

A volley of fire from the Confederates joins the sound of Minié balls from their rifles striking the Duck from the other side. Montoya decides he has had enough as well and opens fire. His M-60 is doing as much damage to the rebels as Tucker's is on the Yanks. Rees looks toward the Confederate line, but can see nothing through the heavy smoke produced by the rebels' black powder weapons.

Shepard and Tosseti start firing their M-16s, adding to the slaughter of Union soldiers. Shepard loads his M-203 and fires a 40mm high explosive round with a resounding "thump" that lands with deadly accuracy.

Rees is impressed. That shot was maybe 350 to 400 yards away. Shepard fires two more rounds before taking a musket round in the leg. Dropping his weapon, he starts screaming. Rees runs to him and attempts to stem the blood flow. Tosseti stands over them and fires, covering them until Rees can get Shepard's leg tied off with his own belt and heft the wounded sergeant into the Jeep.

"We gotta get out of here! There are too many of them!" Rees yells.

"I agree," Tucker shouts over the din. "We've got to go through those boys and get some cover. We are way too exposed."

The men inside the Duck fire through the small ports, keeping themselves well-covered. Shouts and yelling erupt from inside the Duck as the M-60 stops firing. Montoya has taken a Minié ball to the head. A few seconds later, Nionee gets into the turret and starts using the weapon.

"Let's go!" Rees shouts over the roar of weapons fire. "We gotta move. NOW!"

Rees sees Kriger emerge from around the side of the Duck and rush toward his position. He stops, raises an LAW (Light Anti-Tank Weapon) and fires it into the mass of Union soldiers. It strikes in front of them and explodes, sending hot shrapnel through them and cutting them to shreds. There is now a large gap in the line where men once stood. Kriger laughs, then runs back and jumps into the Duck before it can leave without him.

"What the fuck was that about?" Rees thinks.

Rees jumps into the Jeep, starts the engine, and heads for the woods. McGuire guns the Duck's Chrysler V-8 engine and begins driving like a madman following the Jeep. Musket rounds are clanking off the Duck and Jeep, but thankfully missing the SPs. Tucker steadily fires the M-60 and hangs on tight as they hit bumps, rocks, and whatever else is on the ground.

Rees drives straight at the Union cavalry, which is charging them. He cannot believe the sight. Dozens of horsemen are coming directly at their armored Duck and unarmored Jeep. Tucker and Nionee fire as fast as they can as the gap closes, hitting their targets with machine gun fire. Men and horses are falling in droves. Bullets don't discriminate when it comes to killing. Horses as well as men scream as they die. Some of the horses keep galloping forward without realizing their riders have fallen off.

There are only a few cavalry solders left when the two sides clash seconds later. Rees is able to duck under a saber swung by a passing horseman, but Tosseti isn't so lucky. He raises his M-16 to deflect most of the strike from another horseman passing his side of the vehicle, but part of the sword connects with flesh. He hollers in pain as the blade cuts deeply across his face. The force of the collision knocks the soldier from his horse and he tumbles away.

"Tosseti, stay with me man!" Rees screams while trying to dodge the horses and catching a glimpse of Tosseti's blood-soaked face.

Rees can hear loud thumps coming from behind the Jeep and turns to see the massive steel Duck run right into the charging horsemen. Blood and gore now obscure the Duck's small windows, and Rees wonders how McGuire can see anything through the mess to drive.

Rees returns his attention forward as Tucker turns his weapon around and is now firing to their rear. They have passed by the Union soldiers and have a clear area ahead of them. Rees drives over a crest and down a slight embankment to a sudden stop. The area in front of them is covered in marshes and swamp. They're not getting through that. The Jeep can drive through water almost completely submerged, but it can also get stuck. Besides, they need to check on Shepard and Tosseti.

The Duck comes over the crest and skids to a stop just short of the marsh. The men inside clamber out and take up firing positions at the top of the crest, even Airman Harris. They immediately have to start shooting. Apparently, the Union guys are not going to give up so easily.

Kriger runs over to check on Tosseti and Shepard. Both are alive, but for how long is anybody's guess. Both men are bleeding profusely. Tosseti is cursing a storm as Kriger applies a thick gauze to his face. Tosseti grabs it, still cursing, and tells Kriger to move on. Rees takes that as a good sign. Shepard has passed out from loss of blood.

Rees runs to join the men on the crest, adding his weapon fire to the others. The Union cavalry has grown with re-enforcements and are grouping for another charge.

"What the hell's wrong with these guys?" McGuire yells. "Don't they see what we did to them? They got a death wish or something?"

"No, they're just drawing our attention and making us think they're going to charge," Rees counters. "Look!"

Rees points to the north, where Union soldiers are trying to flank them through the marshes. They do not need to get surrounded. This must have been how General Custer felt, or will feel, or... whatever at the Battle of Little Bighorn. Rees shakes the thought from his head and tries to think of what they need to do next.

"Concentrate!" he tells himself.

He grabs a grenade, pulls the pin, and throws it has hard as he can toward the Union soldiers attempting to flank them.

"Grenade out!" he yells.

Maybe that will get their attention; let them know they aren't as sneaky as they think they are. He knows it will only hold them off for a little while, so he and his men need to come up with a plan and soon. Rees looks at Bouvier and can tell he is thinking the same thing.

***

Clio proceeds through its power-up stage in a crescendo of low-pitched humming noises. Most of the technicians are focused on their jobs and oblivious to what is happening on the control room screen. They are working feverishly trying to get the men home.

Those without immediate tasks watch in horror at what is unfolding on the screen. The women are almost in a state of panic as the battle displays on the screen in real time. They scream as they witness the carnage and cry at the pain experienced by those they know.

The chief turns his attention back to Clio and flips the switch that he hopes will bring the men home.

Meanwhile, Senator Minten and his M.I.S.S. team have secured the checkpoints and relieved every SP without needing to fire a shot.

"This is going better than I thought it would," he says aloud. "I thought these SPs and were supposed to be an elite group. Apparently, I was wrong."

No one answers.

Minten leads the way into Shelly's office, catching the general's assistant off guard. When she sees the armed men, Shelly reaches for her gun.

Minten raises his hand, waving it in a "halting" gesture.

"Uh, uh, uh," he says. "I wouldn't do that if I were you."

The lead M.I.S.S. agent raises his rifle and aims it at Shelly. She relaxes her grip on the pistol and places her hands on the desktop.

"She keeps a .45 under her desk," Minten tells the agent. "Please be a good man and relieve her of it. We wouldn't want any accidents now, would we?"

The agent walks over, still training his weapon on Shelly as he takes her gun.

"Now Shelly, you be a good girl and stay where you are," Minten says condescendingly. "No need to announce my arrival to the general. I'll do this myself."

General Lucas is watching the battle on the control room screen and has his back to his office door. He turns around at the sound of the door opening and is surprised to see Minten. He is even more surprised to see the men with him, each holding weapons at the low ready.

"What's the meaning of this, Senator?" Lucas demands. "We're in the middle of an operation. Why are there armed men in my facility?"

"Why General Lucas, I'm here to take command of this operation," Minten states. "You and the Bank Council have bungled this thing from the start. I should have had control of this from the beginning."

Minten strolls around the room looking at the pictures, running his hand slowly across the television.

"We should have sent well-trained, heavily armed men on this assignment," he says. "And what idiot thinks to send unsuspecting air police to the Civil War? Good gods. Really, the Civil War? What were you hoping to gain, General?"

"That wasn't my call to make. I will agree with you on that, Senator," Lucas responds. "But what has happened, has happened. There's no going back, and right now we are in a crisis if you'll bother to look."

The general points to the screen and Minten finally notices what is showing on the display.

"Is this a live feed, General? My goodness, it's wonderful. Gentlemen, look at this. Air force pukes getting their asses kicked by nineteenth century technology."

Minten's team members watch the battle quietly.

"Just what in the hell do you think you're doing, Minten?" the general asks angrily. "You don't have the authority to take control of this project. I'm calling security and…"

As Lucas reaches for the phone, Minten grabs his wrist and squeezes. The M.I.S.S. agents raise their weapons and point them at the general. Lucas winces in pain and his eyes widen as realization sinks in, then hatred.

"Your security personnel are in lockdown, General," explains Minten. "We have control of everything now and I will be running the show as I see fit."

***

Major Hess is the first to notice what is happening in the general's office. It takes him a few seconds to realize the gravity of the situation, and then it dawns on him what must be happening upstairs.

"Chief Black!" he calls.

The chief is busy with Clio and not paying attention. The women and Bill hear him, though, and turn to look. They see Hess is looking up at the general's office and they look, too.

"What's going on?" Bill asks. "Who are those people? Those aren't air force guys, are they?"

"No, they're not," Nora says and quickly walks over to the chief.

"Chief, I think we have another situation on our hands," she says, motioning toward General Lucas's office.

This time, the chief pays attention and sees what the others are talking about. He knows what he has to do.

Clio is running full throttle now and the entire building is humming. The room is full of static electricity. Clio is in transport mode and will activate any second. The control room lights dim and return. Light flashes emanate from everywhere, and the humming sound hits a fever pitch. Clio is beginning to grab the men and bring them home.

Minten sees the chief looking at him from below and realizes that

Clio is operating. He turns to his men and points at the chief.

"Get down there and stop that man," he bellows. "Stop that damn machine!"

A four-man team runs out the door and heads to the stairs. It's now a race between Clio, the chief, and Minten's henchmen.

***

Rees hears a loud pang and sees Airman Nionee fall back into the Duck as a Minié ball strikes his helmet and knocks it off. Bouvier starts to go to him when suddenly they see Nionee slowly emerge back in the turret. He is holding his helmet and examining the large dent made by the ball. He shakes his head and puts the helmet back on, acting as if nothing happened. The roar of the M-60 starts up again as Nionee gets back to work.

"Lucky bastard. Bet he's got a headache from hell though," Rees thinks to himself before returning his attention to the battle.

"Sergeant?" says Harris, who is lying next to Rees.

"Harris, what the hell are you doing here?" Rees asks incredulously. "Get back in the Duck."

"I'm fine," Harris assures him. "I don't know what happened. One minute I'm lying there groggy, and the next thing I know I feel like a million bucks. I swear, Sarge, I'm fine. Honest, I'm good to go. Now let's get busy killing these bastards."

Rees relinquishes the debate and re-engages the enemy. Harris grabs Rees's arm and points toward the cavalry, which is in line and appears to be ready to charge.

And charge they do. The airmen continue to shoot with renewed vigor, and their advanced weaponry is having the same effect it did earlier. The problem is they are now stationary and the Union cavalry has more men than the security policemen can handle this time. The Union soldiers on the left are firing from the woods with no effect, but it will keep the SPs pinned until the horsemen overrun them.

Rees takes a bead on one of the Union soldiers flanking them when he feels a familiar sensation across his body. He looks at his arm and sees the hairs rising. Gazing up and around their position, he notices the haze return and envelope them. It is forming a bowl over them. He scrambles over to Bouvier.

"I think it's happening again!" Rees shouts over the shooting.

Bouvier stops firing, looks around, and grimly smiles.

"Thank God," he says. "I hope you're right."

The air becomes thick and acidic, and static electricity is everywhere. The humming begins and the men's ears become stuffed.

Rees hollers at the Union boys, "Fuck you!" and throws another grenade.

Pressure begins filling his head and the pain intensifies. He can't focus on the Union soldiers anymore despite the fact they are gaining ground. He drops his M-16 and covers his ears in an attempt to stop the pain and paralyzing pressure, but to no avail. He screams and rolls into a ball.

The hallucinations he experienced last time return, as does the voice of Bob Seger, this time singing *Night Moves.* Rees can hear him, but not see him. An old man appears, who Rees understands to be their guardian through time. He is beckoning for Rees to follow, but Rees's feet feel as though they are mired in clay. The old man reaches out and grabs Rees's hand, pulling him forward.

Rees looks away briefly, and when he returns his gaze, the old man has been replaced by an image of Nora. He is happy to see her and notices she looks older than he remembers. She holds his hand, and Rees feels safe as she pulls him away from the past and toward where he needs to be.

***

Chief Black sees the M.I.S.S. team leave the general's office and knows they are headed for the control room. For what purpose, he doesn't know, but he knows it can't be for anything good. He grabs Bill's arm.

"You four go into that side room and wait for me," he orders.

They look at him stunned and don't move.

"Now!" he exclaims.

This time they run.

The chief looks at Clio, then the screen, then at the M.I.S.S. agents as they come through the control room door. Raising their weapons, the lead agent begins making his way toward the chief.

"Stand down, sir. Stop what you're doing," the agent commands. "This facility is now under the control of M.I.S.S. and Senator Minten."

The chief doesn't like what he is about to do, but he has no choice.

He reaches in and grabs the Inabular, pulling it out. Clio instantly shuts down. The control room lights become brighter, static dissipates, and the room goes silent except for technicians murmuring in confusion. The chief takes the Inabular and runs behind a shield of machinery into the side room before the agents can react.

"What's going on?" Ivy asks. "Who are those people? What do they want?"

The chief ignores her and walks swiftly to a computer bank that doesn't seem to be operating. That's because it isn't a working computer bank. He reaches behind the console and flips a switch. The fake computer bank moves, and the chief pulls it open to reveal a tunnel.

"Quick! Come on. Let's go!" he exhorts them.

The foursome hustles into the tunnel and the chief pulls the console closed behind him. He grabs a ready flashlight and walks by the stunned group, ignoring their repeated questions and telling them to follow him. He opens a metal door at the end of the tunnel that leads outside. He sticks his head out to ensure all is clear and motions for them to follow.

Holding the Inabular in one hand, the chief pulls a small control box out of his pocket with the other.

"I'm sorry. Really, I am," the chief says to confused silence from the group.

He flips open a cover on the small console and presses a button.

"I'm sorry, but the men won't be coming home right now," he continues.

"What in the hell are you talking about?" Skylar demands. "What is going on?"

"Yeah," Nora adds. "Why not? What did you just do? Who are those people and where are our men? Tell us!"

"Those men inside want to take control of Clio and I can't let them," the chief says, and then holds up the Inabular. "This device is what makes Clio work. It's her brain. Without it, she can't do a thing. She shut down as soon as I removed it."

The four look at each other in shock.

"What about the men? They were in the middle of transport, weren't they?" Nora asks. "Where did they go?"

"I'm not positive," the chief replies in a heavy-hearted voice. "But we believe they are in limbo."

"What the hell does that mean?" Nora demands, her brow furrowed with emotion. "And who is we?"

"It means they are floating around out there," the chief says as he waves his hand around him and at the sky. "They are in limbo. Until I can get another time machine up and running, they are in a kind of suspended animation. At least that's what the other scientists and I believe. We tested it with fruit, vegetables, and animals, leaving them in limbo for weeks and months at a time. When we finally returned them, the fruits and vegetables were just as they were when we sent them. They didn't ripen or spoil at all. The animals seemed to have done well, too. They didn't die of starvation or dehydration. We... I hope the results are the same with the men."

"Can't the air force seize control of the time machine?" Bill asks. "Then you can put that thing back in?"

"Sorry, no, but they can't," the chief explains. "When I pushed this button on the control box, I fried every system inside Clio. She is no more. I can't take the chance of M.I.S.S. or that senator getting their hands on her. If they did, sooner or later they would figure out how to start her up again. And even if they did, they wouldn't return the men. They would leave them there forever. At least now they are still alive. Somewhere."

"Oh, that's great, you asshole!" Nora yells and strikes the chief on the chest with her fist. "You hope? You fucking hope?"

Nora strikes him again and again until Bill pulls her away. She breaks down in tears as Skylar goes to comfort her.

"What do we do now, Chief?" Bill asks.

"There's a vehicle stashed over there," the chief says, pointing to a nearby building. "We can use that to get off the base. I'll take you wherever you want to go."

"What about you?" Bill presses. "Why can't you just go to the police or base commander, or whoever?"

"I've got to go into hiding," answers the chief. "I'm the only one who knows everything about Clio. All the others only know bits and pieces. They must never get their hands on a time machine. They will do nothing but harm to the space-time continuum. I can't trust that Senator Minten hasn't influenced others to join him. There's no telling how far up this goes."

The chief looks at Bill and grabs him by the shoulders.

"You've got a story to tell," he says. "You have to tell this story."

"Yes, I do, but who's going to believe me?" Bill says. "I've got no proof. The men are not here to speak for themselves. I've got three women that the military or the government will discredit. You know good and well this will be covered up."

Bill looks at the ground dejectedly, kicks a pebble.

"I'll try though. I'll still try," he says and then suddenly looks at the chief. "Hey, you'll be a wanted man if you go AWOL. You can't just take off like that, can you?"

"Don't worry about me," the chief says. "That's been taken care of. We've always known this could happen. Once I'm gone, it will be as though I've retired. In effect, I will be retired. The paperwork's already completed. After thirty days, I'll be free and clear. If I don't return within the thirty days, the system will retire me. It's all good. My family gets my retirement pay for the rest of their lives."

The group looks at the chief in disbelief.

"What, do you think I spent my entire adult life just working on this time machine?" he laughs. "Sorry, I did have a life outside of the air force. I am divorced and my ex-wife has my son. I won't get to see him grow up, of course, but I'll keep tabs on them. It's all good. Now, we need to go. Are you coming with me or staying here?"

The four gather themselves and follow the chief to the hidden vehicle. It's time for them, at least, to go home.

***

General Lucas and Senator Minten can do nothing but watch the scene unfold below them. The agents bang on the locked side room door, but are stymied until they finally break it open. Several men enter the room, weapons raised, but come out moments later looking confused. The lead agent looks up at Senator Minten and shakes his head in the negative. Minten raises his hands with a quizzical look.

The lead agent picks up the phone to General Lucas's office and Minten motions for the general to answer it. Lucas sighs and presses the intercom button.

"You're on," he informs the agent.

"Senator Minten, the room is empty and we are unable to find the escape door," the agent says."

The general's smirk draws the ire of the senator.

"Where the hell are they, General?" Minten roars. "What kind of games are you playing?"

"What can I say, Senator? Contingencies," Lucas replies with a wry smile.

Minten's face turns red and he moves closer to the intercom.

"Search that damn room again," he orders. "They are in there or there's a trap door or something. Find it."

The agent takes a couple of other agents with him and heads back into the room. At the same time, Clio's consoles are sparking and flaming. The technicians back away from their areas of responsibility as each piece of equipment begins to smoke and shower the room with sparks.

"Now what?" Minten says in a frustrated panic as he rushes to the window. "Wipe that smirk off your face, General, and tell me what's happening."

"As I said, contingencies are in place. Did you think we would allow anyone to take control of Clio?" replies the energized general. "The chief implanted a self-destruct mechanism in each piece of the machinery. Everything that is needed to operate Clio is now fried, melted, and destroyed beyond repair. The chief knew something like this could happen and was ready in case some crazed lunatic like you would try to control her. Sorry, Senator. You lose."

Minten is incredulous. This can't be happening. All his planning and manipulating is for naught.

"I will not be outsmarted by some enlisted man and a puny general," he fumes. "I am in control, not you peons."

Minten knows he has to think of something and quickly. He must turn this around in his favor. Then it comes to him.

Before he can act, however, he sees the M.I.S.S. agents walk out of the room and the lead agent head back to the phone. Minten picks up the general's phone without asking permission.

"What did you find?" he asks the agent.

"You were right, sir. There is a trap door they used to escape. My men followed it outside, did a quick search of the area, but came up empty."

"Get your men and all your gear. We're through here," Minten says. "This inspection and exercise are completed."

Minten looks at General Lucas with a smile that could chill a snake.

"Good to see you, General. I'm sorry for this unannounced inspection and exercise," Minten says, unsuccessfully hiding his sarcasm. "You did an exceptional job and I'll be sure to mention that in my report. I am sorry your little play toy got broken during the exercise, though. I wasn't expecting such dedication from your people. We'll just see ourselves out."

"If you think you can get away with this, you've got another thing coming," General Lucas fumes, pointing his finger at the senator.

Minten looks at the general like he is a pathetic child.

"Now General, don't be a sore loser. You got to see your project work, so there's that," Minten says. "Of course, you did lose several men, but really, who cares? If it gets out that you bungled this experiment – well, you and the Bank Council bungled it together – I can foresee you losing everything. Rank, retirement, maybe even get some jail time."

Minten's evil smile turns into a nasty sneer.

"Don't even think of fucking with me, General. I'll eat you for breakfast, lunch, and dinner. Take this as a learning experience and leave it alone. You stay out of my hair and I'll leave you alone. As a bonus, we will leave that reporter and the three dames alone as well. Things will be just as they are, except you won't have your time machine anymore. Tell the chief goodbye for me, will you?"

Minten turns and casually walks out the door.

***

General Lucas is angry, frustrated, worried, and sad. He knows the chief is gone and won't be back. His friend of many years has been run off like the family dog by an asinine neighbor. The men he's responsible for are stuck in time and there is not a thing he can do about it. The Clio project is finished. Years of research and development are gone within a few minutes.

He knows Minten is right, too. He is responsible for this, not the senator. He let his guard down. He didn't keep an eye out for a possible attack. Instead, he let his ambitions and ego get the better of him. Now he is done. He will put in his papers immediately, before any inquiries or hearings can take place. Not that there will be anything made public anyway. This project will be hidden away and swept under the rug as tightly as anything that ever took place at Area 51. The air force will make up a story for why the men disappeared, most likely a plane crash over the ocean, no survivors, no bodies.

The men. He feels for the men. Never to know what happened to them. They are part of an experiment gone wrong. They didn't ask for it. He feels sorry for them, and then he thinks of the three women he met and how he assured them he would get their boys home.

"Liar," he scolds himself.

Shelly knocks on the door and jolts him out of his self-pity.

"Sir, are you all right?" she asks with real concern.

"Yes, Shelly, I'm fine," he says softly. "We have a lot to do. Please inform the Bank Council that their presence is needed here. All of them, and no excuses for not showing. They are in this sinking boat as well as I am. Do not take no for an answer."

"Yes, sir. I'll get right on it," Shelly replies.

"Have the security police been released from wherever the M.I.S.S. agents were keeping them?" he asks.

"Yes, sir. The captain in charge would like a word with you, though. And from what I'm told, there are some pretty angry cops out there."

The general snorts a small laugh.

"I bet there are," he chuckles. "Please inform the good captain that I'll see him shortly. Oh, Shelly?"

"Sir?"

"How are you doing? I'm sorry about this sordid affair. Must have given you a start."

"I'm fine, sir. No harm," Shelly responds with a smile. "They stole my gun, though."

"I'll get you another," the general says. "It's the least I can do."

"That's all right, sir," Shelly replies. "I assume I'll be moving to another position, as I'm sure the project is over. Maybe I'll get a job at a real bank. I think Wells Fargo is hiring."

Shelly smiles and shuts the door behind her.

"Well, no time to cry over spilled milk," the general thinks, and then a smile crosses his face. "The good senator may think this is over, but…"

Chapter 30

Rees awakens to the familiar smell of pine, but something is different this time. He doesn't feel the sting of needles pressing into his face. The pine smell is fresher, cleaner. It's not natural pine, it's antiseptic. Pine cleaner? He's also more comfortable than he expects to be. He's lying face down on... a bed? What is happening?

He confirms there is a pillow under his head, and then jerks awake to what he believes to be the sound of rifle fire. No, it's not rifle fire. That was in the past. But where is he now? A white room greets his slowly opening eyes and his head throbs.

"Oh my, it was a dream," Rees thinks." I'm home in bed, but this isn't my apartment."

He tries to sit up and is hit with a wave of vertigo and nausea. He closes his eyes in an attempt to avoid vomiting. Too late. Seeing a bucket on the white-tiled floor, Rees leans over and grabs it just in time to collect whatever he is spewing. He hates throwing up. He heaves a couple of times, but there is not much in his stomach. Dry heaves. He finishes and drops the bucket back onto the floor with a clang, and spits into it once more. He looks up through bleary eyes and sees a rag on a table next to the bed, along with a plastic cup of what he hopes is water.

"Well, that's convenient," Rees thinks while reaching for the rag.

The rag is even slightly damp, like someone knew he would need it. He wipes his mouth and drops the rag onto the floor beside the bucket. Feeling slightly better, he slowly sits up and dangles his legs over the edge of the bed. He's wearing a dress. No, wait. It's a hospital gown. Okay, he's in a hospital. But why?

Rees hears a noise behind him and turns to see a man and a woman standing there. He adjusts his eyes by blinking and takes some deep breaths.

"Are you feeling better, Sergeant Rees?" the man asks.

He's wearing a white lab coat. Is he a doctor? The woman is wearing one also, and underneath is a blue air force uniform. Another doctor?

Rees tries to speak, but his throat is dry and all that comes out is a hoarse sounding "Whhhhhh?"

He shuts his mouth and closes his eyes, still fighting the dizziness. When he opens his eyes again, the woman is standing in front of him with the cup of water and a straw. She holds it to his lips and he drinks greedily. He finishes and nods his thanks. Sitting up a bit straighter, he takes a couple of more breaths, relaxes, and feels his senses returning.

"Take your time, Sergeant," the man says. "You've been through quite an ordeal. Your body needs to re-adjust."

Rees nods his head despite not really understanding, and sits still for a few more minutes. Finally, he feels he can rejoin the world and looks up. Both people are now standing in front of him. He notices there are wires attached to his body to monitor his vital signs. The setup is impressive, unlike any he's seen before, even on TV.

"You feel up to talking, Sergeant?" the man asks.

Rees clears his throat and struggles to answer.

"Yes, ah-um, yes. I guess I am," he replies in a raspy voice.

"Good," the man continues. "I know you are confused as to where you are and what has happened. I know you will have a hundred questions."

"A thousand," Rees answers sarcastically.

"I'm Lieutenant General Eugene Watkins, United States Air Force, commander of the hospital wing of this facility. And this is Colonel Michelle Thompson, Chief Medical Officer."

Rees can't help but notice that Col. Thompson is a very pretty woman, but her rank quickly erased that thought from his head. She noticed the change in his attitude upon hearing her rank and smiled a little at his disappointment.

"Sergeant Rees, I'm glad to meet you. Finally," she says. "I'm also glad to see you are recovering nicely."

Rees has no idea what she is talking about. Recovering from what?

"Where am I?" he asks. "What happened? Where are the rest of my guys, Bouvier, Shepard, Kriger, the others?"

The memories of what he just went through are beginning to flood into his consciousness.

"What the hell happened to me? To us?" he adds.

Rees starts to get out of bed and is rewarded with another bout of dizziness and nausea.

"Take it easy, Sergeant," Gen. Watkins suggests. "You're not a hundred percent yet. Please stay seated and we'll try to explain some things to you."

Rees follows the general's advice and sits back on the bed. Col. Thompson gives him some more water, looks into his eyes, grabs his wrist, feels his forehead, and then stands back.

"What's the last thing you remember?" Gen. Watkins asks.

"Um, the last thing I remember was being in a firefight with Union cavalry soldiers," Rees replies, realizing how crazy that sounds. "I remember looking at Sergeant Bouvier and saying something to him right before I started hallucinating, and then I blacked out."

Rees looks at the two officers as he comprehends what he just said.

"Then I wake up here," he continues. "What did you do to me? Did you drug me? LSD or some type of hallucinogenic drug to make me see things? Was this some type of military experiment? No way were we fighting Civil War soldiers."

Rees catches them sharing a knowing glance before returning their attention to him.

"I'm sorry, Sergeant, but we can't answer any questions you have right now," Gen. Watkins says.

Rees starts to object, but the general raises his hand to stop him.

"All your questions will be answered, but not by us," he explains. "We are only here to make sure you are well. We want to check you out first, then you may get dressed and we will have an orderly escort you to an area where someone else will brief you on your situation. Is that acceptable?"

"I guess I don't have a choice, sir," Rees replies, sounding a bit peeved. "Will we be long? I am feeling a lot better as time goes by. Feels like a hangover, and to get through those I usually eat and get moving. Helps clear the head."

"That's good to hear, Sergeant," the general says. When Dr. Thompson is finished examining you, you may get dressed. Your clothes are in the closet. I may not see you again, so if not, just let me say it's been good to have finally met you."

The general comes over to shake hands. Rees is confused. Why are these two officers glad to have met him? He's only a technical sergeant, a security specialist at that.

Col. Thompson finishes her exam, and with a wide smile she tells Rees he is fit and good to go. She asks him if he would like to go outside and have a cigarette first, which is a confusing question coming from a doctor. He starts to say yes, then realizes he doesn't want one. He doesn't even have a craving for one. He's hungry, but not for nicotine.

"Know what, ma'am? I don't want one, and I'm a heavy smoker, too," Rees says, cocking his head in bewilderment. "That's weird, I don't have a craving for one."

The doctor chuckles at Rees's reaction.

"I didn't think you would," she says with a smile. "Since you have been out, we thought you might have been weaned off them. Try to stay that way, will you? Now get dressed and I'll have an orderly here soon."

Rees gingerly gets to his feet and walks over to the closet. There is one uniform hanging inside. Dark blue pants, blue belt with satin polished belt buckle, underwear, t-shirt, socks, patent leather dress shoes, and a light blue shirt with... is that senior master sergeant stripes? No, wait, its seven stripes, but that can't be right. Six stripes are for a master sergeant, but a master sergeant has six stripes each pointing downward. This has five down and two up. What kind of joke is this?

Rees goes to the exit door only to find it locked, of course. He knocks, but no one answers. He can't wear an unauthorized shirt. They must have put the wrong uniform in this room. He gets dressed, except for the shirt. The door opens and a young man sticks his head inside.

"Sergeant Rees?" he asks.

"Yes, that's me," Rees answers.

"I'm Senior Airman Clark. I'm to escort you to a briefing."

"That's fine, but I need a shirt with my rank on it. It seems someone brought the wrong shirt in," Rees says, holding up the shirt. "What's with these stripes? They're all wrong."

The airman looks at the shirt with a hint of embarrassment.

"I'm sorry, Sergeant Rees. Didn't the general or colonel tell you?"

"Tell me what?" Rees asks.

"They were supposed to inform you, but I don't suppose it will be a problem for me to fill you in," the airman replies. "Since everything that has happened, you have been promoted to senior master sergeant."

"What?" an incredulous Rees responds. "What do you mean 'since everything that's happened?' What, the war shit? The drugs, what?"

The orderly looks uncomfortable and does not want to share anything further.

"Excuse me, Sergeant. I'll be right back," he says and hurries out the door.

A few minutes later, Colonel Thompson reappears.

"I am sorry, Sergeant Rees," she says sheepishly. "We were supposed to tell you about your promotion, but it completely slipped our minds. So, congratulations on the promotion, Senior Master Sergeant Rees."

Rees is now more confused than ever, but he can roll with it.

"Okay, ma'am. I can take the promotion for now, but what about these stripes?" he asks, holding the shirt up for her to see.

She looks confused, too. Then it dawns on her.

"Trust me, the stripes are correct," the colonel says with a smile. "You are a senior master sergeant. Please, just finish getting dressed and go with the orderly. Once you get to the briefing room, everything will be explained, including the stripes."

Rees finishes dressing, grabs a new beret, and unfolds it to another surprise.

"Okay, now what the heck? The damn thing is already shaped for me," Rees begins. "And Airman, where's my TAC crest? What's this big eagle cloth crest?"

Rees looks at Airman Clark and quickly realizes he's not going to say a thing.

"Never mind," Rees grumbles. "Lead the way."

Rees and the airman walk past several people on their walk down the hospital hallways. Most eye Rees and smile. He gets the feeling they are observing him, which makes him feel uncomfortable.

"Airman? Why is everyone smiling and looking at me strangely?" he finally asks.

"You're somewhat of a celebrity around here. You'll understand after you're briefed," Clark replies as the two men go into an open elevator.

"Level fifteen," he says clearly.

"Level fifteen," a computer-generated voice confirms from the control panel.

"What was that?" a wide-eyed Rees asks.

"What was what?" Clark responds. "Oh that. It's called voice recognition. There have been a lot of technology advancements since you've been away."

The elevator soon comes to a stop and Rees sees they have dropped fifteen stories in just a couple of seconds. Impossible, he thinks. They exit the elevator and he follows the airman toward the end of the hallway, where a double door is visible.

"Go on in, Sergeant," the airman says, stopping short of the doors. "No need to knock. It's been an honor to meet you. Good luck."

The two men shake hands and the airman heads back toward the elevator. Rees shakes his head.

"An honor?" he thinks. "Why would that be? Something tells me I'm about to find out."

He opens the double doors and enters a spacious, well-decorated room. There is a giant screen on one of the walls and it has a changing view of different parts of the world. The colors are vibrant and crisp.

"That's one nice movie projection," Rees says aloud, walking over for a close-up look at the screen. He looks around and is befuddled when he can't see a projector.

"What the hell is this?" he utters.

"That's a high-definition LED television set. Ninety inches, 1080 progressive scan," a voice behind him says.

"A what?" Rees asks. "Did you say this is a television?"

Rees looks at the television again and then turns his attention to the person speaking. He is a major, from the looks of the gold oak leafs on his epaulets. Beside him is an older gentleman in his seventies, with some of the same facial features as the younger man. Father and son, perhaps?

"I'm Major John Black, Special Operations branch," the younger man states. "I'm part of the reason you're here."

Rees watches the older man while shaking the major's hand. The older man has a slight smile on his knowing face.

"Welcome home, Sergeant Rees," he says.

Major Black asks Rees to have a seat, and the older man sits across from him, watching him intently. This gives Rees the creeps, but he returns the man's smile.

"I apologize, Sergeant Rees," the major says. "Allow me to introduce my father, Chief Master Sergeant Joseph Black, retired."

The chief and Rees reach over to shake hands.

"Good to meet you, Chief," Rees says, wondering where the conversation is headed.

The major lets them stare at each other for a few seconds before getting Rees's attention with a phrase he's never heard before.

"Senior Master Sergeant Rees?" Major Black begins.

"Yes, sir?" replies a stunned Rees. "Sir, about my promotion..."

"Sergeant Rees, please, let me explain everything first and then you may ask as many questions as you want. Is that okay?" the major replies with a smile. "Now if you'll indulge us a minute or two, we're waiting for someone else to arrive."

"Typical military," Rees thinks. "Listen first, then ask questions."

About three minutes later, the door opens and Bouvier walks into the room. Rees smiles and walks over to him.

"Staff Sergeant Bouvier. Damn good to see you," Rees says as the two men enthusiastically shake hands, grasping each other's arms. Rees notices extra stripes on Bouvier's uniform as well.

"Wow, they made you a senior, too? Good for you!" Rees says.

Bouvier starts to say something when Major Black interrupts.

"I'm sorry, Sergeant Rees, those are master sergeant stripes," the major explains. "They changed the rank structure and stripes while you were gone, the thought being that a master sergeant is in management as well as a senior and chief. Since the last two have stripes on top, why not place the master rank on top as well? So airman through technical sergeant now have their stripes pointing down, while master, senior, and chief point up and are on top of the five facing down. You'll get used to it, and everything else."

Rees and Bouvier look at each other's stripes and grin. Major Black introduces his father to Bouvier and asks everyone to have a seat. The major clasps his hands together and leans forward, resting his forearms on his knees.

"Okay, gentlemen. I'm sure you have a million questions," he says.

"I don't even know where to begin," Rees says.

"Well, let's start with my father," Major Black says, nodding to the retired chief. "In the 1960s and seventies, my father invented a time machine. It was first used on you and the men you were working with in August of 1980. The time machine that transported you to 1862 was named Clio II after the Greek goddess of history."

The major clears his throat before continuing.

"The time machine was under the control of, well, some unscrupulous men. Ambitious men who pushed to have the machine tested with live subjects before my father felt it was ready. You were hand-picked for the project. It was not a fair thing to do and those responsible have been held responsible. You and your men were sent to the past and have now returned."

Major Black pauses and looks at his father. The chief nods for his son to continue.

"A complication arose when a certain senator tried to take control of the time machine, by force, while you and your men were being transported from 1862 back to 1980. This resulted in the time machine being destroyed. And since you were in transit, you were stuck in a sort of limbo. You were in stasis, a type of suspended animation we refer to as the buffer."

Rees and Bouvier stare at the major with blank expressions, obviously confused by the tale.

"Okay, do you remember the original *Star Trek* series?" Major Black asks as Rees and Bouvier nod in the affirmative. "You remember how the transporter allowed them to move from one place to another? This was kind of like that. If you recall, there was one episode where Scotty was transporting someone and held him in the buffer. He could hold the person there indefinitely if he wanted. That's kind of what happened to you. All of you were in the buffer."

"How long were we in that buffer?" Rees asks, almost not wanting to hear the answer.

The old chief places a hand on Rees's shoulder and leans toward him.

"Thirty-eight years," the chief says in a stronger voice than Rees anticipated.

Rees's eyes grow wide and Bouvier's jaw drops.

"What!? Thirty-eight years?" Rees says loudly.

Rees's mind is reeling and he begins hyperventilating to the point of having an anxiety attack. The major pours some water for Rees and Bouvier, and the men quickly gulp it down. Rees sets the glass down on the coffee table and stares at it with his mouth agape and eyes wide.

"My God! This is insane!" he thinks to himself. "What's going on? Where are all my friends? Where is Nora? My God, Nora. I saw her only a few days ago, and now they're telling me it's been thirty-eight years? Thirty-eight years!"

The chief intently observes the two time travelers. Rees finally breathes a little easier and returns his gaze. He can see out of the corner of his eye that Bouvier is staring at the chief as well.

"I'm sorry. I know this is a shock to you both," the chief says, taking control of the conversation. "I want to tell you that I am glad you did make it back. Those of you who did."

"What do you mean by that?" Bouvier asks tentatively.

The chief waves his hand dismissively.

"I'm sorry, sergeants," he says. "Everyone who was alive at the moment you were grabbed for transport made it back as well. I'll explain more on that later. Please indulge me a little longer and everything will be made clear."

Still deep in thought, Rees relaxes a little more and accepts what the chief has to say. He senses he can trust the chief.

The chief goes on to describe the development of the time machine up to Clio II's destruction, and then begins filling in the blanks about what has happened in the intervening thirty-eight years.

"After the commotion at the Bank, I took the three young women and the newspaper reporter back to town before I disappeared," he explains. "I left the country and found a safe place where I could work on another time machine. A place without prying eyes. I kept in contact with General Lucas, who was the commander in charge of the Clio project, and he was able to assist me with certain assets I needed.

"It took several years, but finally there were more reliable people in government who could be trusted with what had transpired. A small group of scientific-minded individuals were allowed to assist me in my efforts, although I needed to remain in hiding to be safe. The information was kept top secret, and like 1980, I was the only person who had all the pieces and expertise to make it work."

"What happened to eventually allow us to get us out of the buffer?" Rees asks, taking another sip of water.

"Finally, a forward-thinking congressman gave the green light for me to come out of hiding and initiate the Clio III program," the chief explains. "I had kept in contact with my son the entire time I was in hiding. By this time, he had graduated from the Air Force Academy with advanced studies in engineering, chemistry, and other areas. He was stationed at Area 51 and worked on several top-secret projects, including Clio III.

"The congressman who was overseeing the project did his upmost to get Clio III up and running as soon as possible. Everyone's number one concern was seeing that you and your men returned safely. It took many years to get the program running full steam, but your presence here is evidence that we ultimately succeeded."

Rees closes his eyes and holds up a hand to stop the major. Taking a deep breath, he asks the question foremost in his mind.

"Major, Chief, that's all well and good, but what I really want to know is where is my girlfriend, Nora?"

Major Black takes a deep breath before answering, clueing Rees in to the probability he won't like the answer.

"Nora kept her hopes up for several years that you would return someday," the major explains, looking Rees directly in the eyes. "She went to college and earned a business degree before taking a job with a small computer company that prospered. She invested in the company and became a millionaire. Finally, she settled down and had a family."

Rees looks at the major solemnly for a few seconds before tears begin collecting in his eyes. He takes a deep breath and sighs, losing his fight to prevent the water works. Wiping away the moisture with the palms of his hands, he leans back on the couch and looks at the ceiling as the room waits in uncomfortable silence. Finally, he sits back up and collects his thoughts.

"I'm sorry, guys. I'm just having a hard time with all this," Rees says, looking to Bouvier for support. His friend acknowledges with a nod and puts a hand on Rees's back. "For me, for us, it seems like we've been gone only a few days, not almost forty years. It's just hard for me to get my head around this."

The major nods his understanding and seems hesitant to continue.

"What happened to the rest of our girls?" Bouvier asks. "And what became of your friend, General Lucas?"

"Ivy was married to a pilot who died during a test flight accident at Edwards," Major Black answers. "She returned to North Carolina after that and never remarried. Skylar married a real estate broker who made it big in the properties market. They live on a nice ranch in Idaho. Both women have children and grandchildren.

"As for General Lucas, unfortunately he passed away years ago. He retired shortly after the debacle, ashamed at what had happened to you and the rest of your men. He never got over it and it took its toll on him. He never got to see the fruits of his labor with Clio III."

"That's too bad," Rees says quietly. "After all this time, I'm sure he would have appreciated seeing us."

"Yes, he would have," the chief interjects. "The fact you are here is a testament to his courage."

"Who else can you tell us about?" Bouvier asks.

"The newspaper man, Bill Rogers, wrote an article about their adventures, but was never allowed to publish it," Major Black continues. "He went on to land a job as a White House correspondent for a few years before returning to the *Daily Express News,* where he worked his way up to managing editor. He has since retired and moved to a cabin in the mountains near Asheville, North Carolina."

"I never knew this man, but I'm thankful for all he did for us and our girls," comments Rees, finally having shaken off the initial shock.

"You mentioned earlier that Ivy's brother, Lieutenant McKnight, was helpful as well. I had only met him once, but he seemed like a good guy. Did he get in trouble for his role?"

"Thankfully, no," Major Black responds. "He was found in the M.I.S.S. holding facility in good health. He was more worried about being branded a deserter than anything else. Since the two M.I.S.S. agents your friends referred to as West and Gordon were seen taking him away, he was cleared after a brief investigation. His court testimony was another big nail added to the M.I.S.S. coffin. He finished his service and retired as a full bird colonel."

"And what about that senator? Minten, was that his name?" Bouvier asks. "He didn't get off scot-free, did he?"

"Well, yes and no," the major answers. "Senator Minten was the subject of a secret senate investigation, but because the Clio project is classified, no public charges were ever brought against him. However, he was forced to resign under a claim of poor health and sent on his merry way."

"Sounds like he got off scot-free to me," Bouvier complains.

"Hold on. There's more to his story," the major says. "About six months later, a couple of fishermen found an empty rowboat adrift on a lake near Minten's summer home. The boat contained a fishing rod and a half-empty bottle of Scotch. The police were called, and after an extensive search, authorities recovered his body. The autopsy showed he drowned and had a blood alcohol content of .06, which is under the legal limit. The police concluded he must have fallen overboard and drowned. Un-huh, right."

"Does M.I.S.S. still exist as an organization?" Rees asks.

No, M.I.S.S. was disbanded and several agents were arrested, tried, and imprisoned," Major Black replies. "Their charges included treason, espionage, unlawful entry, trespassing, murder, and a slew of others. John Clayborn, the director of M.I.S.S., was reassigned to another government agency. Clayborn was given a break since he blew the whistle on Senator Minten."

"Major Black?" Rees asks the major tentatively.

"Yes, Sergeant Rees?"

"Sir, what happened to the prisoner we had? Corporal O'Toole? He was inside the Duck when we were fighting. He didn't come back with us, did he?"

The major smiles.

"Yes, he did come back with you. The entire Duck was transported and everyone inside, including Corporal O'Toole, came back. He's in another room. None too happy, I might add. He's very confused, as I'm sure you can understand. It's easier for you to accept being sent back in time than it is for a nineteenth-century soldier being sent forward in time."

"What are you going to do with him?" Rees inquires.

"Everything depends on him," the major explains. "The plan for now is he'll be allowed limited access to the outside world. We have psychologists assigned to him and hopefully they can help him adjust. I think he will acclimate, but it will take time. You may see him later, but we want him to get used to his surroundings first. There are several historians chomping at the bit to interview him."

"Couldn't you just send him back to 1862?" Bouvier asks.

"Yes, we could, and we may if he absolutely wants to," the major replies. "He was listed as killed in action by his regiment. When the war ended and he had not been accounted for as a prisoner of war, they assumed he had been killed in your skirmish."

"But you could send him back before any of this happened, couldn't you?" Rees adds.

"Yes, that would be possible, but he has seen a lot," Major Black cautions. "Not enough where we think he could change the course of history, but he has seen some modern medical equipment, not to mention the Jeep and Duck. If he stays here long enough, he will eventually be seeing much more. It would be inhumane to keep him isolated for the rest of his life, but the more he sees, the less likely we'll ever be able send him back."

Rees and Bouvier nod their understanding.

"What about the butterfly effect?" Rees continues, his mind now racing with questions. "We had to have screwed up something that changed the timeline, didn't we? Has anything changed?"

"Well, we won't know until you see the outside world," Major Black replies. "As far as we know, nothing has changed, but you might notice some differences once you catch up with current events. Since they didn't conduct autopsies back then, no mention was made regarding your bullets, and no one involved in the fight was able to get a good look at you. There's no mention of you at all in the historical record. The incident in town was taken as a random act of violence from some renegade outlaws. We believe that whatever the soldiers saw, or thought they saw, was taken with a grain of salt and credited to battlefield fatigue. No one would have believed them. The soldiers you killed likely would have died during the course of the war anyway, so the butterfly effect would not carry into succeeding generations."

After their discussion winds down, Major Black invites Rees and Bouvier to accompany him to a nearby meeting room, where the rest of their team is waiting. As they walk down the hallway, they pass several security policemen and women. The major informs them they are now referred to as security forces.

They enter a very large conference room and are greeted by the rest of the guys, all excited to see each other. Rees is surprised to see Shepard approach him in a wheelchair. His leg is missing.

"They couldn't save my leg. Too much damage from the Minié ball," Shepard explains, reaching into his pocket to display the offending ordnance. "Gonna make me a necklace out of it."

Shepard doesn't seem to mind the wheelchair and proudly shows off its amazing electrical technology.

"They say they can get me a leg so realistic that you won't even be able to tell it's a fake," he adds in his southern drawl.

Rees tells Shepard he's happy for him, and then realizes he couldn't have woken up just a few hours ago, learned how to use a new wheelchair, and already roll around full of piss and vinegar.

"How long have you been awake?" Rees asks, dumbfounded as to why the rest of the team seems so well-adjusted to events he is still grappling to understand.

Shepard flashes a mischievous smile before answering.

"Caught that, did ya?" he says, executing a well-practiced wheelie circle with his wheelchair. "Hell, I've been up for about six months now. Been wait'n to see when y'all would get here. You should see the look on y'all's faces right now."

Rees quickly scans the room for Bouvier and fills him in on what Shepard said.

"I was wondering the same thing," Bouvier says, clearly as frustrated as Rees. "Why were we the last ones brought back?"

Before they can look for Major Black and hear his explanation, Airman Green comes into the room. He looks great. Doesn't even look like he'd been in an accident. The men clap him on the back, shake his hand, and tell him he looks fantastic. Rees and Bouvier join in the celebration, and then excuse themselves to look for the major.

Major Black and his father are watching the reunion from a corner of the room. When they see Rees and Bouvier headed their direction, they know what's coming.

"You're wondering why the injured men are healed, aren't you?" Major Black asks as soon as the two men get within earshot.

"Yes, we are," Bouvier snarls. "And why were Sergeant Rees and myself just now awakened?"

"Nothing nefarious, I assure you," the major says with a smile. "We actually brought the injured back first. We have the ability now to bring back individuals, not just the whole group at once."

The chief then takes over the explanation.

"We decided to bring back the injured first so we could work on them and give them time to heal before we brought the rest of you back," he explains. "It wasn't a long delay, comparatively speaking. After all, you were in the buffer for almost four decades."

"We apologize for not making this clear earlier," Major Black says. "But maybe this will make up for it. We have a little surprise we thought you would appreciate."

The door opens and in walks Nora, Skylar, Ivy, and Bill. The room grows silent as the two groups stare at each other. Nora sees Rees and a tear runs down her still-pretty, but older face. She crosses the room to him and they embrace.

"I never thought I'd see you again," Nora says through soft sobs. "I waited as long as I could."

"I know," Rees says. "I know."

"You haven't changed a bit, Scott."

"Neither have you, Nora," Rees responds.

She smiles and lightly hits him on the chest.

"That's bullshit and you know it, but thanks anyway," she says with a smile.

The two find a pair of chairs off to the side of the room and sit facing each other, their hands clasped on their knees.

"I'm so sorry you had to go through all of this," Rees says softly. "I, we, were told what you and the others did to try and get us back. I'm just sorry we didn't make it back to you in our own time. I want to thank you for your efforts, and I wish things could have been different."

Nora reaches up and caresses his face, a tender smile on her lips.

"No, Scott, we're sorry for what you men had to endure," she says. "The loss, the killing. I can't imagine what that was like, even though we saw it from the camera's point of view. Do I wish you had made it back sooner? Of course I do, but it didn't happen and I moved on. I did quite well for myself financially, married a good man, and have wonderful children and grandchildren. I also have my sister and Ivy, so no regrets."

Rees looks down and shakes his head sadly.

"I don't know what would have happened between us, Nora. We may have had a life, or maybe not," he says. "We will never know, and that's something neither of us can change. I'm glad you are happy and hope to meet your family someday, if that's all right with you."

"I guess I can introduce you as my young boyfriend and then people can start calling me a cougar," Nora laughs.

"Huh?" Rees asks. "What's a cougar?"

"Never mind," Nora smiles. "Hopefully we can figure something out. My family is not aware of this. They think I'm at a reunion, which I kind of am. But anyway, we'll have to come up with some cover story for you, because this time travel thing is still considered top secret. We'll worry about that later. Let's go back and mingle. I want to talk with the guys and I'm sure you would like to talk with Ivy and Skylar as well."

"That sounds like a good idea," Rees says, perked up by Nora's high spirits.

As he starts to get up, Nora grabs him and kisses him firmly on the lips. Rees is taken by surprise but returns the kiss. They break away and she gives him a wicked smile.

"Sorry, wanted to see if you still had it," she laughs.

Everyone in the room applauds and Rees smirks in embarrassment. Rees catches a glimpse of Shepard and a thought hits him. He excuses himself and seeks out Bouvier, whispering something in his ear. Bouvier listens and a smile crosses his face. He nods in approval, and the two walk over to Major Black and the chief to tell them of their dilemma.

"I'll get the ball rolling right away," the major says.

Half an hour later, Major Black returns and informs Rees and Bouvier that everything is in motion. The major then walks into the middle of the room and asks for everyone's attention. He looks at the smiles on the two men's faces, and then spells out the plan for the room full of people.

***

The men are kept secluded from the outside world during the succeeding weeks. They spend much of their days talking to a "shrink," which the psychologists hate being called, so they do it anyway. Other than being "shrunk," they exercise, eat, and catch up on the past thirty-eight years. They are amazed at modern technology. Portable tablets can research anything from the internet, which did not exist in their time. The encyclopedia has gone the way of the dodo bird. This is information overload.

The United States has been in a few wars, and the Twin Towers came down in the 9/11 attacks of 2001 on American soil. That is something the men never believed could happen. Home-grown terrorists are blowing up buildings and shooting civilians. Something else they never thought they would see.

The country had its first black president; a multiracial golfer named Tiger dominated what had been a white man's game; and more women and minorities had won election to political office.

They missed seeing the space shuttle era, and now there is an International Space Station operated by men and women of several countries. The Berlin Wall came down, the Soviet Union fell apart, and Russia is back to being its own country again. Vietnam has become a tourism destination.

Music is another story. Metallica and the Rolling Stones are still around and touring, Bob Seger was a popular concert draw for more than fifty years, and most of the bands Rees followed have either passed into history or are nostalgia acts today.

Medicines have improved the quality of life and people are living much longer. Things that Rees and his men know as science fiction on television and movies have become reality, such as personal computers, portable tablets, cellphones, and digital books.

Things have changed. Some good, some not so much. Rees wants to focus on the good for now. He's sure he'll see the bad stuff later. He doesn't know if he'll ever completely catch up, though.

***

Even though their enlistments were up decades ago, the military still considers the men enlisted. Rees guesses they could legally fight it, but where would they find a lawyer to take such a case? Would the air force even allow them to contact a lawyer? That's doubtful.

The government wants to keep close tabs on the men, keeping them under watch 24/7. Rees imagines this must be how the president and his family feels, unable to do anything freely without Secret Service shadows.

One thing that makes the situation tolerable is something Bouvier and Rees have discussed, but the others haven't considered. At least they have not heard anyone mention it. Each of them has a boatload of back pay coming to them; TDY pay, hazardous duty pay, medical pay, pay, pay and more pay. They are all rich. They can't wait to tell the guys when the time is right. They can't do anything with the money at this point anyway.

After months of being cooped up, the men are going stir crazy. The time is right for one thing, and that's for Major Black to unveil the plan that Rees and Bouvier suggested during the initial reunion. The major calls a meeting in the conference room, attended by all of Rees's team as well as the chief and some other officers.

"Gentlemen, please direct your attention to the video screen," the major says. "It has come to our attention that you have some unfinished business to attend to."

A video comes on showing an area that looks like a park with a river in the background. The men question each other about what they are seeing when Shepard has an epiphany.

"That's it!" he shouts. "You found it. The spot where we buried our guys!"

"That's correct," Major Black announces. "We took the coordinates you gave us, and a civil engineering team used ground-penetrating radar to locate the grave sites. It took them about a week, but they found them."

The room erupts in cheers at the realization they can fulfill their promise. Rees looks at Shepard and sees tears streaming down his face. Shepard notices Rees watching him and chuckles, wipes away the tears, and raises his fist in triumph.

***

The military transports the men to the park in North Carolina they saw on the video screen. The weather is cool and they stand quietly in drizzling rain, watching men work in and around a tent.

The place where they buried their friends so long ago is now a city park. That is fortunate, since having to dig up a parking lot or excavate under a building or home would have been disastrous. The major and chief didn't waste time making things happen after Rees and Bouvier informed them about the promise they had made.

The captain in charge of the operation comes over and salutes Major Black.

"We are ready, sir," the captain states.

Major Black nods, and the captain salutes and returns to the tent. Rees hears crying and then sees Ivy and Skylar holding onto each other, sobbing quietly. His heart sinks and he feels for Ivy.

A team removes a crate from the tent and takes it to a waiting transport truck. It contains the remains of three rusted and pitted helmets, along with muddy, rusted, and disintegrating M-16s. Shortly afterward, a procession of airmen exits the tent carrying metal coffins, each draped with an American flag. Each coffin carries the remains of their fallen comrades, their brothers in arms. Their friends.

Ivy breaks down, and Skylar and Nora hold her up.

The major calls everyone to attention as the procession passes.

"Present arms!" he commands.

The men hold their salute until the last coffin is placed in the vehicle and the door closed.

"Order arms!" he commands, and they smartly drop their salutes.

They stand at attention as the vehicles drive away, and then slowly disperse once the vehicles are out of sight. The bodies will be examined and identified at the base hospital, and then prepared for a proper military funeral.

Rees watches sadly as Nora visits with some of the guys. His time with her may have been decades in the past for Nora, but it seems only a few days ago as far as he is concerned. She notices his gaze and walks toward him with a smile on her face.

"Well hello, handsome," Nora says with a flirtatious tone.

She can't help but notice him blushing and chuckles at the sight.

"I'm sorry," she adds, "but you're still handsome to me."

Rees returns the smile and they clasp hands. The moment is at the same time painful and wonderful for Rees. He looks Nora in the eyes, privately wishing they were still a couple.

"And you're still beautiful to me," answers Rees, who is struggling to accept the fact that things can never be the same. "I hope life treats you well and we can remain friends."

"Of course," Nora replies. "The Clio project may have robbed us of a chance at being happy together in the past, but that doesn't mean we can't be friends in the present."

After a warm embrace, Nora breaks away to rejoin Skylar and Ivy. Rees can only watch and wonder what might have been. Bouvier understands Rees's emotions and walks over to put a comforting hand on his friend's shoulder.

"What now, do you think?" Bouvier asks.

"I'm not sure," Rees responds. "They can't keep us locked up forever. Well, I guess they could, but I don't see that happening. I don't mind staying in the air force. It was what I was planning on doing, anyway."

"A lifer? You?" Bouvier scoffs.

"Yes, and why the hell not?" Rees replies, acting a bit offended.

"Just never figured you for the type," Bouvier shrugs.

"I'm not sure yet, Jack," Rees smiles. "I'm keeping my options open, but it seems like the right thing to do. Maybe I'll stay with this program. You never know what the future holds, pun intended."

"See you back at the base," Bouvier smiles as he walks away.

"Yeah, see ya in a bit," Rees replies as he stands and looks toward the river.

It's a nice river. This is a pretty spot and he's glad they had found it.

The sound of footsteps breaks Rees from his thoughts and he turns to see two men approaching, one holding an umbrella over both of them. They are well-dressed and carry themselves with confidence as they stop in front of him.

"Sergeant Rees?"

"Yes, I'm Sergeant Rees. What can I do for you?"

"It's nice to meet you," says the older of the two men, shaking Rees's hand. "I wanted to introduce myself. I'm Congressman Olsen and I'm in charge of the Clio project. Well, not so much in charge as I am an overseer. I make sure things happen."

"You must be the congressman I've heard about," Rees replies. "You're the person who helped get us back."

"You are correct. I wanted to talk to you and Sergeant Bouvier, but I see he has left," the congressman says. "We might have need of your services if you are willing, but we'll discuss that at a later date. I believe you met a few of my ancestors, including my great-great-great grandfather, William Olsen. He and his sister, Sarah, passed along a fantastic tale of men from the future visiting the family store in Hendricks Hill one day in 1862. Caused quite a ruckus from the way the story goes. Billy, as he was called at the time, had an even more outlandish tale about being in a large, green, horseless carriage, looking at colorful pictures of naked women and meeting several strangely dressed men, also from the future. Sound familiar?"

"Yes, that sounds very familiar," Rees replies with a smile. "So, that would mean your father is, or was, Judge Olsen?"

"Yes, that is correct. Oh, and by the way," the congressman pauses as he reaches into his pocket. "Please return this to Sergeant Tucker. I think he may have misplaced it. Or it was stolen. One never knows with my family."

Rees holds out his hand and the congressman drops a worn and faded command crest into his palm. It is the crest Tucker lost during their interaction with a young Billy Olsen more than 150 years ago.

"Well I'll be," he smiles.